⇒ RIVALS ⇐

Janet Dailey

—≡ RIVALS ≡—

MICHAEL JOSEPH LONDON

MICHAEL JOSEPH LTD

Published by the Penguin Group
27 Wrights Lane, London w8 5TZ, England
Viking Penguin Inc., 40 West 23rd Street, New York, New York 10010, USA
Penguin Books Australia Ltd, Ringwood, Victoria, Australia
Penguin Books Canada Ltd, 2801 John Street, Markham, Ontario, Canada L3R 1B4
Penguin Books (NZ) Ltd, 182–190 Wairau Road, Auckland 10, New Zealand

Penguin Books Ltd, Registered Offices: Harmondsworth, Middlesex, England

First published 1989

Filmset in Monophoto 11/13pt Sabon and
printed and bound in Great Britain by
Richard Clay Ltd, Bungay, Suffolk

A CIP catalogue record for this book is available
from the British Library

ISBN 0 7181 3191 6

I

SOMEONE WAS watching her. She could feel the weight of a pair of eyes on her. It was hardly surprising in a room full of people – yet she had the strongest sensation . . .

Twenty minutes earlier, Flame Bennett had arrived at the De-Borgs' twelve-room eyrie high atop one of the gleaming towers on San Francisco's Telegraph Hill. Pausing in the marble foyer with her friend and associate Ellery Dorn, she'd hastily begun tugging off her black Fendi gloves, one finger at a time, as she turned to the waiting maid in her starched uniform. 'Has Miss Colton arrived?'

'About fifteen minutes ago, Ms Bennett.'

The reply confirmed Flame's suspicion. They were late, later than even fashion allowed. Tonight's party was more than just an exclusive gathering of the San Francisco opera committee; it was a formal reception for the internationally acclaimed coloratura soprano, Lucianna Colton, the guest diva in the fall season's opening production of *Il Trovatore*. Not being on hand to welcome her was the equivalent of being late for an audience with the Queen. It simply wasn't done.

'What a pity we missed her entrance,' Ellery murmured dryly as he handed his topcoat and white silk scarf to the maid, then brushed absently at an invisible speck of lint on the sleeve of his black jacket.

Flame shot him a quick glance. His faint smile held a hint of mockery. That was Ellery – cynical and urbane and elegant with a wry mocking wit that could be quite cutting. And, as always, he was impeccably groomed with not a single strand of his light brown hair out of place.

'How typical of you, Ellery,' she laughed as he stepped up behind her and slipped the black fox jacket from her shoulders. 'Your tears match your crocodile shoes.'

'But of course.' He gave the jacket to the maid, then tucked a guiding hand under her elbow. 'Shall we make our entrance?'

'We don't have any choice,' Flame murmured with a trace of ruefulness he didn't share.

Leaving the foyer, they passed through the reception hall and entered the small sitting area beyond it. Her glance touched briefly on the sunny yellow traditional sofa and black Regency chairs juxtaposed with a pair of eighteenth-century Oriental cabinets, the room's decor indicative of the genteel blend to be found throughout the spacious penthouse flat. But her attention was drawn to the bright chatter of voices interspersed with soft laughter coming from the main sitting room on the right.

Unconsciously she squared her shoulders as she paused in the arch to the claret-glazed room. Flame was accustomed to heads turning. Long ago, she had come to terms with the fact that her looks attracted stares, both the admiring and the envious kinds. It was more than being model tall and shapely or possessing a strongly beautiful face. No, what set her apart was that rare and striking combination of ivory-fair skin, jade-green eyes, and copper hair with just enough gold in it to tone down the red.

But the looks directed her way now held a hint of disapproval at her tardiness. She knew all the guests. Most were old family friends who had literally watched her grow up. Flame was one of the few at the gathering who had the distinction of being a direct descendant of one of San Francisco's founding families. And that very connection gave her entrée to the elite circles, an entrée that new money couldn't necessarily buy. As Ellery had once caustically observed, the colour of a person's money wasn't nearly as important in San Francisco as the colour of his or her blood. With the latter, one didn't automatically need the former.

Their hostess, Pamela DeBorg, a bright bird of a woman with feathery ash blonde curls, spotted them and swooped over, the shawl scarf to her panne-velvet Blass gown billowing out behind. 'Flame, we had given up on you.'

'It was unavoidable, I promise,' Flame apologised. 'The agency was filming a commercial at the Palace of Fine Arts. Unfortunately, we had some problems.'

'Indeed,' Ellery chimed in. 'Our prima donna was a leopard – or should I say leopardess. I hope yours doesn't turn out to be as temperamental and uncooperative as ours.'

'Lucianna is an absolute dear,' Pamela declared, clasping her hands together in delight, the spectacular diamond ring on her finger flashing in the light. 'You will love her, Flame. She is so warm, so affable . . . what can I say? You must meet her yourself. Come. She's in the Garden Room with Peter.' She caught at Flame's hand, drawing her from the arch, then paused long enough to include Ellery. 'You, too, of course.' Then she was off, somehow managing to stay a half-step ahead of Flame while turning to her, talking all the way. 'Did I tell you she changed the entire travel schedule and flew here on a private jet instead? It was absolute insanity this afternoon trying to get everything rearranged.' Flame smiled sympathetically, aware no other response was required. 'And wait until you see her gown. It's gorgeous. But the necklace she's wearing – a fabulous diamond and ruby bijou that will make you die with envy. Jacqui hinted that she thought it was paste,' she added, dropping her voice to a conspiratorial level when she mentioned the chronicler of San Francisco's society doings, Jacqui Van Cleeve, a former socialite herself before her divorce. 'But those rocks are definitely real, Flame. That necklace reeks of Bulgari's touch. Believe me, I know.'

Flame didn't doubt that. It had been said that Pamela DeBorg's collection of jewellery could rival the Duchess of Windsor's, both in quantity and quality.

Just ahead, a set of French windows stood open, leading into the Garden Room. Pamela swept through them then paused a fraction of a second. The lengthy expanse of glass provided the grandly spacious penthouse with its de rigueur view of the Golden

Gate Bridge and the Bay. Intimate groupings of plushly-cushioned rattan furniture were scattered among a profusion of potted plants and Chinese urns.

In the middle of it all, holding audience, stood the dark-haired diva herself, stunning in a back-plunging gown of scarlet that hugged her generous curves. She turned, giving Flame a glimpse of the ruby and diamond necklace and her much-photographed face, too prominently boned to be considered beautiful, although it undeniably commanded attention.

She certainly was the centre of it now, Flame thought, glancing at the committee members clustered around her, including their host, the sandy-haired financier, Peter DeBorg.

'There she is,' Pamela said needlessly and pushed forward. 'Forgive me for interrupting, Lucianna, but I have someone from the committee I want you to meet – Flame Bennett.'

'How nice.' Her glance swung to Flame, her dark eyes showing a perfunctory interest that matched her smile as she said, 'It's my pleasure.'

'I assure you it's all mine, Miss Colton. And I hope you'll accept my apologies for not being here to welcome you when you arrived tonight.'

'Yes,' Pamela rushed to explain. 'Flame was filming a commercial and they had some sort of problem with a lion or leopard or something.'

'You're an actress then.'

'No,' Peter DeBorg spoke up. 'Flame works for Boland and Hayes, a national advertising agency with offices here in San Francisco.'

'I'm not sure I understand.' Her questioning look ran from one to the other. 'Are you a model?'

Flame smiled faintly. 'No. I'm a vice-president with the company.'

'A vice-president.' Her full interest was now focused on Flame, sharply reassessing. 'How wonderful to meet a woman with power.'

Flame acknowledged the compliment with a gracious nod then half turned, directing the attention to Ellery. 'I'd like to introduce you to another officer of the company and my closest friend, Ellery Dorn.'

'Miss Colton.' Ellery stepped smoothly forward and took her

scarlet-nailed fingers, raising them to his lips. 'We are looking forward to your Leonora. Although, if I may be so bold to suggest, instead of having San Francisco at your feet as you do here' – with a gesturing sweep of his hand, he indicated the glitter of city lights beyond the glass panes of the penthouse windows – 'you will have them *on* their feet.'

'Ellery, how very clever of you!' Pamela exclaimed, clapping her hands together.

'And flattering.' Lucianna Colton added with a regal incline of her head.

'I prefer to think of it as a portent of things to come,' Ellery insisted as more guests strolled into the Garden Room, not to admire the view of the storied city but to have a closer look at the famous lady in scarlet. Catching sight of them, Ellery lightly took Flame's arm. 'As much as we would like to monopolise your time, Miss Colton, I'm afraid we must deny ourselves. There are too many others eager to shower you with the same accolades.'

After exchanging the usual pleasantries, Flame and Ellery withdrew. Almost immediately their place was taken and Flame heard Andrea Crane gush, 'I was at La Scala last year when you performed so divinely in *Tosca*.'

As they crossed the threshold into the main sitting room, Ellery glanced back and smiled wryly. 'Amazing.'

'What is?' Flame eyed him curiously.

Drawing her to one side, he nodded at the collection of guests, some seated, some standing. 'Tonight's guest list reads like the Who's Who of San Francisco society. Yet . . . there they are fawning over a woman from some little Midwestern town who can hit a high F without screeching.'

'It's a bit more than that,' she replied, momentarily distracted by the odd feeling she was being watched. 'She is an extremely talented artist.'

'Artistic talent is the elevating factor, isn't it?'

That sensation of a pair of eyes on her persisted, stronger than before. 'Is this going to turn into a philosophical discussion, Ellery? Because if it is, I don't think I'm up to it.' She half turned, trying to discern the source of the eerie feeling, and came face to face with a waiter, a hawk-faced man in his mid-forties. For an instant she was unnerved by the piercing study of his deep-set hazel eyes, hooded by a heavy brow. Then his glance fell as he stepped forward and extended the salver of wine glasses balanced on the palm of his right hand.

'A glass of Chardonnay?' Not even the smooth, respectful wording could eliminate the rough edge to his voice.

'Thank you.' She took one of the stemmed wine goblets from the tray, her glance running over him again. Had he been the one staring at her? Although she couldn't be sure, she suspected he was. Why had it bothered her? Why had she felt so uneasy? Men customarily stared at her – for all the usual reasons. Why should a waiter be different? He offered wine to Ellery, then moved on to another group of guests.

'Brown shoes and black pants,' Ellery raised an eyebrow in disapproval. 'The caterer should pay more attention to the dress of his help.'

Flame glanced again at the retreating waiter, this time noting the brown of his shoes. Unexpectedly, he turned his head and glanced back at Flame. The instant he realised she'd seen him, he looked away.

A hand touched her arm, then travelled familiarly down to cup an elbow. 'I see you finally made it.'

Recognising the voice, Flame tensed briefly, then flashed a quick and warm smile at the man who was easily her most important and influential client. At fifty-six, Malcom Powell looked it, too – an imposing figure of only average stature but very powerfully built. His dark hair was leonine thick and shot with silver, but that touch of grey only added to the image of an iron man. Some said that was exactly the way he ruled his huge chain of department stores across the country, a family business which he'd inherited and on which he'd built his reputation, although they currently represented only a small portion of his vast holdings.

'Malcom, I didn't know you were back in town.'

'I flew in last night.' His grey eyes bored into her, seeking a reaction, then flickered with irritation when he found only calm. 'I left a message with your secretary this afternoon, but you never returned my call.'

'I was tied up all afternoon filming a commercial. I didn't have time to check with the office for messages. You surely don't think I deliberately ignored your call.' She accompanied her reply with a bright smile. Long ago, she had learned that the best way to handle Malcom Powell was by not letting him intimidate her. Confrontation was always better – if done carefully.

'No, not really.'

'What was it you wanted?'

His glance flicked to Ellery. 'Get Flame another glass of wine.' He took the crystal goblet from her and set it on the lacquered side table along the wall. 'And make sure it's been properly chilled this time.'

'By all means.' Ellery bowed his head with an exaggerated respect. 'I'll even corner the wine steward and express your dissatisfaction to him.' To Flame, he added, 'It shouldn't take more than five minutes.'

When he strolled away, Flame turned to Malcom, the cornerstone to her entire career. She owed him a great deal, and he knew it. She hadn't been hired by the agency eight years ago because of her qualifications or her college degree. She had been window-dressing for the firm – with valuable connections and contracts, someone they could parade before a client during a presentation. That's when Malcom had seen her, over five years ago. Less than a year later – at his insistence – she had been put in sole charge of his account. Plus, he had directed other companies her way, especially ones he did business with. Within three years, she had controlled several of the agency's largest accounts. Naturally, they had promoted her to a vice-president.

She let her gaze run lightly over his face, taking in the broad, square jaw, the jutting chin with its dimpled cleft, the deep set of his grey eyes, and most of all the power that was so indelibly stamped in every line. Gratitude, admiration, respect – she felt all those things – as well as a trace of resentment.

'Have dinner with me Monday night.' The invitation fell somewhere between a demand and command.

'Have lunch with me on Tuesday.'

'Have you already made plans for Monday evening?'

'Yes,' she lied.

'No, you haven't. I had your secretary check when I called this afternoon. We'll have dinner together Monday night.'

'We'll have lunch on Tuesday,' she countered. Again that feeling of being watched returned, but she couldn't let it distract her.

'Why must we always fence over such trivial issues?' Malcom grumbled in irritation. 'Why can't you simply agree to dine with me on –'

'Tuesday at lunch. We made some changes in the holiday layouts. I want to go over them with you.'

The look in his grey eyes took on a wanting quality. 'Do we always have to discuss business, Flame?' he asked, holding her gaze.

'You know we do, Malcom.' The entire conversation was an echo of hundreds that had gone on before.

'So you say, but I'll argue the point with you further – on Tuesday,' he replied, conceding to her with a final dip of his head. 'I'll have Arthur pick you up at twelve-thirty sharp.'

'I'll be ready.'

'So will I.'

Flame knew she'd be in for another contest of wills on Tuesday. And she had to admit, if only to herself, that there was a part of her that enjoyed these stimulating duels of theirs – and Malcom's always challenging company.

As Ellery came walking back, that sensation of someone watching her resurfaced. 'Your wine, m'lady.' He offered a stemmed glass. 'Chilled to precisely thirty-six degrees Centigrade. Or was it Fahrenheit?'

'There is a difference, my fine friend,' she answered as she covertly scanned the room. Just as she suspected, the brown-shoed waiter with the hawk face was on the other side of the room, this time carrying a tray of hors d'oeuvres.

As she started to look away, her glance was caught and held by another man standing on the far side of the room, a shoulder negligently propped against the claret-glazed wall. His hair was as black as the tuxedo he wore. And despite the languid pose, the overall impression was that of a lean and rangy black panther, coiled energy held in check, ready to spring at a second's warning.

He stared back. She took a sip of wine without tasting it, conscious only of the unexpected quickening of her pulse. She thought she knew everyone at the party, but who was he? She looked again, telling herself that her interest was strictly curiosity – and not believing a word of it. His gaze never left her as he nodded absently to the person with him and raised a crystal tumbler to his mouth. For the first time, Flame glanced at the petite blonde beside him. Jacqui Van Cleeve, the columnist. Who was he? Obviously someone of importance.

'The man with Jacqui, Malcom, do you know him?'

But Ellery replied first. 'I believe I heard someone say he's here with Miss Colton.'

'Then it must be Chance Stuart,' Malcom concluded, still trying to locate the pair.

'I think I've heard that name.' But Flame couldn't remember where or why.

'I should think so,' Malcom declared. 'In the last ten years, Chancellor Stuart has become one of the largest land developers in the country. He has an uncanny knack for being at the right place at the right time.' His expression grew thoughtful. 'He's building that new resort complex in Tahoe. I wonder what he's doing in San Francisco.'

'I expect that is precisely what darling Jacqui is trying to find out,' Ellery surmised.

'My reason for coming here is hardly a secret, Miss Van Cleeve,' Chance Stuart let his glance slide briefly to the persistent blonde, recalling Lucianna's warning that the woman was known for three things: her sharp eyes, her sharp nose, and her sharp tongue. He had to agree – everything about her was pointed, including her questions.

'Call me Jacqui,' she invited. 'Everyone does.'

'Then let me explain again, Jacqui. I was on my way to Tahoe to check on my project there when Lucianna mentioned she was coming to San Francisco. I suggested she fly with me since it wasn't that much out of my way.'

'Then you aren't looking for more property?'

'I'm not here for that purpose, but I'm always looking.' He absently swirled the Chivas in his glass, listening to the melodic clink of the ice cubes against the crystal sides. 'If you were on vacation and a hot story landed in your lap, would you ignore it?'

'No,' she admitted.

'Need I say more.' He lifted the glass to his mouth and tipped it, letting the cold Scotch trickle in and burn down his throat.

'You've known Miss Colton for some time, haven't you?'

'A long time, yes.' He lowered the tumbler, his glance automatically straying to the stunning redhead across the room. She had stirred his interest from the moment she'd walked into the room with a stride that had in it the faintest hint of a swagger, with a quick rhythm that synchronised and turned graceful the supple movement of her body. And her shoulders, wide and straight, had been presented squarely in a manner that flaunted serene confidence. She was a woman all the way through – all lace and legs.

'Would it be safe to guess that your on-again, off-again romance with Miss Colton is back on again?' the columnist queried slyly.

'I hate to disillusion you, Jacqui, but all this on and off business is the product of your profession. Over the years, our relationship has never changed.'

'I suppose you're going to try to convince me that you're just good friends.' She openly mocked the cliché.

'It doesn't make good press, does it?'

'If it's true.'

Ignoring that, Chance raised his glass and gestured toward the far side of the room. 'Isn't that Malcom Powell?'

All the photographs he'd seen of the august lion of the retail world had depicted a somewhat stout and stern man. In person, he had a commanding presence, physically vigorous and trim despite that barrel chest.

'Yes, that's Malcom,' the Van Cleeve woman confirmed. 'Truthfully, I didn't expect to see him here. Diedre told me that he'd returned from a business trip only last night.'

'Diedre?' He arched her a questioning look.

'His wife.'

'Is that her?' His gaze sharpened on the pair, irritation flickering through him.

'No, that's Flame – Flame Bennett.' During the brief pause that followed, Chance could feel the columnist carefully monitoring his reaction. 'Gorgeous, isn't she?'

'Definitely.' He continued to lounge against the wall, for the moment content to enjoy his unobstructed view of the woman so aptly named Flame, conscious of the hot, smooth feeling that flowed through him.

'Aren't you going to ask me about her?' The instant the faintly challenging question came out of Jacqui Van Cleeve's mouth, Chance knew she'd give him a complete rundown on Flame Bennett. She made it her business to collect every scrap of information – whether rumour or fact – on every person remotely important. And when a person had that much information, they could never resist sharing it.

'I was always told it wasn't polite for a gentleman to ask questions about a lady,' he countered smoothly.

Her short laugh had a harsh and grating ring to it. 'I have heard you accused of many things, Chance Stuart, but being a gentleman was never one of them. Granted you have all the manners, the polish, the clothes of one, but proper, you're not. You're too damned daring. Nobody's sure what you're going to do next and you move too fast. That's why you make such excellent copy.'

'I'll take that as a compliment.'

Again he felt the speculation in her study of him. 'It will be interesting to see how you fare with Flame.'

'Why do you say that?' He glanced at her curiously.

'Because . . . she's a woman of such contrasts.' Her attention swung away from him, centring on the subject of their discussion. 'She can be as fiery as the red of her hair – or as cool as the green of her eyes – and that quickly, too. I suppose that's part of the fatal attraction she has for men. You always see them fluttering around her like moths. She lets them get only so close and no closer.'

'Why?'

'I'm not sure, but no man seems to last with her. It isn't even a case of off with the old and on with the new. No one sticks around long enough to be old. But there again you have the contrast. These romantic flings of hers are too few and far between. Therefore, you can't call her wild. Her behaviour is definitely unconventional.' After a fractional hesitation, she added, 'Of course she was married briefly about nine years ago. Supposedly, it was one of those young marriages that simply didn't work. At least that was the official line at the time.'

'And unofficially?'

'Truthfully? I never heard anything to make me think otherwise,' the Van Cleeve woman admitted. 'A failed marriage has made more than one woman wary of trying again. It could be as simple as that or it could be her career.'

'What does she do?' Currently careers were fashionable among socialites. But in his experience, Chance had found that the women were rarely more than dilettantes, dabbling in photography or modelling, owning art galleries, antique stores or exclusive little dress shops, invariably managed by someone else.

'Flame's a vice-president with the Boland and Hayes Advertising firm,' she replied, then added, 'Of course, it's common knowledge that she has to work for a living. Even though she comes from one of San Francisco's founding families, there is little or no money left. No doubt a humbling experience but I can assure you she's never suffered any hardship as a result. Like anywhere else, it pays to know the right people.'

'Like Malcom Powell,' Chance guessed.

'She handles his advertising account personally. And – there's been a lot of speculation lately about what else she might handle *personally* for him.'

He detected something in her voice that made him suspect, 'You don't believe it.'

'No,' she admitted. 'By the same token, I don't belive Diedre when she insists that Malcom takes a fatherly interest in Flame. But what else can a wife of thirty-five years say? Believe me, if a father eyed his daughter the way he does Flame, he'd be subject to arrest. He wants her, but he hasn't had her.'

'How can you be so sure?'

'If Flame was having an affair with him, she wouldn't try to hide it. It isn't her style.' Jacqui frowned, as if aware she wasn't making herself clear. 'I guess what I'm trying to say is – if Flame cared enough to get involved with a married man, then she wouldn't let herself feel any shame or guilt.'

'What about the other man with her? Is he her latest fling?'

'Ellery Dorn? Hardly.' She laughed, then explained. 'Ellery is every married woman's choice for a walker when her husband isn't available. He's handsome, witty, charming – and gay. Surprised?' She shot him a knowing glance. 'Not to worry. Few people ever guess that about him. That's what makes him so ideal.'

'Then he's nothing more than a safe escort.' Mentally Chance filed that little piece of information away along with all the rest.

The more he learned about Flame Bennett, the more intrigued he became.

'They're good friends as well. As a matter of fact, Flame is probably closer to Ellery than anyone else. Of course, he's a vice-president in the same agency, so I'm sure the fact they work together has something to do with that.'

'Probably.' With a little push of his shoulder, he straightened from the wall. 'Speaking of walkers, Lucianna is bound to be wondering what happened to me. I enjoyed the chat, Jacqui.'

'So did I. And from now on, I'll be watching your progress with more interest.'

'Not too closely, I hope.' He winked at her as he moved away.

— 2 —

WITHOUT BEING obvious, Flame watched as Chance Stuart leisurely wound his way around the guests. He was tall, taller than he'd first appeared. She found herself liking the way he moved, like an athlete, all smooth co-ordination and easy grace. He certainly had the body of one, wide at the shoulders and narrow at the hips, with lean, hard muscle in between.

As he drew closer, Flame was able clearly to see his face and the dark blue of his eyes. She decided it was the deep blue colour that made the impact of his glance so much like a jolt of electricity. His features could have been hammered out of bronze, beaten smooth without taking anything away from the ruggedness of his cheeks or the hard break of his jaw. But there was something else there too – some indefinable quality about him that stamped him as dangerous, a man who could smile and draw a throaty groan from every woman in the room.

With a faint start, she noticed that he was angling away from her. He wasn't coming over. She hadn't realised how much she'd anticipated meeting him until she felt the sudden sinking disappointment. She struggled to contain it, feeling foolish and a little conceited that she'd taken it for granted that Chance Stuart would seek her out. She realised that she'd read too much into the eye contact, fallen victim to the 'across-the-crowded-room' syndrome. It would have been laughable if she didn't feel so let down.

But there wasn't time to dwell on it as she encountered a glaring look from Diedre Powell. Such looks were nothing new. Most wives regarded her as a threat to their marriages, especially older women like Diedre Powell with husbands who had a history of having affairs on the side.

And like most, Diedre had kept her marriage intact by smiling and looking the other way – until one day she'd seen her reflection in the mirror and fear had set in. Now her skin was pulled smooth, the chin tucked, the jowls gone, the eyelids lifted, her Chanel gown of blue silk crepe flowing over a figure that had regained much of its former trimness. And her hair was once again a lustrous brown – except for the shock of white that streaked away from her forehead.

The woman was living in her own private hell. Flame wondered if Malcom knew it – and if he did, did he understand? She doubted it. That hungry, possessive look in his eyes plainly stated that he wanted her, but she also knew that didn't mean he wanted a divorce. In his mind, there was no correlation between the two.

'There you are, Malcom.' Diedre glided over to them, a smile fixed brightly in place, the Powell sapphires glittering at her throat and ears. 'Sid Rayburn was looking for you a minute ago – something about a meeting at the yacht club on Thursday?'

'Yes, I need to get together with him. Where is he?' With a lift of his head, he glanced beyond her to scan the room.

'When I saw him last, he was over by the dining room.' She waved a beringed hand in its direction.

As Malcom moved away, he briefly touched his wife's shoulder in passing. She turned to Flame, a faintly triumphant gleam in her eyes. 'It's good to see you again, Flame. How have you been?'

'Busy . . . as usual,' she replied evenly, aware that they were both going through the motions of polite chatter, and playing their own separate games of pretend.

'So I've heard.' Just for an instant she showed her claws, then quickly sheathed them to smile pleasantly.

A few years ago, Diedre's attitude would have bothered her, but not any more. Her skin had thickened. Wives invariably blamed her if their husbands started paying attention to her, with or without encouragement. She supposed it was easier to blame the so-called other woman than it was to admit that the fault belonged with the husband and his roving eye. It wasn't fair, but what was in this life?

From the Garden Room, a musical laugh broke above the chatter of voices. The sound drew Diedre Powell's glance. 'I do believe that's Margo with Miss Colton. We've been missing each other all evening.' She started to walk by Flame, then paused and laid a hand on her arm, her fingers closing briefly in what passed for an affectionate squeeze, and smiled at Ellery. 'You really should see that Flame doesn't work so hard.'

Then she was gone, leaving the cloying scent of Giorgio in her wake. 'Such caring, such concern. Amazing isn't it?' Ellery declared in mock admiration. 'I do enjoy intimate little gatherings like these, don't you? – As a matter of fact, I enjoy them so much that I think I need something stronger to drink than this wine. How about you?'

'I'm fine, really I am,' she insisted, and smiled as she lifted her glass to take another sip of the dry Chardonnay.

'If you say so.' He shrugged and went off in search of the bar.

Her gaze followed the slim set of his shoulders halfway across the room, then wandered absently to the dimly lit Garden Room beyond the set of French windows. Chance Stuart stepped through the opening, his gaze making a leisurely sweep of the room in front of him. For an instant, everything inside her went still. As yet, he hadn't noticed her standing to his left and Flame took advantage of it to study the strong, rakish lines of his face and the ebony sheen of his hair, clipped close as if to curb its unruly tendencies. There was a sleekness about him – a raciness that convinced Flame he should be wearing a warning label advising the unwary that here was a man highly dangerous to the senses.

Still perusing the other guests, he reached inside his black evening jacket and took a gold cigarette case from the inner breast pocket. He flipped it open, then hesitated, his head turning slightly as his glance swung directly to her.

'Cigarette?' He held out the case to her.

'Thank you, but I don't smoke.' She accompanied the assertion with a slight shake of her head in refusal.

A faint smile tugged at the corners of his mouth. 'Do you object if I do?'

'Not at all.' With a brief movement of her hand, Flame indicated the crystal ashtray on the side table near her.

She watched his strong, tanned fingers as they removed a cigarette from the case and carried it to his lips, their line as masculine and well-defined as the rest of him. A light flared, then disappeared behind his cupped hand as he bent his head, touching the cigarette to the flame. A thin trail of smoke curled upwards. Flame followed it and again encountered the lazy regard of his blue eyes, all warm and glinting with male appreciation.

'I don't believe we've been introduced.' He wandered over, a hint of a smile now deepening the creases in his lean cheeks. 'I'm Chance Stuart.'

'I know,' she admitted and smiled back, aware of the unexpected – and almost forgotten – sensation of heat coiling through her body. It had been a long time since any man had had that effect on her.

An eyebrow lifted. 'Then you have the advantage on me.' His voice was pitched low, a hint of a drawl in its delivery.

'From what I've heard about you, Mr Stuart, that seldom happens,' she said, softening the slightly pointed remark with a smile and adding, 'I'm Flame Bennett.'

'Flame,' he said, as if testing the sound of it, his glance sliding to the fiery gold of her hair. 'That's much more original than Red.'

'Perhaps like you, Mr Stuart, I'm an original.'

'I won't disagree with that. In fact, it's the first thing I noticed about you.' Chance had the distinct feeling that his every remark, his every look was being weighed by her. However receptive she appeared to be to him – and she was – her guard remained up, a guard apparently few men had ever penetrated. He thought back to Jacqui Van Cleeve's comment about Flame and Malcom Powell. Powell was a man who always got what he wanted, yet this woman had successfully resisted him.

'Really, that's the first thing you noticed about me?' A smile played at the corners of her mouth, drawing his attention to her lips, soft and full at the centres yet strong. 'And what was the second?' There was a hint of challenge in her question.

'The second wasn't so much noticing as it was recognising that I wanted to see more of you.'

Her knowing look simultaneously taunted and encouraged him as she laughed softly. 'I do believe you're making a pass at me, Mr Stuart.'

'No.' He denied that. 'I'm merely stating my intentions. And the name is Chance.'

He detected the faint break in her poise, a break that allowed him to see the pleased look that flared in her eyes, welcoming his interest before her long lashes veiled it. 'Your reputation is obviously well-earned. You do move fast, don't you ... Chance?' She hesitated deliberately over the use of his given name, setting it apart and letting an added warmth invade her voice.

'Am I moving too fast for you?'

'That's a very leading question,' she replied, deftly parrying it without committing herself to anything, although a definite interest remained in her eyes.

'That's why I asked it.' He smiled, his eyes glinting with a wickedly mocking light.

'Will you be staying in San Francisco long?'

'Not this time. I have to fly out first thing in the morning.' Chance regretted that as he studied the tumble of red-gold hair that framed her face in a mass of rippling waves. On its own, the colour was striking enough, but it was made more so by the ivory fairness of her complexion. He wondered if her skin would be as smooth to the touch as it looked. He let his glance stray to the lace top of her dress, ashimmer with black seed pearls sewn on to its scrolling pattern. Here and there the fine mesh revealed a discreet hint of flesh. 'I like your dress.' Almost absently he trailed the tip of his finger down a long sleeve, feeling the heat from her body – and the sudden tension that claimed her. He lifted his glance to her eyes. They were alive to him, returning his look measure for measure. 'I wonder what it is about black lace that stirs a man's blood?' he mused aloud.

'I should think you'd be able to answer that question more easily than I could since you are very definitely a man.'

'You noticed.'

She laughed softly. 'Along with every other female in this room.'

'Excuse me, sir,' A waiter intruded. 'You are Mr Stuart, aren't you?'

'Yes.' He reached over and stubbed his cigarette out in the crystal ashtray.

'You have a call, sir. There's a telephone in the reception hall.' The man stepped back, still keeping his gaze downcast. 'If you would follow me.'

His glance ran briefly to Flame. 'You will excuse me.'

'Of course,' she said, with just a hint of regret in her smile.

With a nod, he signalled to the waiter to lead the way. As they set out, Chance tried to think who would be calling him – especially here. He hadn't left word where he could be reached when he'd left the hotel. But Sam could have tracked him down.

Sam Weber carried the title of Senior Vice-President in the Stuart Corporation, but his role was much larger than even the title implied. Sam Weber was his right arm, his detail man, his backup – just as he'd been when they'd served together in Nam, then later in college and finally in business. Chance made the deals and Sam pulled the loose ends together.

It had to be Sam calling him. He was the only logical choice. But if it was Sam, then something had gone wrong.

The waiter halted short of the hall's square arch and gestured at the contemporary side table standing against the wall to the right of the room's entrance. 'The telephone, sir.'

Chance immediately spotted the brown receiver lying on the table next to the telephone and nodded briefly to the waiter. Dodging the overhanging boughs of the bitter-sweet branches that sprouted from the celadon vase in the centre of the room, he walked over and picked up the receiver. 'Hello –'

Before he could identify himself, a voice on the other end of the line broke in. 'It certainly took you long enough, Stuart.'

Chance stiffened, instantly recognising that distinctive, raspy-edged voice that carried both the sound and the sting of whiskey, its tone as critical and malevolent as always. 'How are you, Hattie?' he murmured tightly, feeling the old slow burn of anger and bitter resentment. He had stopped calling her *Aunt* Hattie nearly thirty years ago.

'Obviously still alive,' came the challenging retort. Without any effort, he had a mental picture of her standing before him, gnarled fingers clutching the gold head of her cane, black eyes gleaming with hatred, white hair curling about a face lined by years of embitterment. Not once could he remember Hattie smiling at him – or even looking at him with anything that passed for approval. 'I'm at your hotel,' she announced. 'I'll expect you here in precisely thirty minutes.'

The imperious demand was followed by a sharp click as the line went dead. For an instant, Chance remained motionless, frozen by the icy rage that swept through him. Then he quickly hit the telephone's disconnect switch, listened for the dial tone, and punched the numbers to Sam's private line.

The call was answered on the first ring. 'Yeah, this is Sam. What have you got?'

'Sam, it's Chance.'

'Chance.' The surprise in his voice was obvious. 'I was going to try to reach you as soon as I heard from –'

'Hattie just called me. She's here in San Francisco.'

'So that's where she went,' Sam murmured, the familiar loud squeak of his office chair coming over the line as he leaned back on it.

'What's going on out there?' Chance demanded.

'That's what I'm trying to find out,' Sam replied, then sighed heavily. 'I know she had a meeting with old Ben Canon this morning. She was closeted in his law office about two hours. When her driver came to pick her up and take her back to Morgan's Walk, he was told she'd taken a cab to the airport. We've been checking the passenger lists of every flight that went out of Tulsa today.' There was a slight pause. 'I guess I don't have to worry about that any more.'

'How did she know where I am?' Chance frowned, giving voice to the questions going around in his head. 'And – why would she want to see me?'

'And what's her meeting with Canon got to do with this trip?' Sam added. 'Chance, I don't like the sound of it. I'd like to believe that maybe she finally wants to make peace, but I can't buy it.'

'Neither can I.' A grimness settled through him. 'It could be Canon found out that I own the holding company that just bought up the Turner land.'

'It would take a corporate genius to unravel that ownership and trace it back to you. Ben's shrewd, but his knowledge of corporate law is as antiquated as he is.'

Chance couldn't disagree with that. 'There's no point in speculating why she's here. I'll know first-hand in another twenty-five minutes,' he said, checking his watch.

'Call me back as soon as you can.'

'I will.'

Hearing the click on the other end that signalled the breaking of the connection, Sam Weber slowly returned the receiver to its cradle, then leaned back in his swivel chair, ignoring its protesting squeak as he rubbed a hand across his mouth in troubled thoughtfulness.

'Well . . . where is she?'

Startled by the prodding question, he shot a glance at the apple-cheeked woman seated across the desk from him. For an instant, he'd forgotten that he wasn't alone. A smile pulled at one corner of his mouth as he realised that he could always count on Molly Malone, Chance's executive secretary and staunchest supporter, to remind him otherwise.

With a shift of his weight, Sam tipped the chair forward and lowered his hand. 'In San Francisco.'

'What? Why?' A rare scowl marred features that were inherently jovial in expression. Not that Sam had ever been fooled by her plump and jolly look. Behind those spaniel-brown eyes was a mind as keen as a newly stropped razor. There were few who could ever put anything over on Molly. If she had any blind spot, it was Chance. She doted on him like a mother – and frequently pointed with pride to the strands of grey in her nut-brown hair, claiming that he had given her every one of them. 'What's she doing there?'

'That's what I'd like to know.' Sam pushed a wayward lock of his sandy hair off his forehead, combing it back with his fingers. But, like the rest of his cowlicks, it refused to be tamed and quickly fell back. 'She called Chance and said she wanted to meet with him. He's on his way to see her now.'

'That – I hesitate to even call that mean old biddy a woman. It's an insult to my gender,' Molly declared huffily. 'But you mark my words, she's up to something.'

'I agree.' Absently, he gazed at the framed photographs of his wife and children that cluttered his desk. 'But what?'

*

Shortly after Chance left, Ellery strolled back. 'I'm not going to ask if you missed me. I noticed you had company. Could it be that the inimitable Chance Stuart is responsible for the glow you're now wearing?' he murmured, raising an eyebrow. 'Talk about "only having eyes for each other".'

'Must you always exaggerate, Ellery.' In truth she did feel passionately alive, but she hadn't realised it showed.

'Was I? You mean you weren't at all attracted to him?'

'Will you stop trying to put words in my mouth – my impossible friend!' Flame demanded with affection. 'I found him very fascinating and, at the moment, that's all there is to it.'

'If you say so.'

'I do.' Smiling, Flame tried to keep an eye on the entrance to the sitting room, certain Chance would be returning any minute.

But her view of the archway was unexpectedly blocked by Lucianna Colton when she emerged from the Garden Room, surrounded by her coterie of admirers. She paused, looking about the room as if trying to locate someone. 'I know Chance was here only a moment ago,' she declared to no one in particular, then swung around to face Flame, her dark eyes piercing despite the smile on her lips. 'Wasn't he talking to you a moment ago?'

Before Flame could say that he'd been called to the phone, Chance appeared in the doorway. 'There he is, Lucianna,' Pamela DeBorg drew the soprano's attention away from Flame.

His moving glance sought her out, lingered briefly, then shifted to Lucianna as she crossed the room to meet him. Reluctantly, Flame watched as Chance manoeuvred Lucianna away from the others and spoke to her privately. She stared at the two dark heads bent so closely together. Lucianna smiled and nodded agreement to something Chance said, then reached up and lightly stroked her fingers down his strong jaw – as if it was her right.

When the couple rejoined the other guests, his hand moved across Lucianna's back-plunging gown and hooked itself to the side of her waist with the ease of long familiarity. Seeing that, Flame wondered if he'd meant any of what he'd said to her. Maybe it had all been a game to him, a way to pass the time. She didn't want to believe that, yet it seemed all too possible now. Perhaps her ego deserved it. There was one certainty, however, the pleasure she'd felt earlier was gone.

Dimly she heard them offer parting comments to their hosts. When someone protested that it was much too early for them to leave, Chance replied, 'For you, perhaps, but you have to remember Lucianna is still on New York time. She has rehearsals tomorrow. And I know her. If she stays much longer, she'll talk herself hoarse. We can't have that.'

There was one moment before they left when his eyes briefly locked with hers. But this time, Flame wasn't so foolish as to read something significant into it.

She drank the last of her wine and set the empty glass on the tray of a passing waiter. As she started to turn to Ellery, she noticed Diedre Powell looking her way. No doubt Malcom was somewhere in the vicinity, she thought and sighed inwardly.

'Let's leave, shall we. It's been a long day and I'm tired.' Oddly enough, it was true. She felt drained, physically and emotionally.

Ellery seemed about to make one of his cuttingly astute observations, then appeared to think better of it. 'Yes, it has been a long day,' he agreed. 'Why don't you make our apologies to the De-Borgs while I get the car.'

'All right,' she smiled, a trace of weariness showing.

'I'll pick you up in the front of the building in say ...' He turned back the cuff of his jacket sleeve to look at his watch, then hesitated, his glance darting to something on the floor near her feet. 'Is that slip of paper yours?'

'What paper?' Flame stepped back as Ellery reached down and picked up the square of paper folded neatly in half.

He flipped it open. 'How cryptic,' he murmured, an eyebrow arching.

'What is it?'

He hesitated, then handed it to her. 'Perhaps it is yours after all.'

'Now who's being cryptic?' she chided, then looked at the paper, tensing when she read the hastily scrawled message inside: 'Stay away from him!'

'Short and sweet, isn't it?' Ellery murmured.

'Very,' Flame agreed tightly and shot a sharp glance in Diedre

Powell's direction. Yet it seemed too childish, even for her. But if not her, then who?

'I'm sorry.' Concern darkened Ellery's eyes. 'I shouldn't have let you see it.'

'It doesn't matter.' She closed her fingers around the paper, crumpling it into the palm of her hand. 'Sticks and stones, Ellery, sticks and stones.'

'Of course.'

But both knew it was a child's cry. An adult knew better.

— 3 —

As THE limousine pulled away from the curb, Chance gazed at the mist swirling outside the tinted windows and continued to puzzle over Hattie's unexpected arrival. There was no logical reason for her to fly halfway across the continent. It wasn't to see him. The Hattie Morgan he knew would rather see him in hell first.

A soft sigh was followed by a stir of movement next to him as Lucianna settled back against the plush velour seat. 'I'm glad we were able to slip away from the party early, Chance.' She reached for his hand, sliding her palm over his and lacing their fingers together. 'Those affairs can be so tiring.'

'Especially the endless compliments.' He sent her an amused look.

'Not that.' She poked at his arm in playful punishment. 'That's the one part I like.'

'That's what I thought, my prima donna.'

She smiled and let that go, her expression turning thoughtful as she tilted her head back, resting it against the seat and exposing the long, creamy arch of her throat. 'It's playing the role of the prima donna that's so tiring sometimes. You not only have to dress the part, but you must act it too – always pleasant, always smiling, pretending to be friendly, but never too friendly or you'll lose that air of mystique. But above all, a prima donna must be aloof to criticism. You have to smile and never let them see how it cuts you.'

'You do it well.' Chance studied the mask of self-assurance and confidence that had become a permanent part of her. There was little resemblance between the woman beside him and the hillbilly girl from the mountains of Arkansas he'd met for the first time fifteen years ago singing in a smoky piano bar – the same girl who her pastor once claimed was an angel singing in his church choir. But she'd left all that behind long ago – along with the thick rural accent and the unglamorous name of Lucy Kowolski. Today few would guess at her background – as few guessed at his.

'Truthfully' – sighing, she kicked off her satin pumps dyed to match the scarlet of her dress – 'I'm tired of smiling. I don't know which aches more – my cheeks or my feet.' She turned her head to look at him, a coy appeal in her dark eyes. 'Will you rub them for me?'

'Your cheeks?' Chance smiled, deliberately misunderstanding.

'What a stimulating thought, darling.' She slipped her hand free and lightly stroked his cheek. 'Why don't you start with my feet and work your way up?' she suggested and curled her legs under her to kneel on the seat cushion facing him. 'That's what you used to do. Remember?'

'You never let me forget.' But he didn't object as she shifted to recline longways on the passenger seat and rested a stockinged foot on his thigh. Automatically he cupped his hands around it and began gently kneading its sole and running his thumb along its arch.

A low moan of pleasure came from her throat. 'Mmmm, that feels so good, Chance.' He smiled and said nothing. For a long run of minutes there was only silence. Then Lucianna murmured, 'Was it nine or ten years ago that you pulled off your first really important deal – the one that netted you more than a million dollars?'

'Nearly ten.' He lifted her foot off his thigh and placed it on the seat. Obligingly she raised her other foot for him to rub.

'I tried to be happy for you. In a way, I was.' Her shoulders lifted in a vague shrug. 'But I hated you, too. You were succeeding and I wasn't.'

'I know.' They'd gone their separate ways after that. No longer lovers, and jealousy straining even their friendship.

'Now I've made it, too.' Satisfaction riddled her voice. 'Chauffeured limousines, sable coats, designer gowns, my own personal hairdresser, everything first class – all the accoutrements of success are mine. I'm thirty-five years old. Thankfully that's young for an opera singer. My voice will be good for another fifteen years – longer if I'm careful. But, do you know what's funny, Chance? I have everything I've ever wanted, yet, being with you again, I realise how lonely I've been.'

'Lonely?' He arched her a sceptical look. 'With your travelling entourage of maids, hairdressers, and accompanists? Impossible.'

'It's true. I'm not close to them like I am to you. We should get married, Chance.'

His thumb paused in mid-stroke halfway down her foot. Then he ran it the rest of the way to her heel. 'And do what? Meet each other in airports. You know how much I travel. And you said you were booked for what? – over a hundred performances next year alone. That wouldn't be much of a marriage, would it?'

'But don't you see, Chance, you understand how much this means to me. If I married anyone else, he would object to all the travelling I have to do. Maybe not in the beginning, but in time he would. I've seen it happen with too many other singers, male or female. But you wouldn't mind. You have to admit, Chance, that we are good for each other.'

'You don't really want to marry me, Lucianna.' But he understood what she meant. Over the years they had become comfortable with each other – the way two old friends could be. They slipped in and out of the roles of lovers because it was easy. He knew he could find comfort and affection in her arms – with no demands from her, no strings, no expectations to be fulfilled. 'We know each other too well.'

'Is that bad?' she chided. Yet the very absence of any hurt in her voice proved to him that he was right in what he said. 'We are a lot alike, you and I.'

'Be honest, Lucianna. Do you really want a husband who knew you when you were Lucille Kowolski, a nobody from nowhere with only pride and ambition to her name. We both started at the bottom and clawed our way to the top. We aren't the same people any more. We've put all that behind us. I don't want to be reminded of it every morning. I don't think you do either.'

'I couldn't stand it.' Her voice vibrated with feeling as she turned her head away, presenting him with the power of her profile. 'Although, it did sound like a good idea,' she added, a little wistfully.

Looking at her and feeling the ease of friendship, he thought of Flame, the intriguing green of her eyes, the sculpted bones of her face and the aloof calm of self-control, but, beneath, was an untapped well of emotion. She was a woman of strong will, perhaps even stronger than his own. That alone was a challenge to him, but that alone didn't explain her attraction for him, an attraction that had something to do with the awareness that lay between them. The few minutes he'd spent with her, she'd stimulated more than his desire.

Then he'd received the phone call from Hattie. What the hell did she want? A troubled frown darkened his expression.

The limousine made a wide turn into the private cul-de-sac of the hotel's entrance, its headlights piercing the wispy white fog. Roused from his thoughts, Chance gave Lucianna's silk-clad foot one last kneading squeeze and swung it off his leg. 'Better put your shoes on. We're here.'

'Must I?' Again there was that petulant note in her voice but when Lucianna stepped from the limousine, her feet were once again wedged in red pumps.

Their individual suites were located on opposite ends of the same floor. When they emerged from the elevator, Lucianna paused, angling her body toward him and idly running her fingers up the edge of his jacket lapel, her dark eyes bold with invitation. 'This business meeting of yours can't take much more than an hour, can it? I have a magnum of Taittinger's chilling in my room.'

Chance let his gaze linger on the pouting fullness of her lips. She was a sensual woman, practised in pleasing him. Two hours ago – maybe even less – it would have been a foregone conclusion that he would spend a satisfying hour or two in her bed. But he couldn't summon any interest in the thought now.

'Another time,' he suggested.

A hint of regret was in her smile, yet her look was thoughtful. 'There always is with us, isn't there?'

'Yes,' Chance agreed, recognising that each time they parted it was with the certain knowledge that they would meet somewhere again, sometimes by design, sometimes not.

'Till then.' She rose up to kiss him, old patterns reasserting themselves in the warmly delving contact. Chance responded automatically, his mind preoccupied with his impending meeting with Hattie.

The instant he turned from Lucianna to walk down the corridor to his suite, he forgot her, his thoughts centring wholly on Hattie Morgan, dominating them as she had once dominated him. But no more. That had ended long ago.

Or had it? A wry smile tugged at the corners of his mouth as he realised that again she had commanded him to appear and he had obeyed the summons. This time, however, it had been voluntary. He had to find out what had brought her to San Francisco. He'd always believed that nothing short of death would ever persuade her to leave Morgan's Walk. Obviously he was wrong.

He inserted the key in the lock and gave it a turn. When he opened the door, he heard the soft music playing in the background, the soothing symphony of strings, like the lights left burning in the sitting room, courtesy of the night chambermaid. Stepping inside, Chance closed the door behind him and started to slip the room key into his pocket, then checked the movement.

Hattie sat in the room's wing chair, facing the door – and Chance. His glance skimmed her, taking in the mink-trimmed travelling suit from another era and the sensible low-heeled shoes on her feet. The blue-white of her short hair lay in soft waves about her face. At first glance, she looked like everybody's favourite aunt, but a closer look revealed the stiffness of her spine, the unbending set of her shoulders, and the gloved hand that gripped the handle of her cane like a royal sceptre.

'You're late.' It was more a condemnation than disapproval that threaded through her husky voice.

'So I am.' A muscle flexed along his jaw as Chance remembered the eight-year-old boy who had once winced from the lash of her tongue, confused by the venom in it and the hatred that burned so blackly in her eyes. He glanced at the companion chair, angled to face Hattie's, then moved away from it, walking over to the suite's small bar. 'It's obvious I'll need to have a talk with the concierge about letting strange women into my room.' He picked up a decanter of brandy and splashed some in a snifter. 'How did you manage it, Hattie? Did you convince him you were my sweet old aunt?' Chance mocked cynically as he scooped up the glass, cradling its round bowl in his hand.

'It was much simpler than that,' she retorted. 'I merely bribed the chambermaid to let me in. I've never had to resort to lies to get what I want. I'm not a Stuart.'

He smiled at the gibe, feeling no amusement at all, only a cold anger as he wandered over to stand nearer to the room's centre. 'You have yet to tell me, Hattie, to what do I owe the displeasure of your visit?'

With satisfaction, he watched her lips tighten into an even thinner line. 'You're very confident, aren't you?' she observed. 'You think I have no choice but to leave Morgan's Walk to you.'

'It galls you, doesn't it? – the thought of Morgan's Walk passing into the hands of a Stuart. But you're bound by the conditions set down in your own inheritance of the land. On your death, it must pass to a blood relative. If there is none, then it all becomes the property of the State of Oklahoma. But that condition doesn't come into play, does it?' Chance paused, taking a short sip of the brandy and letting its smooth fire coat his tongue. 'It's a pity you didn't have children of your own, Hattie. Then you wouldn't be faced with leaving it all to a nephew you despise.'

But both of them knew that she had never been able to have children as a result of injuries received in a riding accident in her youth. He had a dim memory of a rare argument between his father and Hattie. In it, his father had shouted obscenities at her and taunted that she was only half a woman, twisted with jealousy and bitterness because she would never have a child born of her flesh. It wasn't until he was much older that he knew what that meant. By then, he'd learned that Hattie's hatred went much deeper than that.

'Morgan's Walk means nothing to you.' It was more a conclusion of fact than an accusation.

'You're wrong, Hattie,' he said softly. 'I have many memories of the place where I lived for eleven years . . . the place where my mother died. Her body wasn't even cold before you threw us out.'

'I threw out a range wolf and his cub. But for my sister, I would have done it much sooner.' Not a flicker of remorse showed in her expression.

'And you never let any of us forget that either. You couldn't even let my mother die in peace,' Chance recalled, along with all the bitterness.

'Others may be fooled by your fine clothes and fine airs – or your beguiling smile – but not me. They may marvel at your ability to spot a weakness and move in, but I am well aware that you were born with the cunning and the instincts of a wolf. Do you think I don't know what you intend to do with Morgan's Walk? A Stuart ultimately destroys everything he gets his hands on.'

Chance slowly rotated the snifter in his hand and absently studied the swirling, amber-brown liquid in the bottom. 'Some things deserve to be destroyed, Hattie,' he said, neither affirming nor denying her veiled accusation. 'A place that's only known hatred is one of them.' Lifting the glass, he bolted down the last swallow of brandy.

Her gloved fingers tightened their grip on the cane. 'Morgan's Walk will never be yours,' she declared in a voice hoarse with anger.

Amused, Chance cynically arched an eyebrow in her direction. 'Short of murder, there's no way you can prevent me from getting it. Like it or not, Hattie, I am your only kin – your only choice for an heir.'

'Are you?' There was a smoothness, a smugness in her expression that he hadn't observed before. 'I wouldn't be too sure about that.'

Chance was instantly wary, and smiled to hide it. 'Is there some significance to that remark?'

'Merely that you may not be my last remaining relative.'

'Am I supposed to believe that?' he mocked.

'It happens to be true.' Her cool statement reeked of confidence.

He studied her with a long considering look. 'It's a nice try, Hattie. But if there was anyone else, you would have mentioned them long ago.'

'Perhaps I just found out about this person myself.'

He didn't wholly believe her, but he didn't like the gleam in her eyes either. He started to ask how she'd found out about this so-called relative, then remembered the meeting she'd had this very morning with the crafty old lawyer, Ben Canon, and checked the impulse, asking instead, 'Is that what – or should I say, who? – brought you to San Francisco?'

'I thought you should be the first to hear the news . . . and I wanted to see your face when I told you. You see' – she paused again for emphasis and rose from her chair, briefly leaning heavily on her cane – 'I know how much you were counting on getting Morgan's Walk. I never underestimate the greed of a Stuart. You would be wise not to underestimate the determination of a Morgan to stop you.'

'I'll remember that.'

When she started toward the door, Chance walked over and opened it for her. The cane ceased its rhythmic tap on the floor as she paused short of the threshold, a hard satisfaction gleaming in her eyes. 'This is one time when I have truly enjoyed seeing you, Stuart.'

'Then you'd better enjoy the feeling while it lasts, Hattie,' he returned, his mouth quirking in a cold smile.

'I intend to.' Again the cane swung out in advance of her stride.

In three steps she was by him and out the door. For a grim second, he stared after her stiffly erect form, then closed the door on her. Turning into the room, Chance hesitated a split second then crossed to the telephone and dialled the number to Sam's private line.

As before, the call was answered on the first ring. 'Hello.'

'Chance.' He identified himself and glanced briefly at the door. 'It looks like we may have a problem, Sam.'

'Hattie.' He guessed immediately.

'Right. She claims another relative exists, one who will be the heir to Morgan's Walk.'

'What?! My God, Chance, you don't think it's true, do you?'

'I don't know, but I intend to find out.'

'She could be bluffing.'

'I can't take that gamble, Sam. The stakes are too high,' he replied grimly. 'Get a hold of Matt Sawyer. Tell him to drop whatever he's doing and get on this right away. If there is a second legitimate heir to Morgan's Walk, then Canon's probably the one who tracked this person down. Tell Matt to start working on that angle.'

'Will do.'

Chance paused briefly, then asked, 'Is Molly there?'

'Sitting right here,' Sam confirmed, a smile in his voice.

His own mouth curved faintly in response to the image that

flashed instantly into his mind of the sweet-faced woman who, only now at fifty-five, had started to count the strands of grey in her brown hair. Widowed and childless, Molly Malone had gone to work for him nearly fifteen years ago, starting out as a part-time secretary, girl Friday and office cleaning lady. Somewhere along the line in those first few months, she had added mothering to her other duties. She ran his office staff now, some said with an iron hand, although she was still butter in his. Time clocks meant nothing to her. She worked all hours; 'Whatever it takes' was her favourite line. She *lived* the Stuart Corporation – not out of loyalty to her job but because it was his. Chance knew that. Just as he knew that no woman could be more devoted to her son than Molly was to him – even to the extent of making his enemies her own, and of them she hated Hattie most of all – almost obsessively so.

He glanced at the gold Rolex on his wrist. 'It's already after midnight there in Tulsa. I suppose she stayed to find out what Hattie wanted with me.'

'You got it.'

'Since she's there, tell her to get on the phone and start calling all the hotels in San Francisco until she finds the one where Hattie's staying. As soon as she does, relay that information to Matt. He's bound to have an investigating firm that he works with here on the West Coast. I want to know her every move – her every contact, from the time she arrived to the time she leaves.'

'You don't believe that Hattie flew all the way out there just to see you, do you?' Sam declared with dawning awareness. 'You think this alleged long-lost relative might live out there.'

'It's a possibility we can't overlook.' Without a break, Chance continued, 'I'm flying out to Tahoe first thing in the morning. I'll probably be tied up most of the day with the architect and engineer going over the design problems we have on the main hotel and casino structure. Hopefully we won't have to make any changes that will affect the companion ski lodge and chalets. But you know how to reach me if anything comes up. Otherwise, I'll be back in Tulsa late Sunday night. Tell Matt I'll expect him in my office nine o'clock Monday morning with a full report.'

'Done.'

As Sam's parting 'Take care' faded, Chance hung up the phone.

For a moment he stood there idly studying the empty brandy glass in his other hand. Then he turned and started across the room, loosening the knot of his black tie and unfastening the collar button of his shirt as he went. At the bar, he reached for the decanter again and poured a half a shot of brandy into his glass. With his fingers curved around the bowl, he picked up the snifter, then paused. Swivelling at the hips, he turned, slanting his shoulders at the wing chair that Hattie had occupied.

'You didn't really believe it would be over so easily, did you, Hattie?' he murmured. 'You should have remembered the promise that eleven-year-old boy made you. Maybe you've seen the last of me, but Morgan's Walk hasn't.'

===4===

THE SATIN caftan whispered softly about her legs as Flame wandered into the black-and-white living room of her Victorian flat, absently nursing that first cup of morning coffee in both hands. With sleepy-eyed interest, she surveyed the casually intimate grouping of furniture around the zebra stripe wool rug, the eye-catching white on white motif of the overstuffed sofa repeated on the cushions of the dramatic horn chairs finished in gleaming black lacquer accented with solid brass.

There was an awareness that the room's decor was a subtle reflection of her own personality, the airy and open effect of white contrasted sharply by the dynamic and sensual impact of black. And Flame also knew that the sleekly contemporary look on the inside was at odds with the ornate gingerbread trim of the building's exterior. The turn-of-the-century house had supposedly been a wedding present from a doting father to his beloved daughter, like so many others that had been built on Russian Hill, so named after a cemetery for Russian sailors that had occupied its summit during the city's early history. Twelve years ago, the mansion's many rooms had been converted into spacious, individually owned apartments.

Looking around her, Flame realised that this flat was the one good thing that had come out of her disastrous marriage. It was hers now. Although at the time, she would have willingly given it up along with anything else just to obtain a divorce. Fortunately, that hadn't been necessary.

The buzzing ring of the doorbell cut sharply through the morning stillness. Flame frowned at the black mantel clock above the white marble fireplace. It wasn't nine o'clock yet. No one came to visit this early on a Saturday morning. Her friends knew how much she relished her weekend mornings – waking up at her leisure, dressing when she pleased, and going out if she chose. During the weekdays she adhered to a set schedule of appointments, meetings, and business luncheons, but the weekends when she wasn't working on a rush campaign or on call, she spent strictly on impulse, shopping or sailing with friends, occasionally taking in an exhibition she wanted to see or simply lolling around the apartment and catching up on current novels. The evenings were different, usually with some private dinner party, social function or benefit interspersed with concerts and theatre performances.

When the buzzer rang again, more strident in its summons the second time, Flame set her cup down on the glass top of the black lacquer and brass occasional table and ran lightly from the living room into the foyer, her bare feet making little sound on the honey-coloured parquet flooring. Out of habit, she glanced through the front door's peephole. On the other side stood an elderly lady, a pillbox hat of loden green perched atop a soft cloud of white hair. Despite the slight distortion from the thick glass, Flame was certain she didn't know the woman.

The woman started to ring the doorbell a third time. Flame pushed the tousled mass of her hair away from her face with a combing rake of her fingers and began unfastening the series of security locks and chains. In the midst of the third ring, she swung the heavy oak door open.

'Yes?' She glanced expectantly at the elderly stranger, certain she had come to the wrong address. Yet the avid stare from the elderly woman's brightly black eyes inspected every detail of her appearance, skipping over the purple and pink of her caftan to centre on her hair. 'Were you looking for someone?' she prompted when the silence threatened to lengthen.

For an instant she doubted the woman had heard her and briefly wondered if she might be deaf. Then an awareness seemed to enter the woman's expression.

'Forgive me for staring,' she said, a pleasant huskiness in her voice. 'But – your hair, it's exactly the same shade of strawberry blonde as Kell Morgan's. His portrait hangs over the fireplace in the library.'

'Who are you?' she challenged, a fine tension rippling through her as she suddenly realised why those eyes looked familiar. Her father's had been just as brilliantly black, always shining with life. But that was impossible. She didn't have any family left – no aunts, no uncles, no cousins.

'I'm Harriet Fay Morgan,' she announced, a pleased smile curving her lips and emphasising the tiny fracture lines that aged the parchment-like fineness of her skin. 'And you are undoubtedly Margaret Rose Morgan.'

'Bennett.' The correction was an automatic response.

'You're married?' A pepper-grey eyebrow lifted in sharp question.

'Divorced.'

'Yes, yes, I remember now. Ben told me that.' Irritation briefly darkened her expression at the momentary memory lapse. And that hint of vulnerability prompted Flame to notice that – for all the woman's alertness – she had to be in her late seventies or early eighties . . . too old to be made to stand outside, especially when there were a dozen questions Flame wanted to ask.

'Won't you come in, Mrs Morgan?' She swung the door open wider and stepped to one side, allowing her to pass.

'Thank you.' With an unhurried dignity, the woman entered the foyer, her small shoulders square and straight beneath the jacket of her fur-trimmed suit, its stylish cut reminiscent of a fashion popular twenty years ago. The cane seemed to serve as a prop rather than a support as she turned to Flame. 'I must insist that you call me Hattie. I never married so to be called "Miss" at my age seems inappropriate.'

'Of course.' Flame led the way into the living room. 'I have fresh coffee made. Would you like a cup?'

'I prefer hot tea if you don't mind.'

'Not at all. Please, make yourself comfortable. I won't be a minute.'

But it was closer to five minutes before Flame returned with a pot of tea, the attendant cream, sugar and saucer of lemon as well as a teacup and saucer balanced on a tray along with a cup of coffee for herself. In her absence Hattie Morgan had enthroned herself on one of the horn chairs. Catching back a smile at the thought, Flame realised that there was a certain hauteur about Hattie that bordered on the regal.

'Lemon, cream or sugar?'

'Lemon, please,' she replied, taking the delicate Sèvres cup and saucer from Flame, her glance lightly sweeping the room. 'This is pleasant,' she observed, her attention returning to Flame as she lifted the dainty cup from its saucer. 'Of course, it's nothing at all like Morgan's Walk.'

'Morgan's Walk is your home?'

'Our family home, yes. It's stood for nearly a hundred years, and, God willing, it will stand for a hundred more.'

'Where is that?'

'Oklahoma, about twenty minutes from Tulsa.'

She volunteered no more than that, leaving Flame with the impression that Hattie was waiting for her to ask the questions. 'You mentioned a man named Ben earlier. Who is he? For that matter, who's Kell Morgan?' Flame took her coffee and moved to the corner of the sofa nearest to Hattie's chair.

'Ben Canon is the family lawyer, and has been for years. It was through his efforts that I located you. And Kell Morgan' – again those bright eyes took note of the glinting red lights in Flame's hair – 'was my grandfather. His brother was Christopher Morgan.'

The latter was said with a sense of import, yet it meant nothing to Flame. 'Should I know that name?'

'He was your great-grandfather.' She sipped at her tea, eyeing Flame over the cup's golden rim. 'You aren't familiar with your father's family history, are you?'

'Not very,' she admitted, her frown thoughtful and wary. 'All my father ever told me about his grandfather that I can remember was the story of how he'd come to San Francisco shortly before the turn of the century and fallen hopelessly in love with Helen Fleming, the daughter of one of the city's founding families. Within three months, they were married. Other than that . . .' Flame shrugged, indicating her lack of knowledge, and settled back against the sofa's plump white cushions and curled a leg underneath her. For all her relaxed poise, inside she was tense. 'I know several of my friends have become deeply involved in tracing their family tree and finding out all they can about their ancestors. It's as if they must in order to have any sense of who or what they themselves are. I've never agreed with that. In my opinion, everyone has their own separate identity. Who my ancestors were or what they did has nothing to do with who I am today.' But even as she made her slightly impassioned disavowal, she was aware that her own actions frequently contradicted that. Because of who her family was, she had a certain prestige. She hadn't earned it; her ancestors had. And even while a part of her resented it, she used it to open doors, to mix with the right people, and to further her own career. She stared at the coffee cooling in her cup, conscious of the silence and not feeling particularly proud of her accomplishments. 'If I offended you, Hattie, I'm sorry. Obviously you share their interest in family trees or you wouldn't be here.'

'Their interest, perhaps, but not for the same reason. And I'm certain we differed in our approach. You see, it was a living descendant of Christopher that I was anxious to find.' But she didn't elaborate. 'Believe me, that wasn't easy. Soon after Christopher Morgan left Morgan's Walk and went West all those years ago, the family lost touch with him. For all we knew, he might even have changed his name.'

'Why would he change it?' she frowned.

'Who knows?' Those sharply bright eyes never once left Flame's face, their burning intensity somehow mesmerising. 'It was hardly uncommon for a man who went West to change his name and take on a whole new identity. Frequently it was to conceal a criminal past, but sometimes it became a symbolic way to start a new life.'

She understood such reasoning. After her divorce, she had elected to keep her married name, as if by doing so she was no longer a Morgan. But everyone knew she was.

'Tell me about yourself,' Hattie urged. 'I understand you work.'

'Yes, I'm a vice-president and account executive for a national advertising company here in the city.'

'A vice-president. You must be very intelligent.'

Was she? Or had she finally got smart and stopped fighting the family name and started using it instead to get what she wanted? As a vice-president, she received an excellent salary, but even on that she wouldn't have been able to afford half of what she owned. Practically all the expensive furnishings in her flat and nearly her entire wardrobe of designer clothes she'd purchased from agency clients, but never at retail. No, she used her position, both with the company and in society, to obtain special discounts. That was the way the game was played, and she'd learned to be good at it. It was a form of urban survival today.

'It helps to know the right people, too,' she replied, lifting her shoulders in an expressive shrug, a little uncomfortable with the compliment.

'I understand you are an only child.'

'Yes.'

'And both your parents are gone.'

Flame nodded. 'They were in an auto accident eleven years ago. My father was killed instantly. My mother was in a coma for several days. She died without ever regaining consciousness.' After all this time, the sense of loss was still acute. Even now, she missed them. There were moments when she could almost hear her mother's laughter – and her dad's teasing voice. They had loved her. Not because of her bloodline or because she was beautiful, but for herself. Since she'd lost them, she'd learned just how rare that kind of love was.

'You and I are a lot alike, I think,' Hattie observed. 'We've both had to learn to be independent at an early age. My mother died a few hours after my baby sister was born. I was fifteen at the time – with a baby to take care of and a household to manage. Then I lost my father when I was nineteen. Suddenly Morgan's Walk was mine. I not only had a baby sister to raise, but an entire ranch to run.'

'Morgan's Walk is a ranch.' Flame was surprised by that. 'I thought it was some sort of an estate.' Although what kind of estate there could be in Oklahoma, she had no idea. Certainly it had never occurred to her that it was a ranch.

'It's both. There's almost twelve hundred acres of land within its boundaries. Once it was twenty times that size, but time and circumstances have whittled away at it. Most of it is river valley, some of the lushest, greenest land you'll ever see.' Where before Hattie's demeanour had been marked by a watchful reserve, there was now animation, a rapt excitement lighting her face and putting an even brighter glow in her eyes. 'It's beautiful country,

Margaret Rose, all rolling hills and trees unbelievably green against the blue of the sky. And the main house sits at the head of the valley. Oh, and what a house it is – three storeys of brick with towering white colonnades. Your ancestor Christopher Morgan is the one who designed it before he came to California. All the bricks came from a kiln right on the property and they used the land's red dirt to make them. Wait until you see it. I know you'll love it.'

'I'm sure I would.' Flame smiled, touched by the woman's obvious love for her home. 'Although it's not likely I will.'

Hattie seemed startled by that. 'Oh, but you will. You must. Morgan's Walk will be yours when I die.'

For a stunned instant, Flame stared at her. 'What did you say?' she managed at last, certain she had misunderstood.

'Morgan's Walk will be yours when –'

She didn't need to hear any more. 'You can't mean that. You don't even know me,' she protested.

'You're a Morgan. I knew that the minute I saw you. It was more than the red of your hair and the high cut of your cheekbones. It was the strength of pride and the determination to succeed that I recognised in you.'

'That doesn't explain anything.' She frowned. 'It doesn't even make sense.'

'But it does. You see, Morgan's Walk must pass to a Morgan. If there is no direct descendant, then the land becomes the property of the State. That's why it was so important that I find you. For a time I thought –' She caught herself up short, and dismissed the rest of the sentence with a shake of her head. 'But I don't have to worry about that now. I found you.'

It sounded logical. Almost too logical. Flame couldn't help being sceptical. People just didn't ring somebody's doorbell and announce that they were inheriting a ranch – in Oklahoma or anywhere else.

'Is this some elaborate con to get money out of me?' she demanded. 'Because if it is, you're wasting your time.'

'You're suspicious by nature. That's good,' Hattie stated, a satisfied gleam in her eyes. 'Morgan's Walk will definitely be safe in your hands. You won't let . . . anyone take it from you.'

Flame caught that faint hesitation. 'Is someone trying to get it from you?'

— 41 —

Hattie leaned forward and pushed her teacup and saucer on to the coffee table's glass top. 'As I said, it's rich land. There will always be someone who wants it. People have fought over land since before the time of Moses, haven't they?' She smiled smoothly. 'As for money – I won't pretend that Morgan's Walk is as prosperous as it once was. It isn't. At best, you'll receive only a small income from it after all its costs are paid. Of course, you may run into some sort of inheritance tax situation. You might want to check into that.'

She kept talking as if it was a matter of course. Couldn't she see how absolutely improbable it sounded? Flame tried to explain. 'Hattie, I'm a city girl. I don't know the first thing about cows or ranching.'

'I am eighty-one years old. You surely don't believe that I chase cows at my age. I grant you, I can still climb on a horse and ride out to look things over, but I have a foreman who oversees every-thing – a ranch manager, if you will. Charlie Rainwater is a good man – as honest and loyal as the day is long. You leave him in charge and you won't have a thing to worry about. In time, you'll learn from him everything you need to know. Now.' She folded her hands together in a gesture that seemed to indicate it was time they moved on to more important matters. 'How soon can you come to Morgan's Walk?'

That was the last question Flame expected to hear. 'I don't know that I can. After all I do have –'

'Forgive me,' Hattie interrupted. 'I didn't mean that you should drop everything and fly out with me today. I know that you have certain responsibilities and commitments you have to honour. But surely you can arrange to have a long weekend off and come for a visit. It's selfish I know, but I want the chance to show Morgan's Walk to you myself.'

Unwilling to commit herself, Flame said, 'I'll have to check my schedule.'

'You'll come,' Hattie stated confidently. 'You're a Morgan. And whether you want to admit it or not, your roots are buried deep in that land. It will pull you back.'

'Perhaps,' Flame conceded, although she personally wasn't cer-tain she believed any of this.

With her mission complete, a few minutes later Hattie said her goodbyes and left for the airport. Flame offered to call her a cab, but Hattie said, no, she had a car and driver waiting outside for her.

Alone again, Flame returned to the living room. But the quiet of the morning was gone. In its place was a feeling of unreality – as if the last hour hadn't really happened, that it had all been her imagination. Had it? No. The teapot was there on the tray next to the cup and saucer Hattie had drunk from. But that still didn't mean any of it was true. For all she knew, Hattie was just some crazy old woman. She probably didn't even own a ranch. No, it was all too far-fetched.

Still . . . Flame looked around the room and felt a loneliness wash over her. It was all that talk about family. She hesitated, then walked over to the white lacquered bookcase and took down the family photo album. She hadn't looked at it in years, not since – She shook the memory aside and flipped the book open.

She smiled at the photo of a four-year-old girl, a new Easter bonnet perched atop her carroty curls, too fascinated by the shiny black of her patent leather shoes to look at the camera. Those were simpler times, happier times. She kept turning pages, pausing now and again to gaze at a snapshot of her with her mother or her father or the rare few when all three of them were in the same photo. They were all there, past Christmases and birthdays, ski vacations in the Rockies or the Sierras, sailing trips along the coast, her first dance recital, her first communion, eighth-grade graduation, dances, proms, boyfriends. And in every picture, there were smiles and laughter.

Tears welled in her eyes as she looked at the last photo. She was standing next to her father in front of a fiery red Trans Am, a graduation present from her parents. It was jammed to the ceiling with her clothes and the thousands of other things she was certain she would need at college. It hadn't mattered that she was only going across the Bay to Berkeley. She had to take it all. Her father had his arm around her shoulders, laughing and hugging her close.

A tear rolled down her cheek. With the back of her hand, Flame scubbed it away, sniffed back the runny wetness in her nose, then laughed softly, remembering the time when she'd been seven and taken a tumble on the slopes, banging her knee. She'd cried and her father had given her his handkerchief. She'd blown her nose, then asked him one of those impossible questions, 'Daddy, why does my nose run every time I cry?'

He'd had an answer for her. He always did, not necessarily the correct one, but an answer just the same. 'Maybe because it's sad that you got hurt.'

'Then why doesn't my mouth run?' She'd wanted to know. 'Isn't it sad, too?'

'Your mouth runs all the time. Jabber, jabber, jabber.'

And she'd laughed and laughed. He'd always made her laugh.

A soft sigh trembled from her, wistful of that time when she'd been happy and loved . . . and so very sheltered. Although she hadn't known it at the time.

The next pages were missing, ripped from the book in a fit of wounded rage. She fingered the ragged edges of the stiff paper, not at all sorry they were gone. She didn't need photos to remind her of Rick.

The sudden loss of her parents had been a brutal shock. For days after their separate funerals, one on top of the other, she'd been too numb to feel anything. Then came the grief, the pain, the terrible loneliness. But more than that, she'd felt lost and alone, with no anchor and no direction. To have their love wrenched from her so suddenly had left an awful, aching void. She'd desperately needed to be loved again. She had started reaching for it, grasping for it everywhere and anywhere. On campus the talk had been that she was a little wild. Maybe it had looked that way, but she hadn't been, not really.

Then, at a fraternity party, she'd met Rick Bennett. That night he'd made her laugh – the way her father used to do. And he had dark eyes and dark hair, like her father. And he'd been handsome in a clean-cut all-American way that spoke of solidness, steadiness. Rick had taken her home that night, back to her sorority house, then called to say goodnight. He'd phoned the next morning, too, to tell her good morning.

Almost from the beginning, they'd been inseparable. The only thing they hadn't done together was attend the same classes. He'd been a post-graduate student in law, and she'd been only a lowly sophomore – majoring in Rick was always what she'd laughed and said then. Which had been the absolute truth.

In retrospect, it seemed appropriate that Rick had proposed to her on April Fool's Day. Of course, he had made it sound very romantic by claiming that he'd picked it because he was a fool over her. During their short engagement, he managed to pass his bar exam and persuaded Flame to introduce him to a very senior partner with one of San Francisco's most prestigious law firms, who was also a long-time friend of her family. Whether out of friendship or sympathy for Flame or an objective evaluation of his qualifications, Rick subsequently had been invited to join the firm.

Then came the wedding. Rick had insisted it be a lavish affair. Flame had argued against it. Without any family of her own, she hadn't felt right about it, but he'd urged her to remember she was a Morgan – and to be practical and think of all the wedding gifts they would receive, items they wouldn't have to buy to set up house. She could have told him that gifts of silver and Baccarat crystal would hardly be practical for a young couple, but in the end, she'd relented, and the guest list for the wedding had read like the Who's Who of San Francisco society.

On her marriage, Flame obtained absolute control of her parents' estate, which amounted to a little more than a quarter of a million dollars. The first purchase they'd made had been this pricey flat – no boxy condo in a concrete and glass high-rise for them. And second they'd bought a Porsche for Rick. He'd always wanted one, and an aggressive young attorney needed to project the right image. And that image had meant clothes. Brooks Brothers suits hadn't been good enough for Rick; it had to be Cardin, Blass, and Lagerfeld.

Oddly enough, she had never minded the money they'd spent. The apartment was a good investment as well as a comfortable home. As for the car, she'd loved Rick and wanted him to have it because he'd always dreamed of owning one. And the clothes, she'd been just as guilty of wanting to wear only the best.

No, the money hadn't been their problem. As soon as they'd returned from their honeymoon in Greece, Rick had urged her to renew her family contacts and persuade some of her friends to recommend him for membership in the yacht club. Soon they were going out nearly every night – to this party or that dinner, a gallery showing or a ballet, a charity benefit or a gala opening. They'd dined only at the trendiest restaurants and partied only at the 'in' spots.

In the beginning, she'd accepted his reasoning that it was important to his career for him to mix with the right people. San Francisco was full of brilliant young lawyers, but without influential contacts few of them would ever achieve their potential. And Rick had no intention of being a brilliant older lawyer still waiting to be made a partner in the firm. She'd agreed with him – and allowed him to organise her daytime activities, too – becoming involved in the 'right' charity and civic organisations, lunching, playing tennis or going shopping with wives whose friendships he wanted her to cultivate.

After seven months on that social merry-to-round, Flame had grown weary of it and rebelled. There had been some charity ball they were supposed to attend but when Rick had come home from the office that evening, she hadn't been ready.

'Why aren't you dressed?' He looked at her with some surprise and glanced at the gold Piaget wristwatch she'd given him for Christmas. 'You'd better get a move on or we'll be late.'

'No, we won't.' Ignoring his look of impatience, she went to him and firmly placed his hands on the back of her waist, then wound her own around his neck. 'Instead of going to the ball, let's stay home and have a romantic evening together . . . just the two of us.' She leaned up and nipped at his ear. 'We haven't done that in a long time. And I have a bottle of Dom Perignon chilling in the fridge, along with some Beluga caviar. Later we can fix some fettucini, or maybe a steak. You slip out of that tie and I'll –'

As she started to loosen it, Rick stopped her. 'I love the thought, darling, but we'll have to do it some other time. Tonight we have this charity thing. They're expecting us.'

'You make it sound as if they'll cancel the ball if we don't show up. I assure you they won't,' she teased with a cajoling smile. 'So why don't we just skip it?'

'No.' He set her away from him, a finality in his voice and his gesture that rankled.

Still Flame persisted. 'Why not?'

'Because we said we'd be there and we're going.'

'Rick, it's a charity ball, for heaven's sake. How many hundred functions like it have we attended these last six months? I'm tired of them. Aren't you?' She frowned.

'Whether I'm tired of them or not is immaterial,' he retorted, yanking at the knot of his tie. 'Affairs like this are important to me. I thought you understood that.'

Stung by his tone, Flame was tempted to ask if they were more important than spending time with her, but she checked the angry impulse and turned away instead, feigning a shrug of indifference. 'Then you go. I'll stay home by myself.'

'Don't be ridiculous, Flame,' he snapped. 'You're a Morgan. You have to be there.'

You're a Morgan. How many times had she heard him say that? She'd lost count, but this time, the phrase sunk in. She swung on him in full temper. 'My name is *Bennett*. Or had you forgotten that little detail?'

He flushed guiltily. 'You know what I meant.'

'No.' She shook her head in firm denial. 'I don't think I do. Why don't you explain just how you see me? Am I your wife? Am I the woman you love? Am I your life's partner? Or – am I your social entrée?' she challenged, suddenly remembering the thousand little conversations that had taken place over the past months – and the way Rick had always drawn her family name into them. She realised that he knew more about the history of her family than she did.

From that point on, the confrontation had degenerated into a shouting match, insults and accusations hurled on both sides. In the end, Rick had stormed out of the flat, and for days afterwards they'd been cold to each other. Eventually they'd gone through the motions of making up, but it had never been the same after that.

As the weeks wore on, Flame had gradually come to see that she'd unwittingly hit on the truth. If Rick loved her at all, it was because she was a Morgan and, therefore, his passport into a world that would have otherwise barred him from entering. He didn't love her, not for herself. He never had. Two months later, she'd filed for a divorce.

She'd walked away from the marriage scarred but much wiser. She'd learned a valuable lesson, one that she found many oc-casions to apply. Over the years, she'd discovered that few people sought her company for its sake alone. Some, like Rick, saw her as a passport to power and prestige. Some were outright social climbers. Others were attracted by her beauty and regarded her as a prize to be paraded on their arm. And to others, like Malcom

Powell, she represented a conquest that had eluded him. All of those people she had eliminated very quickly from her life, dropping them the instant she discerned their reason for wanting to be with her – which was much easier than most supposed. As a result, her circle of friends was small indeed. And, of them, she regarded only Ellery as her one true friend. He'd never asked anything of her and never once taken advantage of their friendship. On the contrary, Ellery had always given – of his knowledge, his understanding, his time and his company.

Slowly Flame closed the photo album and hugged it tightly to her. That old need to love and be loved was still there, but, of necessity, buried deep inside. Friends, a beautiful home, gorgeous clothes, and an unquestionably successful career weren't enough to fill the emptiness. Without someone to share them with, they meant little. But who?

Instantly an image of Chance Stuart flashed in her mind. Suddenly she could see again that faintly wicked glint in his blue eyes, the raffish charm of his crooked smile, and that aura of virility he wore so casually. She smiled, realising that he'd made a very definite impression on her – and wondered if she would see him again or whether it had been a line, forgotten minutes after it was said. Probably.

Sighing, Flame returned the photo album to its place on the shelf, her fingers lingering for a moment on its worn, leather-bound spine. As she turned, her glance fell on the horn chair. That strange visit from Hattie Morgan had started this rush of memories with all her talk about family. How odd that it had taken a stranger to remind her.

— 5 —

THE BLACK marble and glass of Stuart Tower loomed tall and proud, adding its own bold statement to the progressive skyline of cosmopolitan Tulsa. Like everything else Chance Stuart owned, it carried his name, emblazoned in gold leaf to gleam in the sun for all to see. More than one had suggested, not entirely in jest, that he should take that scrolled 'S' and put a line through it, turning it into a dollar sign because everyone sure as hell knew that the name Stuart and money were practically synonymous.

When the silver Jaguar wheeled into the entrance to the underground parking garage, the brash young attendant in the booth quickly sat up straighter, threw a one-fingered salute at the driver, then gazed after the car with a mixture of longing and envy. It rolled to a smooth stop in the space marked: RESERVED, C. STUART. Chance stepped out and crossed to the private elevator. It made only one stop – on the twentieth floor, the office of the Stuart Corporation.

The elevator whisked him silently to the building's top floor and opened its doors on to Molly's office, the private entrance allowing him to avoid the public reception area and the many offices of the company's various departments. As always, Molly was already seated behind her desk, guarding the door to his office, her chubby cheeks rounded in a smile of welcome when he walked out of the elevator.

'Morning, Molly. Has Matt Sawyer arrived?' he asked, heading straight for his office.

'Not yet.'

'Show him in the minute he does.' Chance opened the door, then paused. 'And let Sam know I'm here.'

'Right away.' She reached for the intercom.

Without waiting, Chance entered his office and automatically closed the door behind him, then crossed the bleached wood floor to his desk in the corner. He glanced briefly at the stack of telephone messages and letters waiting for his attention on the desk's granite top. Turning his back on them for the time being, he walked to the smoke-tinted glass that enclosed two sides of the immense room.

His corner office overlooked buildings that represented some of the finest examples of the art deco style architecture so popular in the thirties. Once those buildings housed the offices of such oil giants as Waite Phillips, Bill Sinclair and J. Paul Getty. Chance studied them briefly then lifted his glance to the city sprawled over the rolling hills of Oklahoma's Green Country.

Many had questioned his decision to make Tulsa his headquarters when he could just as easily have picked Dallas or Denver if it was a central location he wanted. Few knew of the affinity he felt for this city. It had come a long way from its humble cowtown beginnings, a wide spot along a dusty trail – and from its wild and rowdy days as an oil boomtown. All its rough edges had been smoothed. Now it stood sleek and sophisticated with its alabaster skyline, a high-tech city in a high-tech world. He and Tulsa had much in common. It was more than a home-town boy coming back after he'd made good – much more.

There was a quick rap on his door followed by the click of the latch. Chance swung around expecting to see Sam walk in. But it was Molly, a steaming cup of coffee in her hand. 'I knew I had missed something. Nobody makes coffee as good as you do, Molly.'

'You're only saying that to make sure I don't go on strike and refuse to make coffee for you any more.' She crossed the room and set the cup on his desk beaming at his praise, her round cheeks growing rounder, and reminded him of the time he had teased her about being his all-round girl – round cheeks, round eyes, round face, and round body. Then her look faded to one of faint disapproval and he knew he was about to be lectured on something. 'One thing's certain. That Lucy woman –'

'Lucianna,' he corrected, transferring his attention to the phone messages in his hand.

'Whatever she calls herself now, she didn't bring you any coffee in the morning.'

'No. Room service did.'

Molly ignored that. 'You've known this Lucianna a long time, I know, but she won't make you a good wife. And it's time you got married.'

'What can I do? I keep asking and you keep turning me down.' He walked back to his desk.

'You're impossible.' She pretended to be angry with him. 'When are you going to wake up to the fact that you're thirty-eight years old? You not only don't have a wife, but you don't have any children either.'

Sam strolled into the office, lanky and trim with a thatch of unruly light brown hair. 'At least, none that you know about, Molly.'

She turned. 'If he had any, I'd know. Everyone would, because you can bet the mother would file a paternity suit.'

'If it's a child you want, Chance, Patty and I will loan you one of ours. You can take your pick. Right now I think Patty would willingly give all four of them away. It was a bad weekend at home. I'm glad I spent most of it here.'

Chance straightened from his desk, fully alert. 'Did you come up with anything?'

Sam shook his head. 'I've already filled you in on everything I know. Until Matt gets here . . .' He shrugged the rest.

'Molly, see if Matt Sawyer's here yet.'

'Of course.' Easily she slipped back into the role of the efficient secretary and left his office to return to her own.

Sam watched her go, then turned back to Chance, grinned and shook his head in amusement. 'She never gives up, does she?'

'Not Molly.'

Sam wandered over to the desk and sat down in the charcoal suede chair that faced it. 'Did you get everything worked out in Tahoe to your satisfaction?'

Chance smiled crookedly. 'Let's say I got everything worked out. Whether it will be to my satisfaction remains to be seen.' The Tahoe project was his most ambitious to date. When completed, it would be a year-round resort complex, with a palatial hotel and gambling casino adjacent to the marina and yacht club, with a luxury ski lodge coupled with chalet-style condominiums and an array of ski runs and trails.

'I talked to Kiley this morning,' Sam said, referring to their construction manager on the project site. 'He mentioned you had a little run-in with Nick Borrello.'

'You could call it that,' Chance conceded. 'Among other things, he accused me of stealing his casino.'

Admittedly he'd bought it from the man at a bargain price, but the casino had lost money the last three years – for a number of reasons. Poor management was one of them, and another was its location on the fringe of Lake Tahoe's main gambling area. As a small, independent casino it couldn't compete with those operated by the big hotels and it couldn't siphon away enough of their trade.

As a casino alone, Chance wouldn't have been interested in it. But he'd looked at its lake frontage, the surrounding forest, the jutting mountain behind it and its proximity to the gaming centres, and knew immediately that the site was – in the argot of land developers – a 'Tiffany location'.

'He's certainly changed his tune, hasn't he?' Sam remarked. 'Not six months ago, he was so happy to have you take it off his hands that he would have gladly kissed your feet.' A smile spread across his face, boyish in its charm. 'For that matter, most of your competitors were convinced you'd bought a lemon.'

'I know.' Chance smiled back, aware that he hadn't been quick to correct that impression either. Instead, he'd waited to announce his plans for the site until three days after the Nevada gaming commission had given him their nod of approval. At that point, he inked the lease he'd arranged with the Forest Service, giving him the mountain behind the casino. With that in hand, he held a press conference and announced his plans.

Suddenly everybody had sat up and taken another look at the deal he'd put together. That's when they realised that not only had he bought it at a rock-bottom price, but he also didn't have a dime in it himself. A major hotel chain anxious to get into the area had fronted all the money, and a national insurance company was waiting in the wings to fund the rest of the project. By the time the development was completed and in operation two years from now, his profit from it would be in the hundreds of millions. Most developers had walked away, shaking their heads and grumbling that they hadn't seen the same potential – and admitting, however grudgingly, that he'd pulled another rabbit out of the hat with typical Stuart style.

But not the former owner, Nick Borrello, who had initially bragged about the deal he'd made. Now he was screaming foul. But Chance was used to that.

The door to his office swung open, and Molly stepped in briefly to announce, 'Mr Sawyer's here.' She moved to one side, allowing the man to enter.

Few people would look twice at Matt Sawyer, and fewer still would guess that the former FBI agent had left the Bureau to head one of the more reputable private security agencies in the country. He was a nondescript man of average height, build and colouring, but his investigative skills were widely regarded. Five years ago, Chance had hired him for the first time to locate the owner of a small, but vital piece of property whose whereabouts were unknown. He'd had his own people on it for nearly a month. Matt Sawyer had located the man in less than forty-eight hours. Since then, Chance had employed his services on numerous occasions, and he'd proved himself invaluable more than once in tracking down much-needed information.

'Hello, Matt.' Chance came around the desk to greet him, briefly gripping his hand, then motioning towards the small grouping of sofas and armchairs where he held many of his informal meetings. 'What did you come up with?'

'Not a lot yet, but we're working on it.' He gave his trouser legs a hitch as he sat down on the cerulean-blue chair and placed his briefcase on his lap. 'I did talk to Ben Canon's secretary. She was fairly co-operative, but there was a lot she either didn't know or wouldn't tell me.' He snapped open the case and took out two folders. 'She did confirm that Canon had a meeting with Hattie at nine on Friday but she claimed she didn't know what it was about. She said Canon instructed her to hold his calls and closed the door to his private office so she didn't overhear any of the meeting. Which, according to her, lasted about ninety minutes. She was sure of the time because Canon had an eleven o'clock appointment and Hattie was gone before that client arrived.' He passed one of the folders to Chance and gave the other to Sam. 'Somewhere around nine-thirty – she wasn't certain of the exact time – Canon buzzed her on the intercom and asked her to make reservations for Hattie to fly to San Francisco that same day. And she also arranged for a cab to take Hattie to the airport. But, according to her, no explanation was given for the trip or the urgency of it.'

'She has to know more than that.' Chance tossed the folder and its detailed report on the coffee table without opening it, knowing that it would obtain merely facts and he wanted impressions as well. 'She's his secretary. She sees everything that passes over his desk. She's bound to know what he's working on.'

Matt shook his head. 'Not the way Ben Canon operates. The way she described him, he keeps everything pretty close to the chest and never confides in her about a client. He opens all the mail himself and has a set of locked files in his office where he keeps any correspondence or paperwork dealing with current cases.' He paused, a wry smile quirking his mouth. 'And you aren't going to believe this. He has an old manual typewriter that he uses to type any important correspondence himself.'

'Why does he even bother to have a secretary then?' Sam frowned.

'To answer the phone I guess.' Matt shrugged.

Chance continued to eye Matt closely. 'You found out something from her, didn't you?'

Matt looked at him and allowed a rare smile to show. 'In addition to answering his phones, she empties the wastebasket in his office. On Friday night she found a large Manila envelope in it from a Whitney or a Whittier or a name similar to that. She noticed it because the return address was Salt Lake City and she has an aunt living there. She thought the man might be a doctor – a gynaecologist maybe. She wasn't sure, but she remembered something like that being printed below his name. And I'm guessing that it didn't say gynaecologist. Instead it read genealogist.'

'Someone who studies family histories – genealogy.' Sam sat

up. 'I'll bet you're right, Matt. I'll bet Canon hired him to try to locate anyone who might be related to Hattie.'

'It's logical,' Matt agreed. 'They have amassed quite a collection of family records in Salt Lake City, second only to the archives in Washington, I understand. Anyway, if there is a genealogist named Whittier or Whitney there, he shouldn't be too hard to find.'

'What about Hattie's stay in San Francisco?' Chance wanted to know.

'We weren't quite so lucky there. As you know, she stayed downtown at the Cartwright. By the time my associate in the Bay area was able to get someone over there Saturday morning, she'd already checked out. A little after eight, the desk clerk said. The doorman remembered that she was picked up by a man driving a dark green saloon. He wasn't sure of the make or model, but he thought it had California plates. About two and a half hours later, a car matching that description dropped her off at the airport. The agent didn't get close enough to get the licence number. Unfortunately we don't know what she did, where she went, or who she might have seen in that two and a half hours between the time she left the hotel and arrived at the airport.'

'No description of the driver?' Chance asked.

'None. But obviously either she or Canon knows somebody in San Francisco. I have a contact in the telephone company checking to see if either of them made any long distance calls to the Bay area in the last week.' He closed the briefcase, snapping it shut with an air of finality. 'Like I said, we don't have a lot of hard information for you right now, but I have a lot of things we're working on.'

'This has to have top priority, Matt,' Chance reminded him, the hard gleam in his eyes leaving the man in little doubt that he meant it. 'If you can't find the information one way, then try another, but find it. Don't let locked files stand in your way.'

'I understand.' Matt nodded quietly, not needing any elaboration on that statement.

After he'd gone, Sam turned to Chance, his hands thrust deep in his pockets in a troubled and thoughtful pose. 'It doesn't look like Hattie was running a bluff does it? But you never thought she was. Why?'

'You didn't see her. She was like a cat still busy licking the cream off her whiskers.' He picked up the report from Matt and carried it to his desk.

'I still don't believe it,' Sam declared, raking his fingers through his hair. 'To have some long-lost cousin wind up with Morgan's Walk . . . Chance, what are you going to do?'

'I'll buy it if I have to.'

'What if this person won't sell?'

'Everybody has a price, Sam. That's where Hattie made her mistake. Whoever this relative is – they aren't going to give a damn about Morgan's Walk. All they're going to care about is how much they'll inherit.'

'But if Hattie's already talked to them, she could have turned them against you already. And if she hasn't, you can damned well bet she will.'

'It won't matter. We'll use a third party to make the deal. They'll never know they're selling it to me.'

'I wish I could be as sure as you are.'

'It's a hand we'll have to play when we find out who this relative is and get some background on him. Maybe by the time I fly back to San Francisco for Lucianna's opening night this Friday, we'll know. Which reminds me . . .' He picked up the phone and punched the intercom line to Molly's phone.

'Yes?' came the crisp response.

'Molly, I want you to send some flowers for me.'

— 6 —

TENSION GRIPPED the small meeting room off the agency's
graphic arts department as Flame studied the rough sketches
spread across the long table in front of her. Proposed layouts for
new print advertising lay side by side with storyboards for tele-
vision commercials. A shirt-sleeved artist with rumpled brown hair
shifted uneasily in his chair, the strain of waiting for a reaction
from her finally showing. The movement drew a sharp but sympathetic look from the copywriter. Ellery ignored both, and Flame
didn't even notice either, the whole of her attention focused on the
concepts before her. Slowly and reluctantly she shook her head.

'You don't like it,' Ellery concluded, his remark covering the
half-smothered curse from the artist.

Flame breathed in deeply and released the breath in a regretful
sigh. 'Truthfully? No.' She picked up the storyboard. 'This idea
for a new commercial is merely a slicker version of the one we've
been airing.'

'It's been very successful.'

'I know it has, but we've been reworking this same theme for a
year now. We need a new slant, something that will appeal to
younger crowds. The results from the market research and demo-
graphic study we did this summer indicated that a very low
percentage of people in their twenties shop at Powell Stores. In

my opinion, that should be our target market. The whole point of any advertising campaign is to increase sales and broaden the consumer base. If there's a segment of the market we're not reaching, then we go after it.'

'Any ideas on how we might accomplish that?' Ellery walked over to stand beside her.

'Ideas are your province.' A smile played at the edges of her mouth as she handed him the storyboard. 'My job is to point you in the direction our client wants to go.'

'Thanks,' he muttered sardonically.

The copywriter paused in her doodling and pushed her glasses higher on the bridge of her nose. 'This survey you mentioned – did it say why they don't shop at Powell's?' She hooked an arm over the back of the chair, training her entire attention on Flame, her thoughts already focusing on the problem at hand.

'Basically, their reaction to Powell's fell into two categories. One, they saw Powell's as being too staid, too conservative. Second, and not too surprisingly, they thought it was too expensive.' She paused to glance at Ellery. 'I'll get a copy of those reports to you.'

'That might be helpful.'

'I think it will.' She nodded. 'The objective of this new campaign has to be to give Powell's a youthful, modern image – *without* alienating its established customers. I think you should begin to think about a new logo – something to relate to the 1990s and the year 2000. That will lead to new copy and new visuals.'

'A piece of cake,' the artist snorted, lifting his shoulders in a mock shrug of unconcern. 'We can do that in our sleep, can't we, Andy?' he said to the copywriter. 'Problem is, we're not going to get much sleep.'

A knock at the door interrupted the discussion. Flame turned as the door opened and her assistant, Debbie Connors, poked her head inside, her long blonde hair swinging forward in a mass of crinkly waves. 'Sorry, Flame, but you asked me to remind you about your luncheon appointment with Mr Powell. The car's out front now and waiting for you.'

Flame glanced at her watch and sighed. 'Tell them I'll be right down.'

'Mustn't keep the great man waiting,' Ellery murmured dryly.

There was irony in the look she sent him. 'You may be jesting, but it happens to be the truth.' She started to the door. 'I'll have Debbie drop those reports by your office. If there's anything you need clarified, we can talk after I come back from lunch this afternoon.'

Ellery nodded, then added with a sly smile, 'Have fun.'

The sleek grey limousine, polished to a gleam, was at the kerb waiting for her when Flame emerged from the building. The stocky chauffeur hurriedly tossed his cigarette aside and reached to open the rear passenger door for her.

'Afternoon, Ms Bennett.' He touched his cap to her, a smile wreathing his broad face.

'Hello, Arthur.' She returned the smile and automatically handed the portfolio case to him. 'How are the grandkids?'

'Just fine, ma'am.' Pride widened his smile even further. 'Growing like weeds, they are.'

She laughed at that, partly because it was expected. 'They have a way of doing that.' She lifted her glance to the strip of blue sky visible between the towering canyon walls of the street's flanking high-rise buildings. 'Gorgeous day, isn't it?'

'Indeed it is, ma'am. Indeed it is.' His hand was at her elbow politely helping her as she bent to climb into the rear seat. He waited until she was comfortably situated then closed the door. The blare of traffic on the streets intruded briefly when he opened the front door and slid behind the wheel, laying the slim case on the seat beside him. Then there was silence, broken only by the whisper of the air-conditioner as the car turned into the flow of traffic.

Leaning back in the plushly upholstered seat, Flame took advantage of the quiet to relax from an unusually hectic morning. Absently she gazed out of the window at the rush of people on the crowded sidewalks, caught in the lunch hour bustle.

On either side, skyscrapers stretched upwards, walling in the streets. The agency's offices were strategically located on the fringes of both the city's financial district, referred to by many as 'the Wall Street of the West', and the elite shopping area around Union Square with its high-fashion stores and de luxe hotels. Flame smiled, recalling an observation Ellery had once made concerning the proximity of the two areas, finding it singularly appropriate since on one side, the buildings were sky-high and on the other, the prices.

'Where are we having lunch today, Arthur?'

With a turning lift of his head, he made eye contact with her reflection in the rear-view mirror. 'I don't know ma'am. I was told to bring you to the store.'

'I see.' She sat back, briefly wondering at this break from the normal routine. Usually they lunched at Malcom's club. Still, she didn't mind. In a way, she almost welcomed it. A change of scene might satisfy some of this restlessness that had been bothering her these last few days.

A short five minutes later, Arthur let her out at the front entrance to the main Powell's store from which all its many national branches had sprung. With portfolio case in hand, Flame entered the store, breezed past the perfume counter with its barrage of scents, and went straight to the executive offices located on the mezzanine level.

When she entered Malcom's outer office, the stern-looking brunette behind the desk glanced up and allowed a smile to cross her expression. 'Go right in, Ms Bennett. Mr Powell's expecting you.'

'Thank you.' At the door to his office, Flame hesitated a split second, then walked in without knocking.

A Tabriz carpet covered the parquet flooring and every vertical inch was faced with hand-selected California pine that had been painted, laboriously stripped, then waxed, imbuing the expansive and imposing office with the aura of a captain's cabin. That feel of a mariner's room was subtly reinforced by the framed map of the China Seas that hung on the wall behind the massive antique desk at the far end of the room, a desk that failed to dwarf the man seated behind it, for all its size. Malcom rose from his chair as Flame approached, the tap of her heels muffled by the heavy Persian rug.

'As usual, you look lovely, Flame.' His grey glance ran over her in swift appraisal. 'I especially like that suit you're wearing.'

'You should.' Smiling, she briefly lifted a hand in a model's gesture to show off the Adolfo suit of turquoise blue knit. 'It's from your fourth floor.'

He smiled back, the cleft in his chin deepening. 'I always knew you were a woman of discriminating taste.' His look was covetous, revealing his desire to add her to his list of possessions.

Seeing it Flame kept her smile in place and murmured a deliberate, '*Very* discriminating, Malcom . . . in all things.' She set the leather portfolio on to the seat of the stiff-backed chair in front of his desk. 'Shall we go over these changes before lunch?' Assuming his agreement, she started to unfasten the metal clasp.

'Has Harrison approved them?' he asked, referring to his marketing director.

She nodded affirmatively. 'I went over them with him last Thursday.'

'Then there's no need for me to look at them. If he's satisfied, so am I.'

His reply was unexpected. In the past, Flame had always gone over such things with him, however minor they might be. It had been a means of maintaining the guise that these were business luncheons, even though she'd known all along that business had nothing to do with his desire for her company. This change to something openly social, something personal – what did it mean? She wasn't sure. Perhaps an increase of pressure from him to coerce her into a more intimate relationship.

Inwardly she was on guard, but outwardly she retained her easy smile as she relatched the case with a decisive click. 'If you don't want to see them, that's fine with me, Malcom.' Turning to him, she let her smile deepen. 'I never argue with a client.'

'That's very wise, Flame.' His grey eyes were thorough in their close study of her. 'Because a customer is always right. And if you don't believe that, try doing without him.'

Was that a threat? It certainly had the sound of one, but the warm light in his eyes seemed to deny that. Flame chose to regard it as nothing more than a clever rejoinder.

'You should include that in your next company newsletter as a proverb by Powell. Coming from the CEO, it would definitely make good copy.'

'I might do that.'

'You should.' She paused to pick up her leather case. 'So, where are we going for lunch today? You haven't said.'

'We aren't.' He came around the desk to stand before her. 'We're going to eat here. I decided it was time I made use of my private dining room for something other than dry and boring business luncheons. Do you mind?'

'Of course not.' Flame didn't allow the faintest glimmer of misgivings to show even though this was the first time she would be lunching with him at somewhere other than a public place. 'At least we shouldn't have any reason to complain about the service today.'

'Or the food, I hope,' Malcom added, a glitter of rare humour in his look.

'With a chef as superb as yours is reputed to be, I'm sure we won't have to live on bread alone.'

'Shall we find out?'

Taking her by the arm, he ushered Flame into the anteroom he'd converted into a private dining room at a rumoured cost of fifty thousand dollars, although it was too tastefully done to show. The wood-panelled splendour of his office was repeated in the anteroom. This time the decor's nautical feel was reinforced by a massive oil painting of a China clipper ship running before a sea storm that hung above the Edwardian side table.

Irish linen covered the small round table in the centre of the room, its leaves removed to accommodate more comfortably a party of two. But no candles gleamed and no roses bloomed from crystal vases, and the brass chandelier overhead was turned to full bright, eliminating any suggestion of romantic intimacy. Noting that, Flame breathed a little easier.

As soon as they were seated, a waiter opened a bottle of wine. Malcom waved aside the presentation of the cork and the offer to sample the wine, gesturing instead for the waiter to fill both glasses with the bottle's deep red wine. Malcom lifted his glass to her in a typically silent salute, then waited, watching as Flame sipped from hers.

'A Cabernet,' she said with approval.

'Do you like it?' The tone of his question implied that if it didn't meet with her approval, they'd have something else.

'It's excellent.' Although many considered it fashionable only to drink the dry white wines, Flame had always preferred the full-bodied taste of a good red.

'It's fine.' Malcom nodded to the hovering waiter, then finally tasted his own.

'Would you like me to begin serving now, sir?'

Again Malcom nodded affirmatively. The waiter withdrew to the serving pantry, then returned almost immediately with a salad of fresh spinach and strawberries for each of them. Flame smooth- ed the linen napkin over the lap of her turquoise blue skirt then reached for her salad fork.

'How was your weekend?' Malcom inquired.

'Quiet, thankfully. Which is just the way I like it.' Using her salad fork, she folded a spinach leaf on to its tines. 'Oh, but Malcom, I did have one rather bizarre visitor.'

Briefly Flame told him about the elderly woman who had called on her Saturday morning, claiming to be a distant relative. When she mentioned the supposed inheritance of a ranch in Oklahoma, Malcom agreed that it was all too far-fetched, that the old woman was probably having delusions – if not senile.

'What about your weekend?' she asked. 'Did you have your usual complement of house guests?'

His wife's penchant for entertaining was legendary, and an invitation to the Powell family residence in the exclusive island community of Belvedere was highly coveted, both for the 'in' status it implied and for the island's balmy climate and scenic vistas of San Francisco's alabaster skyline to the south and the famed Golden Gate Bridge to the west. Established by the old guard of affluent San Franciscans shortly before the turn of the century to escape the summer fog, Belvedere had become renowned for its historic homes, narrow, winding roads, and beautiful gardens, and a life – typical of most island communities – that centred on the water, becoming the home of the elite San Francisco Yacht Club.

'Not this weekend,' Malcom replied. 'Like yours, mine was quiet. As a matter of fact, I took the boat out for a last sail.' The vessel he so casually referred to as a boat was a sleek forty-foot sailing yacht that had competed in the America's Cup some years earlier. 'The way my schedule looks these next few months, I probably won't have another opportunity to take it out again before winter sets in.'

Sailing was a topic of mutual interest. Their conversation revolved around it through the salad course. The waiter returned with the entrée and placed it on the table before Flame. 'Veal with a green peppercorn sauce, this is one of my favourites,' she declared, directing a quick smile at Malcom.

'Don't you think by now I know what you like?'

At that instant, Flame realised the entire menu had been selected on the basis of her personal preferences, everything from the choice of wines and the salad to the entrée and – 'Then we must be having chocolate soufflé for dessert,' she guessed, trying to sound offhand to hide the fact she was impressed that he'd cared enough to notice her likes – that he'd wanted to please her.

'What else?' His look gleamed with confidence and satisfaction.

She laughed softly, aware that her mood had lightened considerably, much of her earlier tension gone. She decided it was the combination of the excellent wine and food, the room's rich, yet comfortable atmosphere – and, perhaps most importantly, Malcom's subtle attentiveness to detail.

Through the rest of the meal, both the anticipated chocolate soufflé for dessert and the coffee afterwards, they chatted about business in general with a few side trips into politics and the economy. It was this exchange of views and opinions, typical of most of their past luncheons together, that Flame enjoyed, the talk stimulating in a quiet sort of way and providing a diversion from the endless shop talk at the agency – and the sniping gossip.

'More coffee?' Malcom started to reach for the silver pot the waiter had left on the table.

She refused with a faint shake of her head, then smiled. 'Need I say that the luncheon was superb?'

'I'm glad you enjoyed it.' His glance ran swiftly over her, admiring in its assessment. 'That particular shade of turquoise is an excellent colour on you. It brings out the green of your eyes. You should wear it more often.'

'If you always serve up flattery after a meal, we'll have to make it a point to lunch here more often, Malcom,' she declared, smiling as she folded her napkin and laid it on the table.

'I'll remember that,' he replied, then paused briefly. 'Speaking of remembering, I have something I want to show you.' Pushing his napkin on to the table, he rose from his chair. Joining him, Flame walked back into his office. 'For some time, I've been considering expanding the line of furs we carry at our major stores.' Malcom stopped to close the doors to the dining room. 'Naturally I'm concerned about maintaining the Powell reputation for quality. That's why I'd like your opinion on this coat.'

The request wasn't unusual. In the past, Malcom had frequently consulted with her on such things, reasoning that she represented both ends of his market – the working career woman and the socialite.

Her interest piqued, she followed when Malcom walked to the

small conference table on the far side of the pine-panelled room. A luxurious dark fur lay across one of the chairs. He picked it up, then turned, draping it over his arm for her inspection. The instant Flame saw the dark, almost black, full-length fur, she felt as if the air had been snatched from her lungs.

'Malcom, it's exquisite,' she murmured and reached out to touch it, then darted a quick, dawning look at him. 'It's sable, isn't it?'

'Russian sable, yes. Try it on.'

Needing no persuasion, Flame turned and let Malcom help her into it. As she ran her hands under the stand-up collar of the coat and down the front, letting her fingers slide through its thickness, she was certain there was no sensation quite like the sensual feel of a fur – soft, silken, and utterly luxurious. Nothing else could make a woman feel so feminine, so elegant – so incredibly alluring.

Impulsively she turned to Malcom. 'It's stunning.'

'On you, it is.'

His response was hardly effusive, but the look that blazed in his eyes more than made up for it. She swung away knowing she shouldn't have invited him to notice, but feeling too recklessly glorious to care. She wrapped the coat tightly around her and hugged it, burying her fingers deep in its fur.

'I have a suggestion.' The weight of his hands settled on to her shoulders. 'Why don't you wear it to the opera Friday night?'

Briefly she allowed herself to be tempted, then sighed in regret. 'I couldn't. It wouldn't be right,' she said with a firm shake of her head.

She hadn't noticed the slight pressure that had drawn her back against him until she felt the warmth of his breath near her ear. She should have moved away from it, but she didn't.

'It couldn't be more right.' The pitch of his voice was low and caressing. 'It belongs on you, Flame.' His lips moved against her hair, a feathery sensation gliding towards her neck.

Instinctively she turned her head to deny him access. 'Don't.' The protest sounded weak to her as his mouth found the shell of her ear instead, the sensitive nerve ends reacting to the unexpected contact and unleashing a cascade of shivers.

She hadn't realised how vulnerable she was – how susceptible. She shouldn't have spent so much time alone this past weekend, thinking and remembering how much she wanted to be loved, recognising that there was no lonelier sound than laughter that was heard only by the one who laughed, that there was no hollower victory than the one celebrated by the victor alone. There was no such thing as independence when there was no one standing beside you; there was only loneliness. The touch of Malcom's hands and the brush of his lips against her skin were reminding her of that all over again.

'I want you, Flame.' His breath heated the side of her neck. 'I have from the moment you walked into this office three years ago. I vowed then to make you mine. You belong to me, Flame. It's time you admitted that.'

She realised that she'd been ripe for this moment. And Malcom had set the stage perfectly with the wine and the food, the easy conversation and the sable coat that had reminded her she was a woman with normal, human needs. But could she trust him? Was it her needs he sought to fulfil? Or, like Rick, did Malcom want her to satisfy his own ends?

His hands glided down the fur sleeves, following the bend of her arms to enfold her while his mouth brushed tantalisingly over her cheek and ear. But it was less his caresses she responded to then the stroking words he murmured.

'Haven't I shown you how it can be with us? Quiet dinners together. Intimate evenings with just the two of us. It will be so very wonderful, Flame, if you'll just let it.'

She wavered for the briefest of moments. 'No,' she said, then more decisively, 'No.'

In one quick step she was free of his arms, and in two more, there was distance between them. Hurriedly she shed the coat, then turned and thrust it back at him, holding herself absolutely rigid so he wouldn't discover how badly she was shaking inside.

'The fur is beautiful, Malcom, but I don't care for the conditions that are attached to it.'

'You didn't offer any objections to them a moment ago,' he reminded her, a confident gleam in his grey eyes.

Unable to deny that, Flame ignored it. 'We've been through this before.' When he failed to take the fur from her, she tossed it on to the back of a nearby chair. 'I am not going to become your mistress,' she insisted stiffly. 'I won't be used like that.'

'*You* won't be used.' Anger flared, hardening the grim set of his features. 'Who the hell do you think you are? Without me, you're nothing but another impoverished socialite with a lot of pride. Your job, your salary, your vice-presidency, your so-called career, I'm responsible for every bit of it!'

She'd pushed him too far and she knew it. But there was no turning back – even if she wanted to. 'I never asked you for any favours, Malcom.'

'But you were damned quick to accept them. I've bought and paid for you ten times over.'

'When you wanted me to handle the Powell account, I made it clear that if you thought you were buying anything else, I wasn't interested. I promised you that your account would have my absolute priority. And it has. I have jumped every time you've called. The only place I haven't jumped has been into your bed – and I won't!'

His smile was anything but pleasant. 'Even if it means losing the Powell account . . . and all the others I sent your way? I opened corporate doors for you, Flame, and I can close them just as fast – and make certain they stay closed to you.'

'Is that an ultimatum, Malcom?' The thin thread that held her temper snapped. 'Are you telling me that either I go to bed with you or you'll destroy my career? Do you want me so badly you don't care that I'd be hating you all the while you were making love to me? A hostile merger, is that what you want?'

'No, dammit, it isn't!' He half swung from her, raking a hand through the silver-tipped mane of his hair.

Flame stared at him, conscious of the rawness inside, and the trembling of hurt and anger. Abruptly she pivoted on her heel and walked stiffly to the high-backed chair in front of his desk. She retrieved her portfolio case from its sea cushion and started for the door. But Malcom was there waiting for her. She halted an arm's length away.

'I honestly don't think you can complain about the job I've done for you, Malcom. Or the agency, either. If you think you're entitled to more than that, then pull the account. Don't hold that threat over my head.'

'I never intended to,' he stated impatiently.

'No?' She smiled without humour. 'It sounded remarkably like a power play to me.'

In one stride, he closed the space between them and caught her arms. 'Dammit, Flame, you're not indifferent to me. You proved that when I held you in my arms.'

'I've never denied that I enjoy being with you. I've always admired and respected you, Malcom – and liked you, too. And that's precisely the reason I won't become your mistress.'

'You're not making any sense.'

'Aren't I? Malcom, I don't have any illusions that it would be anything more than an affair. Maybe I'm greedy but I'm not interested in being some man's mistress – not even yours. I don't want a brief affair where I'm just another possession. I want more than that – something that offers me the promise . . . or at least the hope – of a lasting, fulfilling relationship with someone who cares about *me*.' She looked at him, more conscious than ever of the void in her life. 'Maybe you'd make me happy for a time . . . I don't know. But sooner or later, you'd get tired of me and it would be over. Then where would I be? We couldn't work together any more. It would be too awkward – for both of us. Ultimately you'd take your account to another agency. And I'd lose you – and it, too.'

'You don't know that.'

'Let's not kid ourselves, Malcom. That's precisely what would happen.' She was still angry but now there was an icy edge to it. 'Either way I'd be on the losing end. I've known that all along.'

His hands relaxed their grip on her arms, then released her altogether. 'You wouldn't lose, Flame, I can be very generous.' The look in his eyes was just as strong with the desire to possess as it had been before. Nothing she'd said had made any impression on him.

'I'm not an object to be bought, Malcom. I thought I'd made that clear,' she retorted, then gave up, recognising further argument was pointless. 'If you'll excuse me, I have to get back to my office.'

He didn't argue. 'I'll have Arthur bring the car around.'

'I prefer to walk, thank you.'

And walk she did, covering the dozen or so blocks between Powell's and the agency at a brisk pace, thinking she could walk off her anger. But it didn't work. By the time she reached her office, she was angrier than before – angry at Malcom for attempting to threaten her, and at herself for giving him the opening. How could she have been so stupid – so weak?

When she sailed into the small outer office occupied by her assistant, the young blonde looked up from her desk, a look of relief rushing across her face. 'Am I ever glad you're back –' Flame walked right by her and pushed open the door to her office, then froze in shock. '– the florist delivered some flowers,' Debbie finished lamely.

Some flowers? They were everywhere! Not a foot of flat surface failed to have a vase on it, cascading with boughs of Phalaenopsis orchids. Haltingly, Flame entered her office, still stunned by the fragrant profusion of white orchids.

'Incredible, isn't it?' Debbie murmured from the doorway.

Flame turned, finally recovering her voice. 'Who sent them?'

'There's a card on your desk.' Belatedly the girl realised that the top of it couldn't be seen for the orchids. 'I put it on the phone.'

As she crossed to the desk, it suddenly occurred to her that there was only one person she knew who would indulge in such extravagance. She snatched up the card and ripped it open, muttering under her breath, 'So help me, if Malcom thinks –'

Then she read the message inside: 'Till next time we meet,' signed Chance Stuart.

Stunned, she leaned against a corner of the desk and tried to catch back the incredulous laugh that bubbled from her.

'Who's it from?' Debbie asked as Ellery appeared at her shoulder.

'Is Flame back?' Then he saw the orchid opulence in the office. 'Hello, what is this? Are you turning your office into a jungle paradise or did you get the FTD account?'

The telephone rang. 'I'll get it.' Debbie hurried back to her desk in the anteroom.

'Isn't it incredible, absolutely incredible?' Still faintly awe-struck, and almost at a loss for words, Flame trailed a hand under an arching bough, its whole length strung with exotic white blooms.

'Who sent them? Tarzan of the jungle or Merlin Olsen?' Ellery wandered into the room, his glance centring on the card in her hand.

'Chance Stuart.' She was still trying to believe that.

Debbie poked her head in the doorway again. 'Flame, there's a long distance call for you from a Mr Stuart. Line two.'

For an instant, her glance locked with Ellery's. Then she turned and tried to find the telephone again amidst the tangle of trailing orchids. Locating it at last, she picked up the receiver and punched the button with the blinking light, conscious all the while of the silly flutters of excitement in her stomach.

'Hello.' She tried to sound natural, but who could when her office was inundated with flowers and the sender was on the line.

'Flame. Chance Stuart. How are you?' The rich timbre of his voice seemed to travel right through the wires, all lazy and warm with the potent smoothness of hot brandy.

Instantly her mind conjured up the image of his dangerous smile and his rakishly handsome face. 'At the moment, I'm engulfed by cascades of orchids. They're everywhere – and they're beautiful.'

'I'm glad you like them.'

'I do.'

'I called because I happen to have an extra ticket for the opera on Friday. It's an excellent seat in the parterre . . . right next to mine. Could I persuade you to use it and attend the opera with me?'

Hesitating, Flame glanced at Ellery, aware that she had planned to go with him, but she was more aware of the way her first and only meeting with Chance Stuart had ended. He'd left the De-Borgs' party with his arm around the opera's guest diva.

'What about Miss Colton?' she asked with forced casualness.

'Lucianna will be on stage singing, I believe. But whether she is or not, I'm still asking you. Will you come?'

'I have made other plans.' She looked again at Ellery. He smiled wryly and motioned for her to accept. 'But I think I can change them without any difficulty.'

'Good.'

After supplying him with her address and agreeing on a time, Flame echoed his parting words, 'Till next time.' Then she hung up, her fingers lingering on the receiver for a moment, his card still clutched in her other hand.

'Do you know' – Ellery tilted his head back to eye her thoughtfully – 'you have the very definite look of a woman in love?'

'That's ridiculous.' Yet her cheeks felt unusually warm. 'I don't even know him.'

'My dear Flame, love is not an opinion. It's a chemical reaction. Either something happens between two people or it doesn't.'

'Are you talking about love or spontaneous combustion? Not that it really matters,' she shrugged. 'Both can blow up in your face.' She'd had too much experience with such things to be guided by her own feelings. 'I've found it's much safer to do a little testing first. It can save a lot of hurt.'

'Careful, my dear. Your scars are showing.'

'I'll cover them up with powder,' she replied, then looked around the room at the profusion of orchids, again overwhelmed by the sheer number of them. 'What am I supposed to do with all these?' she wondered out loud.

'Enjoy them, my dear,' Ellery offered drily. 'Simply enjoy them.'

Flame shot him a glance of wry amusement. 'You know, Ellery, I'm almost convinced you're a romantic masquerading as a cynic.'

He smiled and winked slyly. 'Just like you.'

His reply startled a laughing breath of instinctive denial from her. But Ellery paid no attention to it as he strolled out of her office. Flame shook her head in mock exasperation and turned to the nearest vase of orchids, a vague wistfulness for shattered illusions entering her expression as she breathed in their fragrance, the card from Chance still in her hand.

7

LANTERNS gleamed from the ornate wrought-iron gateposts that marked the entrance to the courtyard of the imposing War Memorial Opera House. Its towering arched windows blazed with lights, announcing to the world the fall opening of the opera. Outside, sleek limousines, Rolls Royces and Mercedes lined Van Ness Avenue, while more notables gathered inside.

The cultural event signalled the advent of San Francisco's social season. Everybody who was anybody, along with the few who wanted to be somebody, attended the gala. They came to see and be seen – to the eternal delight of every couturier around the globe. And they were all there, de Ribes silk brushing against the taffeta of Ungaro, Valentino velvet rubbing shoulders with the satin of St Laurent. Adding to the dazzle of it all were the glittering diamonds, the gleaming rubies and sapphires, and the sparkling emeralds that adorned the fingers, wrists, throats and ears of the opera's patrons.

When Flame arrived on the arm of Chance Stuart, notice was duly taken of the high sweep of her hair, the diamond clusters at her ears, and the strapless sheath gown of de la Renta ombrebeaded silk crepe topped by a matching bolero jacket with long sleeves and wide shoulders. But it was her escort, clad in black evening attire, who stirred their interest with his dark good looks,

electric blue eyes and naughtily wicked smile. For once Flame
was the one who received the green glances of envy. And she
accepted them with pleasure.

A flashbulb went off, its bright flare of light momentarily blinding Flame. She held up a hand to shield her eyes and blinked
rapidly to clear them. 'I think I'm going to be seeing spots in
front of my eyes all evening, especially after the gauntlet of pap-
parazzi we ran outside.'

'I don't blame any photographer for wanting to add a picture
of you to his private collection,' Chance murmured, his glance
running warmly over her.

Her smile mocked his highly flattering but untrue statement. 'I
have the feeling they were more interested in the devilishly handsome man I was with.'

'Devilish – is that how you see me?' The grooves in his lean
cheeks deepened, suggesting amusement but stopping short of a
smile.

'In some articles I read about you recently, it was suggested
that you have the devil's own luck . . . and, the way your smile
can evoke the most wicked thoughts, it occurred to me you might
have traded in your tail and horns for a black tuxedo tonight.'

He held her gaze, his look becoming decidedly intimate, shutting out everything else around them. 'Maybe that explains it
then.'

'What?' She was surprised by how breathless she felt.

'A devil's always drawn to fire – the hotter the better.' His
mouth slanted in a smile. 'This could prove to be one helluva
night.'

'Flame, darling.' Jacqui Van Cleeve pounced from the crowd.
Flame swung her attention away from Chance, more disturbed
by his suggestive comment then she cared to admit, and focused
it on the society columnist, dressed in a slightly outrageous charcoal and pink floral gown of silk damask with a back bustle that
seemed singularly appropriate to Flame considering how much
Jacqui's tongue already wagged. 'I missed you at the Guild's pre-
performance dinner gala. Ellery assured me you would be here
tonight. Of course, there's no need to explain your absence now.
I can see why you weren't there,' she declared, turning to Chance.
'Welcome back.'

'Jacqui.' His dark head dipped in acknowledgement as he gave her one of his patented smiles. 'You are very eye-catching this evening.'

She laughed, the large bangled hoops at her ears swinging with the movements. 'I definitely don't blend into the wallpaper – unless it's Victorian.' She paused, her eyes sharpening on him with a knowing air. 'I honestly wasn't sure San Francisco would see you again. I'm glad I was wrong.'

'What can I say? I was drawn back like a moth,' he replied, his glance sliding naturally to Flame, the glitter in it as much as his words indicating that she was the reason he'd returned.

She tried not to look as pleased as she felt. And she tried, too, not to let her expectations rise too high, something she'd fought all week. But it was proving to be very difficult, especially now that she was with him and discovering all over again that his company was every bit as stimulating as she remembered.

'I can see you deserve your reputation for moving fast,' Jacqui observed in a low murmur.

'I've never found anything to be gained by waiting,' Chance countered smoothly. 'Have you?'

'No,' she conceded, then cast a reporter's eye over the be-jewelled crowd around them. 'They really dragged out the rocks tonight, didn't they? It's amazing how easy it is to tell who's wearing the real thing. All you have to do is look for a burly bodyguard hovering nearby – one with an unsightly bulge in his jacket.' She paused, a smile breaking across her face. 'This re-minds me of the time I attended some exclusive charity ball in Dallas. There was a woman there, positively draped in diamonds. I made some remark that I thought it was a bit much. And this sweet little Texas gal informed me in this drawling accent of hers, "Jacqui, honey, when it comes to diamonds, less is not necessarily better." If tonight's any indication, I'd say the senti-ment seems to be universal. Look.' She laid a hand on Flame's arm, drawing her attention to the slender blonde near the arched windows, dressed in a LaCroix creation that was all froth and chiffon. 'There's Sandra Halsey. Isn't that a divine gown she's wearing?'

'It is,' Flame agreed.

'She had it flown in on the Concorde for the occasion. Talk about conspicuous consumption,' Jacqui declared, then paused, her lips thinning in faint disapproval. 'I do wish someone would tell her to stop sprinkling her conversation with French phrases. It's so terribly déclassé.'

'And déclassé isn't?'

But Jacqui Van Cleeve was completely impervious to the light jibe. 'No. We stole it from the French too long ago. Now it's as American as sabotage. Would you both excuse me? I'd swear she's wearing the Halsey rubies and Claudia vowed they would never touch her neck. Wouldn't it be something if those two have finally settled their feud after all this time?' Then she was off, her bustle wagging like the tail of a bloodhound hot on a scent.

Smiling faintly, Flame turned to Chance. 'In case you haven't noticed, the only difference between our Jacqui and an ordinary newshound is the diamond-studded collar she wears. Other people's secrets are her stock in trade, printable or not.'

'No doubt many that people wished she didn't know.'

'That's putting it mildly,' she murmured, and wondered to herself what Jacqui knew – or thought she knew – about her.

It was a question that grew stronger when she noticed Malcom Powell coming toward them, his stride unhurried. She hadn't seen or spoken to him since she'd walked out of his office on Tuesday. She met his glance, conscious suddenly of the aura of power he exuded. He didn't like being denied anything he wanted. She watched as his gaze sliced from her to Chance, then back again, the look in his eyes hovering somewhere between a demand and an accusation.

'Hello, Malcom,' she greeted him first, keeping her voice cool but pleasant.

'Flame.' He inclined his head briefly, the strands of grey in his dark hair catching the overhead light from the chandeliers and giving it a silvery cast.

'I believe you met Chance Stuart last week –' she began.

'Yes, at the DeBorgs',' Malcom confirmed and extended a hand. 'I wondered if you would fly back to catch Miss Colton's performance.'

As they gripped hands, Flame felt the tension in the air – like that of two adversaries meeting for the first time and quietly sizing each other up.

'For that among other things,' Chance replied.

'Oh?' There was a challenge in that single sound from Malcom but Flame missed it, distracted by the odd feeling that she was being watched.

'Where's Diedre? Isn't she with you?' Flame asked, instantly using the inquiry as an excuse to scan the crowd and locate the party staring at her.

'The wind mussed her hair. She went to the powder room to repair the damage.'

But Flame only heard the first part of Malcom's explanation as her glance initially swept by the man in the navy suit, then came back catching his watchful gaze fastened on her. His face, there was something familiar about its hard, pointy lines, yet she couldn't place who he was or where she had seen him before. Abruptly, almost guiltily, he turned and walked away. His lack of formal attire prompted Flame to wonder if he was part of the building's security. But, security usually wore black suits.

Why was she letting it bother her? Strange men had stared at her nearly all of her adult life. She forced her attention back as Malcom said, 'There's Diedre. If you two will excuse me . . .'

'Of course.' Flame smiled, still slightly distracted. Just for a moment she let her gaze follow Malcom as he walked away.

'Your agency handles the advertising for his stores, doesn't it?' Chance remarked.

'Yes,' Flame admitted, wondering if he'd heard the rumours about her alleged affair with Malcom. But there was nothing in his expression to indicate that the question was anything other than an idle one. 'As a matter of fact, we've been working on the store's holiday ads and commercials for the past month. For us, Christmas starts well before Thanksgiving.'

'That's getting into the Christmas spirit early.'

Mockingly she corrected him. 'Ah, but we're dealing with the commercialised version of Christmas – the one that promotes the belief it's more blessed to give than to receive, and inspires the ringing of cash registers instead of silver bells. Our advertisers tend to spell Christmas with dollar signs.'

'Scrooge would be proud of them.' He grinned.

Flame laughed at that and added, 'Too bad no bah-humbugs are allowed. He'd fit right in now.'

'What about you? Are you a bah-humbug person?' Chance asked, eyeing her curiously.

'Not really.' She sobered slightly. 'Although I admit, without any family left, Christmas has lost much of its meaning for me.'

'You don't have any family?'

She shook her head. 'I lost both my parents several years ago. And, since I was an only child . . .' She shrugged off the rest of the sentence and the twinge of loneliness that came with it, and switched the focus to him. 'I suppose you're from a big family.' None of the articles about him had contained any mention of family. In fact, Flame couldn't recall any reference to his background other than the mention of a tour of duty in Viet Nam.

'No, like you, I'm an only child with both parents gone. And holidays don't mean much to me either.' A smile curved his mouth, but it was the look of understanding in his eyes that touched Flame.

Sid Barker stood squarely in front of the pay phone and puffed impatiently on his cigarette, his right shoulder twitching in a nervous shrug. His gaze moved constantly, his hazel eyes darting restless glances at the well-heeled guests that passed him.

Uncomfortable among this moneyed crowd with their fancy airs and superior looks, he unconsciously rubbed the top of a brown shoe along the back of his navy trouser leg, trying to give some polish to its scuffed toe. He smoked the cigarette all the way down to the filter, then took a last drag and exhaled the smoke out of the long beak of his nose.

As he started to stab the butt into the sand of the ashtray stand, the phone rang. He dropped the cigarette instantly and snatched the receiver from the hook before it could ring again.

'Yeah, it's me,' he said, the roughness of the street in his voice. 'What took you so long?' . . . 'Right, I saw them together not five minutes ago. I think she made me though.' . . . 'If you say so,' he said, moving his head in disagreement. 'But I don't think it's going to do much good. With that red hair of hers, she don't strike me as the kind that scares easy.' . . . 'If that's what you want, that's what I'll do. It's your money.'

He hung up, cast a quick look around to see who was about, then turned and slicked a hand over his thinning hair, the twitch back in his shoulder. With another scanning look, he headed back to find the redhead, his mind racing to find a way to get her alone.

For once, luck was on his side. Just when he figured it would be hours before the right moment presented itself, there it was. She was standing to one side, listening but not appearing to take part in the conversation.

Moving as quickly as he dared without drawing undue attention, Sid Barker circled around and approached her from the side. He was two steps away when she finally noticed him, her glance at first startled, then probing. Maybe she hadn't recognised him after all. He stopped close to her and furtively slipped her the note from his pocket.

A frown flickered across her smooth forehead as her green eyes dropped their probing inspection of him to glance at the paper. Immediately he moved away and plunged into the thick of the elegant crowd.

'You'd better wise up before it's too late and stay away from him. You'll regret it if you don't.'

Stunned by the threatening message scrawled across the paper, Flame stared after him, the phrase 'stay away from him' echoing in her head. Those were the same words that had been written on the torn piece of paper at the DeBorgs' party last week. As the milling crowd closed in behind him and hid him from her view, she caught a glimpse of his brown shoes. The waiter with the hawk-like features, the one she'd caught staring at her so rudely – it was the same man.

But the message made no more sense than it had before. Stay away from whom? From Malcom? From Chance? And who could have sent it? If *him* referred to Malcom, then Diedre was the logical choice. But if it was Chance, then who? Lucianna Colton? Did she consider Chance her private property?

Or could it be . . . Malcom. He didn't like competition of any sort. The more she thought about it – and remembered the veiled threats he'd made on Tuesday – the more it sounded like him. He wasn't above using intimidation to get what he wanted. Obviously nothing she'd said to him on Tuesday had made any difference. He wanted her. And her feelings, her future, didn't enter into it, no doubt rationalising it all away with some vague thought of seeing to it that she was well taken care of.

'I think it's time we took our seats.' The suggestion was accompanied by the touch of a hand on her back, both startling her. With a quick turn of her head, she encountered Chance's warm look, a look that immediately sharpened. 'Is something wrong?'

'No.' She smiled quickly, perhaps too quickly. 'It just occurred to me that you'd probably like to go backstage and wish Miss Colton luck tonight.'

Chance smiled and shook his head. 'Lucianna goes into total isolation for at least three hours before a performance. Her hair-dresser and the wardrobe lady are the only people she allows in her dressing room.'

'You've known her quite a while, haven't you?' It was some-thing in the ease of his answer that made her suspect that.

'Longer than either of us care to remember.' The hand at the back of her waist increased its pressure slightly, an altogether pleasant sensation. 'Shall we go in?'

Smiling, she lifted her head a little higher, determined to let none of this spoil her evening. 'I think that's an excellent sugges-tion, Mr Stuart.'

Shortly after they'd taken their seats, the house lights dimmed and the orchestra began the opening strains of the prelude to *Il Trovatore*, The Troubadour. There were the last-minute stirrings and whispers as those who had lingered took their seats. Then the curtain lifted on a fifteenth-century setting of a castle and its gardens in Aragon surrounded by the mystery of night.

The captain of the guard, in a resonant bass voice, recounted to the retainers gathered around him the lurid tale of an old gypsy woman, burned at the stake for the crime of casting an evil spell on one of the Count's two infant sons, and how, to avenge her mother's death, the daughter of the gypsy steals the other child and, according to the story, throws it into the fire that had killed her mother, thus establishing Verdi's melodramatic plot of a gypsy's vengeance.

At the end of the guard's tale came the ominous tolling of the midnight hour. Then Lucianna Colton made her entrance in the role of Leonora, a noble lady of the court.

As applause greeted her appearance, Flame stole a glance at the man beside her. In the darkened theatre, the lights from the stage cast the angles and planes of his face into sharp relief, high-lighting the prominent bones of his cheek and jaw, and hollowing with shadows his lean cheeks. She was conscious of the strength in his smoothly carved profile – and she was conscious, too, that he showed little reaction to Lucianna's appearance. She'd won-dered if he would – if he'd had some sort of disagreement with the soprano – if he had invited her tonight in retaliation. Yet she could read nothing into his expression that suggested any of those things. He looked pleased by the applause Lucianna received, but no more than anyone would be when they knew the performer.

A little ruefully, Flame realised that it wasn't going to be so easy to put those obscure warnings out of her mind and simply enjoy the evening. As if sensing her gaze, Chance turned his head slightly to return the look. In that moment, she became conscious of the scant inches that separated them, their shoulders nearly touching. Fleetingly, she wished the opera was ending instead of just beginning, then forced her attention back to the stage as Lucianna Colton, staying in character, waited for the burst of applause to fade, then began her opening aria, a song of love and emotions awakened.

The second act curtain opened to a dawn scene of the gypsies' mountain encampment and the famous strains of the Anvil Chorus. When it faded, the gypsy's daughter, now an old woman, began to sing her impassioned version of her mother's death at the stake.

Chance listened to the gypsy's hatred and bitterness and the ringing cry to 'Avenge Thou Me', but his attention ultimately strayed from the mezzo-soprano's aria. There was too much in the character that reminded him of Hattie, all twisted with a hatred that seemed to feed on itself.

He could have dealt with that but not the frustration that a week's worth of digging had failed to provide him with the name of Hattie's new heir, the one who would deny him Morgan's Walk. Matt Sawyer had learned the identity of the genealogist in Salt Lake City, a certain Bartholomew T. Whittier. Unfortunately the man had gone to England to trace the ancestors of one of his clients. Matt had finally located him in some remote village in the North of England, but Whittier hadn't been much help. Yes, he'd remembered compiling the information on the West Coast branch of the Morgan family, but the attorney he'd dealt with in Tulsa had demanded that he forward all his notes along with the information he'd obtained. So, no, he didn't have any records. However, he was quite certain that the only living descendant of that branch had been a woman, although she had married and her name wasn't Morgan any more. No, he couldn't remember what it was now – not without his notes. But he could gather all the information again. This time it shouldn't take him so long since he knew many of the sources he'd used previously. Yesterday the genealogist had flown back to Salt Lake City, at Chance's expense, to begin the search for the Morgan descendant all over again.

Originally Chance had hoped that when he flew out here this weekend, he'd have the name of this long-lost Morgan. He didn't, but there was some consolation in knowing that he would be dealing with a woman. The odds were in his favour that a woman in California wouldn't be interested in owning a cattle ranch in Oklahoma, however romantic it might sound to her. Sooner or later the novelty of it would wear off and he intended to make certain it happened sooner rather than later.

It would mean more trips to San Francisco but – he glanced sideways at Flame – he had a feeling he'd be making more of them anyway. Why not combine business with what was certain to be pleasure?

8

AFTER THE performance, Flame accompanied Chance backstage and joined the throng of friends and admirers crowding into
Lucianna Colton's dressing room to shower her with their plau-
dits. Flame couldn't disagree with a single one of them. The brilliant shading of the cadenzas, the wonderful colouring of the trills,
the breathtaking use of the rubatos, and the free, liquid quality of
her voice convinced Flame that she deserved them all.

She watched as Lucianna Colton, still in heavy stage make-up
and gowned in an emerald-green kimono, rushed to embrace
Chance. 'I was wonderful, wasn't I?' she declared with refreshingly honest arrogance.

'You were more than wonderful. And if fifteen curtain calls
don't prove that, nothing will,' Chance straightened from the embrace with a streak of scarlet lipstick on his cheek.

'It was glorious, wasn't it? They just kept applauding and applauding. I thought they'd never stop.' She noticed the lipstick
stain on his cheek and made a rueful little moue with her mouth.
'Look what I've done. I've left my mark on you, darling.' She
reached up to wipe it away with her thumb, but succeeded only
in smearing it.

'Don't worry about it.' Using the handkerchief from his pocket,
he wiped at the stain himself.

'I'm not,' she murmured, a faintly smug smile curving her red lips.

'It was a brilliant performance, Miss Colton.' Flame inserted. 'Your name deserves to be spoken in the same breath with Callas, Sills, and all the other bel canto greats.'

'That's kind of you.' But the very coolness of her gaze made Flame wonder if the diva didn't resent her being with Chance. Immediately, Lucianna swung her attention back to him. 'You will be at the party, won't you?'

'Maybe later.'

'Lucianna, darling.' A man burst into the room, throwing his arms open wide in exaggerated adoration. 'You were divine, superb, truly nonpareil.'

'Oscar,' Lucianna cried in welcome and rushed to meet him. 'You loved me?'

'Loved you? Darling, you made my heart cry,' he exclaimed as Chance took Flame's arm and steered her through the crowd and out the door.

Lucianna's dark eyes watched him leave. Maybe later, he'd said. But she knew him too well. He wouldn't be coming to the party. He'd be with that redhead instead. And the thought turned her cold inside – the hot cold that burned. Why? She'd seen him with other women before. Yet some instinct warned her this one was different. Had she lost him?

No. She wouldn't accept that. They had been lovers – and friends – for too many years. No woman would ever love and understand him as well as she did. He would come back to her.

She tilted her chin a little higher and turned on a bright smile. 'I am fabulous, aren't I, Oscar?'

Once clear of the adoring crush, Chance said, 'I took the liberty of making a late dinner reservation for us. I hope you don't mind.'

His announcement caught her off guard. She thought he intended to whisk her home after the comment he'd made to Lucianna about the party. 'Not at all.' She smiled quickly, brilliantly.

But obviously he noticed the split second hesitation that preceded her answer. 'If you prefer to attend one of the parties, I can cancel the reservation.'

'No. Although I thought you might want to toast Miss Colton's triumph tonight.'

'Why would you think that?' He arched a dark eyebrow in her direction, a curiosity in his look.

'The two of you are close.' She attempted to shrug off the answer. 'That's common knowledge.'

'You've been listening to rumours.' He reached in front of her to open the door, then paused with his hand on the latch, his body angled towards her. 'You, of all people, should know better than to put much stock in rumours.'

It was said gently, with a mere hint of a chiding smile. And Flame realised instantly that he'd heard the rumours about her and Malcom Powell. He'd heard them and dismissed them. She smiled, suddenly at ease with both herself and him.

Those who elected not to attend one of the post opera parties usually went to Trader Vic's or L'Etoile or one of the other currently popular gathering spots, assuming, of course, they were well enough connected to get a seat. To Flame's surprise, Chance had made reservations at none of those. Instead he stopped the Jaguar in front of an intimate little French restaurant with a reputation for serving excellent nouvelle cuisine.

'Do you approve?' he inquired as he helped her out of the car.

'Very much.' Her glance skimmed the baroque doors that marked the café's entrance. 'Although I wasn't aware it stayed open this late.'

'It doesn't.' A hint of a smile grooved his cheeks. 'They made an exception tonight.'

There was a flicker of disbelief, then amazement at the implication that he had arranged for the restaurant to open specifically for them. But when they walked through the doors, Flame saw that it was true. The tables beyond the foyer were empty, and lavish sprays of orchids cascaded from every vase in the foyer – Phalaenopsis orchids – the very kind he'd sent her.

'The florist had a few left over.' His remark was one of those throwaway answers not to be fully believed, and Flame didn't. Every bit of this had obviously been planned in advance.

Before she could say anything, a slim man with the thin face and Gallic nose of a Frenchman glided forward to greet them. 'Monsieur Stuart, Madame Bennett, welcome to François's. The opera, you enjoyed it, yes?'

'Very much, Louis,' Chance replied, giving his name the French pronunciation.

'Your table, it is ready. If you would follow me, please.' He led them to a table for two, aglow with flickering candlelight. At Flame's place setting stood a crystal bud vase with a single orchid spray arching from it. After he had seated them, Louis stepped to the silver champagne bucket on its legged stand, removed the bottle being chilled in ice, and held it out to Chance for his inspection. 'Carlton's Pêcher, as you ordered, monsieur.'

'Excellent, thank you, Louis,' he replied, nodding his approval.

With practised deftness, he uncorked the bottle of peach champagne and filled their fluted glasses with the effervescent wine, then withdrew. Chance lifted his glass.

'Shall we drink to the next time?' he suggested.

'Till next time,' Flame echoed the message that had accompanied the orchids, and touched her glass to his. She took a sip of the refreshingly light yet heady wine, then laughed softly. 'I think I'm a little overwhelmed. Orchids, a café to ourselves, imported peach champagne. Do you always go to such lengths to impress a woman?'

'Only when I consider it important.' Again there was that gleam of amusement in his eyes that was so much more seductive than the lascivious looks some men gave that said they could hardly wait to get her into bed.

'I'm flattered.' More than that, she was conscious of the bright sparkle of electricity between them, an electricity that gave new life to rare and half-forgotten feelings and evoked a desire to please, to share, to touch and – to love.

But there was always the risk that these feelings were one-sided. Hadn't past experience shown her that? There were any number of reasons Chance sought her company. Although she didn't think a desire to be seen with a beautiful woman was one of them. And if it was her contacts he was interested in, they wouldn't be here in this restaurant. But, he'd known about Malcom. For all she knew this could be some sort of power play. Maybe he wanted to take something he knew Malcom Powell wanted.

She hated these suspicions, but that wariness had spared her a lot of hurt in the past. Once burned had equalled two hundred times shy in her case.

'You don't look flattered,' Chance observed. 'If anything, you look troubled about something. What is it?'

— 85 —

'Nothing,' she denied. 'I suppose I was wondering why you did all this. It's wonderful but – it wasn't necessary.'

'That depends on your definition of necessary,' he replied smoothly. 'Take the orchids for example. By surrounding you with them, I could be certain of having your undivided attention when I called to persuade you to change your plans and come with me tonight.'

She laughed. 'That is an understatement. You had more than my undivided attention; you had my interest totally piqued.'

'And as for coming here' – he smiled – 'you'll have to admit that if we'd gone anywhere else, we would have been constantly interrupted by friends and acquaintances. Here, we can dine quietly just the two of us. So, while all this may seem extravagant on the surface, it's really very logical.'

Finding it impossible to argue with him, Flame lifted her glass. 'To logic – Stuart-style.'

After that, Flame found it amazingly easy to relax and enjoy the champagne, the meal, and the company. There didn't seem to be any lack of things to talk about.

'You saw the new Franco Zeffirelli production of *Turandot*,' she exclaimed with envy. 'I've been dying to see it. I've heard the stage design is magnificent.'

'It should be, considering the cost of it reportedly ran upwards to a million,' Chance replied dryly. 'I've often wondered if the money wouldn't have been better spent getting some of the great name stars to appear at the Met.'

'That's true,' she agreed. 'Now if you want to see them, you have to go to Europe.'

'That's where the money is. They get paid more over there than they do here.'

'I know, but it's still a shame,' she said, then sighed wistfully. 'I had tickets to see *Turandot* the last time I was in New York. Unfortunately I wasn't able to go at the last minute and wound up giving them to a friend.'

'Were you in New York on business – or pleasure?'

'Business. The agency's corporate headquarters are in New York and I was there for a meeting.'

'Do you go there often?'

'Three or four times a year. What about you?'

'About twice that . . . sometimes more.'

'Where do you stay?' she wondered curiously.

'At the Plaza Athenee.' He tipped his head to one side. 'Why do you ask?'

Smiling faintly, she swirled the champagne in her glass, watching the bubbles breaking on the surface. 'I wondered if you stayed at your competitor's hotel.'

'My competitor?' His gaze narrowed in puzzlement.

'Donald Trump.' She grinned teasingly at him over the rim of her glass.

He smiled at that. 'We may be in the same business, but I don't regard him as a competitor. I'm not interested in any development in Manhattan or Atlantic City. He's welcome to do whatever he's big enough to do there. I'll take the rest of the country for my territory.'

The glint of amusement in his eyes eliminated any hint of arrogance from his statement and drew a soft laugh from Flame. 'I'm surprised you didn't say the world.'

'I have to leave some room for growth,' he chided, grooves dimpling his lean cheeks.

'Now why didn't I think of that?' she declared, feigning a sigh.

A discreet distance from the table, a waiter stifled a yawn. Flame caught the sudden movement of his hand and quickly looked away, wishing she hadn't seen it. She didn't want to be reminded of how very late it must be.

'What are you doing tomorrow – or perhaps I should say, today?'

Meeting his gaze, she noticed the quiet, masculine insistence of it. And she noticed a dozen other things at the same time – like the ebony sheen of his hair in the low candlelight and the innate strength of his tanned fingers curved so gently around the bowl of his brandy glass.

'The Museum of Modern Art has an architectural show by Mario Botta that I've been wanting to see. I'm told it's quite impressive.'

'Could I persuade you to change your mind and drive down to Carmel with me for lunch?'

'I hope you don't intend to accomplish that by inundating me with orchids again,' she declared laughingly. 'I don't know what I'd do with more.'

'I won't – if you'll agree to come with me to Carmel and – in the words of its famous mayor – "make my day".'

Laughing, she lifted her hands in mock surrender. 'I'll come quietly.'

'Good.' His smile widened. 'I have some calls to make first thing in the morning. I can pick you up – say, around ten-thirty?'

'Wonderful. We can take the scenic route along the coast high-way and still be there in plenty of time for lunch.'

The waiter returned to their table, trying his best to look alert. 'May I bring you anything else? More brandy, perhaps?' he sug-gested, glancing at Chance's nearly empty glass.

'Not for me.' He looked at Flame, but she shook her head, echoing his refusal. 'That will be all, I believe.'

His reply signalled the end of the meal and the evening. Much of the drive back to her Victorian flat was made in silence, an oddly comfortable one. At the front door to her flat, he held out his hand for the keys. 'May I?'

Willingly she surrendered them to him and watched as he un-locked her door. When he turned to give them back to her, she knew – even without the sudden acceleration of her pulse to tell her – that the moment had come. There was a sameness to it, wondering if it would be awkward, if her expectations had been raised too high by the easy intimacy of the evening – if she would like being kissed by him.

As his hand glided on to the curve of her jaw, she tilted her head back in age-old invitation. His face was there before her, sculpted in bronze, his gaze moving slowly over her features.

A faint smile softened the line of his mouth. 'Ten-thirty tomor-row.'

There was a promise in his voice, but not nearly as much as she found in his kiss as he rubbed his mouth lightly over her lips then came back to claim them in a sensual tour de force.

And the sensations lingered long after he'd gone.

9

AT QUARTER past ten, the doorbell rang. Flame hurried to answer it, hastily tying the folded ends of the silk scarf into a knot beneath her hair in the back, and finishing just before she reached the door. When she opened it, there stood Chance. Her heart did a crazy little flip-flop at the sight of him.

Previously, he'd always been in evening clothes. This was the first time Flame had seen him in casual dress with his shirt unbuttoned at the throat, revealing a smattering of dark chest hairs and black denim trousers fitting smoothly over slim hips and muscled thighs. A windbreaker in the same shade of blue as his eyes hung over one shoulder, held by the hook of his finger. The result was less smooth sophistication and more rugged virility.

'I'm early.' His mouth quirked in that now familiar smile as his gaze made a slow sweep of her. 'You look rested and refreshed.'

'I am.' Although she wasn't sure how much sleep she'd actually got. Not that it mattered since she'd wakened with the feeling that she owned the world. 'Let me get my jacket and I'll be ready.'

In the living room, she retrieved the matching jacket to her full skirt of stone beige twill. As she started back to the foyer the phone rang. More than likely it was Ellery wanting to know how her evening had gone. Shrugging that she could talk to him later, she ignored the ring and walked swiftly back to the foyer.

Leather-bound tomes lined the bookshelves in the library at Morgan's Walk, their weighty presence adding to the room's sombre tone. Behind the Victorian pedestal desk of mahogany, a museum piece itself, Hattie Morgan listened to the unanswered rings and impatiently tapped a finger on the leather arm of her chair.

'Where is that girl?' Angrily she pushed the receiver back on to its cradle, breaking the connection and stopping the irritating brr-ings in her ear. Turning, she cast a disgruntled look at the portrait of Kell Morgan hanging above the fireplace mantel. The accumulation of dust and grime over the years had muted the bright copper shade of his hair, but she remembered the oil's original colour – and the number of times she'd wished that colour had been her own. But that girl, Margaret, had it.

'I should have called earlier. I shouldn't have waited.' She reached for the gold handle of her cane, propped against the desk within easy reach. Gripping it with her gnarled fingers, she pounded it once on the hardwood floor, venting her frustration and anger. 'How did he find her so quickly? She'll see through him. She has to.'

She struck the cane on the floor again, but the loud thud made the pain in her head worse. The prescription Doc Gibbs had given her would alleviate much of it, but she didn't like taking it. She didn't like the dullness that came with it, especially now when she needed to think.

Tucked among lush Monterey pines with the Pacific Ocean at its feet, Carmel-by-the-Sea had long been a favourite retreat of writers and artists drawn to the site by the simple charm of its village-look and the wild beauty of its surroundings. Strolling along the sidewalk crowded with tourists, passing shop after quaint shop, Flame decided its true appeal was its wonderfully eccentric character. Here was a town that turned down its thumb at such things as billboards, neon lights, and large retail signs, and turned its back on such customary amenities as sidewalks and kerbs on its side streets, then pointed with pride at its dearth of streetlights and traffic signals.

Yet, as she glanced in the window of a gourmet foods shop, Flame knew the village community wasn't capable of supporting the one hundred and fifty-odd shops in the town, more than a third of which were galleries carrying the works of local artists. They had to rely on the tourist trade. Carmel wasn't adverse to progress – as long as it came on its terms. Maybe that's what she liked best about it, more than its charm or its picturesque setting.

'Look out,' Chance's warning came simultaneously with the tightening pressure of the arm hooked casually around her shoulders.

In the next second, she was hauled against him and out of the path of a nine-year-old racing his bike. By the time Flame saw the boy, he was gone and she was moulded firmly to Chance's side, an altogether pleasant discovery.

Looking up, she saw the grooved smile he directed at her, all lazy and warm like the look in his eyes. 'There's nothing more dangerous than a speeding nine-year-old.'

'I don't know about that,' she said, well aware that the rapid beat of her pulse had nothing to do with nearly being knocked down by a child. 'I can think of one or two other things more dangerous.'

'Can you?' His gaze strayed to her lips and lingered there. 'I can only name one. We'll have to compare notes later and see if we agree.'

'Or the ways we differ,' she suggested, unconsciously staring at his mouth.

As his arm loosened its band around her, Flame recognised that there was no more reason for her hand to be braced against the rock-hard flatness of his stomach. Reluctantly she withdrew it and turned to resume their stroll down the busy street. But she continued to feel the comfortable weight of his arm draped around her shoulders when they began walking again.

'Hungry?'

She almost laughed at that leading question. The touch of him, the warmth of him, the feel of him beside her had made her hungry, ravenously so. But she couldn't tell him that.

'A little,' she admitted instead. 'If I remember right, there's a charming Italian restaurant a little further down the block. We could go there.'

'Why not?'

Her memory proved accurate and after a five-minute wait, they were shown to a table in the corner of the room. Flame smiled when she saw the predictable red-checked tablecloth and the Chianti bottle dripping with multicoloured wax from the candle lodged in its neck.

'This place hasn't changed a bit,' she said, recognising a familiar print of Naples on the wall as she sat down in her chair. 'The last time I was here, it was with a group of my sorority sisters just before spring break. Then two carloads of guys from the fraternity followed us down. We all came in here to eat. First someone threw a meatball, then we were flinging spaghetti in each other's hair. Before long, it turned into a food fight, Italian style. I'm surprised the place survived that. It's amazing the insane things you do when you're young and foolish.'

'I guess it is.'

'What college did you attend?' she asked curiously, then held up a hand quickly to check his answer. 'No, let me guess. I used to be very good at this. It was in the Midwest, right?' He nodded, watching her with an amused look. She smiled. 'I was positive it wasn't an Ivy League school. It was probably a Big Ten. Ohio?' she guessed.

'Wisconsin.'

'I was close.'

'Where did you go?'

'Berkeley.' She knew her smile faded a little, but she had too few good memories attached to that time in her life. 'My mother wanted me to go to her alma mater Vassar, but I rejected that, insisting that I wasn't going to leave sunny California for the frigid East. I picked the Berkeley campus of the University of California instead – the home of the free spirit right across the Bay. I think I chose it because even though I wanted to leave the nest, I didn't want to stray too far. I'm glad I didn't.' She hesitated, then explained, 'I lost both my parents in an auto accident the following year.'

'It must have been a difficult time for you.'

'It was. It's not something you ever really get over, but I've learned to accept it.' And she'd accomplished that by not letting herself dwell on their deaths but, rather on their lives. 'I wish you could have met my father. He was a wonderful man.' She paused to smile. 'I know. All daughters say that about their fathers, but in my case it was true. Every time I think about him, I remember that perennial gleam of laughter in his eyes. Even in serious moments, it was there – just below the surface, ready to break through.'

Picking up the new lightness of her mood, Chance observed, 'And I'll bet one look from those baby greens and he gave you anything you wanted.'

Laughing, she admitted, 'Most of the time. What about you? What were you like when you were a little boy?' She had the feeling he'd probably been one of those charming rascals, full of the devil, in and out of mischief all the time.

An eyebrow lifted in mocking challenge. 'Who said I ever was one?'

Before Flame could respond to that, the waitress stopped at the table to take their order. As she opened her menu. Flame began to wonder if Chance had actually been joking when he'd said that. Something – some underlying edge in his voice suggested that the remark made in jest was the truth. Belatedly she remembered that he'd told her his mother had died after a long illness. He'd been eleven at the time. Which meant she'd obviously been ill through much of his childhood. Perhaps he'd even helped to take care of her – as much as a seven-, eight-, nine- or ten-year-old could. It certainly wouldn't have been a happy or a carefree time.

Lunch turned into a long, leisurely affair as they lingered at the table over a cup of capuccino, talking about everything and nothing. It was mid-afternoon when they finally emerged from the restaurant and headed for the beach to walk off the meal.

Seagulls wheeled and swooped over the rolling surf, tumbling headlong towards the shore. Idly Flame watched their acrobatics as she wandered over the white sugar sand with Chance, his arm around her shoulders and her own curved to the back of his waist, a thumb hooked in the belt loop of his denims. There was wild, classic beauty to the setting with white-capped waves crashing on to the long, curving stretch of beach, a beach guarded by ancient Monterey cypress, all twisted and bowed by the ceaseless sea wind.

It was a place that appealed to the senses – the wind whipping at her hair, sharp with the tang of the ocean, the muted rumble of the waves rolling on to the beach, the diamond sparkle of the sunlight on the deceptively smooth waters of the bay. And all of it seemed to make her more aware of the man beside her, like the casual rubbing of his hip against hers with each stride they took, or the pervading warmth of his body heat. She was forced to admit that she was more conscious of Chance than she had been of any man in a long time.

'It's beautiful, isn't it?' she said, needing to break the silence no matter how mundane the comment.

'Very.'

'I'm glad they haven't built a lot of hotels and condominiums along the beach. It would spoil the natural beauty of it.' Her comment drew a low chuckle from him.

'And I'm glad not everyone shares that opinion or I'd be out of business along with many other developers.'

'That's what you do, isn't it?' she realised with a trace of chagrin. 'Build fabulously large resort complexes. How did you get into that? There are so many other kinds of things you could have chosen instead – residential, industrial, retail centres.'

'A combination of things, I suppose.' He paused, his gaze turning thoughtfully to their surroundings, a seriousness in his expression that she rarely saw. 'From the time I can remember, the importance of land was drilled into me. But the resort aspect,' Chance went on, 'came about while I was at college. Have you ever heard of the Wisconsin Dells?'

'Vaguely I remember the name but I don't know anything about it.'

'It's a vacation area in Wisconsin, very scenic, very commercialised and very popular with residents in the surrounding states. Seeing the Dells as a college student and being exposed to Playboy's famous resort at Lake Geneva made me realise that people love to play – young, old, rich, and poor – and everyone in between. Whether the times are good or bad, they still play. If anything, the need to escape becomes even stronger during the bad times – the wars and depressions. That's why they flock to the beaches and the mountains – or any place where they can be surrounded by beauty, atmosphere, and preferably, luxury.'

'Which is exactly what a Stuart resort provides,' Flame guessed, then tried to remember, 'How many resorts carry the Stuart banner now? Is it six?'

'Seven,' he corrected, directing that lazy, lopsided smile at her again. 'Plus the one in Tahoe under construction and two more in development.'

'Very impressive,' she murmured, dipping her head to him in mock homage. And it was, especially when she recalled from the articles about him that he'd built all of his multimillion dollar resorts in less than twelve years, and considering that some had taken two years to construct, that was quite an accomplishment.

Abruptly he halted their stroll. 'Why is it that we always seem to be talking about me? What about you and your life?'

'Mine isn't nearly as interesting as yours.'

'To you maybe, but not to me,' he said, slowly shaking his head as he turned towards her, his hand automatically sliding under her jacket on to her waist. At the moment, Flame wasn't sure if she was more aware of the warm pressure of his hand on the curve of her waist or the hard feel of his ribs beneath her own. 'There are a dozen things I've yet to find out about you.' His voice was pitched low, faintly mocking yet provocatively challenging.

'Such as?'

'Such as . . . how did you manage to become a vice-president without becoming hardened by all the dirty infighting of corporate politics?' His gaze moved slowly over her face, blatant in its interest. 'Who put that wariness there that I sometimes see in your eyes? How could your ex-husband have been so foolish as to let you go?' As she felt the brush of his fingers in her hair, he asked, 'Does your hair always look like spun fire in the sunlight? Did your mother have lips like yours? And does every man find it as hard as I do to keep my hands off you?'

All sense of caution fled as she moved into his arms, her mouth lifting to meet his more than halfway. There was none of last night's sensual exploration. This time her lips rocked with his in need, tasting the trace of salty spray on them and discovering the hot satin of his tongue. Everything quickened and rose inside her, the blood rushing through her veins and suddenly heightening all her senses.

Her hands had long ago found their way under his windbreaker and now splayed themselves over his back to feel the flexing play of its muscles. Arching, she leaned into him, letting him take all her weight and intensifying the soaring feeling. There was a dim recognition of his hands moving expertly over her body, but she didn't try to keep track of them. It was enough that they were spreading the intimacy of the kiss over her.

When his mouth rolled off her lips and began to trail a series of warm, wet kisses over her face, Flame felt herself tremble, a passion she had always known she possessed but that had gone too long unused, surfacing. Who had been the last to ignite it? She couldn't remember. But she had the feeling that none had ever aroused it as thoroughly or as quickly as Chance had. Did she want that? Could she afford it? She felt his mouth at the corner of her lips again and turned into it. Her mouth opening to take his tongue and let the hot, soft sensation of it fill her.

Then came the jarring blare of rock music from a ghetto-blaster, drowning out the undulating rumble of the heavy surf. She sensed a matching reluctance as Chance disentangled his mouth from hers and pulled away. The sea wind felt suddenly very cool against her kiss-heated lips. She kept her face turned to him, catching that flash of irritation in the look he threw at the trio of giggling girls, sauntering down the beach darting glances over their shoulders at them. But there was no sign of that irritation when his glance came back to her, the blue of his eyes darkened by the thing that had happened between them – something too private, too intimate to be continued in such a public place. Yet his arms stayed around her, not letting her go immediately.

'Do you have any plans for tonight?' he asked, a faint huskiness in his voice.

'I don't know,' she replied softly, the smallest of smiles curving her lips. 'Do I?'

The grooves in his hard, lean cheeks deepened. 'Indeed you have. Dinner with me and . . . whatever else happens to follow it.'

The desire to bed her was in his eyes and he made no attempt to conceal it, silently letting her know that the final decision was hers to make. For her to take that step, emotions had to be involved. But weren't they already? Why couldn't she be honest with herself and admit that she felt a great deal more than mere lust? She wanted to trust. She wanted to believe, especially now that she already cared.

'In that case, maybe we should start back,' she said, smiling lightly and moving back from him. 'I'd like to shower and change before we have this special dinner.'

In silent agreement, Chance turned to head back across the heavy sand already marked by the indentations of their previous footsteps. He kept an arm around her, drawing her with him to walk again at his side. For a time, Flame studied the twin set of tracks before them, one large and one small, noticing how close together they were and thinking how right it looked.

Then she lifted her gaze to the clump of cypress ahead of them, their gnarled trunks gracefully bowed by the wind. At the base of the nearest one stood a man in a tan windbreaker, smoking a cigarette and . . . watching them. She was sure of it. Abruptly he dropped the cigarette, briefly stepped on it, then swung away and started walking in the same direction they were going. But when he'd turned, his hawk-like profile had been clearly outlined.

It was the waiter with the brown shoes, the same man who'd delivered that message of warning last night. Stunned, Flame faltered slightly, breaking the ambling rhythm of their steps and throwing Chance off-stride as well.

'Careful.' His arm tightened in support as if he thought she had stumbled over something. She felt his glance move to her and quickly tried to eliminate the look of shock from her expression. But obviously not quickly enough. 'Is something wrong?' he asked.

'No.' She couldn't very well tell him that some man had followed them all the way to Carmel – especially if, as she suspected, it turned out to be Malcom who was paying this man to tail her.

'Are you sure?'

'Of course.' She gave him a wide smile. But she wasn't sure he believed her.

═ IO ═

IN THE dimly lit lounge, a small combo played a dreamy ballad, all soft and bluesy with longing. A handful of couples moved slowly around the handkerchief-sized dance floor frequently described as intimate. Flame fully agreed with the description as she danced with Chance, not a breath of space between them, their feet moving indifferently to the rhythm, their heads bent together, with Chance now and then turning his mouth against her temple or cheek in discreet caresses.

Idly she ran her fingers along the corded muscles at the back of his neck, letting them glide into the clipped ends of his black hair. There was a wonderful forgetfulness in his arms that allowed her to block out the memory of the dark green saloon that had followed them back from Carmel three cars behind – and the memory of the same car parked at the corner when Chance had picked her up. None of that had any place here, not with his arms around her and the dreaminess of the music drifting through her.

As his mouth lightly rubbed itself against her forehead, Flame smiled. 'Walks along the beach, candlelit dinners for two, orchids by the jungleful, soft music, soft lights, and cheek-to-cheek dancing – I have the feeling that I'm being very thoroughly romanced,' she whispered, and felt the curving of his mouth into a smile.

'It couldn't possibly be because you are,' he murmured dryly, the huskily low pitch of his voice as caressing as the hand on her back.

'Then you admit it?'

'When subtlety fails, bold moves are required.'

'And you know how to move boldly, don't you?' The teasing lightness in her voice was simply a part of the word game they played – a way of masking the mounting tension, a tension that was both exciting and stimulating. 'I do believe you're trying to take advantage of me, Mr Stuart.'

'Wrong.' His head moved faintly in denial. 'I'm trying to persuade you to take advantage of me.' Drawing back to watch her reaction, Chance studied the strong, pure lines of her face, knowing how the mere sight of her moved him, a feeling intensified by the softly rounded shape of her body pressed so easily against him.

For the first time, he saw no wary hesitation shadowing the green of her eyes. They looked back at him bright and clear, shining with a promise that nearly broke through his restraint. He managed to check the impulses that pushed at him, and obeyed instead the instincts that had warned him from the beginning that this wasn't a woman who could be forced into giving or swayed by lavish compliments and passion-filled kisses.

He was a man of the land. He always had been. And land taught a man patience, a virtue necessary to give something the time it needed to grow and ripen. Not even buildings sprung up overnight.

'That's an intriguing thought,' she murmured softly and his glance fell immediately to her lips, faintly parted. Today, at the beach, he had come close to tasting the fullness of their response. And Chance knew that he'd never be satisfied with anything less than all of it. 'Taking advantage of *the* Chance Stuart.'

'Interested?' He raised their linked fingers and lightly rubbed his mouth over hers.

She watched him, a half-smile forming as if secretly amused by some thought that had just occurred to her. 'There's this little voice inside my head that keeps saying "Take a chance".'

'I like that voice. Maybe you can persuade it to speak a little louder.'

'I don't need to. I want to take a chance.' She raised her head to him, her upturned lips seeking his mouth.

— 99 —

He had barely tasted the honeyed gloss of her lips when the band stopped playing and a scattering of faint applause broke around them. Chance pulled back slightly breaking the contact but not letting her go. 'Why don't we continue this at a place that's less crowded and infinitely more private than here? Like my suite.'

'I think that's an excellent idea.'

Chance unlocked the door to his suite, then stepped back to let Flame precede him. Without hesitation, she walked by him and wandered into the sitting room, then paused and turned back to him with a model's grace, the tiered flounces on the skirt of her slim black silk dress briefly flaring out. The collar of her fur jacket was high around her throat, the sooty black of it contrasting sharply with the copper gold of her hair.

Deliberately she looked around the room, then brought her glance back to him, something playful about the soft line of her mouth. 'I thought I might find a room full of orchids waiting for me again. Or, at the very least, peach champagne on ice.'

He went to her, a smoothness inside him that wouldn't last any longer than it took to touch her. 'We don't need those props, Flame,' he said, his hands gliding along her jaw and into the hair behind her ears. 'Not when we have this.'

He kissed her with a long slow warmth that gradually took possession of both of them. For him, he knew there could be no orchid half as fragrant as the perfumed scent of her hair, and no wine half as intoxicating as the taste of her on his tongue.

This time there was no hesitation, no testing to see if the ground could support what was being built. Instead it was a meeting of two forces, each strong in its own right, and in the silent probing of the other's strength, uncovering feelings that didn't require passion to achieve intimacy.

As she leaned into his kiss, Chance felt the heaviness of her body settle against him, the thickness of the fur preventing him from feeling the womanly shape of her. Reluctantly he straightened, his hands sliding down to slip the jacket from her. He gave it a toss on to the closest chair, his gaze never leaving her face, all the while highly conscious of the nameless feelings that surged through him, powerfully aroused yet oddly tender, too.

For an instant, he searched for something to say, but all of it had been said before – in some other hotel room, to some other woman. He didn't want to use those same words with Flame. There was a flicker of surprise at the realisation that he wanted it to be different with her.

But there was a pattern to things that couldn't be changed, and he recognised that, too, as he picked her up, cradling her in his arms and carried her into the bedroom. There, he set her down and kissed her again, rediscovering the earthy and stimulating pressure of her lips.

When he pulled back to loosen his tie, she held his gaze with an eloquent ease and raised her hands, reaching behind her neck to unfasten the top hook of her dress. Leaving his tie half undone, Chance turned her around and slowly slid the zipper all the way down to the base of her spine, watching with interest the back of her dress separate and reveal the creamy white of her skin and the lacy black of her teddy. He slid the dress off her shoulders and down her arms, stimulated by the silken texture of her skin. As he bent to nibble at the white bareness of a wide, straight shoulder, the dress fell the rest of the way to the floor in a rustling whisper.

While his fingers edged the thin straps of her teddy off her shoulder, his nibbling mouth followed its ridge to the base of her neck. Her head was thrown back and to the side, allowing him to explore at length the rapidly pulsing vein in her neck. He was conscious of the disturbed shallow breaths she took, and the faint tremors she tried to contain. He wanted more, so much more.

He turned her into his arms and found himself confronted with the rest of the racy nothingness of her teddy. 'Black lace,' he murmured, gazing at the wispy pattern of dark threads that so thinly veiled the slow but agitated rise and fall of her breasts.

'You said black lace on a woman did things to a man's blood.' There was a disturbed edge to her voice that reached out to him. 'And I wanted to affect you that way.'

'You do.' His own voice vibrated from some place deep inside him.

With infinite care, he dispensed with the fragile garment, prolonging the moment to heighten the anticipation for both of them. Anticipation became realisation as she stood naked before him, pooled in the light coming from the doorway to the sitting room.

For a moment it was enough just to gaze at the picture she made, her lips faintly parted, her eyes on him, the light shining on the rounded contours of her body and shadowing its hollows. Then he had to touch and prove that this statuesque figure was real.

He started at her neck, his fingertips gliding down the slender arc of her throat to the hollow at the base of it. Separating, his hands moved along twin paths to the jutting roundness of her breasts, their fullness a wondrous and lusty surprise to him as they spilled over the cup of his hands. He felt her breathe in sharply, deeply, then hold it, her lashes fluttering down. He rubbed his thumbs over the erect points of her nipples, drawing a tremor from her, followed by a sound that fell halfway between a sigh and a moan, a purring quality to it that matched the way she arched her body towards him. He let his hands trail lower, on to the flatness of her stomach, muscles contracting inwardly at his touch. Then he spread them over the cradling protrusion of her pelvic bones and around, on to the firm cheeks of her bare bottom, and drew her to him.

There was no more doubt now. She was very real, the outline of her rounded breasts pressed firmly to his chest, the sensation of them penetrating through his clothes. She was all heated flesh moving under his hands as she came to him, her lips seeking his and breathing their drugging sweetness into his mouth. He gathered her in, briefly giving way to the pressures inside. Her lips parted under the stroke of his tongue, her own mating with his, hot and soft, tasting of wine and some other intoxicating flavour uniquely her own. At last, he set her away from him and his own clothes made a pile on the floor next to her, her admiring eyes watching him all the while, their look heavy-lidded with desire.

As he lifted her for the last time, her arms wound themselves around his neck. There was silence between them, their eyes, their hands, their bodies communicating much more eloquently than mere words could have done. Chance carried her to the bed, the covers already turned invitingly back. The mattress dipped under his weight centred on the point of one knee as he laid her down, then followed after her.

She rolled to him, her slim hand gliding across his bare chest, and running its fingers through the curling hairs, then sliding up to the back of his neck. The pull of her parted lips brought his mouth down to them, open and hot, eating at him with need.

He slid a leg between her thighs and instantly felt her push against it as he cupped a breast in his hand and played with its nipple, rolling it between his thumb and forefinger and marvelling at its high erectness. Shifting his attention from her lips, he explored the perfumed hollow behind her ear. Taking her delicate lobe between his teeth, he nipped at it gently, then nibbled his way down the long cord in her neck. She was all motion against him, her hands running over his shoulders, neck and back, her body straining towards him, her hips arching in a rubbing rhythm until he was surrounded by heat, pressure pushing at him from inside as well as out.

With the thigh he had wedged between her legs, he lifted her higher in the bed, bringing her luscious breasts within easy range. Her fingers tangled with his hair, digging and flexing as his mouth moved from the hollow of her throat to a tautly erect nipple and traced its round tip with his tongue. Her back arched, her body urging him to take all of it but he needed no such coercion as he drew it in. Aroused by the deep-throated sounds that came from her and the quickened rate of her breathing, Chance let his hand move lower, abandoning its fondling of her other breast to wander over the flatness of her stomach, pausing to investigate her navel then finally sliding into that silken nest of auburn-gold hair pressed so tightly against his thigh.

He wanted her. God, how he wanted her – right now – this minute. He almost let himself be swept away by the force of that need, then finally controlled it. This was their first time together and he wanted it to be theirs, together. He didn't question the why of it – not now – and concentrated instead on prolonging the pleasure for both of them and revelling in the taste, the touch, the smell, the sound – the sight of her in his bed.

When the pressure became an agony neither could endure, he shifted on to her, his weight briefly pinning her. With no barrier to break, he was absorbed into her and she was all tight and warm around him. He brought his mouth down, slanting it across her lips as he lifted her hands high above her head and linked her fingers with his. The need to hurry fled. This was a moment to be enjoyed to the fullest. He moved slowly, making each thrust long and deep and feeling the rise of her hips match each stroke.

As the tempo increased, seemingly, on its own, there was only sensation – the feel of her tongue licking away the beads of perspiration that had formed on his upper lip, and the rake of her teeth across his shoulder before she bit into his muscle, smothering the moaned cry of his name, the urging press of her hands running over his back and buttocks, and the soft, wild suppleness of her body melded so completely with him. There was an illusion of the world spinning and he wrapped his arms tightly around her, not letting her go anywhere without him.

Unable to sleep, Flame carefully eased Chance's arm from her and slid noiselessly from the bed. She paused to look back and make sure she hadn't wakened him. In sleep, there was even more strength in his features, a kind of hard pride that was usually masked by a smile. She stared for a moment, remembering again that absolute rawness of emotion, so powerful and so beautiful . . . much more than excitement, much more than exquisite release.

She turned from the sight of his face and the clean, male lines of hard muscle and flesh. At her feet lay the white of his dress shirt. She hesitated briefly, then picked it up and put it on, smiling at the sleeves that were much longer than her arms. She rolled back the cuffs to her wrists and padded silently into the darkened sitting room, fastening two of the front buttons along the way.

She drifted over to the window and gazed at the nightlights of San Francisco that gleamed back at her from the inky darkness. Absently, she turned up the collar of his shirt and buried her face in it, breathing in the heady fragrance of his masculine cologne.

When she'd come to his suite, she hadn't known one moment of doubt. She'd wanted him to make love to her. She'd wanted him, and she'd had no desire to hide those feelings. For too long she'd kept her own natural passion suppressed. But she'd never expected his lovemaking to unleash this torrent of feeling. It was a little frightening – this depth of feeling she had for him now. She shied from the word love. To use it would mean he had the power to hurt her. But, dear God, if she didn't see him again after tonight, that would hurt, too.

'There you are.' As his voice came to her from the darkness, Flame stiffened, suddenly sensing that he was very near. When she felt his hands settle on to the looseness of the shirt's sleeves, she turned before they could actually close around her arms. There was a lazily possessive look in his eyes. 'I was beginning to think I dreamed you.'

'I couldn't sleep.' Seeing him standing there with that look in his eyes, she felt that swell of incredibly tender feelings again. As his hands curved on to the sides of her waist, she smoothed her own over the hard, flat muscles of his chest, the contact reminding her of his strength – and his gentleness. 'Chance, I –'

But he cut in before she could explain the cause of her sleeplessness. 'It's scary as hell, isn't it?'

Stunned that he could know exactly what she was thinking, she offered no resistance when he drew her closer, cradling her hips against his. 'How –'

'– did I know?' He finished the question for her and smiled. 'Do you think you're the only one it happened to? In case you've forgotten, I was there, too.'

'You very definitely were,' she admitted. 'But I didn't know if it had the same impact for you.'

'It did.' He gathered her the rest of the way into his arms and rubbed his cheek and mouth against her hair. 'Tomorrow is going to come whether we like it or not, Flame. And when it does, I'll have to leave.'

'I know.' Pride kept her from clinging to him.

'We'll both have our share of nights to sleep alone. I don't want tonight to be one of them.'

There was no mocking inflection in his voice, no teasing, no making light of it; he was completely serious. Moved by that, Flame gazed at this man who fitted her as comfortably and warmly as a second skin.

'Neither do I,' she said, certain now that getting through the lonely nights ahead would be difficult as long as she had the stirring memories of this night to keep her company.

'Then come back to bed with me.'

The urge was strong to say something ridiculously romantic like – I'd go anywhere with you. Instead Flame shifted slightly in his arms and curved an arm around the back of his bare waist to turn him towards the bedroom, letting her actions say what would have sounded too foolish coming from her lips.

Back in the bedroom, Flame slipped out of his shirt, and turned to the bed. Chance was already there, his long frame stretched out full length on the mattress, the covers down around his waist revealing the male torso that was all hard, flat muscle and bronze flesh. She paused for an instant, knowing that he was looking at her and knowing, too, that he liked what he saw.

As she climbed into bed, Chance rolled on to his side and reached out to snare her and draw her firmly to his side. His face was inches from her. She watched his gaze idly follow the track of his hand as it glided over her ribcage to cup the underswell of her breast, giving rise again to those initial stirrings of desire.

Then his gaze came back to wander over her face in a thoughtful study. 'I can't seem to make up my mind,' he murmured.

'About what?' She ran her hand over his arm, feeling the bunched muscles.

'If this is where you belong – or where I belong? There's a part of me that wants to put a brand on you and claim you as my private and very personal property,' he said, then paused. 'And there's another part of me that feels very humble. And *that* is a feeling entirely new to me.'

'For me, too,' she whispered.

'Flame.' That was all he said before his mouth opened on her lips taking them whole and devouring them with a bold sensuality that she easily matched. That intense hunger was something she understood too well, and she returned it with equal aggression.

This time when they made love, she was struck by the wild harmony of it, like the fury of a storm that comes, unleashes its torrents, then passes, leaving in its wake the earthy and invigorating feeling of clean, fresh air.

= II =

CHURCH BELLS peeled the call to morning worship as Chance pulled up in front of her flat. At the same moment, Flame saw Ellery coming down the steps to the Victorian mansion. She waved briefly to him, and ignored his halt of surprise as she turned to Chance.

'There's no need to walk me to the door.' She didn't want to prolong the goodbye that had to be said.

'I'll call you.'

And with Chance, that wasn't a line. He never said anything he didn't mean. She'd learned that about him, as well as many other things. 'If you don't reach me the first time, don't give up. Wherever I am, I'll be back.'

'I don't give up on anything.' His hand tunnelled under her hair, cupping the back of her neck and pulling her to his mouth. Flame responded to the heated kiss that was packed with feeling and promise. When he released her, she felt warm all the way through. The glittering darkness of his blue eyes added their own promise to the kiss as he murmured, 'Till next time.'

'Till next time,' she echoed the phrase that had become almost a talisman to her, then reached for the door handle.

When she climbed out of the sports car, she was faintly surprised at how clear-eyed she felt, with no sting of tears, no painful tightness in her chest. All because of that wonderful certainty that there would be a next time. Leaving the car she crossed to the base of the steps then turned to watch Chance drive away.

'Since you're so terribly overdressed for church, this is obviously the morning after a glorious night before.' Ellery came down two more steps to stand behind her.

'What makes you think it was only the night before that was glorious?' She was a little surprised by the lightheartedly smug feelings that prompted her to tease him back. It had been so long since she'd been in love that she'd forgotten how good it could make a person feel.

Ellery drew his hand back, his eyes widening slightly and that eyebrow arching as she turned to climb the steps. 'We are feeling a little cocky this morning, aren't we? – if you'll excuse the expression.'

His remark didn't immediately register, her attention distracted by the sight of the dark green saloon that pulled into the empty parking space on the opposite side of the street. 'Ellery, without being obvious, take a look at that dark green saloon – a Ford, I think – parked about halfway down the hill. Can you see the driver?' She kept her back to the street – and the saloon, and pretended to look through her evening bag for the door key.

'Not very well,' Ellery said after a brief pause. 'Why?'

'Do you remember that waiter with the brown shoes at the DeBorgs' party last week? He had a big hooked nose.'

'I remember.' A silent question remained in his voice, waiting for an explanation for all this.

'Look closely at the driver and see if it's the waiter.'

'He's too far away. All I can see is the shape of a man's head on the driver's side.'

'Never mind.' She shrugged in irritation and took the key from her bag. 'Let's go inside.'

Frowning, Ellery glanced one last time at the car, then followed Flame as she ran lightly up the steps to her door. 'What's this all about? Why would you think that's the waiter?'

'Because he's the sender of that nasty note – or more correctly the deliverer of the note.' She inserted the key in the deadbolt lock and gave it a quick turn, then pushed her weight against the door to open it.

'How do you know that?'

'Because' – she breezed into the foyer, leaving Ellery to close the door behind them, then paused at the door to the hall closet and slipped off her fur jacket – 'he had another message for me at the opera Friday night. That one he delivered in person.'

'Another message?'

'Yes. The gist of it was the same as the first – Stay away from him. Only this time there was an added warning that if I didn't, I'd be sorry.' She was conscious of the brittleness beneath her offhand manner, but she couldn't pretend any more that it didn't bother her. 'On top of that, he followed me everywhere I went all weekend.' Stiffly she draped the jacket on to its shouldered hanger and hung it in the closet.

'Everywhere?'

'No, not everywhere – thankfully.' In spite of her tension or maybe because of it, she glanced at Ellery and laughed, again conscious of her new-found feelings. 'And don't raise your eyebrow at me, Ellery Dorn.'

'Would I do that?' he declared in mock innocence.

'You do it all the time.'

'At least now I know why I wasn't able to reach you all weekend. Although I must admit at the moment I'm more interested in finding out who the *him* is in the "stay-away-from" messages. Was the second more enlightening than the first?'

'No,' she admitted. 'But it has to be Chance.'

'And the sender?'

She hesitated as she briefly let her glance lock with Ellery's. 'I think it's Malcom. Who else is there? Initially I thought it might be Lucianna, but she strikes me as the kind who would come at me with her claws unsheathed if she thought I was taking her man.' She paused, her shoulders sagging in vague discouragement. 'After that ... disagreement ... I had with Malcom the other day, I know he isn't above making threats. And this business of having me followed – it could be his way of impressing me with the lengths he'll go to for what he wants.'

'What are you going to do about it?' This time Ellery was just as serious as she was.

'I know what I'd like to do. I'd like to threaten him with a sexual harassment suit.'

'But you don't dare,' Ellery guessed.

'Not if I want to continue as a vice-president of Boland and

— 109 —

Hayes.' A wry smile of resignation pulled at one corner of her mouth. 'Besides, a suit like that would do more damage to my reputation and career than it ever would do to his. What agency would want to hire me after those kind of headlines? And what client would want to work with me? None. So . . . I don't have any choice but to tough it out with him and show him that I won't be intimidated, not by him or anyone else.'

Ellery set his attaché case on the floor, freeing his hands to applaud her mockingly. 'Marvellous speech darling. Stiff upper lip and all that.'

She threw him a look of mild exasperation. 'If you're quite through, you can tell me what you wanted to see me about. This obviously isn't a social visit or you wouldn't have brought that along.' She gestured at the leather case by his feet.

'My timing may be questionable, but I have with me some new ideas for the Powell holiday ads.' His mouth twisted in a ruefully apologetic line. 'I thought it would be a good idea if we went over them privately, then, if you shoot them down the way you did before, you won't completely demoralise my staff.'

'You're right, Ellery. Your timing is very questionable.'

'If you'd rather wait –'

'No. Just give me a few minutes to shower and change – and forget that without a great deal of effort I could learn to heartily dislike Malcom.' She started down the hall to her bedroom, adding over her shoulder, 'Feel free to make some coffee.'

The aroma of freshly brewed coffee permeated the air when Flame came out of her bedroom, dressed more casually in a pair of brown slacks and an over-sized beige sweater. She hadn't bothered to dry her hair, instead slicking it back from her face, the wetness of it bringing out the red lights. She found Ellery in the living room with all the roughly sketched layouts and storyboards spread over the coffee table.

'I poured you some coffee.' With a wave of his hand, he indicated the cup sitting on the glass top of the occasional table.

'Thanks.' Retrieving it, she sipped at the steaming hot liquid, the smell and the taste of it reminding her of the breakfast she'd shared with Chance in his suite mere hours ago. She'd eaten most of hers while sitting on his lap all because she had tried to decline any food, insisting that she couldn't eat in the mornings. Chance had taken it as a challenge, pulled her on to his lap and proceeded to feed her bites of a pineapple Danish. In retaliation she had done the same to him with a raspberry one. Before it was over they had ended up licking the filling from each other's fingers and kissing it from the other's lips, the flavours of raspberry and pineapple mingling together in the process. It had been the most enjoyable breakfast she'd ever had.

She glanced at the black lacquered mantel clock, deciding Chance was probably at the airport by now. Possibly he could have even taken off already. Idly she wondered when he would call.

'Well?' Ellery prodded her for a reaction. 'Are any of these the slant you wanted?'

With a start, Flame realised that she'd been looking at the sketches without seeing any of them. 'Sorry, I –' The ringing of the telephone interrupted her, and she jumped to answer it, certain it was Chance calling from the airport.

But the whiskey-rough voice on the other end of the line didn't belong to Chance. 'Is that you, Margaret Rose? I've been calling all weekend. This is Hattie Morgan.'

'Hattie.' Belatedly Flame remembered the proud old woman who had come to see her with that wild story about being related and leaving a ranch in Oklahoma to her. She'd thought she'd heard the last of her. 'Where are you?' she wondered.

'At Morgan's Walk, of course,' came the snapped answer.

'Of course. I should have guessed.' She felt a twinge of pity that the poor woman was still clinging to her fantasy. More than likely she was at some nursing home, and all this was just a lonely attempt to reach out to somebody. 'Hattie, is there someone there I could talk to ? An attendant or a nurse?'

'A nurse?! No, there is not!'

'It isn't that I don't want to talk to you, Hattie,' Flame tried again. 'I merely want to –'

'You don't believe me, do you?' came the accusation. 'You think everything I said was the ramblings of a senile old woman. I'll have you know that my mind is as sharp as yours.'

'I'm sure it is –'

'No, you aren't. But I can prove everything I said to you. Do you have a paper and pencil?'

'Yes.' A notepad and pen lay next to the telephone.

'I'm calling you long distance from Oklahoma. Mark this number down.' With a sharp, staccato rhythm, she reeled the numbers off, then commanded, 'Now, read it back to me.'

Flame couldn't help smiling as she repeated the numbers she'd hastily jotted on the pad. The woman was indeed sharp – sharp enough to know that she could have pretended to write them down. Now Hattie knew she had.

'Good,' came the clipped response. 'Now I'm going to hang up and I want you to call me back at that number.'

'Hattie –'

'No. I don't want you to have any doubt that I am calling from Oklahoma. You can check the telephone directory yourself and see that I've given you the area code for Oklahoma.'

'I know that . . .'

'Then do it and call me back. Reverse the charges, if you like.' There was sharp click, then the line went dead.

Frowning with sudden doubt, Flame slowly lowered the receiver to stare at it. Had she misjudged this Hattie Morgan? Was it possible she had been telling the truth?

'Is something wrong?'

Ellery's question deepened her frown. 'I don't know.' She depressed the disconnect switch, held it down for a short span of seconds then released it and waited for the dial tone. When it came, she pushed the 'O' button for the operator. 'Yes, the area code for Oklahoma please,' she requested as soon as a voice came on the line. 'The Tulsa area' . . . 'Nine one eight,' she repeated while staring at the same set of digits she'd written on the pad. 'Thank you,' she murmured automatically as she hung up the phone.

'Who was that call from?' Ellery was now on his feet. 'What's going on?'

She half turned to him, still trying to sort through it all herself. 'Do you remember me telling you about that elderly woman who showed up at my door last week with that preposterous story that I was her last living relative and she was going to leave me her ranch in Oklahoma? That's who just called me.'

'What did she want?'

'She wants me to call her back – and the number she gave me has an Oklahoma area code.' She exhaled a silent laugh of disbelief and doubt. 'You don't suppose all that was true. I thought she had slipped away from some nursing home or private care centre. I mean, she could have easily read somewhere that my maiden name is Morgan – or that my Morgan ancestors married into one of the founding families in San Francisco.' She stared at the phone, remembering how casually she had dismissed the whole incident. 'It seemed so logical that a lonely old woman with no family of her own would want to pretend that she was related to me, especially when she saw that I had red hair, the same colour as some grandfather of hers.'

'You don't really believe she intends to leave you some cattle ranch in Oklahoma?' Again there was that high arch of an eyebrow from Ellery, conveying scepticism and question.

'I don't know what to believe,' Flame admitted and picked up the telephone again, dialling the number Hattie had given her. 'But if she answers, at least I'll know she told me the truth when she said she lived in Oklahoma.'

The first ring had barely ended when a voice demanded, 'Hello?'

'Hello – Hattie?' She felt oddly tense.

'Yes,' came the clipped response, followed by an even sharper demand. 'Is that you, Margaret Rose?'

'Yes, it is.'

'You certainly took your time about calling me back.'

'I did as you suggested and confirmed that the area code you gave me was for Oklahoma.'

'Then you should be satisfied on that score.' No attempt was made to mask the indignation and irritation in her voice.

'I am.' Flame tried to remain tolerant.

'I intended to ask how soon you would be able to visit Morgan's Walk, but it's become quite apparent to me that you neither believe in its existence nor that we are related.'

'Hattie, you surely have to realise how it would all sound to me.'

'I do. Although I thought I had convinced you of the truth of my claim when we talked. After all the searching I did to find you, I . . . But that is beside the point, isn't it? My word is not enough. You obviously require proof, and it's probably best that you do. Keep that wariness, Margaret Rose. It is better that you don't trust anyone too much.'

'You said something to that effect before,' Flame recalled.

'And it's true . . . as you'll find out. But – be that as it may, since it's proof you need, it's proof you shall have. I'll arrange immediately for copies to be sent to you documenting that you and I are of the same Morgan lineage. They should be in your possession no later than the end of the week.'

'Hattie, that isn't necessary –'

'Oh, but it is. It's very necessary. You must learn that everything I tell you will be the truth – and everything can be supported with proof.'

'I believe you,' she insisted with fading patience.

'No. Not yet you don't, but you shall. In the meantime I would prefer that you take nothing on blind faith. Now, when you receive the papers, study them over carefully. Then we'll talk about your trip to Morgan's Walk.'

'What is it that you're not telling me?' Flame demanded, giving way to her growing suspicion. 'There's something I should know, isn't there?'

'There are many things you should know now that Morgan's Walk will be yours when I'm gone. Too many to discuss on the phone. We'll go over everything when you come here.'

'But –'

'There is one other thing I must know, Margaret Rose, and it's very important.'

Flame pressed her lips tightly together, irritated by the way Hattie had sidestepped her question. As the pause lengthened, she realised a response was expected. 'I'm listening, Hattie,' she challenged somewhat sharply.

'I was beginning to wonder,' she retorted. 'Now, tell me, have you mentioned my visit and our . . . little discussion to anyone . . . anyone at all, even in passing?'

'Yes. Was it supposed to be a secret?' She frowned.

'How many people did you tell? Think carefully.'

'Only two.'

'Are you quite sure?'

'I am very sure,' Flame replied, allowing a trace of impatience to enter her voice. 'It wasn't something I went around telling everyone I met.'

'These two people, who are they? And please, you must accept that if it wasn't important, I wouldn't ask.'

Flame paused, wondering whether she might have been right

about Hattie Morgan all along. All this cross-examination and talk of proof was becoming a bit much. 'One was a very close friend of mine, whom I have known for years – a Mr Ellery Dorn. And the other was a client and family friend, Mr Malcom Powell.'

'Those are the only ones you told? No one else?'

'No one. I've already said that.' She tried very hard to remember she was talking to an elderly woman – and a slightly paranoid one at that.

'In that case, I want your word of honour that you will not discuss this further – with anyone. And when you receive the copies of the documents I'm sending you, don't show them to anyone . . . unless, of course, you wish to take them to your attorney to verify their authenticity. But no one else. Do I have your word on that?'

'Why this secrecy? When you were here, you weren't concerned about who I might talk to.'

'I didn't see the need then. Now I do. I have my reasons, Margaret Rose, and I will explain them to you when you come to Morgan's Walk. As I said, I will tell you everything then. And you will understand perfectly why I must ask for your word now. Do I have it?'

She sighed, knowing that this was the only answer she was going to get. 'Yes, you have my word.'

'You won't regret it. Goodbye, Margaret Rose. We shall talk again next weekend, after you have had an opportunity to study the papers.'

'Goodbye, Hattie.' She hung up the phone, still trying to fathom the entire conversation.

'That sounded like a rather bizarre conversation,' Ellery prompted.

Flame turned, lifting her arms in an expressive shrug. 'I'm not even going to pretend I understand. Although I have the feeling that I just took a blood oath not to divulge our conversation to anyone, including you.'

'Why?' His frown was halfway between amusement and amazement.

'I don't know.' She shook her head. 'It's all terribly mysterious and hush-hush. So hush-hush, she won't tell me. Maybe it's a ploy to get me sufficiently intrigued so that I'll fly out there.'

'Intrigue. That's a curious choice of words.'

'And maybe more accurate than I know.'

As Hattie returned the receiver to its cradle, she heard the creak of a floorboard in the great hall outside the study door. For an instant she held herself motionless, listening. After eighty-one years, she knew every creak and groan in this old house, and the sound she'd just heard hadn't been one of its natural grumblings.

'Who's there?'

There was no answer to her demand. Her mouth tightened into a thin line as she grabbed up her cane and pushed out of the worn leather chair. With the tap of the cane giving her walk a three beat tempo, she crossed to the arched opening, the double set of pocket doors flush to the carved frame. Her sweeping glance searched the area to her right, then homed in like an arrow on the stout, grey-haired woman.

'I knew there was someone out here,' Hattie declared. 'You were eavesdropping on my telephone conversations again, weren't you, Maxine?'

The woman turned, indignantly drawing herself up to her full height, her already ample bosom managing to appear considerably larger as she pushed her chest out. 'With all due respect, Miss Hattie, I have better things to do with my time than listen in on your conversations.'

'Then what are you doing out here and why didn't you answer when I called out?' Hattie's gaze narrowed suspiciously on her, not believing a word of that disavowal, however exemplary it sounded.

'I didn't answer because I thought you were talking to someone on the telephone. I didn't realise you expected me to reply.'

'Then you admit you knew I was on the phone.'

'Yes, I knew. And I also knew that this dusting needed to be done. Which is precisely what I was doing.'

Hattie had a moment's uncertainty as she tried to find a flaw in the housekeeper's explanation, but the sudden stabbing pain in her head eliminated it as she paled at the excruciating pain and started to lift a hand to her head, feeling the blackness press in on her.

'You didn't take your pill, did you?' Maxine Saunders accused. 'I'll get it for you.'

'No. No pill. I don't want it.' Hattie fought back the blackness, winning another battle with it.

'You know what the doctor said –'

'Such touching concern, Maxine. One would almost think you cared,' she taunted bitterly.

'After spending the last thirty years of my life taking care of Morgans, it's become a habit, Miss Hattie,' she retorted, almost as sharply. 'I've tried to give it up many times. Maybe one day I'll succeed.'

'Thirty years, is that what it's been?' Hattie struggled to recall despite the throbbing in her head. 'Yes, that's right.' She slowly nodded. 'You were always making sugar cookies for . . . that whelp. Said they were his favourites.'

All expression left the woman's face. 'He was a little boy.'

Hattie harrumphed at that, then stepped back and pulled the pocket doors closed, eliminating the possibility that the house-keeper would eavesdrop on future conversations. The cane swung with each stride, hitting the floor a beat off from her footsteps, as Hattie walked back to the large swivel chair behind the mahogany desk and sat down. Again she picked up the telephone, this time to dial Ben Canon's home number. The housekeeper answered and she waited impatiently for Ben to come on the line.

When he did, Hattie came straight to the point. 'Make copies of the documents and the summary that man from Utah sent us and get them off to Margaret Rose right away. But make certain they don't contain any mention of Stuart. Include my sister's death if you think it's necessary, but not her marriage or the child that came from it.'

'That may not be a wise thing to do under the circumstances, Hattie,' he replied. 'She's seeing Stuart –'

'Yes, yes, I know,' she interrupted impatiently. 'You told me.'

'You need to talk to her, Hattie.'

'I have. That's why I want you to send those documents to her.'

'No, I mean, you need to warn her about Stuart.'

'I can't. She already thinks I'm a senile old woman who doesn't know what she's talking about. She's not entirely convinced we're even related. She thinks I made it all up. Heaven knows why. If I told her the truth about Stuart and tried to warn her that she's walking into a trap with him, she'd never believe me. More than likely, she'd be convinced I was crazy. Worse than that, she'd go to Stuart with the story. He'd twist things around and sweet-talk her into turning against me. No, I need to have her here when I tell her. I need to convince her that what I say is the truth.'

'How do you know Stuart hasn't talked to her?'

'She would have told me if he had.'

'You can't be certain of that,' Ben argued.

'Yes, I can. She would have confronted me with any story he might have told her, but she didn't. She swore she mentioned my visit to only two people, and neither of them was Stuart.'

'He's playing it very cool, isn't he,' Ben murmured. 'I'd still like to know how he found out about her so quickly. We've got a leak somewhere, Hattie.'

'When will you have my new will ready?' she demanded. 'I know Stuart. He'll contest the handwritten one we did in your office.'

'I'm typing up the last of it right now, here at home. I'll bring it out for you to sign as soon as I'm finished. I thought it would be best if no one in my office knew about it.'

'Good. And be quick about those copies, Ben. I'm running out of time.'

'I know, Hattie. I know.'

Then he rang off and once again she was surrounded by the companionable silence of the house. This time she could draw no comfort from it, not when she knew the very walls around her were threatened. Her glance strayed to the pair of antique oval frames that sat on the desk next to the telephone. Silver filigree surrounded a photograph of her parents taken on their wedding day. But it was the picture in the second frame that claimed Hattie's attention. She stared at the photograph of a young, dark-haired girl with big, trusting eyes, her face shining with innocence.

'This is your fault, Elizabeth.' The tenderness of love softened her voice and added an unspoken forgiveness to the words as Hattie reached out and lightly stroked an arthritically crooked finger over the cheek of the girl in the picture, her baby sister.

Elizabeth Morgan had been sickly almost from the day she was born. Countless days and countless nights Hattie had nursed her fragile sister through bouts of colds, fevers, pneumonia and influenza. At times, it had seemed that delicate little Elizabeth had caught every sickness that went around, but with her it had always been worse than for anyone else. Often Hattie had wondered whether her sister might have been stronger if their mother hadn't been so ill before she was born. She gazed at the photograph and the aura of fragility it had captured forever.

'Why did I send you into town that day? Why?' It had been an innocent errand to pick up a few non-essential supplies that could have waited for another day, but Elizabeth had wanted to go – she'd wanted to be helpful instead of always a burden. And Hattie had let her go alone.

Elizabeth was late – later than she should have been. Hattie's imagination worked overtime, envisioning dozens of dreadful reasons – but she couldn't know how dreadful. Cranky with worry, she jumped on Elizabeth the instant she returned.

'Where have you been? Do you realise how late it is? How could it possibly take you this long to run a simple errand?'

Elizabeth laughed at her questions, as usual, not at all bothered by their sharpness. 'Don't fuss at me like I was one of the hired hands, Hattie. I would have been back sooner, but halfway home, I had a flat tyre.'

'A flat tyre.' Her glance sliced to the car, noticing for the first time that the tyre on the left front wheel was darker than the rest – and minus the clogs of dried red mud that marked the rest. 'You couldn't have changed it yourself.' Elizabeth wasn't strong enough to either jack up the car or remove the lug nuts and Hattie knew that.

'No. A man on a motorcycle stopped and changed it for me or I'd still be there.'

'Not one of those hoodlums in a black leather jacket.' She shuddered inwardly at the thought of her Elizabeth in the company of one of those toughs with their disgustingly long hair slicked into a ducktail at the back.

'He was nice, Hattie. And he wears the leather jacket to protect him from flying gravel and things like that.'

But Elizabeth didn't tell Hattie the way he'd looked when he took his jacket off – or the way his muscles had bulged beneath that thin T-shirt when he'd been changing the flat – or the way his shiny black hair had gleamed in the sunlight – or the way he'd swaggered a little when he walked – or the way he'd looked at her like she was a piece of candy he wanted to eat. At twenty-seven, Elizabeth hadn't had much experience with men, seldom dating in high school partly because she'd been sick much of the time and partly because Hattie had been strict about when she could date – and whom. But mostly because she was painfully shy.

And she knew that Hattie wouldn't approve of this boy at all. Although he wasn't a boy; he was a man in his early twenties, younger than her. She'd been a little scared when he first rode up. Everyone knew that the guys who rode motorcycles had a reputation for being fast. But it had been a little exciting, too. That's why she had let him coax her into trying on his black leather jacket. She had liked that – and the way he had smoothed his hands down her arms once she put it on.

'Have you ever ridden a motorcycle?' he'd asked.

'No.'

'Come on. I'll take you for a spin on mine.'

'I – can't.' She knew she shouldn't even be talking to him, let alone trying on his jacket and definitely not riding his motorcycle. Yet he made her feel so daring – and pretty. She wasn't, of course. She was plain – a dark mouse and not vibrant and strongly handsome like Hattie. 'I'll be late as it is.'

'Where's home?'

'Morgan's Walk.'

'You live there?' He looked again at the car, then back at her.

'Yes.'

'What's your name?'

'Elizabeth. Elizabeth Morgan.'

He'd lifted an eyebrow at that. 'You must be the dragon lady's baby sister.'

'You shouldn't call her that.' For an instant, she regretted letting this conversation begin.

'I'm sorry.' He smiled, and it was the kind of smile that made her want to melt. 'If she's your sister, then she can't be all bad.'

'She isn't. She's wonderful.' But guilt set in. 'I'll have to go. She'll be worried about me.' Hurriedly she removed his jacket and gave it back to him.

'You aren't going to run off, are you?' he protested when she moved to the car and opened the driver's door.

'I – Thanks for stopping to help . . . and changing the tyre for me.' Yet the way he looked at her, Elizabeth had the feeling it was more than thanks he wanted. 'I . . . please, let me pay you something –' She reached for her purse on the car seat.

'Keep it,' he said. 'I don't take money for helping a lady in distress, especially such a beautiful lady.'

No one had ever told her she was beautiful. No one.

But she didn't mention any of that to Hattie – or the feeling that her knight in shining armour had just ridden up on a motorcycle. It would have sounded too silly, especially when she didn't know his name.

For days afterward, Elizabeth lived in secret hope of seeing him again. She made up excuses to go into town thinking she might run into him. Finally at the Columbus Day Parade, she found him again. And when he asked her again to go for a ride on his motorcycle, she got up enough nerve to go with him. She loved every minute of it – the racing down the highway at ninety miles an hour, the wind roaring in her ears competing with the wild pounding of her heart, and the hugging him tightly most of all. He turned off on some country road and stopped along a quiet river bank. There, with the sun glittering on the water and a canopy of autumn red and gold leaves overhead, he kissed her.

Afterwards, with her whole body still tingling from his kiss, she whispered, 'I don't even know your name.'

'I don't want to tell you,' he murmured against her neck. 'When you find out who I am, I'll never see you again.'

'No. How can you say that?'

'Because' – he lifted his head, his gaze burrowing straight into her . . . all the way to her heart, it seemed – 'I'm Ring Stuart.'

For a moment, Elizabeth felt cold with fear, knowing what would happen if Hattie ever found out who she was with. It didn't matter to her though, not now that he'd kissed her. 'I don't care what your name is, Ring Stuart,' she declared fervently, and he'd kissed her again, reminding her why she didn't care.

In the weeks that followed, she arranged to meet him whenever and wherever they could, but never often enough or long enough. Yet the very infrequency and shortness of their meetings gave each one an intense sweetness.

Immersed in the fall ranchwork, Hattie didn't guess what was going on, not until she insisted that Elizabeth ride with her out to one of the pastures and check on the winter graze. Charlie Rainwater, one of the ranch hands, rode along with them. He was the one who drew Hattie's attention to the change in her younger sister.

'Does Miss Elizabeth have herself a fella or something?' he asked.

'No,' Hattie denied immediately, regarding the idea as ludicrous. Not that she was against Elizabeth having a beau. She had simply given up on her younger sister ever marrying, convinced that she was destined to be a spinster like herself. After all, Elizabeth was twenty-seven years old and had never had a steady beau. Hattie didn't think it was all that surprising. As much as she loved her, she recognised that Elizabeth was too plain, too thin, too shy, and too sickly – hardly wife material. Yet Charlie's comment troubled her. 'What makes you think she has a boyfriend?'

He shrugged his shoulders and nodded his head in Elizabeth's direction. 'Just watchin' her over there, hummin' to herself and pickin' them bouquets of dry weeds – and lookin' dreamy-eyed as a doe. You put that together with all the trips she's been makin' into town lately and I figured she had a fella stashed away somewheres.'

Hattie didn't miss the implication of that comment – the implication that her Elizabeth was meeting someone on the sly. Her little sister wouldn't do something like that. If Elizabeth had a boyfriend, she'd bring him to Morgan's Walk so Hattie could meet him. Wouldn't she?

She started noticing things after that – little things like the flimsy excuses Elizabeth made to justify her trips to town, the flush that was in her cheeks when she came back, and the shininess in her eyes. Finally, hating the suspicions, Hattie ordered Charlie Rainwater to follow Elizabeth the next time she went to town and find out once and for all whether she had anything to worry about.

'Ring Stuart?! You mean Jackson Stuart's boy?'

'That's the one,' Charlie confirmed when he reported back to her.

'You must be mistaken.' Her Elizabeth wouldn't be with a Stuart.

'There's no mistake, ma'am. It was Ring Stuart, all right. I didn't want to believe it either. That's why I made sure. I didn't think there could be two people who walked down the street like they owned it – like the way he does. And there isn't.'

'What do you mean – she *met* him?'

'Just that, she met him. She took that blouse back to the store like she said she was gonna do. Then she went over to this park, and there he is waiting for her.'

'Maybe it was just a coincidence that he was there.'

'It's possible, ma'am.' Charlie conceded, shifting his weight from one foot to the other and staring down at the pointed toes of his boots.

'But you don't think so,' Hattie guessed.

'No, ma'am.'

'Why?'

He seemed reluctant to answer that, then finally glanced at her from beneath the brim of his battered hat. 'When she saw him standing there, ma'am, she ran right into his arms like she was comin' home after bein' away a long time.'

At that moment, her shock had shown – her shock and that sense of ultimate betrayal. 'That will be all, Charlie.' She dismissed him, unable to ask more, not wanting to hear more – not wanting to know how completely Elizabeth may have betrayed them all . . . with a Stuart!

'I knew you'd react like this, Hattie,' Elizabeth said when Hattie confronted her. 'That's why I never told you. I didn't keep it from you to hurt you. I just knew you wouldn't look at Ring and judge him for himself.'

'He's a Stuart.'

'That's his name, yes. But what does that mean?'

'How can you ask that? You know –'

'All that happened years and years ago, Hattie. I wasn't alive then and Ring wasn't either. You can't hold him responsible for something his father did. Ring's different.'

'He's a Stuart. He's cut from the same cloth and it's bad cloth.'

'That isn't true. Ring is good –'

'Good for nothing like all the rest of them.'

'Stop talking like that. You don't even know him.'

'I know all I need to know about him.'

'How can you condemn him just because his last name happens to be Stuart? Why does that automatically make him bad? Why

— 123 —

can't you forget something that happened sixty years ago? It didn't happen to you.'

'But I saw Stuart after he was released from prison. I was there when he confronted our grandfather. I heard what he said – and saw the hate in his eyes . . .' Just as she saw the indifference in Elizabeth's face. None of it mattered to her sister. She was convinced those long ago threats had nothing to do with her. Hattie knew just how wrong she was. She tried another tactic. 'Have you seen where this Stuart boy lives?'

'No,' Elizabeth admitted, somewhat subdued.

'It's a shack, hidden away in the hills at the end of a long dusty road. When he was a boy, that shack was a haven for every gangster from Clyde Barrow to Pretty Boy Floyd. And during the war, when cowboys from this very ranch were dying on the beaches of Normandy, a black market business was operating from there. Ring Stuart comes from a fine, upstanding family, wouldn't you agree?'

'That doesn't mean he'll be like his father.'

'He was raised by him.'

'But Ring has plans, wonderful plans –'

'To get his hands on Morgan's Walk, just like his father tried to do.'

'That isn't true.'

'Isn't it?'

Hattie was wise enough to see that no amount of arguing, threats or reasoning on her part could sway Elizabeth from her misplaced belief in this renegade. Romantically and foolishly, her naive little sister saw herself and Ring Stuart as star-crossed lovers irresistibly drawn together despite the long-standing rift between their families – in the fanciful tradition of the Montagues and the Capulets. His faults and his failings didn't matter to her, convinced as she was that her love would change him. Hattie knew better. People didn't change no matter how much they might want to – not on the inside where it mattered.

Wisely she stopped short of forbidding Elizabeth from seeing Stuart again, recognising that much of this was her fault. She'd protected her baby sister too much from the harsher side of life, trying to make life easier for her than she'd had it. She'd kept her in innocence even as she'd envied it – and used it as a vicarious means of escaping from the stressful responsibility of Morgan's Walk.

No, the way to put a stop to this disastrous relationship before it went any further was not to prevent Elizabeth from seeing Stuart again, but to pay a little visit on the one who had taken advantage of her sister's trusting innocence.

A crow cawed the alarm and swooped off an oak branch, black wings flapping, as Hattie negotiated the car over the rutted track. A squirrel abandoned its search for nuts among the fallen leaves and raced to the nearest trees, chattering noisily at her when she went by. Ahead the thick tangle of brush and woods crowding both sides of the narrow lane retreated to form a clearing, a clearing cluttered with rusting car bodies, empty oil drums, and piles of worn tyres strewn amongst the yellowed weeds. The landscaping matched the tumble-down house that sat in the middle of it, all the paint long since peeled from its boards, leaving them a dirty weathered grey.

In front of the house, looking distinctly out of place, stood a souped-up motorcycle, a black and shiny machine of sleek power. Kneeling on the ground beside it, tinkering with the motor, was Ring Stuart. He straightened slowly to his feet when Hattie drove in and parked her car ten feet from the big Harley.

When she got out of the car, he took a couple of steps forward and idly wiped his greasy hands on an equally greasy rag. With a steely calm she looked him over, not at all surprised by what she saw. A pair of faded jeans blatantly hugged his narrow hips leaving little to the imagination for a knowing eye. A dirty T-shirt clung to every muscled contour of his chest, its short sleeves rolled up to the points of his shoulders, the right one bulging over a pack of cigarettes. Her glance touched briefly on the revolting tattoo of a knife dripping blood from the blade-tip that ran down his left bicep. Then she examined his face. The devil had given him his lean, handsome looks and hell-black hair, as well as a pair of lightning-blue eyes to go with them.

'Well, well, well, if it isn't the duchess herself.' His lip curled in a sneering smile. 'I kinda figured you'd be paying me a visit, only I expected you to come yesterday.'

'You did,' she murmured, disliking him even more intensely than she'd expected.

'Yeah.' He sauntered a few steps closer, his weight balanced on the balls of his feet giving a cocky spring to his walk. 'I spotted that cowboy you had following Elizabeth right off. You should have seen his eyes bug out of his head when he saw the way she kissed me – and kept kissing me.'

'You're disgusting.'

His smile widened. 'Elizabeth doesn't think so. As a matter of fact, she's crazy about me. She likes it when I kiss her . . . among other things.'

Hattie stiffened at his deliberately suggestive remark. 'You know I'm not going to allow this to continue.'

'There's nothing you can do about it, duchess,' he said, his head tipped arrogantly back. 'She's old enough to know her own mind. She doesn't need your consent or approval.'

'How much?'

'How much?' he repeated on a note of amusement. 'Man, you really are something, duchess. You know I've often wondered what it would be like living in that big house with people waiting on you, serving you coffee in dainty china cups and fetching the morning paper for you. It must be real fine living.'

'How much money do you want, Stuart, to leave my sister alone?'

'You really think you can buy me off, don't you, duchess?'

Pointedly she swept her glance over the weed-choked clearing and the dilapidated house with its front porch askew. 'What's your price, Stuart? Name it.'

'I've already got what I want. I've got Elizabeth. She's mine and you can't take her away from me. If you thought you could, you wouldn't be here talking to me now.' He paused, his confidence growing. 'She was real shy with me at first, but she isn't shy anymore. It kinda surprised me at first. But after meeting you, I'm convinced that she's got all the passion in your family. What kind of sister are you, anyway? She loves me and here you are trying to make me give her up.'

'It would never work between you. Never.'

'Why? Because you think I'm not good enough for her?'

'I know you aren't.'

'She doesn't agree with you. Y'see, the difference is she believes in me, and that means more to me than all the money you could pay, duchess.'

'I'm warning you –'

'No, I'm warning you – you'd better watch how you talk about your future brother-in-law or I just might take your little sister away from you for good.'

She held his gaze for a long minute, then said, 'You're a fool, Stuart,' and turned on her heel and walked back to the car.

Driving out of the clearing, she could see his reflection in the rear-view mirror as he stood in the middle of the track, watching her leave and looking cocksure of himself. At a midway point, the long lane to the shack widened. There, Charlie Rainwater waited in the ranch pick-up along with half a dozen hands from the bunkhouse. Hattie pulled up alongside the truck.

'He wouldn't listen, Charlie,' was all she said.

'I figured as much, Miss Hattie.' He turned the key in the truck's ignition, the engine grinding slowly to life. 'Reasonin' with a Stuart is a lot like talkin' to a mule. First, you gotta get their attention.'

He shifted the pick-up into gear and the vehicle lurched forward on to the rough trail. Hattie sat in the car and waited, listening to the lonely sigh of the wind in the trees. Fifteen minutes? Twenty? She wasn't sure how much time passed before she heard the rumble of the pick-up making the return trip.

Charlie drove up beside her, a cut on his lip and a bruise swelling his cheek, but there was a smile on his face that went from ear to ear. 'He wasn't able t'do much talkin' when we left him, Miss Hattie, but I can guarantee that he got the message.'

When Hattie returned to Morgan's Walk that day, she said nothing to Elizabeth and went about her work as usual. Late in the afternoon, Elizabeth received a phone call from one of her girlfriends. Unbeknown to Hattie, Ring Stuart had called Sally Evans and persuaded her to phone Elizabeth with a message. Sometime after midnight, Elizabeth slipped out of the house and met Ring Stuart. Hattie didn't discover she was missing until morning. She looked for her, but she found no sign of either of them. The next day, Elizabeth called to say that she and Stuart were married, and asked if they could come home to Morgan's Walk.

'You can come home any time, Elizabeth, but not with him. I won't have a Stuart sleeping under this roof.'

'Then neither one of us can come, because I'm a Stuart now, too.'

Two months went by, two miserable and bitterly lonely months for Hattie with memories of Elizabeth haunting every room. She made no attempt to contact her, certain that in time she would come to her senses and see what a terrible mistake she had made. Then came the phone call from Ring Stuart informing Hattie that Elizabeth was ill.

Piles of dirty dishes with food caked on them covered the kitchen counters. Empty beer bottles spilled over the sides of the waste basket and sat next to every chair and butt-filled ashtray in the filthy shack. The thought of her Elizabeth living in this germ- and dirt-infested dwelling sickened Hattie as she followed Ring Stuart down a dingy hall to one of the back bedrooms.

In the bedroom, Hattie stepped around the dirty clothes strewn on the floor. Bedsprings squealed noisy protest under Ring Stuart's weight as he sat down on the edge of it and took Elizabeth's hand.

'Honey, Hattie's here.'

She stopped two feet short of the bed and fought back the bitter tears that stung her eyes when she saw Elizabeth, her wan face as pale as the pillow slip beneath her head. 'This place is a pigsty. How can you live in this filth?'

'I'm sorry. I know it's a mess.' Her voice was barely more than a whisper. 'I haven't been feeling too well lately, and –'

'– and he's too lazy,' Hattie hurled the contemptuous accusation at Stuart.

'Hattie, it isn't man's work,' Elizabeth chided gently.

'I never thought he was a man, and now that I've seen the way he takes care of you, I know he isn't.' She moved to the bed and laid the back of her hand against Elizabeth's cheeks, feeling for a temperature, and completely ignoring the glare from Stuart.

'That isn't fair, Hattie,' Elizabeth protested. 'Ring has tried, he really has. But he can't keep a job and look after me, too.'

'He's certainly done a fine job of looking after you, hasn't he?' she murmured caustically, unable to suppress the rage she felt at her Elizabeth being forced to live in these wretched surroundings. 'Have you called the doctor, yet?'

'I saw him yesterday,' Elizabeth caught at her hand, a frailness in her attempt to clutch at Hattie's fingers. A smile fairly beamed from her face. 'Hattie, we're going to have a baby. So you see, I'm not really sick. I'm pregnant.'

For several long seconds, Hattie stared at the girl she'd raised since birth, inwardly revolted by the prospect of her sister having a child sired by a Stuart. She wanted to scream at her and demand to know if she realised what she had done – the terrible consequences of this.

Instead, she swung on Stuart. 'I want to speak to you. Now!' She turned on her heel and marched from the room. The instant she reached the living room, she whirled to confront him. 'I'm taking her out of this pig hole you call a house, today.'

'She won't go without me, duchess,' he said confidently. Hattie lifted her head slightly, eyeing him coldly. 'Looks like my daddy was right all along doesn't it? A Stuart will have Morgan's Walk.'

'Not you. It will never be you,' she vowed.

'But my son will.'

'God willing, the child will never live to cry its first breath. But you'd better pray that when Elizabeth loses it, she doesn't lose her life as well.'

'Damn you, I love her!'

'Do you? Or is it merely convenient to love her?'

'I love her,' he insisted angrily.

'But not enough to give her up – not enough to do what's best for her. You deliberately got her with child. You knew how fragile her health is yet you risked her life impregnating her.

'Everything will be all right. You'll see.'

'It had better be, Stuart. Otherwise, you'll answer to me.'

Although bedridden through most of her pregnancy, Elizabeth carried the baby to term and gave birth to a remarkably strong and healthy boy. Yet the ordeal seemed to have taken its toll on her own health. As the months went by, she grew weaker. An aemia was the initial diagnosis, but when she failed to respond to treatment, she was admitted to the hospital for tests.

Returning from a consultation with the doctor, Hattie found Ring in the library, his feet propped on the desk and blue smoke curling from the cigar in his mouth. 'Are you wondering what it's like to run Morgan's Walk? If you are, you're wasting your time. You'll never find out,' she declared, jerking off her gloves.

He didn't move from his relaxed position as he smiled at her through the smoke. 'You can't be sure of that, duchess. After all, you aren't going to live forever.'

'I swear I will see you in hell before I let the day come when a

Stuart has the right to sit behind that desk. Now get out of my chair.'

He pulled his feet off the desk top and bowed his head in exaggerated respect as he slowly stood up. 'I return your throne to you.'

'It probably doesn't interest you at all, but the results from the tests came back.'

Reluctantly she observed the leap of concern in his eyes. 'How's Elizabeth?'

Coldly, with no more emotion left, Hattie replied, 'Your wife has leukaemia.' Before her eyes, Stuart crumbled in shock.

'My poor darling Elizabeth,' she whispered to the girl in the silver-framed photograph, then slowly drew her hand away and pushed out of the chair. The loneliness of the old house seemed to press in on her, its weight combining with the tiredness of battling for so long. This time she leaned heavily on the cane as she crossed to the portrait above the fireplace.

'I regret but one thing in my life – that I told them to stop after they had given him a good beating. I should have had him killed.' She bowed her head. 'The fault was mine. It was never Elizabeth's. She didn't know what she was doing, but I did. I should have put an end to it then.'

⟢ 12 ⟣

THE MORNING sun peered through the smoked glass windows of the Stuart Building's top floor, spreading its refracted rays over the small group gathered around the circular burl conference table in the executive office. A slight man with cherubic features and soft spaniel eyes held the floor, his usual reticence forgotten as he spoke about the one field in which he was an acknowledged expert, considered by many to be one of the best, if not *the* best, civil engineer in the country.

'When I passed these preliminary drawings for the dam by Zorinsky at the Corps, he saw a problem in only one area.' Fred Garver riffled through the pages of blueprints on the tall easel until he found the one he wanted, then flipped the ones in front of it back to reveal a cross section of the proposed dam. 'He felt the concrete keys should be another three feet deeper to eliminate any possible undermining of the dam itself. If we do that, we're probably talking about an additional cost of another half-million dollars – depending.' He paused to shoot both Chance and Sam Weber a quick look. 'Without test borings of the site, I can't be sure what we'll run into once we start excavating. I don't know if we'll hit rock, sand, clay or what? All the construction figures I've given you are just rough estimates. And I mean, rough.'

Sam expected Chance to acknowledge that comment. When he

didn't, Sam darted a quick glance in his direction and frowned slightly at Chance's obvious absorption with the scribblings he was making on the notepad resting on his knee. He had been preoccupied through much of the meeting – a meeting he had called to get an update on Garver's progress. Yet he hadn't asked one question or shown any interest in the engineer's drawings. That wasn't like him. That wasn't like him at all.

'Yes, we understand that, Fred,' Sam inserted to fill the void.

'As long as you do.' The engineer shrugged his acceptance and turned his attention back to the cross section. 'Personally, I don't think it's necessary to increase the depth of the keys. Although if we do incorporate Zorinsky's recommendation, then we would probably be assuring ourselves of a quick approval from the Corps. The way I see it we have two choices: we can either make this change now or wait until we get to do some test borings to know what we're dealing with. How soon will you be taking title to the property so we can get on it and do our preliminary site work?'

Sam looked again at Chance, wishing he would field that question, but there was no indication that he'd even heard it. 'We can't give you a date yet.' He didn't think it was his place to admit that Chance might not get title to it at all, not the way things were going.

'Do you want us to just sit tight for a while or go ahead with the change?'

Damn but he wished Chance would speak up. This wasn't the kind of decision he normally made when a project was in its preliminary stage. Looking at Molly, her chair positioned at an unobtrusive distance from the table, Sam wondered what he should do. She grimaced faintly and shrugged her shoulders, unable to offer any suggestion to him. He shifted uncomfortably in his seat and nervously cleared his throat. The sound seemed to rouse Chance, his attention lifting somewhat abstractedly from the notepad before him.

Still, Sam doubted that Chance knew the question. 'Why don't you give us a couple of days to think it over, Fred, and we'll get back to you with our decision?' he suggested, trying to cover for Chance's inattention to the entire discussion.

'That won't be necessary.' Chance contradicted him. 'Make the changes in the design. When the time comes, I'll want to move on this project fast. I don't want anything holding us up.' He shoved his notepad on to the table and rolled to his feet. 'Leave a set of the drawings so I can study them later and send us a copy of any changes. We'll stay in touch.'

As if pushed by some inner restlessness, he left the conference table and walked to the window. His back remained to them, abruptly but effectively bringing a quick end to the meeting.

Sam exchanged another troubled look with Molly, then helped Fred Garver and his young associate gather their materials together, and made certain a full set of the preliminary drawings remained behind. With Fred reverting to his reticent ways, there was little conversation as Sam walked him to the door. No mention had been made of Chance's inattention during much of the meeting, but Sam felt obligated to offer some sort of explanation in his defence.

'Don't mind Chance,' he said at the door. 'He's had a lot on his mind lately.'

'I guessed as much.' Fred nodded, throwing a brief glance over his shoulder in Chance's direction, his mouth curving into a smile of understanding when he looked back at Sam.

After they'd left, Sam hesitated a moment at the door, then turned and walked back to the conference table. Chance was still at the window, staring out, his hands idly shoved in the side pockets of his trousers. Molly quietly gathered up the dirty coffee cups and set them on the serving tray.

Sam picked up the rolled set of blueprints and turned it in his hands. 'Do you want me to leave these here for you or put them on the draughting table in my office with the others?' But his question drew only more silence, and his concern and bewilderment at Chance's behaviour gave way to exasperation. 'Dammit, Chance, you haven't heard one word anybody's said in the last hour, have you?'

'No, he hasn't,' Molly stated quite emphatically as Chance half turned to give them both a blank, preoccupied look. 'He's been doodling on that pad of his. Whenever he starts doing that, you can be sure he isn't listening to anyone.'

'Sorry,' Chance frowned absently. 'I guess my mind is elsewhere.'

'My God, that's an understatement,' Sam muttered, shaking his head in bewilderment. 'Your mind has been *elsewhere* ever since you got back from San Francisco. Exactly what happened out there?'

'It's that Bennett woman, isn't it?' Molly guessed, eyeing him with wondering interest. 'The one you sent all those orchids to.'

Chance held her gaze for several seconds, his look distantly thoughtful and his silence seeming to confirm her statement. Then he turned back to the window. 'It just may be that you're going to get your wish after all, Molly.'

For a stunned instant, she couldn't say anything, then she asked, somewhat tentatively, 'Are you saying that you're thinking about marrying her?'

Like Molly, Sam stared at Chance, not entirely convinced that he really meant to imply that. Chance swung away from the window, his glance briefly touching each of them as a wry smile tugged at his mouth.

'The thought has crossed my mind,' he admitted as if amazed by it, too. 'Is there any coffee left in that pot?'

'I – I don't think so.'

It was obvious to Sam that she was practically bursting with questions about this woman who had managed to capture the heart of the man she loved like a son. For that matter, he was, too. In all the years he'd known Chance, he couldn't remember him ever seriously contemplating marriage to anyone. He always said he was married to his work, that the company was the only mistress he needed. Sam always thought that if anyone got Chance to the altar, it would be Lucianna. His relationship with her went back a good fifteen years. Nothing lasted that long unless there was some strong feeling on both sides. So who was this Bennett woman?

'Get a fresh pot for us, Molly. I have some things I want to go over with Sam. And bring me the notes of the meeting with Garver as soon as you have them typed.' The decisive tone sounded more like the old Chance, the one that placed business first and everything else a distant second.

Molly heard it, too, and reluctantly smothered her curiosity. 'Right away.'

As she left the office, carrying the tray and her notepad, Chance turned to him and gestured at the roll of blueprints in his hands. 'Is that the set Garver left with us?'

'Yes.' Sam nodded, unable to make the lightning switch in conversation. 'Chance, were you serious a minute ago about this girl in San Francisco?'

'Woman,' he corrected. 'Woman, Sam. Intelligent, sensitive, warm . . .' He paused, his expression taking on a faintly rueful look. 'I can't seem to stop thinking about her.' Again there was a faint, bemused shake of his head. 'And no woman has ever intruded on business before.'

'Are you going to marry her?'

'I don't know.' He seemed reluctant to go that far. 'I only know I keep remembering what it was like being with her. Not just being in bed with her, but being with her.' This time the shake of his head was more definite as if he was trying to rid his mind of the memory of her, at least temporarily. 'This isn't getting us anywhere. Unroll the site map. I want to see where Garver thinks the shoreline will be once the lake forms behind the dam.'

Sam spread the sheet with the site drawn to scale on the table, anchoring two of the ends down with the sugar bowl and creamer Molly had left. 'It hasn't changed much from his original drawing, except maybe over here on the north side where the waterline doesn't come up as high on the bluff as he first estimated. Otherwise, it's the same as before – with virtually all of Morgan's Walk under water.' Including the house, but Sam didn't say that.

'That bluff area shouldn't have much effect on Delaney's master plan of the project,' Chance remarked, barely looking up from his study of the site drawing as Molly re-entered his office with an insulated pot of fresh coffee. 'All the same, you'd better make a copy of this and send it over to his office,' he said, referring to the architect and land planner on the proposed resort complex. Then he tapped a finger on the northwest corner of the manmade lake. 'We're definitely going to need the Ferguson property. What's the status on it? Have they agreed to an option yet?'

'They insist they won't sell – at any price. Their son's farming the land for them now and they plan on turning all of it over to him and moving into town next year. It's the same story with the MacAndrews' place.'

'Who holds the mortgages on their farms?'

'One of the savings and loan companies, I can't remember which one right now. I'd have to check the reports.'

'Buy the mortgages.'

'Chance, we're probably talking somewhere in the neighbourhood of a half a million dollars to do that,' Sam protested.

'We need those parcels. We'd pay more than that if we could buy them outright.'

'That's not the point.' Sam hesitated. 'Chance, you have to be realistic. Right now – the way things stand – we can't even be sure you're going to get Morgan's Walk. And without it, we can't build the dam – and without the dam, we don't have a lake – and without the lake ... Let's face it, without Morgan's Walk, we don't have a project. We've spent all this money on adjoining land, site plans, and designs for nothing.'

'We'll get Morgan's Walk. One way or another.'

'I know you keep saying that – and you're probably right. But don't you think it would be wise if we waited at least until Matt tracks down this new heir of Hattie's before we invest any more cash in the project? We've got a ton of money tied up in it now.'

'You're getting conservative on me again, Sam,' Chance chided.

'Dammit, somebody has to around here.'

'Buy the mortgages, Sam, and stop worrying about Morgan's Walk.'

'Stop worrying, he says,' he muttered, catching Molly's eye and shaking his head.

'If Chance says not to worry, then you shouldn't.' Molly was prepared to expand on that thought, but she was interrupted by the long beep of the telephone. Automatically she turned to the extension sitting on the rosewood credenza next to the conference table. 'Mr Stuart's office,' she said, once again assuming that crisp, professional air. Then her glance flashed to Chance, a sudden high alertness entering her expression. 'Yes, he's here. Just a moment.' She pushed the hold button and held out the receiver to Chance. 'It's Maxine. She says she needs to talk to you.'

His head came up sharply at the mention of the housekeeper's name from Morgan's Walk. In two quick strides, he was at Molly's side, taking the phone from her.

'Hello, Max. How are you?'

'Truthfully? There are times I'd like to strangle her. She's been impossible to live with lately.'

'What happened?' He knew something had or she wouldn't risk a call.

'I overheard a telephone conversation she had with some woman she called Margaret Rose. It has to be the one because she was talking about sending copies of documents that prove they're related.'

'Just Margaret Rose. That's all?'

'Yes.' A sigh of regret came over the line. 'If she used a last name, I didn't hear it.'

'When was this?'

'Last Sunday. I would have called sooner but she's been watching me like a hawk. Every time I came up with a reason to come into town, she sent somebody else. Finally I had to break my reading glasses. That's where I am now – at the optical company getting them fixed.'

'When the time comes that I can, I'll make all this right, Max,' he promised.

'Whether you do or don't doesn't matter. I'm not doing this for any reward, Chance. I'm doing it because Morgan's Walk should rightfully go to you when she passes on – not to some stranger in California. It's what your mother would have wanted – God rest her soul. Hattie's just doing this to be mean and spiteful. Of course, she always was that, but it's gotten worse lately.'

'How is she?'

'She's in a lot of pain all the time now. She tries not to let on, but I can tell. I think she's forgotten I was a registered nurse long before I was a housekeeper. Knowing what she's going through, sometimes I can't help feeling sorry for her. I'm convinced that half of what she's doing now is because she's crazy with the pain. She's like a mortally wounded animal, wanting to take something with her when she goes.'

'With your help, maybe she won't succeed.'

'I hope not.'

'Was there anything else?'

'Nooo.' She dragged out the word, as if none too certain of that. 'She did make another call after she'd talked to this Margaret Rose woman. Probably to Ben Canon, although I don't know that for sure.'

'Why do you think it was Canon?'

'Because he came to the house later, that afternoon. When I answered the door, he said she was expecting him.'

'Do you know why he was there?'

There was a pause before she answered, 'I think it was to have a new will signed. I know they called old Charlie Rainwater and Shorty Thompson into the library, probably to witness it. I asked them later, but those two are so close-mouthed I couldn't get anything out of them other than a grunt.'

'I can't say that I'm surprised,' he admitted grimly. 'If anything I thought she would have had a new will drawn up right after she learned about this woman Margaret Rose.'

'I thought you would probably anticipate that,' she said, then paused again. 'I'd better hang up. She sent Charlie into town with me. He could walk in any minute and I'd rather he didn't see me on the phone.'

'You take care of yourself, Max, and – thanks for the information.'

'You know I'll help any way I can. Be good, Chance.'

'I will.' He hung up.

'Hattie's made a new will, has she?' Sam remarked in a grimly troubled voice.

'Yes.' Chance turned to look at him thoughtfully, then glanced sideways at Molly. 'Get Matt Sawyer on the phone for me,' he directed, then commented idly, 'At least we have a first name to give him. I wonder how many women named Margaret Rose are in the San Francisco area – specifically ones with a residential phone. A computer search of the phone company's records should be able to provide us with such a list.'

13

COPIES OF birth certificates, baptismal records, marriage licences, church registers, obituary notices, death certificates – they were all there – spread across her desk top. In between bites of the seafood salad she'd ordered from a local deli, Flame checked the names against the ones that appeared on the ancestral chart Hattie had included in the packet of documents. Although she hadn't had time to verify everyone, the evidence seemed irrefutable. She and Hattie Morgan were related, albeit distantly.

A quick rap on the door pulled her attention from the papers on her desk. 'Yes?'

Almost immediately the door opened and the blonde-haired Debbie Connors stepped inside, her look anxious and agitated. 'I'm sorry, Flame, but Mr Powell's outside. He wants to see you. I didn't know what to tell him.' The words tumbled from her in a rush.

'He's here?' Flame questioned, as stunned as her assistant was.

'Yes, I –' The door behind her started to move, pushing Debbie along with it. She stepped hastily out of the way as Malcom Powell walked through the opening.

Flame rose from her chair, unsure what to make of this unexpected visit. Surely he had to know by coming here, the mountain had moved. 'Malcom,' she said in greeting, then added coolly, 'You should have let me know you were coming.'

He paused in the middle of the room. A hand-tailored grey suit, the same iron-dark shade as his hair, smoothly fit itself over his powerfully built chest.

'I see I've interrupted you in the middle of a late lunch,' he observed, his sharp eyes flicking a glance to the partially eaten salad on her desk.

'I'm finished.' In truth, her appetite had fled when he walked in the door. She picked up the salad container along with its plastic flatware and paper napkin and deposited them in her waste basket. When she turned back to Malcom, Flame caught Debbie's frantic what-do-you-want-me-to-do look. 'That will be all, Debbie. Let me know when Tim Herrington arrives.'

'The instant he comes,' she promised and hurried out the door, this time closing it tightly behind her.

'This is the first time I've ever been in your office,' Malcom remarked, looking around him with curious interest, his glance skimming over the white lacquered desk and attendant chairs, upholstered in a textured fabric of pale cerulean blue, and lingering on the abstract painting behind her desk, the art deco sculpture on the occasional table and a set of needlepoint pillows in a geometric design on the small sofa.

'What did you want to see me about, Malcom?' She could think of only one reason for his unannounced visit as she gathered together the documents on her desk and slipped them back into their Manila envelope.

He walked over to the window. 'I almost called and had Arthur pick you up. Then I thought better of it.' He stood with his hands clasped behind his back in a pensive pose. 'After our luncheon last Tuesday, I had a feeling you wouldn't react well to such a summons. You would have come, but only because you felt you had no choice. You would have resented that. And it isn't resentment I want from you.'

Flame very carefully avoided asking him what he did want. She knew the answer to that. She always had. Remaining by her desk, she waited for him to continue, a fine tension threading through her nerves and matching the slow simmer of her anger.

'I think you should know where I stand, Flame. The Powell account is yours as long is it is handled satisfactorily. I won't hold it over your head.'

Provoked by the tone of largesse in his remark, she challenged, 'Am I supposed to thank you for that?'

He half turned to look at her. 'You should,' he said, his eyes defiantly narrowed in their boring study of her. 'Those were brave words you said last Tuesday, but that's all they were. I know you won't admit it, but I could use the account to get what I want from you.'

'Don't bet on it,' she snapped.

Malcom merely smiled. 'I don't think you realise just how vulnerable you are to that type of pressure.' Then he shrugged, dismissing it. 'But it won't be applied. A victory under those circumstances would be hollow indeed. Which is not to say I'm giving up,' he inserted quickly, a subtle warning contained in the firm advisory. 'I'm only saying that when you come to me, it will be of your own free will.'

Ignoring his latter statement, Flame tilted her head at an aggressive angle and demanded, 'Does that mean you'll be calling off your bloodhound?'

'I beg your pardon.' He turned the rest of the way around, his eyebrows lowering to form a thick bushy line that hooded his eyes.

'You amaze me, Malcom,' Flame murmured with a touch of sarcasm.

'What are you talking about?'

'I'm talking about the man who's been following me for the last week, the one you hired,' she retorted, her anger showing although tightly controlled.

'I didn't hire anyone to follow you. Why should I?'

Both his denial and confusion seemed genuine. She frowned. 'Either you have acting talents you haven't used – or you're telling the truth.'

'It is the truth,' he insisted. 'Who's following you and why?'

She hesitated, still watching him closely. 'A man. I saw him for the first time at the DeBorgs' party for Lucianna Colton. He was a waiter, in his middle to late forties with brown hair and a large, hooked nose. He drives a dark green saloon, a late model Ford.' There was nothing in his expression to indicate the description meant anything to him. 'And twice, he's passed on messages warning me to stay away from Chance Stuart. I assumed . . . you were behind them. But you weren't, were you?'

'No.' His gaze narrowed on her sharply. 'Have you been seeing a great deal of Stuart?'

'When he's been in town, yes,' she admitted.

'Are you serious about him?' A muscle flexed visibly along his strong square jaw.

She waited for a twinge of doubt to come, but none did. 'Very serious,' she stated, amazed by the buoyantly content feelings within that had surfaced with the admission.

Malcom paused, then laughed abruptly. 'My God, I didn't realise I could still feel jealousy.' A slight frown creased his forehead as he gazed at her in thoughtful study. 'I don't know why that should surprise me. With you, it's always been different. Perhaps, in the beginning it was the chase and the conquest that appealed to me, but that changed long ago –'

'Stop it, Malcom,' she warned.

He looked at the sparkle of temper in her eyes and smiled. 'You excite me the way no other woman has – including my wife.'

'I don't care, Malcom! Your feelings are a problem you'll have to deal with – not me. I am not going to be the solution to them.' She struggled to keep her voice down and her temper in check.

Moving away from the window, Malcom crossed to the side of her desk, that aura of power emanating from him and reminding her that he was a force to be reckoned with. She faced him squarely, conscious of the possessive look in his eyes and the slow skim of his gaze as it travelled the length of her.

'Stuart's not the man for you,' he announced.

Infuriated by his arrogant assertion, she snapped, 'That's for me to decide!'

'Right now your eyes are filled with him. But it won't last. You'll come to me . . . in time.'

Momentarily shaken by the certainty in his voice, she fought to dispel it. 'You have forgotten one very important detail, Malcom. Whether Chance Stuart is in my life or not, my answer to you would be the same as it's always been – No.'

He didn't like her answer, but a knock at her door checked his reply. Aware the anger had flushed her cheeks, Flame turned, welcoming the interruption as Tim Herrington, the head of the agency's San Francisco branch, walked in.

'Sorry to bother you, Flame,' he began, then paused in feigned surprise when he saw Malcom Powell. 'Malcom, I didn't realise you were here.' He crossed the room, a hand outstretched in hearty greeting, his eyes big and dark behind the bottle-thick lenses of his gold-rimmed glasses.

'Hello, Tim. How are you?' Malcom responded perfunctorily.

'Fine, just fine. And you? No problems, I hope.' His glance ran to Flame as if addressing the remark to her, concerned that there might be trouble with the agency's biggest client.

'None at all,' Malcom assured him.

'Good.' He seemed to relax visibly, the falseness of his wide smile diminishing.

The two of them chatted about business in general a few minutes longer, then Malcom brought the conversation to a close. 'You'll have to excuse me, Tim. I have another appointment.' He looked at Flame. 'We'll have lunch next week. I'll have my secretary call and let you know the day,' he said, taking it for granted that she would make room on her schedule to accommodate him. Which, of course, she would.

Alone in her flat that evening, Flame again went through the sheaf of documents Hattie had sent her. When she came to the photocopy of her own birth certificate, she paused, her attention centring on her given name of Margaret Rose. A smile touched her lips, softly edging the corners. Her mother had been the only one who ever used that name. To everyone else, she'd always been Flame. But not her mother. Never her mother.

Her glance strayed to her purse lying open on the glass-topped occasional table next to her chair. She hesitated, then reached inside and pulled out the small compact that had been a gift from her mother on her thirteenth birthday. A special occasion called for a special gift, her mother always said. And this one was special indeed. Done in cloisonné art, the design depicted a vase holding a bouquet of daisies and roses. Somewhere, sometime, her mother had read or heard that in French, Margaret meant 'daisy'. At the time her father had joked that the design should have been a candle with a tall flame, but her mother hadn't found his remark all that humorous.

Flame suspected that her mother believed she would outgrow her nickname some day. Once – Flame couldn't remember exactly when any more – her mother had told her she'd picked the name Margaret Rose because it had a certain ring of pride and dignity about it that she liked. Of course, Flame had thought it sounded dreadfully old-fashioned and used to cringe whenever her mother called her Margaret Rose. Now no one ever did – no one, that is, except Hattie Morgan.

The telephone rang.

'Speak of the devil.' Flame murmured, as she reached for the phone. She cradled the receiver against her shoulder and slipped the compact back into her purse. 'Yes, hello.'

'Flame? It's Chance.'

'Chance, this is an unexpected pleasure.' She brought the phone a little closer, holding it with both hands.

'I hope so.' There was the suggestion of a smile in his voice. 'I had a few minutes before I have to be at a meeting, so I thought I'd call and see if you have any plans for the weekend.'

'I hope I do – with you, that is.' She smiled, finding it impossible to play it coy with him. 'Are you flying in?'

'Long enough to pick you up.'

'Where are we going?'

'That's a secret.'

'That isn't fair,' Flame protested, intrigued just the same. 'How will I know what to pack? You have to give me some kind of clue. Will I need snow skis or a swimsuit?'

'A swimsuit. And maybe something simple for the evening and a light wrap.'

'Is that it?'

'You can fill in the blanks from there.'

'In that case I'll bring something lacy and black.' She smiled into the phone.

'Or you could opt for nothing at all,' Chance added suggestively, then said, 'I'll have a car pick you up at work at four o'clock. Is that all right?'

'I'll be ready.'

'So will I.'

= 14 =

As THE limousine drove on to the concrete apron, a fuel truck pulled away from a sleek, white Gulfstream jet, with the distinctive 'S' logo of the Stuart Corporation emblazoned in gold on its fuselage. Flame spotted Chance almost immediately, standing next to the wing with one of the flight crew. There was a turning lift of his dark head when he heard the limousine. A high alertness held him motionless for a split second, then he said something to the stockily built man with him and moved away to meet the approaching limo.

He was at the door when she stepped out. Again, she felt the jolting impact of his blue-eyed glance, followed by the heady warmth of his mouth moving on to hers in a slow, claiming kiss. As he drew back, Flame gazed at the rakish angles of his face, so smooth and yet so rugged. She had wondered if she would experience the same rush of feeling when she saw him again or if a week's separation would have changed that. It hadn't. Her pulse was behaving just as erratically and that vague breathless feeling of excitement was still there. But those were physical reactions easily identified. What was harder to name was the strong pull of emotion, that elated feeling of having come home – the one that had to fit under the heading of love.

The creases in his lean cheeks deepened, suggesting a smile

even though there was little movement of his mouth. 'Hello again.'

She was amazed at how much meaning could be conveyed in that softly murmured greeting. 'Hello again,' she whispered back. She would have gladly gone back into his arms but his glance to the side reminded her they weren't alone.

Half turning, Flame saw the chauffeur as he lifted her two pieces of luggage from the truck and handed them to a second man in a flight uniform, younger and slimmer than the first with a definitely Latin look.

'Juan Angel Cordero,' Chance identified the man for her, giving his name the full Spanish pronunciation. 'But we call him Johnny Angel. He'll be flying the right seat. Johnny, meet Ms Flame Bennett.'

'Glad to have you aboard, Ms Bennett,' he acknowledged in flawless English, his dark-eyed look warm with appreciation.

'Thank you.'

'And our pilot in command, Mick Donovan,' Chance said, directing her attention to the man walking up to them, the one he'd been talking to when she'd arrived. 'Flame Bennett.'

'Hello, Captain.' She noticed immediately that his strong, broad features seemed to be permanently etched in calm, unruffled lines. He had the kind of face that inspired confidence, and the touch of premature grey in the sides of his close-cropped hair merely added to the image.

'Ms Bennett.' A faint smile of welcome lifted the corners of his mouth, gentling the crisply pale blue of his eyes. 'I just received the latest weather report. Looks like I can promise you a smooth flight.'

'To where?' she asked, her own curiosity about their destination resurfacing.

He hesitated, sliding a brief glance at Chance, then smiled. 'To paradise, Ms Bennett – Stuart-style.'

'You still aren't going to tell me where we're going, are you, you devil!' She flashed a mildly accusing look at Chance.

'I'm saving it for a surprise.' He smiled back at her, then turned to the pilot. 'Everything set?'

'As soon as Johnny gets Ms Bennett's luggage stowed, we'll be ready to leave whenever you are.'

'Then let's go.' His hand moved to the small of her back to guide her to the waiting jet.

As she turned, Flame thought she caught a glimpse of the hawk-faced man who'd been following her for the last ten days. She looked again at the man heading toward the office of the private aviation company. At this distance, she couldn't be sure it was the same man, yet a feeling of unease ran through her. She had previously dismissed the man as an irritating annoyance, thinking Malcom was responsible for the tail. But he wasn't. She had no idea now who was behind it. Maybe no one? The city had its share of crazies, and, for all she knew, this man could be one of them. And that possibility was a more frightening one.

When she got back, she'd have to do something about him, but not now. She didn't want anything or anyone intruding on her weekend with Chance. She reminded herself that she couldn't be sure it was even the same man. She could be seeing ghosts where none existed. After all, no dark green saloon had followed her to the airport. Of that, she was certain. Smiling, she walked with Chance to the jet's stairway.

A certain amount of luxury was to be expected in a corporate aircraft, but Flame wasn't prepared for the scale she found when she entered the stylishly appointed cabin. Leather suede in a pale ivory colour covered the walls. The same shade was repeated in the upholstery on the swivel chairs, this time with the addition of threads of sea-foam green accented by French blue. The entire colour scheme served to enhance the array of sculptures scattered through the cabin and invisibly secured, works of Brancusi, Giacometti, and Moore. The collection represented a veritable Who's Who of twentieth-century sculptors. Yet there was no sense of being overpowered by it. Instead the effect was one of restrained elegance.

'Like it?' Chance was directly behind her, his hands warm on her arms, his breath stirring the edges of her hair.

'I love it. It has the feel of a . . . small sitting room in a private home – comfortable, beautiful, a place to relax and enjoy.'

'This is – for all intent and purposes – my second home,' he admitted. 'If the truth was known, I probably spend more time in this one than I do at my house in Tulsa.' Behind them came the grinding hum of the steps being retracted, followed by the closing of the hatch door. 'Sounds like we'd better take our seats,' Chance remarked. 'Once Mick gets the green light, he doesn't like to dawdle. After we're airborne, I'll take you on a tour of my home-away-from-home.'

'I'd like that.'

As good as his word, shortly after the jet levelled off at its flying altitude, Chance showed her through the aircraft. The interior design was a marvel of understated luxury, compactness and high tech. Fine leather, the same creamy pale shade as the suede walls, covered a low coffee table that – at the push of a button – became a conference table. In addition to a full entertainment centre, there was also a work station with a microcomputer that allowed Chance to transmit information to his Tulsa headquarters by modem and remain in constant touch with his business operation.

And the small galley, Chance informed her, was capable of serving a full-course meal for eight. The galley cabinets, covered in the same ivory leather as the tables in the main cabin, contained a complete setting of Italian china and silver, as well as an appropriate quantity of linen.

The powder room had the same combination of suede and leather with its accents of sea-foam green and French blue, plus a carpet of gold on the floor.

Lastly Chance took her into the rear compartment, sectioned off from the galley and main salon area by a door. As she looked around the small executive compartment, Flame noticed a double-width closet built into the wall next to a leather-topped desk, also built-in. Impelled by curiosity, she opened its doors. Inside, there was hanger after hanger holding men's suits, sportscoats, blazers, and slacks.

'I keep a complete wardrobe on board,' Chance explained.

'How convenient.' She swung the doors closed, then turned to survey the plush sofa covered in a velvety fabric of French blue.

'It saves a lot of packing and unpacking,' he agreed dryly, then added, 'The sofa makes into a double bed.'

'How *very* convenient,' Flame mocked suggestively, smiling as she rejoined him by the doorway.

'On international flights, it can be.' His gaze took on an intimately possessive look as he lifted his hands, tunnelling them under her hair to lay on either side of her neck. 'I can't believe how much I've missed you.'

The husky pitch of his voice made it easy for her to admit, 'And I can't believe how much I've missed you, too.'

As she tilted her head back, his mouth found hers with unerring accuracy. Instantly, Flame was conscious of the warm feeling that sprang to life inside her, a feeling he could arouse so expertly without their bodies even touching.

With obvious reluctance, he shifted his attention to the corner of her lips. 'I should have arranged to make this a longer flight. We would have had time then to see if that bed could be put to a more satisfactory use than sleeping.'

'Does that mean we're almost at our destination?' She slipped her hands inside his suit jacket and spread them over his shirt front, feeling the heat that emanated from his lean, hard body.

'We probably have another hour to go yet, maybe more,' he admitted, then forced himself to pull away, as if the temptation of her nearness was more than he could resist. 'But after waiting a week to be with you again, I'm not interested in a quick romp. I want to take my time making love to you.'

'I admit a quick romp would merely be an appetiser,' Flame conceded, eyeing him with a playfully deliberate, seductive look. 'But don't you usually serve your guests an appetiser before you offer them the main course?'

'Yes, but I like everything served in one sitting.' His mouth slanted in a one-cornered smile.

Sighing, she lowered her gaze to his shirt front and slid her fingers under his silk tie to trace the line of buttons. 'I don't suppose there's any way you can get this plane to fly faster.'

'I wish.' He chuckled softly, bringing his hands down to capture hers by the wrists and end their tantalising exploration.

'It never hurts to dream,' she said, offering no protest when he gently directed her back to the main salon area. Then recalling the hurt of previous lost illusions, she qualified that, 'Almost never, anyway.'

'You have to dream,' Chance said. 'Otherwise you'll never have a dream come true.'

'Have your dreams come true?' She wondered curiously.

'Some of them have. I'm still working on others.'

'Such as?' she asked, trying to imagine what he might dream about.

'Getting this jet to fly faster.'

She laughed in full agreement.

═ 15 ═

THE SUN was riding low in the sky, setting fire to the clouds on the horizon when the jet touched down at the private landing strip along the western coast of Mexico. That much Flame had guessed from the southerly route they'd taken from San Francisco, keeping the coastal mountains on their left and the Pacific Ocean on their right. Chance confirmed they were in Mexico but he wouldn't enlighten her further.

Alongside the runway stood a small open-air building set amidst a stand of palm trees and rampant mounds of lavender bougainvillea. As the jet taxied on to the tarmac, Flame had a glimpse of the sign on what was obviously the terminal building. But the glimpse was too brief and her knowledge of Spanish too limited. She still didn't know where they were. Not that it bothered her. On the contrary, this aura of mystery merely heightened her interest and added a further touch of excitement to her weekend away with Chance.

A car waited for them on the tarmac. On the driver's door was the now familiar logo of the Stuart Corporation. In the time it took Flame and Chance to walk to the car, her luggage was transferred from the plane to the limousine's trunk. Less than five minutes from touchdown, they were driving away from the inland airport, following a paved road that wound over the mountain toward the ocean beyond.

As they approached a layby that reminded Flame of a scenic overlook, Chance spoke to the driver in Spanish. Immediately the car slowed and pulled on to the gravelled roadside, stopping well short of the viewpoint.

'Do you still want to know where we're going?' Chance arched an eyebrow at her, his sidelong look glinting with faint challenge.

She sensed his desire to show her, a desire that seemed to be couched in a pride and a need to share. That, coupled with her own curiosity, made it easy for her to answer quickly. 'Yes, yes, yes,' she declared, grinning back at him.

He helped her from the car, then led her to the edge of the overlook, his hand firmly hooked around the side of her waist, keeping her close to his side.

The Pacific sprawled before her, the slanting rays of the sun laying a long golden trail across it. At the end of the sun's trail was a small bay surrounded by a dazzling blaze of gold that spread up the mountain slopes. Flame breathed in sharply at the sight, stunned by the discovery that the golden glitter came from the buildings stairstepping the slopes in tier after tier. Here and there, she saw ruby splashes of cascading red flowers and the emerald fronds of tall palm trees.

'Welcome to Ciudad de Oro de Stuart ... Stuart's City of Gold.'

'Chance, it's phenomenal.' She stared at the golden tower of a multi-storied hotel that stood near a pearl-white beach, its balconies strung with more ruby garlands of red flowers. 'The buildings, they actually look as if they're gilded. They aren't are they?'

'No. After six months of testing, we finally developed a stucco-like compound composed mainly of a micalike substance that reflects the sunlight. It's most effective at this time of day.'

In Flame's opinion, that was an excessive understatement. 'I have the feeling I'm looking at the fabled city of gold.'

'Wait until you see it at night when it catches the silver of the moon and the stars.'

Back in the car, they resumed their journey down the winding mountain road to the secluded resort complex, driving past the bay with its yacht harbour and marina crowded with charter boats for deep-sea and sport fishing. A strolling mariachi band played for the bathers still lingering on the beach to catch the last rays of the sun.

For those who shunned salt water, the high-rise hotel offered an over-sized swimming pool – although Flame hesitated to call it a pool when it resembled a meandering tropical lagoon complete with a cascading waterfall and rock ledges. Across from the hotel, a small shopping village with fountains and an arbored square offered familiar Mexican wares. The tiers of buildings on the surrounding slopes were a combination of condominiums and private villas. It was to one of the latter that the driver took them.

As they drove on to the gated and walled grounds of the villa, Flame was immediately enchanted by its lushness. Bougainvillea grew rampant, its multitude of red and purple blooms nearly overpowering the fragrant scarlet hibiscus and the tall graceful palms. A golden fountain sent a continual spray of water into the air, a spray the sunlight turned into diamond droplets.

Her enchantment grew when she entered the house itself. Built in the grand manner around a coral rock courtyard, the interior abounded with architectural and visual vignettes – recessed window seats, intricately carved cathedral ceilings, antique wooden doors, coral stone fireplaces, and floors of Spanish tile and pegged oak. Scattered discreetly throughout were works of Aztec and Oaxacan art, some like the terracotta pot tucked among the tropical greenery that added to the open-air feel of the cool and spacious villa, and others, like the magnificent hammered bronze sun disc, boldly displayed to dominate the room.

The loggia off the master suite overlooked the mosaic-inlaid swimming pool, surrounded by a deck of travertine marble. Beyond gleamed the bay, reflecting now the scarlet hue of the sky.

'Will this do for a weekend hideaway?'

At the sound of Chance's lightly mocking question, Flame turned from the loggia's panoramic view and tried to match his bantering tone. 'It's . . . simple, but nice.' She feigned a shrug, then found she couldn't maintain the pretence of indifference, not even in jest, and wound her arms around his neck, clasping her hands behind his head. 'It's beautifully perfect and perfectly beautiful, Chance.'

'I'm glad you think so, my love.'

The intensely intimate look in his eyes was answered by the darkening sparkle in her own. As his hands settled naturally on to the curve of her waist, she started to step into his arms, then checked the movement when she spied the stout Mexican housekeeper approaching the opened glass and wrought-iron doors to the loggia.

'Excuse me, Señor Chance.' She halted in the opening, a short round woman made shorter and rounder by the stiffly starched white apron tied around her black uniform. Shy dark eyes glanced briefly at Flame in silent apology. 'Señor Rod is on the telephone. He asks if you have arrived. Do you wish to speak to him now?'

Chance hesitated, arching a look of regret at Flame. 'Yes, tell him I'll be with him in a moment, Consuela. I'll take the call in the study.'

'Sí,' she murmured and retreated from the room.

'Sorry,' he said to Flame. 'Rod Vega is my man in charge down here. I shouldn't be long. Why don't you go ahead and freshen up or whatever, and I'll meet you in the main salon in – say, thirty minutes?'

'That long,' she complained, her lower lip jutting in a playful pout.

'That long.' He smiled.

Again she had to settle for a warm, but brief kiss. She lingered on the balcony a moment longer after he'd left, aware that he'd be back and confident the evening would be theirs. She turned to the view, and breathed in the sharp clean tang of the sea air. Paradise, Stuart-style, Captain Donovan had called it. It was definitely that and more.

She heard the door to the master suite open and realised that if she intended to change and freshen up, thirty minutes wasn't all that long. She walked back inside and found the housekeeper had returned.

'Ramón has brought your luggage,' the woman said, indicating the two cases lying atop a richly carved luggage rack. 'Would the señora wish me to unpack for her?'

'Please.' Flame walked over to the rack and retrieved her make-up case from the smallest bag. 'And when you come to the blue chiffon outfit, would you lay that out for me? I want to change into it.'

'Sí, señora.'

Nearly thirty minutes later, Flame exited the master bedroom, the free-floating chiffon of her blue print skirt swishing softly about her ankles. She caught a glimpse of her reflection in a hall mirror and smiled at the deep plunge of the blouse's softly ruffled neckline. The effect of the loose-fitting blouse of blue-dotted chiffon was subtly risqué, an effect emphasised by the sleeking of her fiery hair into a classic chignon. She loved the wickedly alluring feeling the combination gave her.

As she walked down the wide hall, her high heels clicking across its tiled floor, ahead she could see the march of pillared arches that surrounded the main salon, giving it a galleried look. When she was near to it, she heard the explosive *pop* of a champagne cork. Smiling, she quickened her steps, realising that Chance was already there waiting for her.

With her chiffon skirt wafting about her in a rippling sweep, Flame passed through the first arched opening into the salon. Chance turned to meet her, holding a fluted glass of champagne in each hand. She observed with satisfaction the quick lidding of his eyes as his surveying glance went no lower than the neckline of her blouse that revealed all of her cleavage. When he dragged his glance back up to her face, the flare of desire was strong in the darkened blue of his eyes – the very reaction she'd hoped to arouse.

'You look ravishing,' he murmured when she halted before him.

She took the glass of champagne he handed her, giving him a coy look of mock disappointment. 'And I hoped that I looked like a woman about to be ravished.'

He arched a black eyebrow at her. 'The evening is young.'

'Promises, promises,' she taunted playfully and took a sip of the sparkling wine. The instant it touched her tongue, she recognised its distinctive flavour. 'Peach champagne.'

'Of course.' He smiled and took a drink of his own.

She deliberately looked about the salon, like all the rooms in the villa designed in grand proportion and superb symmetry. 'What? No orchids?'

'I'm glad you mentioned that.' He reached inside his jacket and pulled out a long narrow jewellery case. 'Here.'

She looked uncertainly at the jewellery case he'd given her, then lifted her gaze to the lean, rakish lines of his face, unable to conceal her vague astonishment. 'What's this?'

— 154 —

'Open it,' was all he'd say.

Flame hesitated an instant longer, then set her glass down and lifted the hinged lid. Light blazed from inside with sparkling brilliance when she opened it. She gasped audibly at the sight of the magnificent diamond brooch designed in the shape of an orchid spray and flanked by a pair of matching diamond earrings.

'Now you'll always have orchids.'

She stared at the brooch, tears welling in her eyes, moved as much by the sentiment of the gift as she was by the magnitude of it.

If all he'd wanted to do was give her an expensive present, he could have picked up any bauble. But he hadn't. No, he'd chosen with thought and care, wanting to give her something special, something that signified their personal relationship.

She didn't resist when he took the case from her numbed fingers and removed the brooch from its bed of purple velvet. As he pinned it to her blouse, she looked up at him, the blur of tears softening all the hard edges of his face. With no hurry at all, he unclipped the drop earrings she wore and fastened the diamond pair in their place. When he'd finished, he surveyed the results, his hands settling warmly on the tops of her shoulders, a gentleness and a simmering ardour in his look and his touch that affected Flame as deeply as his thoughtfulness.

'Beautiful,' he pronounced in a husky murmur.

'Oh, Chance, I – I don't know what to say,' she admitted, as mere words failed to describe her astonishment, her joy or her appreciation.

'Then don't say anything.'

She didn't. Instead she wrapped her arms around his neck and kissed him, letting her hands, her lips, and her body show him how much his gift meant to her. His arms gathered her close, his hands moving in a restless and needy exploration over her shoulders, spine and hips, their heat penetrating the filmy fabric of her blouse and skirt. The colour and texture of their embrace quickly changed as Flame responded to the unleashing of emotions and desires held too long in check on both sides. She strained closer, arching to him, her fingers sliding into his hair, pressing and urging until the kiss became rough with need, lips, tongues and teeth tangling together. But it wasn't enough. Maybe it would never be enough. She dragged her lips from his and ran them over his face, lipping the high bone of his cheek and nuzzling at his ear, taking all the liberties with him as he did with her, conscious all the while of the high tension of her body and the loud heart thud in her ears.

'Do you have any idea how much I want you – now – this very minute?' Chance murmured thickly, his heated breath stirring against her ear and sending delicious shudders cascading down her neck. 'I had this entire evening planned – champagne, a candlelight dinner, easy conversation, a stroll in the moonlight . . . a stroll that would ultimately take us to the bedroom. Now, I want to skip everything in between and take you straight to the bedroom – to hell with the rest.'

Flame smiled against his cheek, his feelings and desires echoing her own, but with a difference. 'Where is it written that a woman can't be wined and dined – and taken on moonlight strolls *afterwards*?'

'Where, indeed?' he murmured, drawing back an inch or two to study the swollen softness of her lips and the green of her eyes, heavy-lidded with desire. 'Long ago I learned the value of improvising.'

'Did you?' She trailed the tip of a nail down the line of his jaw.

'Yes.' In one fluidly smooth movement, he picked her up and cradled her in his arms. 'And with you, I always seem to be improvising.'

'I love the way you improvise . . . among other things,' Flame added as she began to nibble on the corded muscles in his neck.

In the master suite, all the raw urgency, all the need for haste that had brought them to the bedroom fled. They stood facing each other, less than three feet apart, bathed in the pool of the single lamp that burned. Without either saying a word, they slowly began to undress, peeling off layer after layer. It was more than their clothes they stripped away and more than their bodies they bared to each other. As they looked, really looked at each other, they exposed their feelings, their hearts and their minds to the other.

When he held out his hand to her, she felt a lump rise in her throat. There was something so beautiful in the moment and the gesture she wanted to cry. As she gave him her hand, they moved toward each other, meeting in the middle of the space, their bodies touching. At last she could feel the heat of his body, the hard muscled wall of his chest and the powerful columns of his thighs. Reaching up, he pulled the pins from her hair and let it spill on to her shoulders as she ran her hands over him, his smooth skin like hot satin to the touch.

He held her gaze, his thumbs idly stroking the hollows behind her ears. 'I love you.' The declaration was a low rumble of intense feeling all wrapped up in a single phrase.

'I love you, too,' she whispered back as she rose to meet his seeking lips.

Later, much later, they opened another bottle of peach champagne, dined by candlelight, and strolled beneath the stars, ending up again in the master suite and rediscovering all the delights of making love.

= 16 =

THE GLASS doors to the balcony stood open, letting in the freshness of the morning breeze. Chance paused in front of them, watching the stout Mexican woman as she added a bowl of fresh fruit to the breakfast table set up on the balcony. His glance strayed to the twin place settings, drawn by the cosy look of matching crystal glasses, china cups, and gleaming flatware silently facing each other. Breakfast for him was usually black coffee and occasionally juice; he rarely sat down to a meal. But this morning was different. He wouldn't be eating alone. He would be with Flame. It was amazing how appetising that sounded.

He fastened the clasp on his watch, then turned his head slightly to bring Flame into view. She sat on the damask-covered bench in front of the lighted vanity mirror, robed in a kimono of peacock-blue silk, a matching band catching the hair away from her face while she applied the last of her make-up.

Looking at her, Chance felt again a powerful surge of nameless tender feelings all wrapped up with the need to touch and protect. A thousand times he had attempted to identify those feelings, but they were too elusive. Being with her was like stepping outside after a summer rain into a world that was suddenly clean and invigorating, livening all the senses. Yes, when he was with her, he felt good, very good.

'It seems we're having breakfast outside this morning,' he re-marked when she caught him looking at her.

'I suggested it to Consuela while you were in the shower. You don't mind, do you? It's such a beautiful morning.' She turned back to the mirror and raised the mascara wand to her lashes.

'And in here, too.' He wandered over to stand behind her and study her reflection in the mirror, admiring anew her bold, vibrant beauty.

Her glance met his in the mirror, a hint of demurring amuse-ment in the greenness of her eyes. 'It will be . . . in just a few more minutes.' She returned the mascara wand to its container and laid it on the vanity table.

Amidst the collection of lipstick, creams, and shadows, Chance noticed a flat cloisonnéd case. 'This is an unusual piece.' He picked it up to take a closer look at the intricate design depicting a vase of flowers.

'Isn't it?' Flame said in an agreeing tone, laying down a cotton swab and picking up a tube of lipstick. 'My mother gave it to me on my thirteenth birthday – when I was finally allowed to wear make-up. Powder, lipstick, and mascara, to be precise.'

'Is this lettering on the vase?'

'My initials – M.R.M. – with the "M" in the centre, of course.' She pressed her lips together, spreading the lipstick evenly, then reached for a tissue to blot them.

'MRM?' Everything inside him went still, his gaze riveted to the lettering.

'Margaret Rose Morgan. That's what I was christened. Daddy's the one who gave me the nickname Flame when I was about a year and a half old. It stuck.' Smiling, she reached up and slipped the band from her hair, giving her head a shake to let the fiery strands spill forward. 'My mother always thought I'd outgrow it in time.'

Her glance flicked to his reflection, expecting to encounter his answering smile. Instead, his expression seemed frozen, the muscles along his jaw tightly corded. Bewildered by his reaction, Flame turned sideways on the bench.

'Is something wrong, Chance?' She noticed the way his hand closed around the compact, his knuckles white.

She wasn't certain he'd heard her. Then his gaze shot to her face, all icy blue and cold. 'Chance, what is it?'

Immediately he looked down. 'I just realised – I have nothing of my mother. Nothing at all.' He held the compact an instant longer then gave it back to her.

The compact had always been special to her. Yet, it was only now, with some invisible hand squeezing her heart, that she realised how very precious it was.

'Chance, I . . .' But she didn't know what to say.

His mouth quirked faintly in an attempt at a smile. 'It doesn't matter,' he said, his expression now shuttered. His hand touched her hair, lightly fingering a red lock as if he was somehow distracted by its fiery colour. A light rap on the door broke his absorption. 'Yes?' There was a sharpness in his voice, making Flame aware of the hard tension hidden just below the surface.

'The telephone, Señor Chance,' came Consuela's partially muffled and heavily accented reply. 'It is for you. Señor Sam is calling. He say is *muy importante* he speak to you.'

'I'll take the call in the den.' He continued to study her hair for another full second before letting their eyes meet. Again his expression was unreadable. 'It shouldn't take long.'

'All right,' she agreed, striving for lightness, recognising that he didn't want sympathy. 'It'll take me a few more minutes to finish dressing anyway.'

He let the lock of hair slide from his fingers, then drew his hand away, lightly touching her cheek in parting before he turned and walked from the master bedroom. Flame looked down at the compact her mother had given her those many years ago.

Rage, resentment, and the wretched irony of the situation all seethed inside him as Chance strode across the Spanish-tiled floor to the massive teakwood desk. Dammit, he didn't want it to be Flame. She was the one untouched thing in his life. With her, he could almost forget everything. Dammit to hell – it wasn't fair! But when had life ever been fair to him? He looked at the jet-black phone on the desk and forced his fisted hand to unclench and reach for it.

'Yeah, Sam,' he said into the mouthpiece, deliberately shutting out all emotion.

'Chance, I'm sorry to call you like this, but . . . you have to know. We've learned the identity of Margaret Rose. Chance, it's Flame.'

'I know.'

'You do? How? When?'

'It doesn't matter.' He rubbed a hand across his forehead, his mind racing now that he had refused to feel anything.

'Does she know who you are? Did she confront you with it? What has Hattie told her?'

'Obviously nothing.' He went through everything Flame had ever said to him. There was nothing that even hinted she was aware of his connection to Hattie. Why? Considering how much Hattie hated him, why hadn't she tried to poison Flame with it? He could think of only one reason: she hadn't had the opportunity yet. Which meant he had to make certain Hattie didn't get it.

'Could it be that Hattie doesn't know you've been seeing her?' Sam ventured.

'How could she?' He doubted that Flame would have mentioned him to Hattie. She wouldn't have any reason to. In this short period of time, it was logical to assume that any conversation between Hattie and Flame hadn't touched on private matters.

'Chance, what are you going to do? She's bound to find out.'

'Maybe not. Maybe I can prevent that.'

'How?'

But it was something he needed to think through first. 'I'll talk to you later, Sam.'

He stood at the wrought-iron rail of the loggia overlooking the bay and the golden resort far below. His stance was that of a man lost in thought, his head drawn back, his gaze fixed on some distant point at sea, and his hands buried deep in the pockets of his slacks. Flame paused, wondering if he was still thinking about his mother, then continued to him. He didn't hear the dull click of her sandalled heels when she walked up behind him – completely unaware of her presence until she touched his arm.

Then he turned, that familiar, lazily intimate look immediately darkening his eyes the instant he saw her – that look that always caused those crazy tumblings of her heart. She smiled, realising that everything was all right again.

'Your phone call must not have taken very long.'

'No.' His gaze wandered over her face as if intent on memorising every detail. Then he bent his head, his mouth brushing over her lips before settling on to them with a driving need that had her leaning into him, supported by the encircling crush of his arms. She felt an edge of desperation somewhere – from her or from him, she couldn't tell. But it was there, a part of this desire to be absorbed wholly into one another. When the strain for closeness became too much, his mouth rolled off her cheek to the lobe of her ear, his breathing as heated and heavy as her own. 'How long have we known each other?' he murmured.

She had to think – which wasn't easy when all she wanted to do was feel. 'Three weeks.'

He lifted his head, framing her face in his hands. 'Yet I can't imagine my life without you in it.'

'I know. I feel the same.' She was a little surprised by how easy it was to admit that.

'Are you as certain of your feelings as I am?'

She searched and found not a trace of doubt. 'Yes.'

'Then marry me. Now. Today.'

If she had bothered to try, she could have come up with a dozen valid reasons not to rush into another marriage. But none of them – not the short time she'd known Chance, not her career or her job – was strong enough, singly or combined, to override the fact that she loved him and, more importantly, he loved her.

'Yes,' she said simply.

'You're certain.' He studied her closely. 'I know women like to have big, elaborate weddings. If you want to wait for that –'

'No.' She shook her head, as much as his cupping hands would allow. 'I've had the white satin gown and veil before. I don't care about the trimmings this time, Chance. Your love is more than enough.'

'I do love you, Flame,' he stated firmly. 'Promise you'll remember that.'

'Only if you promise to remind me,' she teased.

'I'm serious, Flame. I've made my share of enemies over the years. No matter what anyone might tell you about me, I do love you. And I intend to go on loving you for the rest of my life.'

'Darling, I'm going to hold you to that – and to me, for the rest of *our* lives,' she declared confidently, joyously.

═ 17 ═

SID BARKER kept the pay telephone pressed tightly to his ear as he mopped away the perspiration on his forehead and upper lip with his already sodden handkerchief. Damn this tropical heat, he thought and wished for a tall, cold beer. At the continued silence on the line, he started to swear at the Mexican operator for not putting his call through, then he heard the muted brr-ing on the other end, answered immediately by a familiar voice.

'Yeah, it's Barker,' he said and darted a quick glance at the door not ten feet away. 'I managed to locate them in Mexico – finally. But you've got a problem. I'm here at some sort of government building – and they just got married.' He anticipated the shocked and angry response he received – and the doubt. 'It's true, I swear. I was standing close enough I could have been a witness.' . . . 'How could I stop it?' he shot back in sharp defence. 'I didn't know what was going on until it was too late. I thought he was just taking her on a little sightseeing tour of the village to show her how the other half lived – the ones who clean his expensive hotel rooms and wait on his rich guests.' The resentment faded as his voice grew more thoughtful. 'Maybe I should have guessed something was up when I got word his private jet had taken off. Less than three hours later, it was back. I figure now that he had them pick up a ring for her. You should see the rock she's wearing.' There was movement at the door as a pair of beaming government officials escorted the newlyweds out of the room. Barker cupped his mouth to the receiver, speaking in a hushed rush. 'They're coming out now. I've gotta go.'

Without waiting for a reply, he hung up and walked briskly from the building to his rental car, guarded by a pair of enterprising Mexican boys.

The heavy damask drapes at the bedroom windows were partially closed, shutting out much of the afternoon sunlight. Maxine paused inside the doorway, struck by the unnatural stillness in the room. Unconsciously she held her own breath as she listened for the sounds of breathing on the ornately carved four-poster. The pink satin of Hattie's quilted bed jacket trimmed with eyelet lace emphasised the pallor of her crepey skin, pinched and greyed with pain. Pity swept through Maxine, followed by an instant hardening. Hattie Morgan was getting just what she deserved.

Moving silently, the thick rubber soles of her sturdy work shoes making little sound on the hardwood floor, Maxine approached the huge bed that dominated the small room. Hattie had slept in this room ever since she'd left the cradle more than eighty years before, even though the spacious master bedroom right next door has gone unused for more than fifty of those years. Maxine had always wondered at that.

She glanced hesitantly at the woman, then picked up the brown plastic container of prescription pills from the nightstand. She checked the capsules inside, trying to decide how many, if any, were gone.

'You're always snooping around, aren't you?' The caustic accusation shattered the stillness.

Maxine turned towards the bed. 'I thought you were resting.' With forced calm, she set the container back down on the nightstand.

'Then what are you doing here?' A glaze of pain clouded the usually sharp eyes. 'I heard the phone ring. Who was it?'

'Mr Canon. He's still on the line. But I didn't want to disturb you if –'

Hattie released a scornfully loud breath of disbelief and held out an age-gnarled hand. 'Give me the phone, then leave the room.' With lips pressed tightly together, Maxine lifted the phone from the nightstand and placed it on the bed next to Hattie, then turned away. She stiffened in resentment at Hattie's parting shot, 'And I'm not so drugged that I won't be able to tell if you listen in on the extension.'

As the housekeeper moved away from the bed, all Hattie could see was a shadowy dark figure. She could feel the excruciating pressure at the back of her eyes obscuring her vision. She was frightened by it and the dimness of her new world. As she waited to hear the door close behind Maxine, she wondered which was the hardest to bear – the pain or the fear. Interminable moments passed before Hattie heard the distinctive click of the downstairs extension being hung up. She felt for the telephone beside her, fingers closing around the receiver and lifting it to her ear.

'Yes, Ben, what is it?' She spoke harshly, fighting to keep the inner panic at bay.

'They're here in Tulsa,' came the reply. 'He brought her back with him.'

'It's true then,' she said, her voice strained by the fervent hope he would deny it.

'Yes. She married him.'

'She promised me –' Hearing the frantic edge in her voice, Hattie abruptly broke off the rest of the sentence, realising it no longer mattered what Margaret Rose had promised her. 'We'll just have to see what we can do about it, won't we?' she said with forced bravery. 'Right,' Ben Canon replied, an offer of encouragement in the response.

A few minutes later he rang off and the line went dead. Briefly Hattie felt that way inside as she hung up the phone. But she couldn't quit. She couldn't let Stuart win, not when she'd fought so long and so hard – not when she'd come so close. She groped for and found the old-fashioned bell pull next to the bed. She yanked on it impatiently and called, 'Maxine, Maxine!'

Almost immediately she heard the muted sound of running footsteps in the hall outside her room.

The door burst open. 'Are you all right, Miss Hattie?' Concern laced the housekeeper's voice. 'Shall I call the doctor?'

'No,' Hattie snapped. 'Get me Charlie Rainwater.'

'But –'

'Now!' she snapped again. When the door swung shut with a

resounding click, Hattie sagged back against the pillows and muttered dejectedly to herself, 'How could you be such a fool, Margaret Rose? I thought you were smart enough to see through him.' She closed her eyes and pressed a hand against them, trying to suppress the blinding pain in her head.

Her position remained unchanged until she heard the scuff of booted footsteps approach her door nearly fifteen minutes later. She brought her hand down and lifted her chin up, jutting it forward at an aggressive angle.

'Come in,' she responded in answer to the knuckled rap at her door, not letting any of the pain or fear creep into her voice. Pride wouldn't let her permit Charlie to see that she might be beaten. He believed in her. He had all these many years.

He paused beside the bed. 'Maxine said you wanted to see me.'

'Yes.' She wished his face wasn't so blurred to her, but it was enough just to hear the soothing drawl of his voice and smell that mixture of saddle leather and tobacco that always clung to his clothes. 'We have trouble, Charlie. She did marry him.' She caught the sound of his half-smothered curse and smiled faintly before going on to explain about the call she'd just received from Ben Canon.

'What do you want me to do?'

When she felt his work-roughened fingers brush over her hand, Hattie caught at them briefly. 'He's brought her back to Tulsa with him, Charlie. I knew he'd be arrogant. And that is his mistake.'

'Then you don't think it's too late.'

'It can't be.' She clung desperately to that. 'But we'll have to be ready to act at a moment's notice. We don't have much time.'

'You can count on me, Miss Hattie.' He squeezed her hand tightly, emotion thickening his voice.

'I know I can.' She nodded feeling the same tightness and the same vague regrets.

'We'll make it.'

'Of course we will,' she said, more confidently, drawing strength from his belief in her . . . just as she always had in the past. She let go of his hand and lay back, listening to the burring spin of the telephone dial as he placed her call to Ben Canon.

— 18 —

'HELLO ELLERY? It's Flame.' She sat crosswise on Chance's lap, idly and possessively fingering the short strands of his thick black hair.

'How was your weekend of sizzle in the sun? Or was it sizzle in the sack?' came Ellery Dorn's dry reply. From the sound of your voice, I'd say you're still floating on cloud nine.'

She laughed at that, her glance straying to the plane's porthole windows and the puffy white clouds beyond them. 'Actually I am – literally and figuratively.'

There was a pause, then a puzzled, 'Where are you?'

She partially covered the phone's mouthpiece with her hand and looked at Chance. 'Where are we?'

'About thirty thousand feet over Dallas.' A faint smile edged the corners of his mouth as he continued idly to massage the curve of her hip bone.

When Flame relayed the answer to Ellery, he responded with a droll, 'I sincerely hope you're in an airplane.'

'I am, I am.' She laughed again, recognising that she was so happy she could laugh at anything.

'If you're flying over Texas now, that means it will be another two and a half hours or more before you reach San Francisco.'

'That's what I'm calling you about, Ellery.' There was a part of her that was bursting to tell him the news – and another part that wanted to drag out the moment. 'I won't be flying back to San Francisco – at least, not tonight.'

'Why not? Where are you going?'

'To Tulsa.' She couldn't keep it to herself any longer. 'Chance and I got married.'

'What?'

She laughed at the surprise in his voice. 'It's incredible, isn't it?' She ceased playing with Chance's hair and held up her left hand to gaze at the interlocking wedding band and five carat marquise-cut diamond ring set in platinum that now so beautifully adorned her ring finger.

'Incredible isn't the word for it,' Ellery replied. 'Flame, are you sure you know what you're doing?'

She looked once more at Chance. The deep blue of his eyes mirrored all the love that she felt. 'Very sure,' she murmured, swinging the mouthpiece of the receiver out of the way and leaning closer to kiss him, letting their lips cling together for several precious seconds.

'I hope so,' came Ellery's sotto-voce reply.

But it was enough to bring Flame's attention back to the matter at hand. 'Would you mind doing me a favour, Ellery? Talk to Tim in the morning and let him know I won't be in the office for a couple of days. Explain that I'm taking a short honeymoon. And let Debbie know, too, so she can cancel any appointments I have.'

'When can we expect you back?'

'Chance has to leave on a business trip – when did you say? Wednesday?' He nodded in confirmation. 'I'll fly back then. Which means I'll be in the office on Thursday morning. Okay?'

'Your honeymoon is obviously going to be as short as your engagement,' Ellery observed. 'Oh, one more thing, Flame –'

'Yes.'

'Congratulations and happiness, my dear.'

'Thank you, Ellery.'

'And tell Stuart I hope he knows what a lucky man he is.'

'I will. Talk to you Wednesday night.' She returned the phone to its console concealed in the cabinetry next to the couch, then faced Chance, linking her hands together behind his neck. 'Ellery insisted that I remind you what a lucky man you are.'

'Extremely lucky,' he agreed smoothly.

'So am I.' Silently she studied his face, admiring its bronze angles, so strong and clean from the slanting cut of his jaw to the unbroken line of his nose. She noticed the look in his eyes, that look that spoke of a pride of possession. She smiled, feeling it too. They belonged to each other now and how very wonderful that was. Idly she smoothed a strand of hair away from his wide brow. 'How long before we reach Tulsa?'

With an effort he dragged his gaze from her face and looked out the window. 'That looks like the Red River below us, which means we're crossing into Oklahoma. We'll probably be landing in another twenty minutes or so.'

'So soon,' she murmured in mock disappointment.

'Yes.' There was more than a trace of regret in his voice as his glance slid to her lips. Then he breathed in deeply. 'We probably should move back to the main cabin. You'll have a better view from there of your new home when we fly in.'

'That's a shame when I'm so comfortable sitting here,' she declared softly and brushed her lips across the ridge of his cheek, breathing in the earthy fragrance of his cologne.

'We aren't there, yet,' he reminded her as he turned his head, seeking and finding her lips.

Ten minutes later they were interrupted by the buzz of the intercom. It was the pilot, Mick Donovan, notifying Chance that he was about to begin his descent into Tulsa. With some reluctance, Flame traded her comfortable seat on Chance's lap for one of the richly upholstered chairs in the main cabin.

With her seatbelt securely fastened, Flame leaned forward, angling her body to look out of the window at the wide open landscape of rolling hills below. The long slanting rays of the setting sun set fire to its autumn hues intensifying the shades of its golds, rusts, and reds and giving a richness to the land.

Somewhere out there, she remembered, Hattie Morgan lived. She'd have to give her a call while she was here – assuming, of course, that she'd have the time to spare on this short trip.

Then Chance's arm curled around her waist and all thought of Hattie fled as he leaned forward to look out the window with her. 'There's my city,' he said. 'Daring and dynamic. Tulsa.'

Etched against the fiery backdrop of the sunset's red sky, she saw the gleaming towers of the city itself, rising out of the surrounding hills and seemingly throwing them off with a mighty shrug of its shoulders. She stared at the tall sleek buildings, their proud stance reminding her somehow of Chance.

'Well, what do you think?'

She felt the brush of his chin against her hair, and hesitated briefly, wondering how she could tell him that her first impression of Tulsa was of something powerful and aggressive – something lean, tumultuous and restless – the very things she sensed in him sometimes.

But the feeling was too elusive to put into words. She chose a safe middle ground instead. 'I like it already. It's vigorous and alive.'

'That black building on the right is the Stuart Tower, where my company's headquartered.' He pointed it out to her just before the plane banked away to make its approach to the airport. Chance kept his arm around her as they both sat back in their seats. 'In the morning, you can come into the office with me. I want you to meet Sam and Molly.'

'I'd like that, darling.' From the few things he'd said about them she had got the feeling that these two people were the closest thing he had to a family. 'I just hope they like me.'

'They will. Although I probably should warn you that Molly may come off like a mother-in-law.'

'Ah, a potential ogre – any suggestions?'

'Just tell her how wonderful you think I am and you'll have her eating out of your hand.' He grinned, certain that Molly would love her as much as he did and refusing to consider the friction that would arise if she didn't.

And Flame laughed. 'You mean you aren't eating out of my hand?'

'If you think I am, that's all that counts.'

She sensed the shift in his mood to something more serious, more intimate. 'What about Sam? How do I get him to eat out of my hand?'

'Ask him about cars. The man's crazy about anything with four wheels and a motor . . . A little like I am about you.' He kissed her, and Flame wasn't aware of the jet's wheels touching down.

═══ 19 ═══

SAM LEANED against the corner of Molly's desk, one hip resting on top of it. He took another deep drag on his cigarette and glanced anxiously at the doors to the private elevator, then swung his gaze to Molly, watching as she fussed over the fresh floral arrangement on the credenza behind her desk. She stepped back to survey the result, then nodded in mute satisfaction even though Sam couldn't see that she'd changed the placement of a single flower. Turning, she ran the same critically inspecting eye over the room. When he saw it fall on the serving tray with its precise stack of china cups and saucers, the requisite creamer and sugar, lacking only fresh coffee to be poured in its decorative urn, his nerves snapped.

'So help me, Molly, if you touch those cups on that tray one more time –'

'I wasn't even thinking of that,' she denied, flashing him an impatient look. 'I was wondering if I should have had the bakery send up some Danish pastries. Watch your ash. It's going to drop on the floor.'

'God forbid,' he muttered, cupping one hand under the cigarette as he swung it to the ceramic ashtray on her desk, then pulled it back to tap the build-up of ash into the gleaming bottom. 'You'd probably call maintenance and have them bring up a vacuum cleaner.'

'I would not.' Immediately she picked up the ashtray and emptied it into her wastepaper basket under her desk, then snatched a tissue from the box she kept on the credenza and wiped the last speck of ash from the ceramic tray.

'Molly, will you stop this fussing?' He stabbed his cigarette out in the ashtray the instant she set it down. A bundle of nerves himself, Sam impatiently pushed away from her desk.

'I just want to make the right impression,' she retorted, grabbing the ashtray again.

'Where are they anyway?' He pushed back the cuff of his jacket to check his watch. 'Chance said they'd be here by ten-thirty. It's past that now.'

'You didn't expect them to be on time, did you?' Molly chided. 'After all, they are newlyweds.' Then she sighed, her eyes crinkling at the corners, matching the curve of her lips. 'I can hardly wait to meet her.'

Sam shook his head in disagreement and rubbed at the tension cording the back of his neck. 'I'm afraid I can't say the same.'

Molly looked at him with some surprise. 'Why not?'

'Because . . .' Sam hesitated, but he'd held it inside too long. It had to come out. '. . . I have bad feelings about this marriage,' he said, turning to face Molly as he brought his hand down, fisting it in helpless frustration. 'Dammit, I don't understand why he married her – why he didn't talk over his plans with me first?'

'He loves her.' As far as Molly was concerned, no other explanation was necessary.

'But don't you see, Molly, that's the point. This is one time I don't think Chance thought things through too clearly.'

She shook her head, unwilling to listen to his criticism. 'He knows what he's doing.'

'Does he?' Sam challenged. 'Let's forget the fact that he didn't have her sign any pre-nuptial agreement, and concentrate instead on what's going to happen when she finds out about Hattie and the ranch. Do you know that he hasn't told her anything about Hattie? And when I talked to him after they got back last night, he informed me he wasn't going to tell her.'

'Why should he?'

'Because sooner or later, she's going to find out. And if he keeps it a secret from her, think how it's going to look.'

'When the time comes, Chance will handle it. He always does,' she stated with supreme confidence. 'You worry too much, Sam.'

'Maybe.' But the boyish features continued to wear a troubled look as he combed the lock of hair from his forehead, unaware that it fell back. 'I don't know, Molly. I just can't help thinking this is all my fault. Chance relied on me to know what Hattie was up to and I let him down. If only I'd paid more attention to those meetings she was having with Canon, but I thought she was trying to find some legal loophole to avoid willing the land to Chance. I'd already checked that out eight ways to Sunday and knew it couldn't be done. But I never dreamed she was tracking down another heir. It never even occurred to me there might be one. If I had known – if I'd had her followed that day she went to Canon's office, I'd have known about her trip to San Francisco – who she saw – everything. And Chance would have known going in that Flame was Margaret Rose. It's for sure we wouldn't have all these complications we're faced with now.'

'You are such a pessimist, Sam.' Molly clicked her tongue at him. 'You see Chance's marriage as a complication, but I see it as the perfect solution.' The elevator light flashed on, indicating it was in use. 'Here they come.' Molly hurriedly sat down in her chair and grabbed up a pen and notepad, then patted the sides of her peppered grey hair. 'Quick. Look busy,' she admonished Sam.

'Busy?' He frowned in confusion. 'But they're on their way up.'

'I know. But we don't want to look like we've been standing around waiting for her to arrive.'

'Why not? That's what we've been doing for the last twenty minutes.'

'We can't let her know that.' Her glance fastened itself on the front of his suit jacket. 'There's cigarette ash or lint on your lapel.'

Sam brushed it off with a flick of his fingers, amused by her anxious flutters to have everything neat and in order despite his continued concern over the situation. 'I'm surprised you don't want me to spit on my fingers and slick down my cowlicks,' he murmured.

A faint ding accompanied the swish of the elevator doors gliding open, checking any answering retort Molly might have made as she directed a beaming smile at the emerging couple. Sam took

— 173 —

one look at Chance's bride and understood completely how this woman had succeeded in stealing Chance's heart when so many others before her had failed. In one word, she was a knockout. Gorgeous, subtly sexy – especially in that sweater dress of kitteny soft Angora – yet . . . the more Sam studied her, the more traces of Hattie he saw behind that warm and glowing look she wore. Just little things, like the proud way she held her head, the sharpness in her green eyes, and that confident squaring of her shoulders. Trite or not, he had a feeling she had a temper to match the fiery colour of her hair – and all it would take to spark it was someone trying to pull something over on her. He hoped to hell Chance knew what he was doing.

'Am I allowed to kiss the bride?' he asked after the initial flurry of introductions and acknowledgements were over.

'Of course.' The words of laughing assent came from Flame.

Sam darted a quick look of surprise at Chance and struggled to hide the surge of misgivings as he brushed his lips across her proffered cheek, breathing in the spicy fragrance of her perfume. Chance seemed to think nothing of the assertion by Flame, but in Sam's opinion, those were words of warning that here was a woman who knew her own mind and didn't let others do her thinking.

'I have fresh coffee made,' Molly volunteered. 'Would you like a cup?'

'We'll have it in my office,' Chance inserted, then arched a questioning look at Sam. 'You'll join us, won't you?'

'Of course. Which reminds me –' he began, following after them as Chance led Flame towards his office. 'Patty asked me to invite the two of you for dinner on Sunday. She's anxious to meet you.'

'Dinner on Sunday.' Chance looked at Flame, his gaze intimately warm and possessive in its run over her face. 'We should be back by then.'

'Back? From where?' Sam frowned, then remembered. 'That's right. You have to fly to Padre Island on Wednesday.'

A vague nod confirmed it, leaving the impression that Chance was too distracted by his new bride to give the whole of his attention to anything or anyone else. 'While I'm there, Flame's going to fly back to San Francisco and tie up all her lose ends. Which means you'll need to make reservations for her, Molly, on

Wednesday's flight but only one way. I'll meet her on Friday and we can fly back together.'

'I'll make a note of it.'

Not liking the sound of Chance's plans, Sam immediately spoke up, 'And I need to go over some things with you, Chance.' He glanced apologetically at Flame. 'You'll have to forgive me for stealing him away so soon. But it's business. You understand?'

'Of course. No problem.'

'I promise I won't keep him long.'

'Molly, why don't you take Flame on a tour of the offices and introduce her around?' Chance suggested. 'Just remember to have her back by noon. We have a luncheon date.'

'I think I can manage that with no difficulty.'

His arm tightened briefly around Flame's shoulders, a smile tugging at his lip corners. 'Molly's convinced I'm perfect. Try not to disillusion her too much.'

'How could I when I agree with her completely?' she countered, matching his mocking tone.

'I like her already, Chance,' Molly declared.

'I knew you would.' But his smile was directed at Flame, a familiar pride of possession in his look.

'Come on. We'll leave these two to their business.'

Sam noticed the way Chance's gaze stayed on Flame as Molly trundled her off, as if he was reluctant to let her out of his sight although not for the same reason that Sam had. When they turned down the hallway, Chance forcibly turned his attention back to Sam.

'Let's talk in my office,' he said, taking Sam's agreement for granted as he crossed the room to the heavy walnut door. Sam followed him inside and closed the door behind them. Chance went directly to his desk and began leafing through the messages that had accumulated in his absence. 'What's on your mind, Sam?'

'For starters, I don't think it's a good idea for you to let her go to San Francisco alone. What if Hattie tries to contact her while she's there?'

'I've already considered that possibility. I want you to get hold of Sawyer and have him waiting at the gate when she arrives on Wednesday. I want someone watching her twenty-four hours a day and a tap on her phone. If anyone – Hattie, Canon, that detective Barker – tries to talk to her, I'll expect Sawyer to make sure they don't succeed. By Friday, I'll be there.'

'And what about from now until then – or after you get back? You can't be with her every minute, Chance,' Sam argued.

'When she's at the house, Andrews can screen all incoming calls. And if she goes out anywhere – to shop or to play tennis – it will probably be with Patty. She won't know anyone else here. And, until she gets settled in, she won't be seeing anyone other than people I introduce her to.'

'You make it sound so simple – so cut and dried, but it's not that way, Chance.' He lifted his hand in a silent appeal. 'What if it's the other way around? What if Flame's the one who contacts Hattie? She could, you know. She's bound to have her phone number. What's to stop her from calling Hattie, getting directions, and driving out to see her?'

'She'd say something to me about it first.'

'What if she didn't? What if she did it on the spur of the moment?' Sam leaned both hands on the granite top of the desk, trying to press home his point and penetrate that aloof unconcern. 'How would you know?'

'I'll know.' Chance dropped the sheaf of his messages on to his desk, letting them scatter from the orderly stack as he faced Sam across the desk top, his control snapping from the strain of the last two days – the strain of living half the time in heaven and the other half in hell. 'I'll know if I have to bug my own house and have her followed everywhere she goes from now on. Dammit, Sam, I know I can't eliminate the risk but I can minimise the exposure.' The level of his voice didn't change, but rather the tone of it deepened to a forceful pitch. 'And that's precisely what I intend to do.'

'I'm sorry,' Sam began hesitantly, drawing back from that tautly controlled anger. 'It's just that –'

'I know.' Chance cut him off abruptly and swung away, moving to the window and inhaling a deep breath, regretting the anger he'd turned on Sam. 'I found out this weekend just how greedy I am, Sam,' he said, staring out of the window at the sprawl of the city beyond the glass panes. 'I want Flame and I want that land. I'll do whatever I have to do to make sure I don't lose either one.'

'I understand.'

'Do you?' He smiled wryly, unsure that he did.

The beeping ring of the telephone intruded. 'I'll get it.' Sam reached across the desk and picked up the receiver. 'Yes, this is Sam Weber.' Almost immediately he lowered the phone, placing his hand over the mouthpiece. 'Chance, it's Maxine.'

Pivoting sharply, Chance reached for it. 'Let me talk to her.' He took the phone from Sam's hand. 'Yes, Maxine.' A tension kept him motionless as he listened to her hurried message. 'Thanks for letting me know.' Slowly he carried the receiver back to its cradle.

'Letting you know what?' Sam asked, watching him closely.

He let his hand stay on the telephone. 'It's Hattie. According to Maxine, she's very ill. She doesn't think she can hold on much longer.'

Sam let out a long, slow breath. 'I'm not sure I believe it. And I feel guilty for hoping it's true.'

'I don't.'

'It looks like everything's going to come to a head sooner than I thought. It's going to get real touchy, Chance.'

'I know.'

══ 20 ══

SUNLIGHT FLASHED on the marquise-cut diamond on her finger, sending prisms of light dancing across the car's dashboard. Absently, Flame turned her gaze out of the window at the still unfamiliar scenery of big and bold Tulsa. She had yet to explore it – or get used to the huge canopy of pale blue sky that seemed to stretch forever, unmarred by ocean-born cloudbanks or blanketing fog.

It was moments like these when the strangeness of her surroundings made itself felt, that it all seemed unreal. She touched the ring on her finger, the one Chance had placed there. It was physical proof this wasn't a dream. She was his wife.

Flame Stuart. She smiled, liking the sound of it.

Even though she was resigning from the agency, she planned to continue with her career here in Tulsa. Not right away, of course. She wanted to spend as much time as possible with Chance these next few months. Later she'd see about obtaining a position with some local agency. Or maybe she could work with Chance in his company, handling the ad campaigns on his various projects. Either way, she knew she would ultimately want the challenge and mental stimulation of work again.

She smiled to herself, realising that this was a fine time to be thinking about all this. But it had all happened so suddenly – the marriage ceremony coming right on the heels of his proposal, then less than twelve hours later flying here with a new husband to a new home. And what a gorgeous home it was, a 1930s mansion styled after a gracious Palladian villa. She remembered that moment on their arrival when Chance had carried her over the threshold into the marble foyer with its grand, curved staircase – and later, when he'd taken her to the special master suite.

Sighing, she ran her fingers into her hair and flipped it behind her ear with a combing toss of her hand, the enormity of the step finally hitting her. My God, she was giving up her home, her job, her friends – everything that had ever meant anything to her. But she'd known that when she'd married Chance. It hadn't mattered then because he was with her, right at her side.

Overhead, the contrails of a passing jet streaked the sky, reminding Flame that Chance was halfway to Texas by now. She wished he was in the car with her so she could take hold of his hand and have the physical reassurance that she wasn't alone in this. Instead she fingered her wedding ring and sighed her longing.

'Is something wrong?'

Startled by the question that came from the silence, Flame glanced at the man behind the wheel, momentarily at a loss for an answer. She couldn't very well admit to Sam Weber that she was having a slight case of post-wedding jitters, not when she knew that deep down she didn't really have any doubts about her decision to marry Chance.

'No. I was just thinking about all the things I have to do once I get to San Francisco.' Conscious of his close scrutiny, she turned her attention to the freeway traffic in front of them. 'Is it much farther to the airport?'

'Ten minutes, more or less. Which means' he paused to glance at the clock on the car's dash – 'we'll be there a good forty-five minutes before your flight leaves.'

'I don't know why Chance insisted that you take me to the airport. I could just as easily have got a cab or had Andrews drive me. It wasn't necessary for you to do it. I'm sure you have more important things you could have been doing.'

'You're not going to hear any complaints from me.' Sam took his eyes from the road long enough to flash a boyish grin her way. 'As far as I'm concerned this is a very pleasant break.'

'Well, good, Sam.' She hoped he meant that.

At odd times, she'd had the feeling that Sam wasn't particularly happy about her marriage to Chance. It was nothing he'd said. No, it was more the way he looked at her sometimes as if questioning her reasons. She supposed Sam thought she might have married Chance for his money. She hadn't, of course. His wealth didn't matter to her at all, but Sam couldn't know that.

'I'm sorry Chance had to leave so soon after the wedding,' Sam remarked, genuine regret tingeing the glance he sent her. 'The two of you should have gone off on a long honeymoon.'

'I don't mind,' Flame insisted with a dismissing shake of her head. 'I've known from the beginning that his work demands a lot of travel. Maybe it's best our marriage starts out as it will go on.'

'Maybe. But I still believe newlyweds need some time alone. I told Chance before he left that Molly and I were going to take a look at his schedule and see if we can arrange to give you those three or four weeks together. It shouldn't be too difficult – barring any emergencies, of course.'

'Sam –' Flame began, touched by his thoughtfulness and wondering if she had misjudged him.

But he didn't give her a chance to say more. 'You'd better start thinking about where you want to go, otherwise Molly will have it all planned for you,' he warned, humour twinkling in his hazel eyes. 'She's already told Chance that she thinks he should take you to Venice.'

'Is that right?' Flame smiled, amused by the conspiracy that had been going on behind the scenes.

'Yes.' Then Sam seemed to hesitate. 'Molly can be quite bossy at times, especially where Chance is concerned. But she means well. I hope you know that.'

'Chance told me the same thing.' Her smile widened as she recalled, 'Actually he told me that Molly was the closest I would come to having a mother-in-law.'

Sam chuckled. 'That's true enough. As a matter of fact, you know that old cliché about believing the sun rises and sets on someone. As far as Molly's concerned, Chance is the sun. And nobody had better dare to cast a dark shadow over his life or they'll answer to her.'

'I did get that impression. Truthfully, though, I like her.'

'It's impossible not to like Molly. She's quite a woman. Once you get to know her better, you'll understand what I mean.' He paused to slide Flame a sideways glance, a wryly boyish grin pulling up one corner of his mouth. 'I hope I have half of her energy and spunk when I'm her age. Do you know that she was in her forties before she went hunting and fishing for the first time? On top of that, her first time out she bagged a trophy buck. I know. I was there. In fact I was the one who took her hunting. She's something else,' he declared then added, 'and independent as the day is long. When she first went to work for Chance, she was taking a night-school course in auto mechanics. She'd decided that the local garage was taking advantage of her because she was a woman and didn't know anything about cars. Speaking of cars, remind me to show you my vintage Porsche when you and Chance come for dinner on Sunday.'

'He mentioned that your hobby was restoring classic sports cars.'

'Patty would tell you it's my passion.' Again there was a flash of boyishness in his grin. 'I don't know that I'd go so far as to say that, but I do enjoy tinkering with cars. I always have. For me, it's a great way to relax and – it's a hobby I can share with my sons, along with hunting and fishing. Patty and I have four boys. The youngest is eleven and the oldest is sixteen. Right now we're in the process of rebuilding a '76 Corvette for Drake, our oldest.' The brake lights on the car directly in front of them flashed red as the traffic on the freeway began to bunch up. 'Hello, what's this?' Sam frowned as he applied the brake and reached for the gear stick to change down. 'This is the wrong time of the day to be having a tie-up.'

But a tie-up it was as the traffic slowed to a crawl, then came to a stop altogether another hundred yards further.

Flame thought she heard the wail of a siren. 'Do you suppose there's been an accident?'

'Maybe.' With a tilt of his head, Sam peered into his side mirror. 'Here comes a motorcycle cop. I'll see what I can find out.' He rolled down his window and flagged down the policeman slowly wending his way between the stopped cars. 'What seems to be the problem, officer?'

'A tractor-trailer rig jackknifed on the overpass,' came the reply, half muffled by the revving of the motorcycle's engine. 'There's a tow truck on the scene, so it shouldn't be much more than ten minutes before they get a lane cleared.'

'I hope not.' Sam glanced at his watch. 'We have a plane to catch.'

Trapped between freeway exits, they had no choice but to wait it out. Ten minutes turned into fifteen, then twenty. Finally, nearly twenty-five minutes later, the traffic started moving again.

When Sam pulled up to the kerb in front of the airport terminal, Flame had barely fifteen minutes to make her flight. 'With luck, your departure will be delayed. They usually are,' he said as he hurriedly retrieved her luggage from the trunk. 'Just the same, we'd better check your bags at the gate to make sure they're on the same flight with you.'

As they started towards the glass doors, an airport security guard stopped them. 'I'm sorry, sir, but you can't leave your car parked here. This is an unloading zone only.'

'Five minutes, that's all I'll be. I swear,' Sam argued, but he argued in vain. Sighing in defeat, Sam turned to her. 'It looks like you're going to have to go ahead to the gate while I park the car. He won't listen to reason. Can you carry your bags? He claims there are luggage carts inside.'

'I can manage,' Flame assured him.

'Okay.' Reluctantly he transferred the two cases to her. 'I'll meet you at the gate as soon as I can.'

'That's not necessary, Sam –'

He cut her protest short. 'I'll be there anyway – just in case you miss the flight or it's delayed.'

Recognising it would be a waste of time to argue, Flame gave in. With a bag in each hand for balance, she entered the terminal building and walked directly to the monitor screens listing the departing flights and their respective gate numbers.

As Flame scanned the screen for her flight, a gentle drawling voice intruded, 'Beggin' your pardon, ma'am.' She glanced absently at the man who had stopped beside her, an ageing cowboy in a suit of brown polyester with the distinctive yoked front of the western cut. 'You're Margaret Rose, aren't you?' A pair of rheumy blue eyes lifted their glance to her hair. 'Miss Hattie said I'd know you straight off by the red of your hair.'

'Hattie Morgan.' Momentarily she was startled to hear him speak the woman's name. 'I had planned to call her when I came back,' she said more to herself than to the ageing cowboy. 'Do you know her?' she said, then smiled, realising she had asked the obvious.

'Yes, ma'am.' As if suddenly remembering his manners, he doffed the cream-white stetson and held it in front of him, revealing a head of wispy thin white hair, flattened by the hat. 'Miss Hattie said she'd mentioned me to you. I'm Charlie Rainwater, the foreman at Morgan's Walk.'

'She did, yes. It's a pleasure to meet you, Mr Rainwater.' Just for an instant, Flame eyed him curiously, taking in his wiry slim body, the half-moon shape of his white moustache and the deep tan of his skin, leathered by years of sun and wind. He had a strong, lean face – and a kind one, innately gentle, like his eyes. 'How did you know I'd be –' But her question was interrupted by an announcement over the airport's public address system. 'That's my flight. I have to go. Please tell –'

'You can't go, ma'am.' He lifted a hand as if to stop her. 'Miss Hattie needs to see you.'

'But –'

'Ma'am, she's dying,' he inserted firmly over her half-formed protest.

'What?' Stunned by his blunt statement, Flame stared at him.

'It's true, ma'am. I wish it weren't, but wishin' don't make it so.'

'But . . . I talked to her only last week. She sounded fine on the phone.' She struggled to shake off the sense of shock. 'What happened? Did she have a heart attack?'

'No, ma'am.' A dip of his head briefly concealed his expression. 'She has a brain tumour. The doctors told her last spring there wasn't anything they could do.'

'No,' she whispered, remembering the desperation she had sensed in the elderly woman, a desperation she had blamed on loneliness. But that hadn't been the cause at all.

'She's been asking for you, Miss Margaret.' His watery eyes made their own silent appeal. 'Will you come to Morgan's Walk with me? I promised her I'd find you and bring you back. If the good Lord's willing, we won't be too late.'

'I –' Flame glanced uncertainly at the monitor screen. The flashing number indicated her flight was in the boarding stage. But it wasn't imperative that she return to San Francisco on this particular flight. She could catch another . . . later. She turned back to the white-haired ranch foreman and smiled faintly. 'I'll go with you.'

Deep gratitude welled in his look. 'It will mean everything to Hattie. Thank you.' He pushed his hat back on to his head and picked up her suitcases. 'I have a car waiting outside. If you'll come with me . . .'

She hesitated, the thought occurring to her that perhaps she should wait and advise Sam of her change in plans. But the anxious look on the foreman's lined and weathered face revealed his eagerness to be on his way back to Morgan's Walk. And time was of the essence. Nodding her assent, Flame turned and walked to the glass doors.

Approached by a winding road and circular drive, the stately Georgian mansion of red brick stood atop a knoll overlooking a long golden valley flanked by a ridge of hills painted in the gold, scarlet and rust of autumn. Some one hundred yards to the right of it, nestled in a pocket of oak trees, were the ranch's outbuildings, the rustic simplicity of the utilitarian buildings in sharp contrast to the subtle grandeur of the manor house.

Through the car window, Flame gazed at the imposing three-storey structure with its pillared entry and gleaming white shutters. This was Morgan's Walk, designed by her great-grandfather, Christopher Morgan. She frowned, suddenly wondering why he'd left it. Why he'd gone to San Francisco. Hattie had never explained that. In truth, she had never asked his reasons, believing that San Francisco was obviously preferable to the vast nothingness of Oklahoma. But, at the time, she hadn't known he'd left something this special behind. Why?

The Lincoln pulled up behind two cars already parked in the circular drive. Before the engine died, Charlie Rainwater was out of the car and opening the rear passenger door for Flame. Picking up on his sense of urgency, she wasted no time stepping out to join him.

'Doc Gibbs's still here. I hope that's a good sign.' He nodded in the direction of the car directly in front of the Lincoln, then tucked a hand under her elbow and guided her to the mansion's pillared entrance.

'I hope so, too,' she murmured, gripped by the memory of

another hurried trip following the car crash that took her father's life and ultimately her mother's.

Inside, afternoon sunlight streamed through the leaded glass windows and laid a golden pattern across the rich parquet flooring of the spacious reception hall. Absently Flame scanned the ornate ceiling mouldings, the glittering crystal chandelier, and the hall's period furnishings, recognising that the mansion's interior filled the exterior's promise of gracious formality within. Yet it was the silence, the stillness of the house that made the greatest impression. She turned to the ageing foreman as he removed his hat and ran combing fingers through his thin white hair, rumpling its flatness.

'I'll bring in your bags directly, ma'am, but it'd be best if I took you straight up to Miss Hattie.'

'Of course.'

He led her to the gleaming oak staircase that curved in a grand sweep to the second floor. As Flame climbed the steps, she trailed her hand along the smooth bannister, its finish darkened by the oils from the many hands that had touched it before hers . . . Morgan hands. Again she felt a sense of the past, a curiosity for the ones who had lived here.

Your roots will pull you back. That's what Hattie had told her. Was that what was happening to her? Hattie would say so. Hattie. Flame lifted her glance to the second-floor landing, her thoughts now turning to the woman.

At the top of the stairs, she glanced expectantly at the set of double doors that obviously led to the mansion's master suite, but Charlie Rainwater directed her to the right with a wave of his hat.

'Miss Hattie's room is over here,' he said.

This time he led the way. A tightness gripped her throat almost the instant she stepped inside the room – a tightness that came from the sudden rush of fear. All the drapes were closed, shutting out the afternoon sunlight and throwing the corners of the room into deep shadow. A lamp on the dresser cast a feeble pool of light.

'Why is it so dark in here?' She wanted to fling the drapes open and rid the room of this feeling that death lurked in its black corners.

'The light hurts her eyes.' The answer came from a tall,

harried-looking man standing to her right, the cuffs of his dress shirt rolled back and the waistcoat to his suit stretched tautly around his protruding middle.

'This is Doc Gibbs, ma'am.'

Even before the foreman introduced him, the stethoscope around the man's neck had identified him for Flame. A smile touched the corners of his mouth, conveying sadness and regret. 'You must be Margaret Rose,' the doctor said, his voice soothingly low and quiet. 'I'm glad you could come. She's been asking for you.'

Flame stared at the inert figure lying in the four-poster bed, half in shadows. 'Shouldn't she be in a hospital?'

'There's very little that can be done for her now.' The admission came reluctantly, betraying a frustration at his own helplessness that, for all his medical skills, he couldn't deny. 'And this was Hattie's wish – to be here in her own home – in her own bed.' He touched the medical bag on the dresser beside him, a syringe lying at the ready. 'I wanted to give her something for the pain, but she wouldn't hear of it.'

'She wanted to be lucid when you arrived, Mrs Stuart.' The third voice came from the shadows. Momentarily startled, she turned as a short, round man stepped forward into the dim light.

Something about him reminded Flame of a leprechaun. Maybe it was his small height at barely five foot two or the white socks he wore with an old suit or loud green tie or the shiny pate of his balding head partially ringed with a fringe of brown hair or the jovial roundness of his face. Yet he had the shrewdest pair of brown eyes she'd ever seen.

'This here's Ben Canon, Miss Hattie's attorney,' Charlie Rainwater explained.

'Mr Canon,' she murmured the acknowledgement.

As he nodded in return, a thin, thready voice came from the four-poster, 'Who is it? Who's there?'

As if commanded by the faint, demanding cry, the wiry foreman moved swiftly to the bedside. Leaning down, he gently laid his hand on top of hers. 'It's me, Miss Hattie. Charlie,' he said, a touching warmth in his voice. 'She's here. I fetched her just like I promised.'

There was a sigh, followed by an agitated, 'Maxine?'

'Ssh,' the aged cowboy murmured in an effort to quiet her. 'I sent her home this morning; told her she needed to rest after sitting up with you the past two nights.'

'Good.' A weak nod of approval accompanied the comment. Then her voice seemed to gather strength as she commanded, 'Bring her to me, Charlie. Bring Margaret Rose to me.'

The foreman looked at Flame, then hesitated, his glance slicing to the physician standing beside her. 'What about Doc, Miss Hattie?'

'Tell him . . . tell him to leave.' She made a feeble attempt to grip the foreman's hand. 'You and Ben, I want you to stay.'

'We will.' With a jerk of his head, he directed the doctor to the door, then motioned for Flame to approach the bed.

The physician looked none too pleased with the request, but he didn't argue. 'I'll be right outside if you need me, Charlie.'

As he slipped quietly from the room, closing the door behind him, Flame walked slowly to the bed, gripped by a vague sense of déjà vu. The surroundings, the circumstances, the individuals were all different. This was not a hospital room. It was not her mother lying in the bed. There had been no accident. Yet the poignant feeling was the same – the feeling that this was going to be the last time she would see Hattie alive.

Charlie Rainwater stepped to one side, making room for her as Flame came up to take his place next to the bed. The shadows seemed to lift, allowing a clear view of the woman, her head and shoulders propped by a mound of feather pillows. That cloud of white hair was the same, but the face looked older, much older than Flame remembered. That parchment-fine skin was furrowed with lines of pain, lips pinched and pale. And the deathly white of her face was only intensified by the pink satin of her old fashioned quilted bed jacket.

Swallowing to ease the constriction in her throat, Flame smiled faintly. 'Hello, Hattie. It's me – Margaret Rose.'

Her eyelids fluttered open, revealing a pair of dark, nearly black eyes, that tried to focus on her. 'Margaret Rose?' A deep frown creased her already lined brow. 'Come closer. I can't see you.' Obligingly, Flame sat on the edge of the bed and leaned towards the woman. Those dark eyes brightened, relief shimmering through them. 'Your hair.' A gnarled hand lifted briefly, as if to touch Flame's hair, but she lacked the strength, and the hand fell weakly back. 'It is you.' She breathed the words, softly, faintly.

'Yes,' Flame covered the bony, age-spotted hand with her own and squeezed it lightly.

Anger suddenly blackened Hattie's eyes, turning them sharp and accusing. 'You promised me. You gave me your word. How could you do it?'

'Do what? I don't understand.' She frowned, recalling a promise of some sort, but it was all too vague.

Her head moved against the pillows in obvious agitation as Hattie ranted on, giving no sign that she'd heard Flame's reply. 'You swore you wouldn't do anything until we talked. How could you let yourself be taken in by him? I thought you were smarter than that. I tried to warn you about him. I tried.'

'What are you talking about? *Who* are you talking about?' Flame demanded, half convinced the pain was making Hattie delirious.

'Why did you have to go and marry him?' Her fingers closed fiercely around Flame's. 'Why didn't you see through him?'

'Chance? You're talking about Chance?' She stiffened in disbelief.

'It isn't too late, Margaret Rose.' Dark eyes fastened on her. 'We can get your marriage annulled. Ben can get it annulled.'

'I don't want an annulment.' Flame pulled her hand back and shot a quick look at the wiry foreman. 'She doesn't know what she's saying.'

'Listen,' he urged quietly, the white curl of his long moustache moving slightly with the sympathetic smile that lifted the corners of his mouth.

'He's using you, Margaret Rose.' That rasping voice reached out to her again. 'Stuart only married you so he could get control of Morgan's Walk —'

'That's nonsense.' Flame stood up, her whole body rigid with denial.

'It's true, I tell you.' For an instant, there was hard force behind her voice, then Hattie subsided weakly against the pillows, more pain twisting through her face. 'It's true,' she whispered. 'He thought I would have to leave it to him when I died. But I fooled him. I found you.' Her eyes closed. 'He found you, too, though. I don't know how. You can't let him have Morgan's Walk. You have to stop him, Margaret Rose.' Her head moved from side to side against the pillows, her voice growing fainter. 'I promised my grandfather on his deathbed that no Stuart would ever get his hands on this land. You must keep that promise. Do you hear me?'

'Yes, I hear you.' The woman was mad. It was the only possible explanation that made any sense to Flame at all. Chance loved her and she loved him. That was the basis for their marriage – not all this nonsense about Morgan's Walk. But why did she keep going on about it? What could she mean?

'Don't . . . Don't ever trust him. The Stuarts are a ruthless breed. They'll do anything . . . even murder to get what . . . they want.' She was slipping deeper into the blackness of pain. She seemed to know it as she made one last valiant attempt to fight it off. 'Ben will tell you. Ben and Charlie. They have the proof. They'll show you. Won't you? Ben? Charlie?' An edge of fear crept into her voice for the first time.

'We're here.' The old foreman quickly stepped to the bed, the brightness of tears in his eyes as he reached down to cradle her hand between his calloused palms. 'Ben and me, we'll explain everything just like you would have done.'

'The pain, Charlie.' There was a hint of a sob in her voice. 'I don't think I can take it any more.'

'You don't have to, Miss Hattie.' With a turn of his head, he looked over his shoulder at the attorney standing well back from the bed. In a voice husky and thick, he said, 'Take Miss Margaret Rose down to the library, Ben, and have Doc Gibbs come back in.'

'Of course.' Stepping forward, the diminutive attorney lightly touched her arm. Frozen inside with a mixture of grief, disbelief and confusion, Flame let herself be led from the room.

21

THE LIBRARY occupied a secluded corner of the mansion's first floor, its tall, small-paned windows looking out on to the tree-shaded rear lawn. Rich panelling of black oak lined three sides of the room while bookshelves stretched from floor to ceiling on the fourth. A pair of wing-backed chairs, covered in burgundy leather and studded with brass, flanked the imported marble fireplace, the pair of them mates to the chesterfield sofa that faced them.

Alone in the room, Flame wandered over to the large mahogany desk that took up one whole corner. Yet she couldn't escape the sensation that there were eyes following her. She pivoted sharply and faced the portrait that hung above the mantel. There he was, glaring at her in silent accusation. No matter where she went in the room, it was the same.

She stared at the man in the painting. Over the years, an accumulation of smoke and grime had dulled its colours, but it hadn't lessened the impact of that strong-jawed face or those piercing black eyes. And the hair visible beneath the wide brim of his western hat had a definite red cast to it, although Flame wasn't ready to concede that originally it might have been the same fiery gold colour as hers.

'Hattie frequently stared at the portrait like that, too.' The remark came from the library's arched entrance with its set of sliding pocket doors. Flame swung toward them, startled to see the elfin-round attorney in the opening, his short arms laden with a large tray holding a silver coffee service and china cups. 'Imposing isn't it?' He walked into the room, the thick rubber soles of his oxfords making little sound on the hardwood floor.

'I assume that's Kell Morgan.' Her teeth, her nerves, and her temper were all on edge.

'Hattie told you about him?' He sent her a questioning look as he awkwardly set the tray down on the occasional table next to the winged chair, rattling the china cups against each other in the process.

Again Flame observed the innate shrewdness of his eyes and reminded herself that this little man was not as jolly or as harmless as he appeared. 'She mentioned that her grandfather's portrait hung above the fireplace in the library.'

'Yes, of course.' He wrapped a pudgy hand around the silver handle of the coffee pot and picked it up. 'I know you said you didn't use it, but I brought some cream anyway. Charlie made the coffee earlier, and – around here – cowboys like their coffee black and thick. So you might want to dilute yours with a little cream.'

But Flame wasn't interested in talking about coffee or cream. She wanted answers to those ridiculous charges Hattie had made. 'What was all that nonsense Hattie was saying about Chance?'

Ben Canon hesitated a fraction of a second, then finished filling one of the cups with coffee. 'I'm afraid it wasn't nonsense.'

'You're wrong.' He had to be. 'In the first place, Chance would never have expected to inherit Morgan's Walk, even if he knew about the place. She must have been delirious when she said that. She told me that it had to pass to a direct descendant.'

'Your husband is Hattie's nephew.'

'But – how can that be?' She'd always understood that Chance had no family – none at all.

'His mother was Hattie's baby sister.' The lawyer glanced at her, a knowing gleam lighting his eyes. 'Obviously he didn't tell you that.'

'No.' Why? Why hadn't he told her? Why had he kept it a secret? Had he done it deliberately? Or like her, had he simply not got around to mentioning Hattie?

'I'm afraid there are a great many other things that he has failed to tell you as well.'

'That's what you say,' she charged. 'But I don't believe you. I don't believe any of this. Where's all this supposed proof Hattie was talking about? Show it to me – if you can.'

He held her gaze for a long, considering second, then shook his head. 'I prefer to wait until Charlie joins us.'

'Why? What difference does it make whether he's here or not? Or is he your proof?' Flame challenged, armed by the memory of Chance saying, No matter what anyone tells you, remember that I love you. 'You surely don't expect me to accept his word for this, because I won't.'

As if on cue, she heard the clump of booted footsteps in the hall outside the library. Flame glanced at the doorway as Charlie Rainwater appeared. Grief bowed his shoulders and shadowed the faded blue of his eyes.

'Hattie?' That was all Ben Canon said, just her name, but that one word was loaded with question. Flame unconsciously held her breath, bracing herself for the old foreman's answer. However much she might resent Hattie's unfounded accusations against Chance, she couldn't pretend, not even to herself, that she wouldn't be touched by the old woman's passing.

The droop of his moustache lifted slightly as Charlie Rainwater made an attempt to gather himself. 'She's resting for now,' he said. 'The Doc's gonna sit with her.'

The attorney nodded, but made no comment as he turned to the serving tray on the table. 'I brought in some of that coffee you made, Charlie. Would you like me to pour a cup? I seem to have been elected by default to do the honours.'

'I sure would,' he accepted readily, his long legs carrying him into the room, the thud of his heeled boots echoing hollowly in the high-ceilinged room and increasing the feeling Flame had that they had gathered here to keep a lonely death watch.

'Would you like to change your mind, Margaret Rose, and have a cup with us?' the attorney offered again, the spout of the coffee pot poised above the third cup.

'No. And please stop using that name. My mother's the only one who ever called me that.' Her mother – and Hattie.

'That's right. You're known as Flame, aren't you?' Ben Canon recalled, his sharp eyes sliding to the red of her hair. 'A most descriptive sobriquet.'

'I'm really not interested in your opinion, Mr Canon – only in the explanation you promised to give me once Mr Rainwater joined us.'

'Yes, so I did.' He took a sip of his coffee, and peered up at the considerably taller foreman. 'It seems her husband failed to mention that he was Hattie's nephew.'

'He is. That's true enough, ma'am.' Charlie Rainwater took a hurried and noisy slurp of coffee, then wiped at the clipped ends of his moustache with the back of his forefinger. 'He was born right here in this house – in the room right next to Miss Hattie's. If you don't believe me, you can ask Doc Gibbs. He was the one who brought him into this world.' Pausing, he stared into the black of his coffee. 'A sad day it was, too. I don't reckon any of us expected to see the day come when there'd be a Stuart in this house.'

'But his father –'

Charlie never gave her a chance to finish as he looked up, a cold fire blazing in his eyes. 'Ring Stuart was a lazy, no-good hoodlum. He didn't give a hoot about Miss Elizabeth. He just wanted the easy life Morgan's Walk could give him. Miss Hattie tried to tell her that, but Miss Elizabeth wouldn't listen. Her eyes were so full of him, she couldn't see anything else.' He gave a wry shake of his head, but there was little humour in the slant of his mouth. 'That really ain't so surprising, I guess. Them Stuarts always did have more charm in their little fingers than most men got in their whole body. So what does Miss Elizabeth do, but run off and marry him. With her being of legal age, there wasn't much Miss Hattie could do about it. She tried. We all tried. But once she married him, Miss Hattie had no choice but to turn her out. That hurt her. That hurt her bad. She loved that girl. Raised her from the time she was born, and she was just a kid herself.'

'But how could Chance have been born here if Hattie threw his mother out?'

' 'Cause she took her back. Miss Elizabeth got real sick and there he was not taking care of her like he should. Miss Hattie couldn't stand that, and Stuart knew it. I warned her that she was playin' right into his hands when she brought them both back to Morgan's Walk, but she said it was better to have the devil close so she could keep an eye on him and know what he was up to. We all knew what he figured. With Miss Hattie being so much older than Miss Elizabeth, he thought she would die first and his wife would get Morgan's Walk – and he'd have control of it. But it didn't work that way. Miss Elizabeth got blood cancer. Many's the time you could see it workin' in his mind to hurry Miss Hattie's demise along, but he couldn't twitch a hair without somebody seein' it. That's when he started drinking – out of frustration mostly.' He cupped both leathered hands around the delicate china cup. 'I reckon he had reason to be frustrated 'cause he sure didn't get Morgan's Walk like he wanted – like he tried to do.'

'Let me see if I understand this,' Flame murmured tightly. 'Simply because his father married to get control of this ranch, you have tarred Chance with the same brush. Is that your proof?'

'There's more to it than that . . . Flame,' Ben Canon inserted, hesitating fractionally over the use of her name. 'Much more. As a matter of fact, the trouble with the Stuarts goes all the way back to *his* day.' He half turned to look at the man in the portrait.

'I suppose this has something to do with the deathbed promise Hattie referred to.' She caught a jeering note of sarcasm in her voice. Part of her regretted it, yet mockery seemed her only defence at the moment. She couldn't allow herself to take any of this seriously.

'I think it would be closer to say that this addresses the events that led up to it.' His smile failed to conceal the hard scrutiny of his glance. 'Perhaps it would be best if I began by telling you a bit about the founding of this ranch, and the history of this area. After all, Morgan's Walk will pass to you on Hattie's death. It's only fitting that you should know something about it – out of respect for Hattie, if nothing else.'

At the mention of the woman's name, she felt a twinge of guilt, realising how callous she must sound to him. She wasn't. There were simply too many emotions pulling her in different directions – anger, confusion, pity, sadness, and – as much as she was unwilling to admit it – fear. Fear that Hattie might be right – that maybe she was being used by Chance. Because of it, the urge was strong to flee the room and this house so she wouldn't have to listen to any more of their lies about him. But she stayed. Like it or not, she had to know.

'You're quite right, Mr Canon,' Flame stated, tilting her chin a little higher. 'If Morgan's Walk is to be mine, I should know more about it.'

'Good.' He nodded in approval.

Without thinking, she glanced at the portrait and froze, an eerie chill running down her spine. Those eyes – the eyes of the man in the portrait – they'd lost their accusing glare and now regarded her with a pleased look. Flame tried to tell herself that she was imagining it, that her mind was playing tricks with her, yet the impression persisted.

Shaken by it, Flame walked over to the coffee tray. 'I think I'll have a cup after all.'

'Help yourself, by all means.' The lawyer waved a hand in the direction of the silver pot as he crossed to the fireplace.

The coffee was every bit as black as he'd warned her it was, but she didn't dilute it with cream, for the moment preferring the strong brew. With cup in hand, she sat down in the nearest wing chair. Following her lead, Charlie Rainwater settled his wiry frame into its mate, both of them angled to face the diminutive attorney. He stood to one side of the blackened hearth, the top of his head barely reaching the marble lip of the tall mantel. She fixed her gaze on him, refusing to let it stray to the portrait that dominated the room and, currently, her thoughts.

'As you know from the documents I forwarded to you on Hattie's behalf,' the attorney began, 'Kell Morgan – christened Kelly Alexander Morgan – was born in 1860 on a small farm – although a Southerner would call it a plantation – outside of Hattiesburg, Mississippi. When the Civil War broke out, his father, Braxton Morgan, joined the Confederate Army and sent his wife and young son off to New Orleans to stay with his sister and her family. When that city fell into Union hands, she took her son and fled to an uncle's farm near Dallas, Texas. Approximately six months after the war ended, Braxton Morgan rejoined them . . . minus an arm and with a crippled leg. Needless to say, circumstances forced them to continue living with his wife's family. A year later, your great-grandfather, Christopher John Morgan, was born.'

'That was 1866,' Flame recalled the year that had appeared on the baptismal record.

'Yes.' He moved away from the fireplace, his short legs setting an ambling pace as he wandered toward the bookshelves that lined one full wall of the library. 'Much has been written about the Reconstruction years in the South, so it should suffice to say that they were rough times for children like your great-grandfather and his brother to be growing up. I don't know if you read between the lines in that obituary notice I sent you from a Dallas newspaper regarding the death of Braxton Morgan, but it seems he was killed during a drunken brawl – no doubt still defending the honour of the South. That was 1869. Two years later, his wife died, probably from exhaustion and overwork. To her uncle's credit, he kept both boys and raised them. Then, in 1875, Kell Morgan struck out on his own at the tender age of fifteen – although I suppose we should keep in mind that in those days that made him nearly a grown man.'

When he turned to gaze at the portrait, Flame's glance was drawn to it as well. She searched but couldn't find that stern and forbidding quality she'd first seen in his expression. Looking at the man in the painting now, all she could see was the pride and strength of an indomitable will stamped in his hard, angular features . . . that, and those dark eyes boring into her as if trying to press their will on her.

'He signed on as a drover to take a herd of longhorns north to the railhead at Wichita, Kansas,' Ben Canon went on. 'That was back in the heyday of the great cattle drives north. Which isn't to say that Texas cattle hadn't been driven to northern markets before then. They had – as far back as the 1850s. Most of them were brought up the Shawnee Trail, called the Texas Road by some. It cut right through the eastern half of the State and stretched from Texas all the way to St Louis. And a wide road, it was, too. It had to be to accommodate the military supply caravans, freight wagons, and the settlers' schooners that travelled over it.

'But it was the Chisholm Trail Kell Morgan went up that spring. It wasn't until late fall when he was heading home that he saw this part of the country for the first time.' Canon stared at the portrait, absently studying the man in the painting. 'I've often wondered what he thought when he topped that ridge of hills and saw this valley before him – lush with the autumn gold of its tall grass and bright with the silver shimmer of the narrow river running through it. With only three years of schooling he could barely read or write, so his impressions were never committed to paper. But he told Hattie the sight of the valley was an image that lived in his mind from that day on.'

Charlie Rainwater spoke up, nodding his head at the portrait. 'According to Miss Hattie, that painting didn't do him justice – not like seeing him in the flesh. He stood six foot one in his stockinged feet – and she claimed he had a pair of shoulders that were just about that wide. She said that every time she saw him he reminded her of a doubletree standin' on an upright shaft. And nobody ever called him Red – at least, not twice. No, he was always known as Kell Morgan.' His glance darted briefly to Flame. 'I never had the privilege of meeting him, you understand. He passed away long before I ever came to work here. But everybody I ever talked to said he was a hard man, but a fair one. As long as you were loyal to the brand, he'd stick by you right or wrong. Miss Hattie said he never smiled much – that he did all his talkin' with his eyes. When he was mad, they'd be as black as hell, but when he was happy, they'd glow ... like they was lit from inside. And he loved this land, too. He was out riding it and checkin' cattle right up to the day he died. Sixty-five, he was.'

The painting lost much of its one-dimensional quality, the smoky-blue haze of its background now projecting the tall, red-headed man in western clothes from the canvas. And that dark glow Charlie mentioned was in his eyes, those eyes that seemed to look directly at her.

'Although uneducated, Kell Morgan was an innately intelligent man – and a keen observer, too,' Ben Canon inserted, again taking charge. 'When he returned to Texas, he started noticing the changes in the making. The era of the open range was drawing to a close. Every year more and more fences were going up. And the long drives north to the railheads took valuable weight off cattle. Four years in a row, he made the long, arduous trek north with somebody else's longhorns. And each time, he stopped to look at his valley – and stayed longer on every trip.

'Now you have to remember that all this land belonged to the Creek Nation. And I use that term "nation" advisedly. The Creek land was a separate entity with its own boundaries, governed by its own laws. Back in the 1830s, the Federal government or more precisely, President Andrew Jackson, decided with typical arrogance that it would be in the best interest of the Five Civilised Tribes – the Creeks, the Cherokees, the Choctaws, the Chickasaws, and the Seminole – to give up their lands in the South that had been their home long before the first white man set foot on this continent, and move West to escape the corrupting influence of the whites. Through a series of nefarious treaties, they succeeded in removing them to this area.

'Now, according to Creek law and tradition, no individual held title to any given parcel of land. It was all owned in common. Which meant it was impossible for Kell Morgan to buy his valley outright. But during his trips here and his sojourns in the neighbouring Creek village of Tallahassee, which the cowboys on the trail dubbed Tulsi Town, he became acquainted with a politically influential mixed-blood Creek named George Perryman. Through him Kell Morgan succeeded in leasing his valley. With the money he'd put aside from his wages, he managed to buy one hundred head of scrub cattle, drove them north to his valley, wintered them on the rich grass, and made the short drive to market in the spring.' He paused, a certain slyness entering his grinning smile. 'That may not sound like much of a start to you unless you consider that he bought them at a price of seventy-five cents a head and sold them for over fifteen dollars a head. With his profits, he leased more land, bought more cattle, and repeated the process with the same results.

'By 1882, Kell Morgan was justly considered a cattle baron. Three years earlier, the U.S. Postal Service had opened its *Tulsa* Station, subtly changing the town's name once again. And by 1882, the Frisco Railroad had extended its line into Tulsa. No longer did Kell Morgan have to drive his cattle to the railhead; it had come to him.'

Without a break in his narrative, the balding attorney turned and scanned the rows of books on the two shelves directly in front of him. 'During all this time, he hadn't forgotten his little brother, Christopher, back in Texas. By then, Christopher wasn't little any more. He was a strapping lad of sixteen. With his newly acquired wealth, Kell sent him off to college in the East, determined that Christopher would have the education circumstances had denied him.' He extracted a wide volume from the shelf and flipped it open as he swung back toward Flame. 'When Christopher finished college with a degree in engineering, he returned here to Morgan's Walk. In that interim period, Kell had been adopted by the Creeks. Now with full rights to the valley – as full as any Creek had – he had Christopher design and build this house. Prior to that, the only structures had been a dog-trot cabin and a log bunkhouse for his cowhands.' Pausing beside Flame's chair, he handed her the leather-bound volume, an old photo album. 'Hattie thought you might like to see some pictures of your ancestors. Here's one of your great-grandfather, Christopher Morgan.'

His finger tapped the thick black paper directly above an old sepia print pasted on the page. A young man sat in a stiff pose, one large hand resting on his knee and the other holding a dark, wide-brimmed hat. He wore a dark suit and vest, the jacket opened to reveal the looping gleam of a gold watchfob and the white of a starched shirt collar tight around his throat. Although unsmiling, the expression on his smooth-shaven face conveyed an eagerness and a love of life. It wasn't closed and hard like the man in the portrait, although the strong, angular lines of their features were very similar. Their hair colour was different, of course. In the brown-tinted photograph, Christopher Morgan's appeared to be a light shade of brown with even lighter streaks running through it.

'You can tell they were brothers,' Flame remarked idly as she turned the page, curious to see more of the old photographs.

'Miss Hattie said back then they were as close as two brothers could be,' Charlie Rainwater declared with a faintly envious shake of his head. 'They weren't a lot alike, though. About as different as daylight and dark, I hear. But just like daylight and dark go together to make a whole day, that's the way it was with them.'

'In your great-grandfather's case, it was probably hero worship for his older brother,' Ben Canon added. 'And Kell Morgan probably saw in his younger brother the educated man he wished he could be. I understand there was a good deal of mutual sharing of knowledge – Christopher teaching him about history and philosophy and Kell giving him lessons in range lore.'

The next pages in the album contained photographs of the house under construction, some posed and some not. Flame was able to pick out Christopher Morgan in two of the pictures. Then she found a third photograph of the brothers. Side by side, the differences in their personalities were obvious – Kell Morgan looking impatient and uncomfortable and Christopher, happy and smiling.

'I don't understand.' Flame turned her frown of confusion to the attorney. 'If they were so close, why did Christopher Morgan leave and never come back?'

'I'm coming to that,' he assured her.

Impatiently she flipped to the next page, irritated by this air of mystery and dark secrets. She wished he'd get to the point of all this and stop dragging it out. Then her glance fell on the lone photograph on the facing page of black paper.

It was a picture of a young woman in period dress. Dainty and refined were the two adjectives that immediately sprang into Flame's mind. She looked as fragile as a china teacup, and Flame could easily imagine the elegant curl of her little finger when she sipped from one. Her dark hair was swept up at the sides, ringlets peeking from beneath the small brim of her high-crowned hat trimmed with ostrich feathers and shiny ribbons. Her heart-shaped face appeared ivory smooth and pale, needing no artifact of make-up to enhance its doll prettiness.

'This woman, who is she?' Flame glanced expectantly at the attorney.

He answered without looking at the photograph. 'Ann Compton Morgan, Kell Morgan's wife. You see, after the house was finished and all the furnishings arrived, Kell decided it was time he took a wife. Naturally not just any woman would do. He had a shopping list of requirements his future bride needed to fulfil. First of all, he wanted a woman with refinement and breeding, someone with culture and education, possessing style and grace – preferably pretty, but attractive would do. But, above all, she had to be the daughter of a family active in either politics, banking or railroads. In short, his wife had to be a lady and a valuable liaison.' Observing the disapproving arch of her eyebrow, Ben Canon smiled. 'As crude and chauvinistic as that might sound to you, you must remember that Kell Morgan was a pragmatic man. Christopher was the idealist.'

'Obviously,' she murmured.

'In the fall of '89, after the first great land run opened the so-called Unassigned Territory to homesteaders the previous spring, giving birth to the towns of Guthrie and Oklahoma City, Kell Morgan went to Kansas City to find his bride –'

'And his list went right out the window when he met Ann Compton,' Charlie Rainwater declared, punctuating it with a faint chortle of amusement as he pushed out of his chair and walked over to the tray to pour himself some coffee. 'Fell for her like he'd been shot out of the sky, he did,' he said, winking at Flame.

'Is that true?' Flame turned to the attorney for confirmation, not so much doubting Charlie's word as she was surprised by it. Kell Morgan seemed the type who would make a loveless marriage of convenience.

'Indeed he fell hopelessly in love with her. And from the standpoint that her father was a socially prominent physician in the community but without any important business connections in his family, she failed his major requirement in a wife. The fact that he married her anyway after a month-long whirlwind courtship, merely proves that, like most men, Kell Morgan had his weaknesses.'

He walked back to the bookshelves and removed a slim volume, bound in a rose-coloured cloth, its edges threadbare and worn. 'In every other respect, however, she was exactly what he'd wanted in a wife – an educated woman, well-versed in arts and literature, trained in the social graces, and extraordinarily pleasing to the eye. When you read the diaries she kept, you'll see that Kell Morgan swept her off her feet. Although what girl wouldn't be if she was ardently pursued by a handsome and rich cattle baron with a grand and stately mansion on the prairie waiting for the warmth of a woman to transform it into a home. There are frequent passages in her diary that deal with the romantic ideas she had about life on the frontier. She expected it to be an exciting adventure. And it would seem that Kell Morgan had made little effort to dispel those notions. He was too intent on winning her affections – and her hand in marriage.'

When he paused to draw in a deep breath, Flame had the feeling he was doing it purely for effect. 'Later, much later, he blamed himself for her disenchantment. Their first few months of married life here at Morgan's Walk were deliriously happy ones – according to her diary. Then, I suppose, the newness of her surroundings wore off. Nothing had prepared her for the tedium and isolation of ranch life – or the long hours, sometimes days at a time, she spent alone while her husband was out on the range. Growing up in the city, she was used to a constant round of teas, socials, cotillions, or friends stopping by to call. Here, she had no friends; visitors were few and far between; and her nearest neighbour was a half a day's buggy ride away. She had nothing in common with the sun-browned women who lived around her. Most of them had never seen a parasol before she came and knew nothing about the classics or chamber music. Naturally Tulsa was the closest town of any size, but the activities it offered – other than an occasional church social on a Sunday afternoon or parties at private homes – were geared more for the cattlemen in the area, eager to blow off steam on a Saturday; drink, gamble, and cavort with the town's soiled doves.'

Flame absently smoothed her hand over the diary's cloth cover. She, oddly, was reluctant to open the book and read the young woman's innermost thoughts. Somehow it seemed an invasion.

'From everything you've told me about her, I have the impression that she had a great deal more in common with Christopher than she did with her husband.' As she voiced her thoughts, it suddenly occurred to her. 'Is that what happened? Is she the reason he left and never came back?' Then she frowned, even more confused than before. 'What does all this have to do with the Stuarts?'

A smile of amused tolerance rounded the attorney's plump cheeks. 'You're getting ahead of me again, Flame.'

'It strikes me that Annie Morgan would never have been happy here.' Charlie Rainwater crossed to the fireplace and stood with one leg cocked and a hand propped on the smooth marble face as he gazed up at the portrait. 'Course, he always believed that she would have come to love it if she hadn't gotten with child that first year they were married.'

'Yes, the confinement of her pregnancy coupled with the loneliness and boredom she already felt merely added to her unhappiness,' Ben Canon agreed. 'Not even the joy of giving birth to a healthy baby the following year made up for it. That boy, by the way, was Hattie's father, Jonathan Robert Morgan,' he added in an aside, then continued. 'Naturally little Johnny had his own way of keeping Ann close to home, even though she was able to find a wet nurse for him. Kell did his best to keep her happy. All these books, the ebony piano in the parlour, a buggy of her own, and a matched team of high-stepping greys to pull it – he gave her everything but the one thing that might have helped – his company. As she frequently states in her diary, a son is no substitute for a husband. And by the early fall of 1893, you get a very real sense of her loneliness, dissatisfaction, and – desperation, I suppose.' He gestured briefly at the closed diary Flame held. 'Hattie has marked the page where the story begins.'

Flame hesitated, then glanced at the slim volume in her hands, belatedly noticing the thin, age-yellowed tassel draped over the back cover. A chainstitch of thin threads connected it to a hand-tatted bookmark inserted between the pages near the back of the diary. She resisted the attorney's subtle urging to read the woman's private journal, then realised this was part of the proof Hattie had promised.

Reluctantly she slid her fingers along the bookmark and opened the diary to the prescribed page. For a moment she stared at the small, neat handwriting, each letter precisely and perfectly formed. Then she began to read.

═ 22 ═

AUGUST 29, 1893

I am going! Kell has finally consented to let me accompany him when he takes the herd of horses to Guthrie to sell to the homesteaders who have gathered there to make the Run into the Cherokee Strip. He didn't say, but I know it was Chris who persuaded him to change his mind. He was adamant that I must remain at Morgan's Walk the last time we argued, insisting that such events attracted the worst as well as the best, that I despaired of him ever permitting me to go. How fortunate I am to have Chris for a brother-in-law. If he had not championed my cause, I am quite certain I would have gone mad if I had been forced to stay in this house all alone for two weeks.

My darling Johnny will have to remain here with Sarah. I shall miss him dreadfully, but the journey overland would be too much for a three-year-old. It's terrible to be pulled like this, wanting so much to go, yet hating so much to leave my son behind. But it will only be for two weeks.

It should be an experience quite beyond compare. Papa writes that his patients have talked of little else but the opening of the Cherokee Strip to settlers. I have heard that people are pouring in from all parts of the country to take part in the Run. Some are estimating that there may be as many as one hundred thousand people on the starting line when the gun goes off. One hundred thousand! And here I am, hungry for the sight of one.

September 9, 1893

At long last, we have arrived in Guthrie. There were times when I despaired we would ever make it. The heat was – and is – unbearable. It has not rained all summer and the dust is so thick it coats everything. All my travelling clothes are covered with it. I know I resembled a walking powder puff when I arrived at the hotel. Each step I took, dust billowed about me. I fear the rigours of outdoor life shall never be for me. I have been bounced and jarred, jolted and rattled until I marvel that all my bones are still connected. Chris knows how I suffered on that journey, but I dared not say a word to Kell. He would have sent me back to Morgan's Walk on the spot and I would have missed all this excitement. (Although I assure you I shall be making the return by train.)

Excitement there is in great abundance, too. The street outside our hotel window is crowded with people in every kind and type of conveyance imaginable. Many of the wagons have clever little sayings written on their canvas covers. We passed one that read:

'I won't be a sooner, but I'll get thar as soon as the soonest.'
And another said:

> *In God we trusted.*
> *In Texas we busted.*
> *But let 'er rip*
> *We'll make 'er in the Strip.*

The determination – the fervour that is on the faces of these people is something to see. Kell calls it land fever. It is definitely contagious for I feel the same restlessness of spirit. Kell has forbade me to leave the room unless he or Chris accompanies me. He says there are too many desperadoes, gamblers and swindlers in town, come to fleece these poor, unsuspecting homesteaders of their precious savings, and he fears for my safety should I venture out alone. Yet when I look out the window of our hotel room, I see whole families jammed in their wagons, young men on blooded horses, boys on ponies, old men on ambling gennets, and

— 205 —

women – yes, women, here to make the Run all alone! The
thought staggers me. Yet the ones I've seen seem to be a decent
sort – not at all the type one might expect to find.

As a matter of fact, a woman stopped us just as we were about
to enter the hotel. She looked to be in her late twenties and,
despite the layers of dust that clung to her, I could tell she was
stylishly dressed . . .

'Please, will you buy my hat?' The woman fumbled momentarily
with the lid to the hatbox she carried, then lifted it and produced
the hat from inside for Ann's inspection. 'It came all the way
from Chicago and I've only worn it twice. You can see it's just
like new.'

At first Ann drew back from the proffered hat and strange
woman accosting her on the sidewalk. Not that she could possibly
be in any danger, not when she was flanked by two tall, strong
men with Kell on one side of her and Chris on the other. Then
she saw the hat – red felt trimmed in red velvet and adorned with
feathers and grey satin ribbon. It was the perfect thing to wear
with her pearl grey dress.

'It's beautiful,' Ann declared, then looked again at the woman,
conscious all the while of the firm pressure of Kell's hand at her
elbow and his rigid stance of disapproval, but she wouldn't be
hurried inside. 'Why on earth would you want to sell it?'

'I . . .' The woman pushed the receding line of her chin a little
higher, asserting her pride. 'I need another five dollars to pay the
filing fee when I make my claim.'

'Where is your husband?' Kell demanded, much to Ann's embarrassment.

'I have none.'

A spinster. Ann looked at her pityingly, then realised what the
woman was saying. 'You aren't making the Run yourself?' This
was no sturdy farm woman with a complexion turned ruddy and
coarse by the sun. Both her manner and style of dress spoke of
gentility and education.

'Indeed I am,' she stated. 'I intend to have a place of my own –
become a woman of property.' Then she explained that she'd
been a teacher for the last eight years in the backwoods of Texas,
obliged to board with the parents of her pupils. 'I want to sleep
in my own bed, have my own curtains at the window, and cook

my meals on my own stove. And this is my one chance to do it. Please, will you buy my hat?'

. . . Kell bought the hat for me, although afterwards he said he shouldn't have encouraged her to go ahead with her foolhardy plan. He says that it will be a stampede when that gun goes off to start the Run. I'm quite sure he's right. I wonder at the daring she has. I know I could never be so bold as to do such a thing. Yet I understand the desperation I saw in her eyes, that need to break from a way of life she despises before it crushes her spirit completely.

It is nearly four o'clock and I am to meet Chris in the lobby on the hour. I think I shall wear my new hat.

There is so much more to tell. I hope I shall remember it all to write down later, but Chris awaits and I am anxious to be out of this room and among people again.

From the stairs' bottom step, Ann scanned the jumble of people crowded into the hotel's small lobby. With the red felt hat perched atop her freshened curls and a closed parasol in hand, she idly fanned her face with a lavender-drenched kerchief, and dabbed occasionally at the perspiration that gathered so readily on her upper lip. A fan turned overhead, yet it seemed to accomplish little beyond circulating the oppressive heat. She looked but there was no sign of Chris. Usually he was easy to spot in a crowd, like Kell, standing a good inch over six feet which put him head and shoulders above nearly everyone else. It wasn't like him to be late. Perhaps he'd stepped outside for some air. Ann decided to check.

Skirting the crowded lobby, Ann made her way to the double doors, propped open to admit any breeze that was stirring. Outside the hotel, the spectacle of the street greeted her once again. She had never seen anything like it in her whole life – cowboys mounted on snorting, half-tamed broncs, dudes in their checked suits and square-crowned bowlers, and women in their poke bonnets and worn gingham dresses riding in buckboards and prairie schooners crammed with all their possessions. The constant stream of traffic churned the dust and created a cloud that hugged the ground. And the rumble of wagons, the rattle of trace chains, the thunder of hooves, the creak of leather, the crack of the whips, the shouted curses of the drivers all combined to assault the ears, just as the stench of sweating bodies, man and animal, combined to assault the nose.

Ann pressed the lavender-scented kerchief close to her nose and looked about the boardwalk outside the hotel's entrance for Chris. But there was only one man in front of the hotel. Dressed in a black waistcoat and black hat, he stood at the edge of the walk facing the street. He was tall, but not as tall as Chris. Nor were his shoulders as wide. And his hair did not possess the gold streaks the summer sun had put in Chris's. Rather, it was black, that deep shining black of a raven. He turned his head to look at something up the street, giving her a side view of his clean-shaven face. Then, as if sensing her gaze, he turned the rest of the way, the satin brocade of his grey vest gleaming between the parted front of his waistcoat.

Excitement fluttered in her breast. He was quite the handsomest man she had ever seen – and a gentleman, too, judging by his dress. But it was definitely improper for a married woman to be staring at a strange man. With a guilty flush, Ann looked away and attempted to cover her momentary confusion by opening her parasol. As she extended it to one side of her, a stout man in a tweed suit and bowler hat chose that moment to exit the hotel. He walked right into it, knocking it out of her hands.

With her mouth open in dismay, Ann watched it land on the sidewalk practically at the man's feet. She saw him look at it, and observed the faint smile that tugged at one corner of his mouth – and wanted to die of pure mortification. She rushed to retrieve it, ignoring the profuse apologies offered to her by the man who had knocked the parasol from her grasp.

Before she could stoop to pick it up, a black-sleeved arm reached down. 'Allow me.' The warm, low pitch of his voice seemed to vibrate right through her.

Immediately she straightened to stand erect and struggled to regain her composure, succeeding to a degree. Her opinion of his looks didn't change when they finally faced each other. If anything it intensified when she encountered the deep blue of his eyes, darkly outlined by thick, male lashes as black as the wings of his brow.

'Thank you.' She held out her hand for the parasol.

But he didn't immediately give it back to her. Instead he opened it first, then returned it, angled to shade her face from the late afternoon sunlight. The look in his eyes was much too familiar as his gaze wandered over her face.

'It would be a sin, indeed, for the sun to damage skin such as yours. I have not seen the likes of it since I was in St Louis a year ago.' Unexpectedly he reached up and lightly trailed a finger across her cheek. 'It's as creamy white and smooth as a magnolia petal.'

She knew she should object to such effrontery. At the very least, she should be shocked by it. But shock didn't accurately describe her tingling reaction. Thankfully she had the good sense not to comment on either his remark or his feathery caress of her cheek. And she hoped her silence on the matter would correct any wrong impression she might have given.

'Are you here to make the Run?' he asked.

'Gracious, no.' She laughed, mostly to release some of the unbearable tension that gripped her. 'My husband is here to sell some of our horses to the settlers.'

'I am envious.'

'Sir?' She blinked at him in confusion, then fought the sensation that his gaze was absorbing her whole.

'I would be envious of any man who has the honour of calling such a rare and beautiful flower his wife.'

Flustered, she lowered her gaze and attempted a cool, 'You flatter me, sir.'

He cocked his head at a denying angle. 'Truth is never flattery. And it is the truth when I say that you are a rare and beautiful flower, one that a man doesn't expect to find out here on the prairie.'

Nor did she want to be here. She hated its emptiness, its isolation, and its rustic society. She longed for the lawn parties, the literary teas, and the cultural pleasures she'd left behind in Kansas City. Once more she wanted to sit at a dinner party where the guests didn't belch or tuck the napery over their shirts or talk about cows and shipping rates or the bank panic.

Suddenly aware of the lengthening pause, Ann murmured a quick, 'I suppose not,' then smiled with forced brightness. 'I shall tell my husband that when I see him. I'm sure he'll find your observation quite interesting.'

'You're meeting him?'

'No. That is, his brother is meeting me here. Kell . . . my husband will join us later for dinner.'

'Kell. That's his name.'

'Kell Morgan, yes. Do you know him?' she asked curiously.

'I know *of* him,' he replied, carefully qualifying his answer. 'But then, there are few in the territory who have not heard of Morgan's Walk. That is your home, isn't it, Mrs Morgan?'

'Yes.' She held her breath for an instant, wondered if she dared to ask. 'And you are?'

'Jackson Lee Stuart.' He touched the brim of his hat. 'At your service . . . any time.'

A trio of riders raced up the street, whipping their horses and ki-yipping at the top of their lungs as if the race for land on the Cherokee Strip had begun. Distracted by the commotion, Ann glanced at the street and immediately spotted Chris riding toward the hotel. Regret swept through her, sharp and poignant. She knew his arrival would signal the end of her meeting with Mr Jackson Lee Stuart and she didn't want it to be over – not yet.

She forced a bright smile on to her face. 'There comes my brother-in-law now.'

Jackson Stuart looked over his shoulder, then turned back to her. 'Now that you have another protector to look after you, I will take my leave.'

'It has been a pleasure, Mr Stuart.' Automatically she offered him her hand in parting.

'If the fates are kind, we'll meet again.' Her heart skipped a beat or two as he bowed slightly and carried her gloved hand to his lips, his blue eyes holding her gaze. Instead of kissing the back of it, he turned it over and pressed a kiss into the very centre of her palm. She was quite breathless with shock – and that guilty feeling of forbidden pleasure, when he straightened and released her hand. 'Let us hope that they are.'

She couldn't agree to that, not out loud. With a tip of his dark hat to her, he moved off, joining the stream of pedestrians on the boardwalk. With an effort, Ann tore her gaze from him and crossed to the edge of the walk to greet Chris as he dismounted.

'At last you're here,' she declared gaily. 'I was about to decide you'd forgotten me.'

'Never.' Smiling, he looped the reins around the hitching rack and gave them a quick tie, then joined her on the walk. 'But what are you doing out here? I thought we agreed to meet in the lobby.'

'We did.' She switched the parasol to her other shoulder as she linked her arm with his. 'But you weren't there when I came down so I stepped outside to look for you.'

'That wasn't wise, Ann. Didn't I see a man talking to you when I rode up?'

She had difficulty meeting his gaze, and chided herself for feeling so absurdly guilty. She had done absolutely nothing to be ashamed of.

'Yes,' she admitted, quite openly. 'He retrieved my parasol after some passer-by had knocked it from my hand. He was very polite.'

'Just the same, you shouldn't venture out alone. Kell's right. This town is filled with cardsharks and swindlers.'

'I'm sure he is.' Just for an instant, she was angry. She turned on Chris, unleashing her frustrations on him as she always did. 'But I didn't endure that horrid trip just to trade one prison for another. You might as well know that I have no intention of spending my entire time here in that hotel room alone. I want to get out and see things – and do things. So much is happening . . . there's so much excitement. I want to be part of it, Chris.'

'I know.' He covered the hand that gripped his forearm and gave it an understanding squeeze.

Ann looked up, realising that she could always count on his sympathy. Dear, wonderful Chris, so like Kell in looks, yet so unlike him. Both had the same strong features and dark eyes, but on Kell they were hard and cold whereas on Chris, they had a gentleness, a sunniness that matched the dark gold of his hair. She could tell him anything and he would understand.

'Kell worries about you, Ann,' he said. 'You can't blame him. He loves you.'

'I know.' She lowered her gaze, realising that she could tell him anything, but not necessarily everything, and definitely not about Jackson Stuart.

How odd that such a brief meeting should linger in my mind this way. I wonder if I shall see Mr Stuart again. Is it wrong of me to hope that I do?

I must end this. Kell calls me to bed.

— 211 —

The horses are selling well now that Kell has moved the herd twenty miles north to the small town of Orlando. That is where the registration booth is located for this area so all the settlers have gathered there to sign up for the Run. Kell keeps the horses groomed and grained, so they look sleek and fast. Already he has sold all but ten of the one hundred horses he brought. Which is truly remarkable when one considers that he sells them for two hundred dollars each. Six months ago he asked thirty dollars a head for the same stock!

Now that the horses have become such valuable steeds, guard must be kept on them at all times. And with literally thousands of people crowded into that small community, there are no accommodations available so I have been obliged to remain here at the hotel in Guthrie. Either Chris or Kell rides the twenty miles back every night so that I at least have company for breakfast and dinner.

I chafed so at being forced to rely on newspaper accounts to know what was happening outside my hotel door that Kell finally consented and allowed me to accompany him to Orlando today and see for myself the spectacle of all the 'strippers' – that is what the newspapers are calling the settlers intent on making the Run on to the Cherokee Strip.

I admit that within minutes of embarking on the journey to Orlando, I questioned the wisdom of it. The temperature soared to one hundred degrees in the shade – if one could find any. And a wind blew constantly, as hot and dry as everything else. Need I mention that the dust was unbearable. I can still feel the grit of it on my skin.

But the sight I beheld at the end of the morning's journey staggers my mind even now. Tents were pitched everywhere, transforming the prairie into a sea of brown canvas that rippled like waves in the incessant wind. And there were vehicles of every shape, size, and description – buckboards, covered wagons, buggies, pony carts, even a racing sulky. I read that there may be as many as ten thousand people camped at Orlando. To me the number seemed much larger than that. Add to all that teeming humanity, their animals and the entire scene becomes one beyond words.

Most pitiful of all, however, were the hundreds upon hundreds of people waiting in line to register. Some had been in line for as much as forty-eight hours. They dared not leave or they'd lose their place in line. And it was a line that grew by the hour instead of diminishing as the ones in front received their certificates. How they could stand there hour after hour in that infernal heat with gale winds swirling that choking dust around them – with not a speck of shade to offer them a respite from the blazing sun – I shall never know. Many succumbed to the heat, collapsing into the dust where they stood. It was a sight that would have torn at my poor papa's heart – especially the women. One was the woman who sold me her hat. She had changed so that I barely recognised her . . .

Ann pulled back on the buggy reins and stared at the woman in the torn and bedraggled gown. Her face was black with a mixture of dirt, sweat, and tears that had caked, melted and caked again. Her hair hung in a lank, tangled mess about her shoulders. Ann couldn't believe it was the same woman. But it had to be. That brightly beaded reticule, clutched tightly in both hands, was the same as the one in which the woman had put that five dollars that Kell had given her for the hat. It was doubtful that there could possibly be two like it.

The woman turned her head and stared at the hooded buggy with blank, bloodshot eyes. Then, as Ann watched, the woman's pupils rolled back and she sank to the ground in a heap. Ann gasped in horror, and that horror increased when she realised that no one was going to risk losing their place in line to come to the woman's aid. Hastily she wound the reins around the whipstand, gathered up her skirts and clambered from the buggy, not taking the time to call to the cowboy Kell had detailed to escort her.

She ran to the woman and knelt in the dirt beside her, for the moment mindless of the heat and the blinding dust. She tried to lift her off the hard ground and cradle her in her arms, but the woman was too heavy for her.

'Please.' She scrambled to her feet and appealed to the others in line. 'Someone get a doctor. There must be one in town. She's fainted from the heat. She needs help.'

'Here.' The man in front of her shoved a dirty blanket into her hands. 'Wad that up and stick it under her head. She'll come around in a few minutes.'

Stunned by his callous indifference to the woman's plight, Ann stared at him, but he turned his back on her and shuffled forward as the line moved its foot at a time. Ann turned to the next man as he started to walk around her and rejoin the moving line.

'No.' Impulsively she caught at his arm. 'You can't walk by like that.'

He stared at her with red-rimmed eyes. 'You sure as hell ain't gonna stop me, missy. An' yo' ain't gonna steal her place in line neither. If yo' want to register, you can just git yore fancy ass to the back of the line.' His talon-like fingers dug into her shoulder and gave her a rough push towards the rear, the suddenness and the violence of it sending her sprawling hands first into the dirt.

Shocked as much by his vulgarity as by his roughness, Ann lay there for a stunned instant then pushed up on her knees just as a big black stallion slid to a prancing stop not three feet from her. A man vaulted from the saddle. Her heart somersaulted at the sight of Jackson Stuart, jacketless in the heat with just a thin cotton shirt, wet with perspiration, covering his arms and torso.

He was at her side in a stride, catching her by the shoulders and pulled her upright as if she weighed no more than thistledown. 'Are you all right, Mrs Morgan?' His hat was pulled low on his forehead, its brim shading the gleaming bronze of his face and intensifying the sharp blue of his eyes.

'I'm ... fine.' She nodded shakily, aware that her hat was askew and her beautiful gown was smudged with dirt. As she reached down to brush uselessly at the dust, Ann noticed the holstered gun strapped to his hip. She was surprised to see him wearing one. Kell, yes – a gun fit him as naturally as the hardness of this land, but not Jackson Stuart. It was the moment's pause the gun gave her that kept her from mentioning the unconscious woman lying on the ground only a few feet away.

And in that moment, Jackson Stuart spun around and grabbed the man who had shoved her. 'I believe you owe the lady an apology.' There was a coldness in his voice that stunned Ann, but the man just looked at him with torpid eyes, his senses too dulled by the heat to catch the threatening tone. In a lightning move too quick for Ann to detect any singleness of action, the gun was in his hand, the muzzle pressed under the point of the man's chin and the hammer was back. 'I said – you owe the lady an apology, mister.'

Suddenly everything was still around her except the wind-swirled dust. Someone up the line called out, 'Better do it, Joe. That's Blackjack Stuart.'

What did that mean? Was he some sort of desperado? Ann stared at him in confusion, barely noticing at all the poor settler's wide-eyed look of alarm as he stammered out an apology.

'That's better.' Jackson Stuart smiled smoothly and gently eased the hammer down, then released the man and holstered his gun all in one fluid motion. When he turned to Ann, his look was warmly apologetic. 'Sorry. Sometimes they need to be reminded of their manners.'

'Of course,' she murmured, not knowing what else to say. 'Please, there's a woman over here suffering from heatstroke. We need to get her out of the sun – and to a doctor if there is one.'

'There's a tent down the way that passes for an infirmary. We can take her there.' He crouched down on one knee beside the unconscious woman, his hands tunnelling under her shoulders and her skirts to pick her up.

'Put her in my buggy,' Ann instructed as her escort came riding up.

'Sorry, Mrs Morgan. I didn't see you stop.' The cowboy grabbed at the creased front of his hat brim in a quick gesture of respect, then struggled to control his mount as it shied away from the flapping skirts of the woman Jackson Stuart carried. 'What happened?'

'This woman collapsed. We're taking her to the doctor.'

Jackson Stuart nodded in the direction of the black stallion, standing quietly with its reins dragging the ground. 'Tie my horse to the back of the buggy. And if you've got any water in that canteen, we'll need it.'

'Yes, sir.' He untied the canteen from the saddle and handed it to Ann, then walked his horse over to the stallion and scooped up the trailing reins.

Ann climbed into the buggy unaided, then turned to help Jackson manoeuvre the woman on to the seat. She was limp as a rag doll in Ann's arms. Then Jackson Stuart crowded on to the buggy seat and relieved her of the heavy burden.

'Open the canteen for me,' he said.

Ann removed its cap and handed it to him, watching as he held it to the woman's parched and cracked lips tipping it slightly to let the warm water trickle into her mouth. He was so gentle with the woman that Ann found it difficult to conceive that a moment ago this same man had held a gun to a man's head. He didn't look at all sinister. In fact, were it not for the absence of a jacket, he had the appearance of a polished gentleman – and an extraordinarily handsome one at that.

'Here.' He gave her back the canteen, then loosened the yellow neckerchief from around his throat and pulled it free. 'Wet this for me. We'll see if we can't cool her down a bit – and get some of this dirt off her face.'

The smile he flashed her was the sharing kind that made her feel warm inside – just like the sound of 'we'. It was the two of them helping, but Ann hadn't thought of it that way until he'd said it. Quickly, she moistened the cloth, then gently bathed the woman's face with it.

The woman stirred, roused perhaps by the coolness of the water on her hot skin or the shade of the buggy's protruding hood. 'Where . . . Where am I? What happened?' Feebly, she lifted a hand, her eyes still glazed.

'Ssh. You fainted,' Ann explained softly, glancing briefly at Jackson as he reached forward and unlooped the buggy reins with one hand, giving them a slap. The buggy lurched forward. 'We're taking you to the doctor. You'll be fine.'

'No,' she moaned, her head rolling from side to side. 'I can't. My place . . . I'll lose my place . . . No,' she sobbed, her arms reaching, her body lifting with its last bit of strength to get back to the line.

'Stop it. You're in no condition to go back there.' Half-frightened by the woman's crazed reaction Ann tried to make her lie still, pushing her back against the buggy seat.

The woman tried to resist, but the effort was too much. Instead her dirty-nailed hands clutched at Ann's gown. 'My land,' she whimpered, her shoulders shaking with great, silent sobs. 'I was so close . . . so close.' Her voice was so faint Ann had to strain to hear it above the hot, blowing wind and the constant din of the settlers' camp. 'It would have . . . been my turn.'

Ann pried herself loose from the woman's clutches and poured more water from the canteen on to the already damp cloth, the rolling bounce of the buggy causing her to spill some of it on her skirt. She darted a quick look ahead of them, then swung it to Jackson. 'How much farther is it?' She was a doctor's daughter, but she'd never had to cope with a sick person. 'She's out of her head, raving on about losing her place in line and her land. She needs quiet and rest, but I can't make her calm down.' There was an edge of panic in her voice, part of it picked up from the woman and part of it from her own sense of helplessness.

'Here.' He took a slip of paper from his pocket and handed it to Ann. 'Give her that. It'll quiet her.'

'What is it?' Ann frowned at him.

'A registration certificate.' He whoaed the grey, stopping the buggy in front of an open-sided tent. 'That's what she was stand-ing in line to get so she could legally make the Run on Saturday.' He wrapped the reins around the whipstand and swung to the ground, then turned back.

'But' – she remembered the line of people standing in the blaz-ing afternoon heat, a line that got longer instead of shorter – 'it's yours.'

His mouth quirked in a quick smile as he reached to lift the semi-conscious woman from the buggy. 'I'll get another.'

He hefted the woman from the buggy seat and cradled her limp weight in his arms. Belatedly, Ann stoppered the canteen and scrambled down to join him, fighting her layers of skirts and ignoring the outstretched hand of her dismounted escort rider. The precious slip of paper was still clutched in her gloved hand when she reached Stuart's side.

'How will you get another?' she repeated. 'You surely aren't going to stand in that line?'

His glance moved over her face, taking in the concern for him. The sight of it pleased him and he toyed with the idea of letting her worry a little longer, then decided against it.

'It isn't necessary, not if you have the cash to spare to buy one. You'd be surprised how many people in that line sell their certifi-cate after they get it, then go back and do it over again.'

'Why?' She couldn't imagine anyone enduring the agony of that line.

'To make extra money.' He carried the woman inside the tent

and laid her on an empty cot. Mumbling more protests, she tried to rise, but he gently pushed her back on to the cot, then took the slip of paper from Ann and folded the woman's fingers around it. 'Here's your certificate.'

With an effort the woman focused her reddened eyes on it. Relief cracked through her dirt-streaked face as all resistance went out of her.

'Thank you,' she whispered, her body shuddering with dry sobs, but there was no welling of tears in her eyes. She had none to spare.

'I'll put it in your bag.' He loosened the beaded, drawstring pouch looped around her wrist and tucked the certificate inside, then placed the reticule in her hand, closing her fingers around it. She clutched the small bag tightly to her breast and closed her eyes.

A man with shirtsleeves rolled and a checked vest straining to surround his protruding belly wandered over to the cot, mopping the perspiration that streamed down his bewhiskered jowls. With an air of disinterest, he looked down at the woman.

'Sunstroke,' he grunted, then looked at the two of them. 'Are you kin?'

'No,' Ann replied. 'I believe she's here alone.'

'Another single woman.' He grimaced tiredly. 'It's hardest on them. Chivalry vanished out here after the first day. Now it's everyone for him- – or her- – self.' He ran the sweat-damp handkerchief around the inside collar of his shirt. 'What's her name?'

'I don't know,' Ann realised with a trace of chagrin.

He sighed and shook his head, something wry and cynical in the smile that twisted his mouth. 'I had a man die of sunstroke earlier today. We're still tryin' to find somebody that knows his name.' Then he seemed to gather up some energy. 'Well, you done your share. Now I'll do what I can for her. Won't be much. I haven't got any help here. Nobody does. They all quit to make the Run and get a piece of land of their own – or die tryin'.'

He took hold of the woman's wrist, locating her pulse as he pulled a gold watch from his vest pocket and flipped it open. His air of unconcern chilled Ann. Where was his compassion? His solicitude? Sapped from him by this sweltering prairie as it had been from the others in the line?

'He's right, Mrs Morgan. There's nothing more you can do for

— 218 —

her.' Jackson Stuart's hand lightly gripped the back of her arm, its faintly insistent pressure urging her to leave.

She let him steer her from the tent, then halted outside its supporting poles, still within the shade of its canvas. The buffeting wind pushed at her, its breath hot like the blast from a furnace. Settlers plodded by, their heads bowed, their shoulders hunched against the wind, and their faces blurred by the haze of dust.

'All these people,' she murmured. 'Half of the ones I saw in the line looked like they belonged in the infirmary. How do they endure these conditions?'

'I've been told it's worse along the Kansas border at Arkansas City. Two, maybe three times as many settlers are gathered there. In just one day fifty collapsed from the heat, and six of those died before nightfall.'

She turned to him. 'Why? Why do they do it?'

His gaze was turned outward, thoughtfully surveying the scene. At her question, he directed it to her. 'For a piece of land to call their own, what else?' The corners of his mouth deepened in wry amusement. 'You should see them at night, sitting around their camp-fires, poring over maps of the Strip, studying every wind and bend of a river or creek, deciding which plot of ground they're going to claim, tracing a route to it, then memorising the terrain around it so they can find it once the race begins . . . assuming, of course, that someone else doesn't get there first. It's all they talk about – all they think about – all that keeps them going.'

'But why?' She remembered the woman he'd just carried inside – dirty, bedraggled, half-dead from the heat, yet she'd been frantic to get back in that line. She hadn't cared about her dishevelled appearance or the grime and sweat that blackened her face or the agony of standing hour after hour in the full sun – not as long as she got that silly scrap of paper. 'Why does it mean so much?'

He gave her a long, considering look, then once again faced the dusty scene before them. 'You're looking at the losers of this country, Mrs Morgan, the losers and the dispossessed. Former slaves from the South, and Johnny Rebs who came back to burned-out homes and Reconstruction, and the people who came West too late to get the rich lands in Iowa, Kansas and Missouri – or else tried and failed. This is the only cheap land left for them, the only place where a man or a woman can file a homestead claim on as much as one hundred and sixty acres for as little as one dollar an acre depending on the location of their claim. This is the only chance a store clerk, a school teacher or a livery boy has to own a piece of land. This whole territory is being settled by losers. They have nowhere else to go, and they know it. If they don't get their chunk of ground here, they likely never will. That's why they're so desperate – why they cling so tenaciously to those certificates.' He paused briefly. 'It's no place for the faint of heart, though.'

'No,' she murmured in absent agreement, recognising that she was one of them. She hadn't been faint of heart, not in the beginning. When she'd married Kell, she had been as eager and excited as these people were about her new life on the frontier, thinking it would be one long adventure. 'But they don't know what it's like here. They don't know how isolated, how monotonous – how very primitive it is,' she declared, inwardly longing for the life she'd left behind in Kansas City.

Jackson Stuart wasn't surprised by the undercurrents of dissatisfaction and despair in her voice. He'd pegged her from the start as an unhappy woman left too much alone. And the interest – the curiosity she'd shown towards him outside the hotel that afternoon in Guthrie had merely confirmed it. A contented woman might have cast an admiring glance his way, but she wouldn't have been curious. More than that, she wouldn't have had that hunger for attention in her eyes.

No, the mistress of Morgan's Walk was a very lonely and unhappy woman. Which raised some very interesting possibilities.

'Why are you here?' Ann stared, recognising that he wasn't like the others. He was too aloof, too detached from all this. Yet he'd had a registration certificate. 'Is it the land you want, too?'

'It's the sport of it that's drawn me here, I guess. The high-stakes gamble of it. It's a race of sorts – with the prize going to the fleetest, the cleverest, and the luckiest. And, it's going to take all three – a fast horse, smart riding, and Lady Luck riding on our shoulder – to claim the choice sites, especially the town lots.' He carefully avoided mentioning that nearly every would-be settler had brought their life savings with them – and that the sack in his saddlebags contained nearly two thousand dollars he'd managed to glean from them in the past two days during friendly games of chance.

'Is that what you want? A town lot?'

'Yes.'

'What will you do with it?'

'More than likely sell it to someone who arrived too late to claim one for himself – at a profit, of course.'

'Then you won't build on it?'

'No.'

'Exactly what is it that you do, Mr Stuart?' She tilted her head to one side, regarding him curiously. 'Back there, some man referred to you as "Blackjack" Stuart.'

'I'm a gambler by profession, Mrs Morgan, and *vingt-et-un*, better known as blackjack is my game . . . hence the name.'

'I see,' she murmured.

'I doubt that you do, Mrs Morgan. A gambler's life is a lonely one. It isn't without compensations, however, for I have travelled the length and breadth of this country. St Louis, San Francisco, New Orleans, New York . . . I've been to them all at one time or another – stayed at the finest hotels, dined at the best establishments, smoked imported cigars, and supped the best wines. Diamond stickpins, suits from a St Louis tailor – I even own the fastest horse in the territory.' He nodded his head in the direction of the black stallion tied behind the buggy, impatiently pawing at the ground. 'But all of life's luxuries are meaningless if you have to enjoy them alone.'

'I . . . I have heard that said before.' She tried not to let him see how much his words echoed her feelings.

'It's been my fate to be extraordinarily lucky at cards, but a woman's love has always eluded me.'

'I find that very difficult to believe. Mr Stuart. Forgive my boldness, but you are a handsome man. I'm quite sure you could have your choice of women.'

'But it's been my misfortune that when I have found a woman I could love, she already belongs to someone else.'

. . . And he was looking directly into my eyes when he said that. It flustered me so, that I must admit I could think of no suitable reply. Although he didn't actually say that woman was I, his meaning was unmistakable. Under the circumstances, I had no choice but to take my leave of him. To stay might have led him to think I would welcome his advances. Which I did not. I am, after all, a married woman. Yet I did feel pleasure that another

— 221 —

man – a stranger – could be attracted to me. I expect that is terribly vain of me to say, but it's true all the same.

The most exciting thing has happened. Kell has secured seats for us on one of the passenger coaches. I shall get to see the start of the great Run after all. There has been so much confusion and rumour of late, saying first the trains will run, then they won't, then they will but only settlers with certificates can board – that I began to doubt I would witness the launching of these hordes of settlers. What a bitter disappointment that would have been too, after spending this entire week here in Guthrie, caught up in the contagion – the madness – of the pending land rush, then not to see this moment in history.

Now I shall. Unfortunately Kell wasn't able to arrange for us to have a private car. They aren't allowed for some reason. I expect the authorities fear the owners of the private cars will profit from them by selling space to settlers and, thus, deprive the railroad company of revenue. Nevertheless we are going. I wonder if I shall see Jackson Stuart.

Cordoned from the crush of fellow sightseers by a human wall of a half-dozen cowboys from the ranch, Ann sat on the very edge of her seat, facing the train's open window. She was certain that nothing in the annals of history could compare with the sight before her. Covered wagons, light buggies, two-wheeled cars, sulkies, horses and riders, heavy wagons drawn by oxen, and a few foolhardy souls on foot, stretched in a ragged column as far as the eye could see – and each one positioned so close to the other that there wasn't space to walk between them.

On the train itself – three locomotives strong with forty-two cars in tow – there was barely room to breathe, let alone move. Settlers bound for the Strip literally packed the cattle cars with more hanging off the slatted sides and piled on top of the cars. Not two windows from her seat, a man clung to the windowsill, his feet on a crossbar.

Just recalling the insane scramble that had ensued when the settlers had been allowed to board the train drew a shudder. It had been a veritable stampede, with everyone pushing and shoving, grabbing at anything and tearing clothes, knocking people down then trampling on them in ruthless disregard of age or sex. And there had been naught the poor trainmen and officials could do but stand back or be bowled over.

Now they all waited as the sun steadily climbed higher in the sky. Stationed in front of the endless long line, troopers of the U.S. Cavalry sat their horses, standing guard until the appointed hour. Although, according to Kell, their presence hadn't been particularly effective the night before when hundreds of so-called 'sooners' had eluded the cavalry patrols and illegally slipped across the line under the cover of darkness to lay claim on the choicest parcels 'sooner' than anyone else.

'It's almost time, isn't it, Kell?' She gripped the fingers of his hand a little tighter, unable to take her eyes from the scene. So many people, yet all of them so still, so quiet, so tense, bodies and hearts straining – she could feel it. Unconsciously, she held her breath.

'Almost,' he confirmed.

At precisely high noon, the eight million acres known variously as the Cherokee Strip or the Cherokee Outlet, would be thrown open to settlement. The morning newspaper claimed that over one hundred thousand settlers would enter the Strip from various gathering points along the northern and southern boundaries.

In the unearthly silence of the moment, the pounding of her heart sounded louder than the puffing chug of the idling train. Here and there an impatient steed pawed the ground or champed restlessly on the bit in its mouth. Noises that once would have been lost in the din of the thousands gathered here now seemed unnaturally loud, jangling nerves already thin with stress. Again, Ann scanned that long ragged line, certain that Jackson Stuart was among them somewhere – but where?

A hundred yards distant, a horse reared and lunged ahead of the column, the bright sunlight glinting on its shiny black neck, wet with sweat. The man upon its back effortlessly wheeled the anxious animal back into line – a man wearing a black hat and a gun strapped to his side, like so many of the other riders. Although she had only a brief glimpse of him before he was swallowed up by the line, Ann felt certain it was Jackson Stuart. She leaned closer to the window, trying to locate him again.

As the trumpeter blew the first sweet, swelling notes on his bugle, the staccato crack of rifle fire broke all the way up and down the line. Instantly the jagged line erupted, bursting forward in a seething rush of humanity. The thunder of thousands of pounding hooves, the rumble of rolling wheels, the rattle of moving wagons, the shriek of the locomotives' whistles, the neighs of panicked horses, and the yells, shouts, curses, and screams of the settlers all melded together into one terrific roar – a roar of agony and madness suddenly unleashed on the world, frightening in its fierceness and stunning in its volume. Red dust rose in a mighty cloud, momentarily enveloping the stampeding horde that left in its wake overturned wagons, fallen horses and downed riders.

Paralysed by the sight and sound of it, Ann stared. For an instant she was certain that all had been swept away by the red billowing sand. Then a scattered line of horsemen broke from the devilish cloud and raced with the wind ahead of it. And one of them – yes, one of them was Jackson Stuart. The fear that had knotted her nerves dissolved in a rush of relief. He was safe. More than that, he was in front, streaking across the prairie on his swift black stallion.

More and more wagons and riders emerged from the settling dust cloud and fanned across the empty plains, the horrendous din from their numbers fading to a rumble dominated by the fierce chugging of the train. Talk broke behind her in a flurry of awed comments.

'So many dreams racing across that prairie,' Chris murmured.

'But more than dreams will die before this day is over,' Kell replied in a hard, dry voice.

Jackson Stuart wouldn't be one of them. He was there in front, leading the way. He would succeed. Others might fail, but not he. Swept by a feeling of elation, Ann swung from the window to face her husband.

'It was glorious, Kell. Simply glorious. A sight never to be forgotten. An experience I wouldn't have missed for the world.' So much danger and excitement – observed from a safe distance, it was true, yet she'd been part of the moment, feeling the heat and the wind, the heart-pounding tension and strain, the thunderous roar of the masses and panicked need for speed.

'Then I'm glad I brought you with me.' His mouth curved

slightly in one of his rare smiles. 'Tomorrow we'll head home –
back to Morgan's Walk – and enjoy a little peace and quiet for a
change.'

*He looked at me with so much love in his eyes that I felt ashamed
of myself for wishing, even briefly, that we didn't have to return.
What is wrong with me? I long to see my son again and hold him
in my arms, yet I loathe the thought of spending day after day in
that house again.*

= 23 =

A BLOTCH OF ink stained the remaining third of the page, giving Flame the impression that Ann Morgan had cast the pen down in agitation and frustration. She felt the same tormented mix of emotions, the same sense of dread. She had no desire to read more, certain that she could guess the rest of it.

As she started to close the diary, she was pulled sharply back to the present by Ben Canon's remark, 'Interesting reading, isn't it?'

'Yes,' she responded automatically, suddenly aware of the cheery crackle of the fire blazing brightly in the fireplace and the pungent aroma of pipesmoke drifting through the air.

Window panes, darkened by the shadows of evening beyond them, reflected the light from the lamps that had been turned on. From some other part of the house came the muted bong of a clock, slowly tolling the hour. Flame wondered if Ann Morgan had listened to that same bell mark hour after hour in this house.

'Would you like another cup of coffee, Flame?' The attorney stood next to the massive marble fireplace, a briar pipe loosely cupped in his hand. He used the chewed stem to point to the silver coffee service. 'I made a fresh pot so I can guarantee it won't be as strong as the last.'

A smile rounded his shiny cheeks, but the bright twinkle in his eyes had a sly look to it. Each time she looked at him, Flame expected to see pointy ears poking through the fringe of hair that ringed his bald crown. It was a bit of a surprise when she didn't.

'If you're gettin' hungry' – Charlie Rainwater volunteered, comfortably ensconced in the twin to her chair, positioned close to the hearth – 'they'll be bringin' sandwiches from over the cookshack in another hour or so.'

'No, I don't care for anything.' She glanced down at the partially closed diary on her lap, the pages held apart by the finger she'd wedged between them. 'And I don't think it's necessary to read any more of this journal. Obviously she abandoned her husband and ran off with this – Jackson Stuart.'

'Nothing is obvious,' Ban Canon asserted with a certain knowing quality. 'I suggest you read a little further. If you've passed the part about the land rush, then skip ahead to the month of – November, I believe it was, somewhere around the tenth.'

Irritation rippled through her. 'Wouldn't it be quicker and simpler if you just told me what happened back then, Mr Canon?'

'Yes,' he agreed quite readily. 'But, under the circumstances, *Mrs Stuart*, it would be better if you learned about it from a source other than myself. I wouldn't want to be accused of bias or prejudice.'

Flame responded to his smile with a glare, then directed her attention back to the diary. Fighting this strange sense of forboding she had, she opened the book again and flipped ahead to pages bearing a November date.

November 9, 1893

Two absolutely wonderful things happened today! This morning at breakfast, Kell announced that we will go home to Kansas City for the holidays! I have longed for this, hoped for this, prayed for such a trip almost from the day I arrived here. That first year, we couldn't go because I was anticipating the arrival of my precious Johnny. And the second and third year, he was much too small to take on such a trip – and I couldn't leave him. And I don't think Papa would have welcomed me if I had come without his grandson. But this year, Johnny is a sturdy three-year-old, and we are going, all three of us. Kell has already made ar-

rangements for us to have a private car for the journey. We will leave on the third of December and spend at least a month there.

The holiday season in Kansas City . . . I can hardly wait. There will be so many parties and gatherings, so many festivities to attend, such a gay and glorious time we'll have.

But what to take and what to wear? Living out here, I fear my dresses have become hopelessly outdated. I will have no choice but to peruse at length my most current issue of 'Harper's Bazaar' and see if I can rectify the problem. There is time to do nothing else, and I refuse to go back and have all my friends regard me as a country bumpkin.

I had no opportunity to do anything about my wardrobe today because . . . we had a visitor. And you will never guess who it was. I could not believe my eyes when I saw him. After Johnny had awakened from his nap, I took him outside to play. It was such a warm and bright afternoon – the finest autumn weather – that I thought the fresh air would be good for him. Heaven knows, in another month that dreadful north wind will come howling across this country, bringing along those dreary grey clouds filled with ice and snow – and it will be much too cold to venture out.

Anyway, by pure happenstance, while Johnny was frolicking with the puppies of one of Kell's hunting dogs, I wandered on to the front lawn. Why? I don't know. It's as if I was drawn there by some mysterious force. When I glanced down the lane, I saw a man leading a lame horse. From his manner of dress, I knew instantly it was not one of our cowboys or a neighbour. And I also knew, even though at that distance I couldn't see his face, that the man was Jackson Stuart. How often I have thought of him these past weeks and wondered how he had fared that day of the great Run. The newspapers were filled with accounts of those murdered in apparent disputes over land claims. Some were 'sooners' and deserved no better fate, but others were legitimate settlers like Mr Stuart. So many times, I had hoped he was alive and well – and there he was.

Mr Stuart was on his way to Tulsa when his beautiful stallion went lame. Fortunately he remembered he was near Morgan's Walk. Considering the lateness of the hour, I knew he wouldn't reach Tulsa before dark and suggested to Kell that Mr Stuart *spend the night with us and continue his journey in the morning on one of our horses. Naturally, Kell agreed with me.*

Dinner that evening was easily one of the most enjoyable – if not the most enjoyable – Ann had experienced since her arrival at Morgan's Walk. Rushed as she'd been trying to prepare everything for their unexpected, but much welcomed guest, she hadn't been able to spend as much time at her toilette as she would have liked. But judging from the frequent appreciative glances Jackson Stuart sent her way, he obviously found a great deal about her appearance to admire. She felt like a flower blossoming under the sun of his attention.

Naturally, the topic of conversation at the table centred on the great land Run into the Cherokee Strip, an experience they had all shared in, either as a participant or observer. For the first time, Ann felt free to chatter away, recounting her many and varied impressions of the start of the race.

'The din was quite deafening,' she insisted. 'I have heard that others likened it to a mighty artillery barrage. I really couldn't say if it was so or not, but I do know that the noise was so great that one felt completely consumed by it. I cannot imagine how it must have sounded to be in the middle of it. Was the start of the race truly as dangerous as it looked? You were there in the midst of all that chaos, Mr Stuart. Tell us what it was like.'

'Insanity. Everyone on that line was of one mind – to get in front quickly and escape the crush. But in those first few jumps after the gun went off, wheels locked, horses bolted, wagons overturned, riders collided.'

She remembered that scene of horror and shuddered expressively. 'All for the dream of owning a piece of land. I can't imagine risking your life for a dream.'

'What is life without a dream?' Jackson Stuart challenged lightly. 'Mere existence, Mrs Morgan, with no hope for anything more. And there has to be more. Otherwise, why go on?'

'What is your dream, Mr Stuart?' Chris inquired.

Jackson Stuart leaned back in his chair and looked around the dining room with its long cherrywood table and glittering chandelier overhead. 'To own a house as fine as Morgan's Walk someday, to travel and see the sights.'

'That's a tall order,' Kell observed.

'Why dream small, Mr Morgan?' Stuart reasoned. 'You didn't.'

Dinner that evening ended much too soon for Ann. She wished she could linger at the table another hour and enjoy more of Jackson Stuart's stimulating company, but when Kell rose, she had no choice but to follow his lead. Hardly had she made the first movement to rise and Jackson Stuart was there to pull out her chair. She acknowledged his assistance with a faint nod of her head, conscious of those black lashes screening a look that was much too bold in its admiration, screening not from her but from her husband. Trying to control the sudden pitter-patter skip of her pulse, she turned to Chris and walked with him from the dining room, the lampas skirt of her golden brown Bengaline gown whispering softly with the gliding movement.

'What was the situation in the new territory when you left it, Mr Stuart?' At the inquiry from Kell, Ann suppressed a sigh. Business. Sooner or later, the conversation always turned to cattle and crops or politics.

'There were still a large number of disputes over the ownership of various claims. It will probably be months before all that's settled. But the rest of the homesteaders are looking to spring. If you have more horses to sell, especially work animals, you'd find a ready market for them, Morgan. After the race, it's been hard to find a horse in the territory that isn't wind-broke.'

'That might be a good idea, Kell,' Chris spoke up. 'We probably have a dozen or so head we could spare from our haying teams. Maybe keep the younger stock and sell off the older animals.'

'It's something to consider,' Kell agreed, typically non-committal.

At the drawing room arch, Ann paused and turned back, her glance automatically running to their handsome guest. 'If you gentlemen will excuse me, I'll leave you to your brandy and cigars.'

For an instant, Jackson Stuart seemed taken aback by her announcement, but that brief flicker of surprise was quickly smoothed from his expression. 'In all honesty, Mrs Morgan, I wish you wouldn't. I noticed the piano earlier and had hopes you might play this evening. You do play, don't you?'

Modesty prevented her from admitting that she was a competent pianist. 'A little, yes.'

'Then, may I impose on you to play for me? It's been a long time since I've heard anything other than someone pounding on a bar-room piano.'

'I . . .' She glanced at Kell, but she could read no objection in his bland expression, 'I should be delighted to play for you, Mr Stuart.'

'You do me honour, Mrs Morgan.' He bowed slightly from the waist, the gleam in his eyes most stimulating.

Aflush with pleasure, Ann entered the drawing room and walked directly to the ornate piano of elaborately carved ebony. She sat down on its bench and arranged the fall of her skirt, then reached for the sheets of music propped on its stand.

Conscious of the crystal clink of the brandy decanter and the subdued murmur of voices behind her, Ann glanced over her shoulder. 'Was there a particular selection you would like to hear, Mr Stuart?'

'No,' he demurred, briefly lifting his brandy glass to her. 'I'll leave the choice to you.'

'Perhaps something by Bach, then.' She chose a concerto filled with suppressed passions and began to play, all the while conscious of her audience and determined to acquit herself well.

Stuart applauded briefly when she finished. 'Beautiful, Mrs Morgan. Simply beautiful.' She glowed under the praise that was in both his voice and his look. 'But I beg you not to stop now.'

'Yes, play some more, Ann,' Kell urged as he pushed out of his chair, rolling fluidly to his feet. 'If you'll excuse me, Mr Stuart, I'll leave you in my wife's capable care. I have considerable paperwork waiting for me in the library.' He turned briefly to Chris. 'I'll need to talk to you before you turn in tonight.'

Ann started to protest his departure, then firmly pressed her lips together, recognising that it would do no good. It never had. That's what was so vexing. He'd spend all day riding over his precious ranch, then most of the evening hunched over its ledgers and account books, leaving scant time for her.

She turned back to the piano and began to play, unconsciously choosing a particularly volatile piece. Halfway through it, she saw Chris leave the room, tossing a quick smile in her direction that promised he'd be back. She doubted it, not once Kell got his hands on him. But what did it matter? Jackson Stuart was here. She smiled, aware that at least she had his undivided attention.

Chris Morgan walked into the library. 'I just realised who that is in there, Kell.' Unconsciously he lowered his voice to conspiratorial volume. 'That's Blackjack Stuart. He's supposed to be connected with the Dalton gang.'

Kell showed no surprise at the news as he briefly looked up from his ledger book, each entry made in a laboured scrawl. 'That connection was obviously broken last year when the Dalton gang was wiped out in Coffeyville.'

The Indian Territory had long been a haven for outlaws. Emmett, Grant, and Bob Dalton had lived in Tulsa most of their lives. The locals rarely commented on the presence of the notorious in their midst. Too much time and trouble was involved in reporting them to the nearest Federal authorities in Fort Smith, Arkansas, one hundred miles away – four days by horseback or one by train. And usually by the time a U.S. Marshal would arrive on the scene, the outlaw would have been warned and gone. Judge Parker, the so-called 'Hanging Judge', had done his best to bring law and order to the territory, but he was only one man with seldom more than forty marshals at any one time to police an area that easily required twenty times that number to do the job adequately.

Chris stopped before the big mahogany desk. 'You've known who he is all the time, haven't you?'

'Yes.'

A frown creased his forehead as he half turned from the desk, running a hand through the streaked gold of his hair. 'If you knew, then why did you invite him to stay the night? Blackjack Stuart supposedly funnelled information to Dalton on gold shipments and the like. Maybe he's doing it for someone else now.'

'Ann invited him. Under the circumstances, I couldn't very well turn him away and risk offending him. The Daltons may be gone, but Stuart still has friends. And we don't have enough men at this time of year to mount a nightguard on the cattle if he decided to retaliate for some imagined slight.'

Chris couldn't argue with that logic. For years there'd been a gentlemen's agreement of sorts between the locals and the marauding element. Asylum was offered in return for protection. In theory it worked. In practice, banks were still robbed, travellers were still waylaid, and cattle were still rustled, not always by outlaws taking refuge in the area. The general lawlessness of the area contributed to the current agitation to have the land of the Creeks brought solely under the jurisdiction of the United States Government, and bring an end to the current system of dual authority.

'Do you think you should say something to Ann? It may be more than a coincidence that his horse went lame so close to Morgan's Walk.'

'Maybe,' Kell conceded. 'But he isn't the first man with a questionable past to stop here. We've even had some work for us. I don't see any point in saying anything and causing her needless worry. Stuart will be gone in the morning.' He returned the ink pen to its desk holder and nodded at the chair in front of his desk. 'Sit down and tell me how the meeting went today.'

Chris paused, drawing in a deep breath and making the mental switch in topics, then took a seat in the leather upholstered armchair. 'About the way we expected. The Creeks aren't changing their position. They refuse to have any discussions with the representatives from the Dawes Commission. Fortunately or unfortunately, depending on your point of view, the Dawes Act that was signed into law last March calls for *negotiations* with the Five Tribes to reach an agreement for the extinction of their communal titles to the land and the allotment of one hundred and sixty acre parcels to individual heads of families. The Creeks aren't going to negotiate. Like the others, they're going to fight it.'

'Where does that leave us and Morgan's Walk?'

'In the middle,' Chris lifted his hand in a helpless gesture. 'We both know it's inevitable that the tribal lands will be broken up. The way they swarmed over the Strip shows just how land-hungry people are. And for all the thousands who made the Run, there are that many and more who missed out. Now they're looking in this direction. The government has already said that all the excess land will be sold to settlers.'

'I intend to keep this valley, Chris.' It wasn't so much a statement as a vow.

'I know.' Sometimes Chris had the feeling that Morgan's Walk meant more to his brother than life itself. 'We'll just have to make certain we're first in line – and that we have a lot of friends in high places.'

When Christopher Morgan remained absent midway through the third piece, Jackson Stuart wandered over to the piano and lounged a hip against it, still absently nursing the brandy in his glass. Ann found his nearness most disconcerting, especially the sensation of his gaze examining every detail about her from the ornate tortoiseshell comb in her hair to the Bengaline front of her corsage. She stumbled briefly over a particularly difficult passage, then completed the piece without another error.

'Beautiful,' he murmured. 'Absolutely beautiful.'

Conscious that his gaze had never left her, Ann had the very warm feeling that he wasn't referring to the music. She drew her hands away from the keys and forced them to lay serenely together on her lap. 'I'm glad my playing pleases you.' She lifted her glance, a breathlessness attacking her throat when she encountered the full force of his gaze.

'It's more than your playing that pleases me.' The smoothness of his voice was like the caressing stroke of a hand. 'The first time I saw you outside that hotel in Guthrie – amidst all that coarse mob of settlers – I sensed instantly that you were out of your element. This is the setting for you – a richly furnished drawing room surrounded by a host of admirers.' He paused, his glance making an idle sweep of the room before coming back to her, humour glinting in the blue of his eyes. 'At the moment, I'm afraid it's a host of one.'

'I should be angry with you for saying such things,' she declared, showing a hint of a smile. 'But I find it quite impossible.'

'That's because I speak the truth. You were not born to this wild, uncouth land, Mrs Morgan. Your manner of dress, your taste in music, your air of refinement, all speak of a more cultured environ.'

'That's true.' Ann didn't attempt to deny it as she rose from the piano bench, the damask-like fabric of her dinner gown settling about her in a whisper of richness. 'Kansas City is my home.'

'You must miss it very much.'

'At times, yes.' Pride wouldn't allow her to admit how unhappy she often was here. 'The parties, the theatre . . . Have you ever been to Coates Opera House? Oh, it's magnificent,' she declared without giving him a chance to answer. 'I do hope a production will be staged while Kell and I are there in December. I so dearly long to see one.'

'You . . . and your husband are going to Kansas City?'

'Yes, in December for a month long visit.' She swung to face him, all her joy at going bubbling through. 'We shall be spending the holidays with my father.'

'You must be very excited.'

'Oh, I am. I haven't been home in more than four years – although at times it has seemed much longer than that.'

'When do you leave?' He absently swirled the brandy in his glass, watching her with contemplative interest, his mind already scheming.

'The third,' she answered blithely.

Chris returned to the drawing room and Jackson Stuart immediately begged to be excused. 'It's late and I have imposed on your good company long enough. It's time I turned in before I wear out my welcome.'

'You could never do that, Mr Stuart,' Ann assured him, quite sincerely.

'I hope not.' He took her hand and, for a moment, lightly held her fingers. 'I will be off early in the morning, long before you arise, so I will pay my thanks to you now, Mrs Morgan. This has been an evening I will long treasure. Thank you.' He lifted her hand to his lips and kept it there an instant longer than was proper.

There went her heart again, fluttering madly against her breast at the pervading warmth of his lips and the boldness of his actions in front of Chris. 'Your company has been most welcome, Mr Stuart,' she replied, fighting the breathy quality in her voice.

With a nod to Chris, he left the room. Ann listened to the sound of his footsteps moving towards the staircase, then turned, feeling Chris's eyes on her. Their look was much too penetrating.

'He's such a polite man, isn't he?' she remarked, striving to sound offhand.

'He's a stranger, Ann,' he reminded her.

'But a very charming stranger.'

True to his word, Jackson Stuart was away before Ann finished her morning toilette. From her bedroom window, she watched him ride away from Morgan's Walk on one of their sturdy brown cow ponies. She tried to tell herself it was foolish to feel such a sense of loss at his leaving. But foolish or not, she did.

Four days later, Jackson Stuart returned to pick up his stallion. Ann was in the dining room, helping Cora Mae polish the silver. A loathsome task, but it was the only way to ensure the lazy woman removed every trace of tarnish. When she heard the uneven tattoo of a horse's hooves drumming on the lane's hard clay, Ann frowned and crossed to a front window, certain it was much too early for Kell to be returning.

She caught back a breath at the sight of the black stallion coming up the lane, lunging at the bit in an attempt to break out of a trot. Jackson Stuart sat astride the horse, a dark figure in his black waistcoat and hat, the silver brocade of his vest flashing in the sunlight. Again she was struck by the handsome, dashing figure he made as she watched him rein the restless stallion in and dismount at the foot of the front steps.

He was coming to the door! She swung from the window and took one eager step towards the entry, then stopped abruptly, looking down in horror at the work apron tied over her house dress of striped brown wool – and the gloves on her hands, blackened by tarnish. From the foyer came the rapping sound of the brass knocker rising and falling against the front door.

'Cora Mae, answer the door – quickly!' she snapped to the black maid as she hastily stripped the gloves from her hands, silently praying the black grime hadn't penetrated the cloth.

'Yes'm.' The slim black woman hurried from the dining room, glad to leave the hated task.

Ann pulled off the apron and tossed it, along with the gloves, on to the table, then ran to the doorway, stopping short of its carved oak frame to smoothly pat the upswept sides of her hair and make certain no strands had escaped. When she heard Cora Mae open the door, she pinched her cheeks to put colour into them. Although she wasn't sure it was necessary, as flushed with excitement as she felt. Then, straining to appear serenely composed, she glided into the reception hall.

'Who is it, Cora Mae?' she called cheerily.

The coloured woman held the front door open, but remained squarely before it, denying admittance as she looked back at Ann.

'It's a Mr Jackson Stuart. He's asking for Master Kell, but I told him he ain't here just now.'

She moved quickly to the maid's side and dismissed her with a curt nod, then turned a warm smile on the man standing outside the door, conscious of the heart thudding in her chest. Immediately he removed his hat in her presence, revealing the gleaming black of his hair.

'Mr Stuart, what a pleasant surprise,' she declared. 'Won't you come in?' She swung the door open wider to admit him.

But he smiled and shook his head in refusal. 'I think not, Mrs Morgan.' Yet there was no mistaking the regret in his voice and his expression as his glance moved over her with that familiar covetous look. 'Your housemaid informed me your husband isn't at home, and I wouldn't want to compromise your reputation if some neighbour should happen by and think you were entertaining an admirer in your husband's absence.'

'You're right, of course.' She felt hot all over, realising that was exactly what she did want – not the neighbour part – but the other, the stimulation that came from entertaining a male admirer, the fending off of compliments in a way that encouraged more, the pretending that a hand hadn't been held too long – that whole thrilling aura of anticipation. After four years of marriage, all that had gone from her relationship with Kell. In truth, her husband had never looked at her the way Jackson Stuart did – as if he longed to ravish her.

'Will you pass along my thanks to your husband for the loan of a horse and the care for my stallion?' Jackson Stuart asked.

'Of course,' she agreed, much too brightly.

'Then I'll bid you *adieu*, Mrs Morgan.'

As he started to bow over the hand she automatically extended to him, she felt a panic grip her throat. 'Will I – we – ever see you again, Mr Stuart?'

His lips barely brushed the back of her hand before he straightened. 'I have the feeling our paths are destined to cross again, Mrs Morgan – if Fortune is with me.'

As he rode down the lane, Ann fervently hoped he was right, realising – quite shamelessly – that she wanted to see him again.

— 24 —

KANSAS CITY – the noise, the gaiety, the bustle, the crowds – Ann couldn't get enough of it. Horse-drawn carriages battled with cable cars and vendors in their pushcarts for the right of way on the paved streets. Wood and stone buildings – three, four and five storeys high – towered on either side; stout and sturdy buildings, not the flimsy false-fronted kind they built in Tulsa. People crowded the sidewalks, hirsute men in top hats or bowlers and women in their fur-trimmed coats and muffs. And everywhere the clang of cable cars, the cries of boys hawking newspapers, the rattle of carriage wheels, and the clamour of a city on the move.

The first four days were one round after another of shopping, lunches, afternoon teas, dinners, private receptions, and parties. By the fourth day, Ann talked as knowledgeably as her friends about the fantastic electric light display at the Chicago Exposition, had memorised the words and music to 'A Bicycle Built for Two', and wondered how she had ever survived at Morgan's Walk all this time without a telephone.

Garbed in a long dressing sacque to cover her combination, petticoat, vest, and her new evening corset elaborately trimmed with lace frills and rosettes, Ann stood beside the bed and studied the two gowns laid out for her inspection. She vacillated between the two, holding up first the *ciel*-blue damask, then the Nile-green

China crepe. Hearing the firm tread of footsteps in the hallway, she turned towards the door, her unbound hair swinging freely about her shoulders. Her look of heavy concentration lifted as Kell walked into their private suite of rooms in her father's house.

'I'm glad you're back,' she declared, turning away as he gave his hat a toss on to a swan chair and absently ran a hand through the waving red of his hair. 'I need your help.' She stepped back to frown thoughtfully at the two gowns again. 'Which do you think I should wear to the Halstons' dinner tonight?'

'We aren't going out for dinner again tonight, are we?' A frown sharply creased his forehead, drawing his auburn brows together in a thick, disapproving line.

'To the Halstons', yes. I told you about the invitation this morning.' She picked up the damask gown and held it against her, then turned to look at her reflection in the free-standing full-length mirror. 'The colour of this one suits me, don't you think?'

'Ann, do you realise that we have been here four days and not once have we had dinner with your father?'

'Of course, we have,' she insisted, not taking her eyes from the mirror. 'He was at the Taylors' and the Danbys'.'

'That isn't the same as having dinner here.'

'Perhaps, but Papa understands,' she retorted, aware that her husband had already tired of this constant round of social affairs. But she didn't care. After four miserably lonely years on that ranch, she was entitled to one month of fun and she wasn't going to let Kell spoil it for her.

'He would understand a great deal more if you spent an entire evening with him.'

Ann ignored that as she critically studied the style of the five-year-old gown. 'The colour's fine, but the bust – it protrudes much too far. I wish my new gown was ready,' she complained. 'Everyone will take one look at me in this and know it was part of my bridal trousseau. If only there was some way to alter it – but I don't dare take it to the seamstress. Her tongue's as fast as her needle. In two days all of Kansas City will know it's an old dress I've had restyled.' She chewed at her bottom lip, trying to think how it could be salvaged. Then she remembered her father's housekeeper. 'Mrs Flanagan, of course. She's excellent with a needle. I'll have her look at the dress.'

With her problem solved, she tossed the damask gown on to the bed and picked up the China crepe. She heard the quick set of footsteps in the hall outside their door and started to turn, then decided no, she'd speak to Mrs Flanagan tomorrow. If it was to be the Nile-green gown, she needed to choose her accessories. Perhaps the feathered fan of rose and white, with the matching aigrette for her hair.

The bustling footsteps came to a quick stop outside their door and a sharp, demanding rap, rap, rap followed. Ann paused briefly in her silent debate as Kell walked to the door and opened it. The short, chubby Irish woman stood outside, a white ruffled cap covering red hair that the years had thoroughly shot with silver.

' 'Tis sorry I am to be disturbing you, Mr Morgan, but this wire just come for you. And I be thinking yourself would want to be reading it straight away.'

'Thank you, Mrs Flanagan.' Kell took the telegram from her.

'No trouble, Mr Morgan. No trouble at all.' With a dismissing wave of her hand, she was off, scurrying away on some other urgent business.

'A telegram,' Ann repeated, mildly curious. 'Who's it from?' She glanced indifferently at Kell's frown of concentration as he struggled to read the message.

'Chris,' he answered, then appeared to grow impatient with his own slowness in reading the words and handed it to her. 'Read it for me.'

She was a bit startled by this rare admission that his reading skills were less than adequate. Usually he was too proud to acknowledge his lack of education – at least in front of her.

' "HIT BY RAIDERS STOP HORSES STOLEN STOP LITTLE BILLY AND CHOCTAW DEAD STOP THREE WOUNDED STOP NEED HELP STOP . . ." ' Slowly Ann lowered the telegram, a dread filling her as she spoke the message's last line, ' "CAN YOU COME STOP" '

She had never seen his face so stony grim before or his eyes so hard. Even before he said it, she knew what was coming. 'We'd better start packing.'

'No.' Her fingers curled around the telegram, crumpling it into her palm, but she wasn't aware of it as she swung away from Kell, fighting the hot tears that stung her eyes. 'I won't go! You promised we'd stay a month. It's only four days.'

'Ann, someone has stolen our horses and murdered two of my men – and wounded three more. For all I know, Chris might be one of the wounded.'

That possibility gave her pause but still she insisted, 'I don't care.'

'You don't mean that. You can't,' he snapped. 'And you can't expect me to stay here and go to your dinners and parties when I'm needed at Morgan's Walk!'

'Then you go!' she hurled at him, then faltered, realising that she had stumbled on the answer. Turning, she repeated it with less anger. 'You go, Kell, and let me stay here.' She went to him, now all appeal, tears running unchecked down her cheeks, her fingers gripping the lapels of his frock coat in silent entreaty. 'Please, Kell. Please let me stay. There's nothing little Johnny or I could do there.'

He gazed at her upturned face, her dark eyes shiny with more tears. She was his weakness. He'd never been able to refuse her anything. And he couldn't now.

Kell caught the next train south by himself. Ann remained at her father's house in Kansas City with their son.

The bon ton of Kansas City filled Coates Opera House for the special performance of *Manon*. Between acts, they mingled to see and be seen, to talk and be talked about. Men in their black evening dress gathered in groups, striking negligent poses of elegant ease and puffing on their Havana cigars while they bragged about their latest business coups and groused about the failing banks, often taking malicious delight in the economic fall of a competitor. Women in their best silks and satins glided about, whispering behind their fans about this person and that and lavishing compliments on one another.

'Ann, how good to see you again.' A blonde-haired woman glided up to her, dressed in a gown with lace and feather trimming that was so tightly corsetted Ann wondered how she could breathe. Not that she cared. Helen Cummings had never been a friend – not since she had stolen Ann's beau five years ago, then compounded the offence by marrying him.

'Helen, how are you?' She smiled politely and prayed that the woman was miserably unhappy.

'The same – deliriously happy.' She waved off the question

with a sweep of her lace and feather fan. 'I heard only yesterday that you were back for a visit. When did you arrive?'

'A week ago.'

'That explains it,' Helen declared. 'Bobby and I were away.'

'Yes, I believe someone mentioned that you were in New York.'

'I don't need to ask how you're managing in the wilds of the Territory. You look simply ravishing in that gown,' she remarked, somewhat grudgingly. 'I was admiring it earlier and someone mentioned it was a Worth.'

Actually it was patterned after an illustration Ann had seen of a gown designed by Worth, but if Helen Cummings chose to think it was an original, Ann wasn't about to correct her. In truth, she knew that her gown of Parma-violet damask was the most elegant gown of any worn that night – and distinctive, too. The corsage was pointed in front and trimmed all around the low neckline with white tulle and lace. A double garland of beads sewn on tulle with delicate crystal pendants curved from the bust to the right side of the waist, fastened there by clasps in the shape of St Jacques shells. Similar garlands of beads and crystals were strung diagonally across the damask skirt above a flounce of embroidered lace. She wore her dark hair parted in the middle and drawn back in large waves to form a high coil, then adorned it with twists of beads to match the gown.

Helen Cummings was clearly envious of the result and Ann intended to keep it that way. 'It is beautiful, isn't it? My husband saw it and insisted that I have it, regardless of the cost,' she lied. Kell had cast only a cursory glance at the illustration and hadn't laid eyes on the finished gown yet. She'd got it from the dressmaker's only this afternoon – after much screaming and railing on her part.

'Speaking of your husband, where is your wealthy cattle baron?' the blonde inquired with a touch of snideness.

'He was called away – on some sort of urgent business.' Ann shrugged, pretending she didn't know what it was all about.

'You surely aren't here this evening by yourself?' Helen looked properly shocked.

'No.' Ann smiled smoothly. 'Papa brought me.'

'Your father – it's been ages since I've seen the good doctor. Where is he? I must say hello.'

'He's –' Ann glanced towards the end of the room where the men were gathered in small clusters, a miasma of cigar smoke hanging over them. Her gaze immediately became riveted on a man dressed in a single-breasted waistcoat in black, a small white bow tie around his neck and studs marching down the front of his stiff shirt. He stood with one leg slightly cocked, his hair gleaming blackly in the flickering gaslight and his eyes – his blue eyes . . .

'My dear, you're gaping,' Helen chided. 'Who is it that has so caught your eye?'

Ann recovered her surprise and astonishment at seeing Jackson Stuart, and broke into a smile. 'Why, it's a dear friend,' she replied, stretching a truth a little. 'I had no idea he was in the city.'

To her immense delight, Jackson Stuart noticed her and immediately made his way towards her. She could hardly wait to introduce her dashingly handsome acquaintance to Helen Cummings and watch the woman's envy. Then she experienced a moment's unease and shot an anxious look at the petite blonde, the daughter of one of Kansas City's oldest and most influential families – and the daughter-in-law of another. If Jackson Stuart showed so much as the slightest interest in her, Ann swore she'd never speak to him again.

But he took no notice of Helen as he halted before her. 'Mrs Morgan. I wondered if our paths would cross during my sojourn in Kansas City.' He bowed over her hand, holding her gaze with his warm look.

Helen Cummings stirred beside her, fluttering her fan to gain his attention. Ann knew the woman was just panting to be introduced to him, but she deliberately ignored her. 'It seems Fortune was kind to both of us, Mr Stuart.'

'Indeed.' He straightened and bestowed on her that faint smile that somehow managed to be so incredibly sensual. 'How quickly time passes. It seems such a short time ago that I stayed with you and your husband at Morgan's Walk, but already a month has passed.' Then he paused, his glance flickering elsewhere. 'Is your husband somewhere about? I don't remember seeing him.'

'No, Kell's away on business. It will probably be a week or more before he returns.'

'Really?' Jackson Stuart pretended he hadn't known that . . . just as he pretended he didn't know the cause for Morgan's absence. But his money belt bulged with his share of the proceeds from the sale of the stolen horses to a less than scrupulous trader in the Cherokee Strip. Thanks to the fleetness of his black stallion, he'd made it back to Tulsa in time to see Kell Morgan get off the train – alone. He couldn't help feeling a certain smugness that his plan was working so well. He vaguely regretted that it had been necessary to kill those two cowboys, but it had been the only way he could make sure Kell Morgan came back – and that he might consider it too dangerous to have his wife and son return – in the event the night raiders struck again, going for the cattle herd. He'd been certain Ann Morgan would agitate to remain in Kansas City – and he'd obviously been right.

'Helen, may I present Mr Jackson Stuart, late of the Oklahoma Territory.' As Ann Morgan introduced the blonde woman with her, Jackson caught the slight edge in her voice and noticed she failed to identify the woman as a friend. 'Mrs Helen Cummings. We both attended the same finishing school.'

'Mrs Cummings.' He acknowledged the introduction with a polite bow and nothing more.

'Mr Stuart, it is such a pleasure to meet a friend of Ann's . . . especially such a handsome one,' the woman declared, looking at him through the long sweep of her top lashes.

Although it went against his nature, he didn't flirt back and, instead, merely smiled. Out of the corner of his eyes, he observed the flicker of satisfaction that fleetingly crossed Ann's expression, and knew she approved of his aloofness.

But Helen Cummings wasn't to be put off. 'What is it exactly that you do, Mr Stuart?'

'I dabble in many things – blooded horses, cattle, land . . .' He let it trail off as if his interests were too many to mention.

'What brings you to Kansas City?'

He was spared from answering that as an older man walked up to them. 'There you are, Ann. I've been looking for you.'

'Papa, I'm so glad you're here. There's someone I want you to meet.' She quickly hooked her arm with her father's and drew him forward.

Jackson Stuart looked with interest at the next obstacle he had to overcome as she introduced him to her father, Dr Frank Compton. He was somewhere in his fifties, a little below average height. Grey silvered his dark hair at the temples and streaked the moustache and goatee he wore. His eyes were the same brown-black colour as his daughter's and his features possessed a certain benign softness that befitted his profession. Although, at the moment, he appeared somewhat distracted as if he had other things on his mind than meeting Jackson Stuart – despite the fact that Ann Morgan implied that he was a long-time personal acquaintance of her husband, an implication that couldn't have fitted better with his plans.

'Delighted to meet you, Mr Stuart, but I'm afraid you'll have to excuse us,' he declared, politely but briskly.

'Papa, what's wrong?'

'I'm sorry, child, but I'm afraid we must leave.' He patted the hand that clutched at his arm. 'It's Mrs Stanhope's time. Their carriage is waiting out front for us.'

'But – must we leave now? The opera isn't over yet,' Ann protested pleadfully. 'There is still the third act to come. There is such a beautiful aria in it, can't we stay? What will another hour matter?'

'A great deal to Mrs Stanhope,' her father chided, an indulgent smile lifting the corners of his mouth.

'Must I go too?' There was a decidedly petulant droop to her lower lip.

'You know it wouldn't be proper for you to stay. An unescorted lady. Unless, of course, Mrs Cummings and her husband –'

Jackson Stuart broke in before the doctor could suggest that Ann join the Cummings party. 'With your permission, Dr Compton, I would be honoured to serve as Mrs Morgan's escort for the remainder of the evening.' He did his best to appear harmless and respectful under the doctor's sharply assessing look. 'As a matter of fact I would welcome the opportunity to repay the accommodations and hospitality your daughter's husband has extended to me in the past.'

'How very thoughtful of you to offer,' Ann fairly beamed at him, not taking her eyes from him as she said to her father, 'I assure you, Papa, Mr Stuart is a most honourable man. Were Kell here, I'm sure he would vouch for him as well.'

The good doctor hesitated, then smiled, 'In that case, it would be churlish of me to refuse your offer, Mr Stuart. I leave my daughter in your capable care.'

'I promise you won't regret it.'

'I'm sure I won't,' he replied and turned to his daughter. 'Advise Mrs Flanagan that I likely will be very late, but I hope to be home before morning.'

'I will.'

Well before the third act began, they took their seats in the private box with Jackson Stuart occupying the one that had previously been taken by her father. Although she pretended not to notice, Ann knew they were the cynosure of all eyes. The whole house was a-twitter, fans spreading as everyone speculated about the handsome stranger sitting next to her. She loved the attention. She'd gone too long without it. The last time she'd created such a stir among her friends had been when Kell had courted her – another stranger, but one with red hair ... a rich cattle baron from the Indian Territory. Not a single one of her friends had thought she would marry so well – not after losing Robert Cummings to Helen Thurston. She'd proved them wrong. Now, with Jackson Stuart sitting beside her, they would all wonder what her life was like at Morgan's Walk. Nor for anything would she tell them the truth. She preferred to have them think she commonly entertained the likes of Jackson Stuart.

As far as Jackson Stuart was concerned, the evening couldn't have turned out better if he had planned it. During the ride in the closed Hansom cab to her father's residence, Ann inquired after the length of his intended stay in the city.

'That will depend on how much I find to keep me here,' he replied. 'I had thought about travelling on to Chicago, or New York – or maybe south to a warmer clime, like New Orleans. And you? You will be staying – what? Another three weeks?'

'At least,' she confirmed.

'Then perhaps I will, too.' He smiled at her undisguised glow of pleasure at his answer.

'The Throckmortons are having a reception tomorrow afternoon. If you have no plans, perhaps you'd like to attend.'

'If it means having the pleasure of your company, I'd be delighted.'

The cab waited while he walked her to the door and chastely kissed her gloved hand. When he walked back to the Hansom, he silently congratulated himself on his luck. She couldn't know that she was playing right into his hand.

'Where to now, mister?' the driver asked from his perch behind the cab.

Jackson Stuart looked up at a night sky so black that it seemed to possess a velvet shine. And scattered across it, like crushed and loosely strewn crystals were the stars. The night was young and he was on a winning streak. Long ago, he'd learned to ride it for all it was worth.

'I've heard Madam Chambers has a blackjack table,' he said idly, then smiled at the driver. 'Fourth and Wyandotte.' The address was squarely in the heart of the city's bon-ton block of sin. He climbed into the cab, wondering if Annie Chambers, the madam of the swank and exclusive brothel, would remember him.

25

During the next ten days, Jackson Stuart became her
constant companion, escorting her everywhere and anywhere she
went – shopping expeditions, skating parties, dinner receptions
and gala holiday balls. There were only two places he didn't take
her, and that was to church – and to bed. But the latter would
come . . . in due time. Everything was progressing exactly the
way he'd anticipated, including the familiar usage of their given
names, begun almost a week ago – at her behest.

'I have never seen you look more beautiful than you do tonight,
Ann,' he declared as he swirled her around the ballroom, holding
her close, no longer concerned about keeping the proper distance
between them. Neither was she, he noticed, aware that she frequently invited the brush of his lips against her temple and cheek
when they danced.

'Nor have you looked so handsome.' She flirted with him
openly now – if discreetly.

'If you were the only woman to think so, I would forever be
content.' Deliberately he inserted a seriousness into his manner,
then observed the quick breath she drew before she melted closer
to him.

He said no more as he gazed into her eyes and guided her steps
through the last few measures of the song. When the music stop-

ped, an immediate flurry of voices rose to fill the silence. He was slow to lead her off the floor, then halted at the edge of it and let his glance sweep the ballroom, decorated with garlands of holiday greenery trimmed with red velvet bows.

'Do you remember what I said to you that evening at Morgan's Walk?' He continued without allowing her an opportunity to respond. 'After seeing you here in this setting, I am more convinced than ever that you don't belong in the Territory.' He held up a hand to stave off the comment she was about to make. 'It's true, Ann. You're a precious jewel wasted in that nothingness, hidden by that dulling red dust. But, here, tonight, the fullness of your lustre and sparkling brilliance shines for all to see and admire. This is where you should be, always – in a setting, like this with chandeliers glittering and violins playing.'

'I wish it could be so.' She attempted to mask the hint of longing in her voice. 'But Morgan's Walk is my husband's home . . . and mine.' Belatedly she linked herself to the man whose name she now carried.

'So?' Jackson shrugged. 'Let it remain your home – your wilderness retreat. There's no reason you have to spend every day of your life there. Your husband can – as many others have done – instal a manager to run the place for him. Or better yet, leave his brother, Christopher, in charge while the two of you travel. That's what I would do if I was in your husband's place.'

'You and I are very much alike, Jackson,' she declared wistfully, then grimaced prettily in regret. 'I only wish Kell thought as we do. But he would never consider leaving Morgan's Walk for any length of time. He loves that place.' A bitterness crept into her low voice as she averted her glance, a shimmer of tears in her eyes. 'Certainly more than he loves me.'

'Ann –'

Her head swung back, a rare defiance glittering in her eyes. 'Morgan's Walk is far from here and much too boring a topic. Dance with me, Jackson.'

Again he took her into his arms and swept her on to the floor, secretly smiling in satisfaction. Yes, it was all going perfectly.

Close to midnight, they joined the throng of departing guests leaving the ball. Sometime during the evening, it had begun to snow. A mantle of white covered the ground while more soft, fat flakes fell as they made their way through the snow to the hired carriage and Jackson assisted her inside, then climbed in himself and spread the fur robe over the skirt of her evening cloak.

As the carriage pulled away from the mansion still ablaze with light, the trilling voices of other departing guests faded into the stillness of the snowy night. Despite the crunch of the carriage wheels in the fallen snow and the jingle of the team's harness bells, a magical, hushed quality permeated the air. Ann could almost believe they were the only two people in the world.

Bundled warmly in her evening cloak of black satin, its hood and cap trimmed with black marten fur to match the muff she carried, Ann leaned forward to gaze out of the carriage window, her breath rising in wispy puffs of vapour. 'Look, Jackson. See how white the snowflakes appear against the black of the night. Have you ever seen anything so beautiful?'

'I know of only one thing that rivals it.'

She turned her head and discovered he was right there, looking out of her side of the carriage, his face only inches from hers. She was instantly conscious of the rapid palpitations of her heart . . . and the heady rush of excitement she felt as his gaze moved over her face.

'What's that?' she asked, fully aware a compliment was coming – and aware, too, that she had invited it.

'The pure white of your skin against the velvet dark of your hair, it's perfection.' His voice was as soft as a caress.

Yet there was perfection, too, in the noble straightness of his nose, the rise of his cheekbones, and the sculptured slant of his jaw. Secretly she thrilled to the intimate messages his eyes so frequently sent her. He made her feel things she shouldn't. She was a married woman. Yet, looking at the well-shaped line of his mouth, she understood why the apple had looked so very tempting.

'Ann.' That was all he said – just her name. But how many times had he said it just that way and made her feel that she was the most desirable woman on earth. Wicked thoughts she had. Wicked, wicked, wicked thoughts. But, oh, they felt so good.

She wanted to be kissed. He saw it in the tension of her, the motionlessness. The signal was always the same whether given by the most proper of ladies or the most pocked and painted of whores. All women were at the mercy of the same signals. Most men expected a difference, but Jackson Stuart knew better.

Her lips felt cool beneath his, chilled by winter's breath. As he went about warming them, he felt her hesitation and that vague, never completely formed impulse to turn away, but she stayed with the kiss. Soon she was reaching into it, bending like a supple willow, her lips all eager and soft. He pressed the advantage, taking her beyond herself, taking her farther than she wanted to go until she broke away, suddenly heavy, her gloved fingers clutching at the front of his coat, her face averted from him.

'No.' Her faint protest was near a moan. 'You mustn't – we mustn't.'

'I know.' He sought her temple, grazing his lips over it. Satisfaction, smooth as the best whiskey, ran through him at the swiftly indrawn breath she took. 'That's what I've been telling myself for days now, but it doesn't change the way I feel.' He continued to brush his mouth over her, speaking all the words against her skin and feeling the faint tremors of longing. 'Ann, you must know – you must have guessed that I came to Kansas City because you were here. I wanted to see you again, talk to you – if only for a moment. I couldn't believe my luck when you said your husband was away. But was it luck, Ann?'

'I don't know,' she whispered.

'Neither do I. I only know that I've fallen in love with you.'

'No.'

He ignored her faint protest, his hands tightening to check her feeble attempt to pull away from him. 'It's true. I love the look of you and the glow of your smile. I love the fragrance of your skin and the perfume of your hair. I love the sound of my name on your lips and the beat of your heart next to mine. I love the feel of you and, yes, the taste of you. Ann, my sweet, my darling.'

There was such agony, such aching intensity in his voice that she was enthralled by it. These last days he had flirted with her often and said bold things, but she never dreamed she had inspired such a depth of love. The discovery was heady and thrilling, just as his kiss had been. She turned her head slightly, letting him find her lips again, no longer frightened by the desire that had flamed within her, now welcoming the forbidden feelings and the excitement of them.

His mouth was all over her lips, not like the last time with a tenderly persuasive ardour, but with hunger – tasting, eating, devouring until she felt wholly consumed by his kiss. But what a delicious feeling it was – so beyond her experience, leaving her completely bereft of thought and breath, her heart pounding until she was quite weak.

When he lifted his mouth from hers, she sagged against him and rested her head against his shoulder, limp with feeling and aware that it had never been like this with Kell – never. The band of his arms remained tight around her, keeping her close while his restless, kneading hands moved over her shoulders and back, alternately pressing and caressing.

'What am I to do, Ann?' he murmured, his lips brushing the elaborate coil of her dark hair. 'I can't bear the thought of letting you go back to Morgan's Walk. I know how miserable and lonely you are there. Yet, how can I ask you to come away with me when I have nothing to offer?' A groan of despair came from his throat. 'When I think of the fortunes that have passed through my hands at the gaming tables, I curse myself for not realising the day would come when I'd meet an enchanting creature like you. What money I have is enough for me, but not enough to lavish you with the beautiful gowns, the jewels, the furs you deserve to have – or take you to all the beautiful places you deserve to go. I would give anything to have your husband's wealth – anything but my heart for you already have that. Ann, Ann.' He murmured her name in husky urgency as he lifted her head, cupping her cheek in his hand and gazing at her. Her face had a dreamy sensuousness, her lips parted, eyes heavy. He'd won her over. 'What a fool Morgan is. What a fool.'

'I wish –' She was afraid to say the rest, afraid to admit she had chosen wrong when she married Kell. He loved her, and, in his way, he had been good to her. It was selfish of her to want the life Jackson had described – and it was sinful of her to enjoy his kisses, but, oh, she did. She did.

'I wish it, too, my love,' he declared. 'But I can't ask you to leave your husband when I can offer you so little. But – if I should find a way – tell me that I have cause to hope.'

'You do, yes.' She couldn't deny it.

Again she was swept away by his kisses, carried off by their languorous heat that produced such feverish longings. All too soon the carriage stopped in front of her father's house. One more time they kissed within the shadows of the closed carriage, then Jackson walked her to the door and bid her a proper goodnight.

She swayed toward him, not wanting him to go, but he stayed her with a smile and a promise. 'Till tomorrow.'

'Yes, tomorrow,' she whispered and watched him walk away amidst a swirl of falling snowflakes. In that instant, she was convinced there was no feeling stronger than the sweet ache of love.

The next two days were the happiest Ann had ever known, filled with secret looks, whispered words of love and stolen kisses – and every moment heightened by the risk of discovery. But the latter only served to make the rest that much more exhilerating. Truly it was an enchanted world.

But on the morning of the third day, the spell was broken – shattered, sending Ann into a thousand scattered pieces. Distraught, she hurried down the hotel corridor, checking the room numbers on the doors and constantly glancing over her shoulder, fearing that she might be seen – or worse, recognised despite the veiling net of her hat. At the door marked twenty-two, she paused and looked down the hallway once more then rapped lightly and quickly.

'Just a moment,' came the muffled but impatient reply, the voice unmistakably Jackson's.

She waited anxiously outside the door, the seconds ticking by with interminable slowness before she heard the approach of his footsteps. She leaned toward the door in nervous eagerness as it swung open.

'Yes, what is it?' The instant he saw her, Jackson Stuart halted in the middle of pulling on his white linen shirt. 'Ann?!'

He sounded as shocked at seeing her as she felt at seeing him in a state of partial undress. She stared at the smattering of dark chest hairs, then turned her head away, hot with embarrassment at the prurient thoughts that raced through her mind.

'I – I shouldn't have come.' She made a half-hearted move as if to leave, but he stopped her, catching at her arm and drawing her back.

'Don't go. Come inside before someone happens by.'

She didn't resist when he pulled her into his room and closed the door. The front of his shirt swung together, hiding his naked chest, but she continued to keep her eyes downcast, her heart pounding like a mad thing.

His hands gripped her arms near the elbows, just below the

exaggerated pouf of her coat's velvet sleeves. 'Ann, you're trembling. What is it? What's wrong?' He bent his head to look under the brim of her hat and through the screen of its black veil to her face.

'I – I didn't know what to do.' She hesitated, then pulled the folded telegram out of her muff. 'This came early this morning. It's from my husband.' He released her to take the telegram, a stillness coming over him. She didn't wait for him to read the message. 'He arrives on the afternoon train.' The raw feeling of desperation that she'd managed to hold in check thus far, now broke from her. 'I had to let you know. I couldn't let you come to take me to the Willets' reception and find Kell there. I had to see you. I had to –'

'I know,' he said, stopping the rush of words.

She looked up, her gaze clinging to his. 'I won't be able to see you any more, Jackson.'

He smiled lazily, unable to believe she was actually here in his hotel room. Although why he doubted his luck, he didn't know, considering the way he'd bucked the tiger last night and walked away from the faro table a big winner.

'What time does his train get in?'

'It's scheduled to arrive at two-ten this afternoon.'

'Then we have three hours.' He tossed the telegram on to the floor, then loosened her veil and rolled it over the brim of her hat. 'Let's not waste them with words, Ann.'

The hat soon went the way of the telegram, to be followed shortly by the muff and the long velvet coat. Dispensing with her dress of striped changeable silk was easy, too, as long as his lips stayed close enough to smother the beginnings of any vague protest.

She felt drunk with his kisses, a dreamy looseness taking over all her limbs. She clung to him for support, letting the arm hooked around her tightly corseted waist take all her weight and thrilling to the feel of his muscled flesh beneath the linen of his shirt.

As he continued to shower her eyes, cheeks, and lips with kisses, his fingers moved to the lace–trimmed throat of her high corset cover. When the top button sprang free at his touch, Ann caught back a breath, aware that his deft fingers had already moved on to the next. She had never been assisted out of her clothes by anyone except her personal maid. Not even Kell had taken such liberties. At finishing school, she'd been taught that a woman of gentility didn't expose her private areas to a man, not even her husband. Voluminous nightgowns with long sleeves and high necks satisfied the need for modesty in the marriage bed, however awkward and cumbersome they sometimes proved to be.

But she would have no such protective garment with Jackson. She went hot at the thought, aware that just to be seen in her petticoats by a man was considered scandalous. Worse, the heat she felt wasn't embarrassment. What a wicked woman she was to want to expose herself and excite him further. But that was exactly what she desired. Exactly.

The corset cover hung loose about her. She moaned softly as he pushed her arms down to the side, then slipped the silk garment from her, his hands smooth against her skin, not calloused and rough like Kell's. Unerringly his fingers moved to the laces at the back of her corset. Some distant part of her idly marvelled that the workings of a woman's undergarments held no mysteries for him. Then she was drawing her first unfettered breath, a breath that ended in a tiny shudder.

With the corset vanquished, he untied the strings to her rose-coloured petticoat of quilted satin and let it fall about her legs in a rustling whisper. When he picked her up and lifted her out of it, she felt as weightless as a babe. Held close to him, she made another discovery. The fine muslin of her combination and its frills of torchon lace proved to be no barrier against the sensation of his hard muscled body pressed against her flesh. She could feel every flexing ripple through the thin fabric as he carried her the few feet to the bed. There, he slowly lowered her feet to the floor, turning her to face him as he did so and letting her body slide upright against him, making her aware of every masculine contour in the process.

She could hardly breathe, her senses assaulted on all sides by him. And the affliction wasn't eased by the quick claiming of her lips in another intimately delving kiss. Its power was such that at first she wasn't aware of the deft manipulations of fingers at the front opening of her combination. Then she felt the touch of his hand against her bare skin. Reaction splintered through her in needle-sharp tingles of surprise and delight. She sagged against him, letting him take all her weight, but he sank under it to sit on the edge of the bed, drawing her with him to stand between his straddled legs.

Dazed, she looked down, her hands clutching at the ridges of his shoulders for balance. A tension gripped her as she watched him spread the front of her combination open, starting at her stomach and gliding up through the valley between her breasts, then branching to expose the bones of her shoulders. She brought her arms down to her sides so he could slip it off, her breath now running shallow and fast, matching the ragged, quick-hammer beat of her pulse.

As he pushed the one-piece garment over her shoulders, the fine muslin briefly caught on the hardened points of her breasts, then sprang free of them. She saw the way his eyes devoured her breasts, and closed her own, a melting heat starting somewhere in her midsection and spreading. She waited to feel the caress of his hands as he slowly pulled the combination chemise and drawers down her arms. Just below her elbows, he stopped and gave the back of the garment a twist, pinning her arms out straight behind her, throwing her shoulders back and her breasts forward.

Startled, Ann looked down, her lips parting in a question that she never had a chance to form as he spread a hand over her flat stomach and moved it up, up, up, then finally reached the under-swell of a breast. He glanced up and saw her watching him. The darkening light in his eyes almost made her want to swoon, but she didn't want to miss any of the delights his eyes promised. And delight there was as he began to nuzzle her breasts, kissing and licking at their nipples until Ann quivered in reaction, an ache coiling ever tighter and centring ever lower in her stomach.

With one final pull of the garment, he freed her arms. Immediately she dug her fingers into his hair and pressed his face to her breast, ending the teasing of his lips. She bowed her head against the awesome pressure that continued to build inside her. Through heavy, half-closed eyes, she watched him tug his shirt off and give it a fling across the room. Then his hands were back on her, rolling the undergarment down over her hips. She was aware of his actions yet she wasn't. As in a dream, everything blurred together, things happening without her paying attention to the how of them – like the way she ended up on the bed.

Yet, as in a dream too, certain things stood out very sharply, a single moment held in time – like the way he had left her to strip off his trousers and drawers, then came back to fill her vision. She had never seen a man unclothed before. She stared at his wide shoulders and leanly muscled chest with its smattering of curly dark hairs. Her glance drifted lower to the hard flatness of his stomach, then lower to his stiffened organ. A breath caught in her throat. She hadn't known a man's body could be so beautiful. Some distant part of her wondered if Kell looked like that beneath the long nightshirt she'd always insisted he wear to bed.

But the thought no more than registered and it vanished as Jackson lowered himself on to her, using his legs to wedge hers apart. The fever that had heated her body cooled somewhat under the settling weight of him on top of her and the sensation of his bony hardness against her inner thigh. This part she knew all too well. She felt the first lick of disappointment as his lips teased the corner of her mouth, his warm breath rolling across her skin. But there was no positioning of her hips, no awkward probing attempt at entry. Instead his hands were busy touching and stroking, moving over her with wayward ease, their path unencumbered by any voluminous nightgown. Ann began to relax and enjoy once more, taking advantage of the chance to run her hands over the bareness of his muscled arms and shoulders and revel in the sensation of skin against skin.

When his mouth transferred its attention from her lips to her neck and the hollow of her throat, she moaned in soft pleasure, liking the little shivers his nibblings sent dancing over her flesh. And she arched in eagerness when he bent his head to again suckle at her breasts. But they didn't seem to satisfy his hunger for the taste of her skin as his grazing mouth wandered lower, feeding on each curve of her ribs. When his moist lips travelled on to her stomach, her muscles contracted sharply, that curling ache intensifying until she wanted to cry out at the tormenting sweetness of it. And Jackson was doing nothing to ease it. On the contrary, his only interest seemed to be in kissing every inch of her.

When she realized his exploring kisses were taking him into a forbidden area, she made a panicked attempt to stop him. 'Don't. You –' Jolted by the sudden hot sensation that swept through her, Ann jammed a fist into her mouth and tried to bite back the animal sound that rose from her throat.

A wildness claimed her. Unable to control it, she abandoned herself completely to it, writhing and twisting with eyes closed, fingers digging at the bedcovers beneath her, a sheen of perspiration breaking out all over her. When the pressure within built to an intolerable level, suddenly he was on top of her again, sliding effortlessly in and burying himself deep. This time she didn't even try to check the soft cry – or any of the other raw sounds that rolled from her as he began to move inside her.

Sprawled across the bed, a bedsheet half-heartedly draped across her hips, Ann felt gloriously limp and empty. Still faintly dazzled by the wonder of the experience, she turned her head to look at the man who had shared it with her. He was watching her, the glint in his eyes holding both a trace of satisfaction and amusement. She rolled on to her side and arched close to him, feeling like a purring cat as she threaded her fingers through the silken hairs on his chest.

'Proud of yourself, are you?' she murmured, peering at him through the tops of her lashes. 'Now that you've had me.'

Reaching out, he snared her waist and pulled her closer still. 'Aren't you?'

'Deliciously so.' She rubbed her head against his shoulder, feeling even more like a contented feline. 'I didn't know it could be like that.' She smiled, convinced she'd discovered the most incredible secret.

'All you needed was a man to show you.'

She sighed an agreement to that, recognising that her husband certainly never had. By nature, Kell wasn't a demonstrative man, his feelings invariably contained behind that hard wall of reserve. She thought back to the times she'd lain with him, remembering the tender restraint of his kisses and his touch. Never once had he attempted to take her out of herself – not the way Jackson Stuart had. In fact, she'd always had the impression that Kell never expected her to enjoy any of it – that he got it over with quickly out of deference to her.

But was that her fault? she wondered, recalling their wedding night and how rigid with fear she'd been. Kell had showered her with ardent kisses that night; the caress of his hands had been eager and bold, but she'd been stiff and completely unresponsive. Too many of her married friends had hinted at how awful it was.

Even her father had lectured her on her wifely duty to submit to her husband's demands, implying that his exercise of conjugal rights was something to be endured. And that terrible, ripping pain had confirmed everything they'd said. Afterwards she had cried and cried, resisting all of Kell's attempts to console her, hating to feel even the touch of his hands let alone to be taken in his arms.

Perhaps it wasn't surprising that her husband had become something less than an ardent lover. It was what she'd wanted. She didn't want to think about Kell – not now. But she had to. He'd be arriving this afternoon.

Suddenly she was assailed by a whole host of doubts and uncertainties. 'Jackson, will I – will I see you again?' The possibility that she wouldn't seemed unbearable.

He tucked a hand under her chin and lifted her head from his shoulder, his gaze warmly possessive as it moved over her face. 'Do you think I could stay away from you now – after this?'

The tension left her in a faint tremor of relief. 'I didn't know. I wasn't sure,' she admitted, smiling at her doubts. But the smile faded as a new thought occurred to her. 'But how? With Kell here –'

'Not here. Not Kansas City.' His fingers moved caressingly over her face, stroking her cheek and her lips, tracing their curves and hollows in loving detail. 'When your husband arrives this afternoon, I want you to convince him that you're tired of the city, that you miss the peace and serenity of Morgan's Walk – that you're eager to go home.'

'He'd never believe me.' She turned from his hand, loathing the thought of going back there, but Jackson wouldn't let her pull away.

'He'll believe you,' he stated confidently. 'He'll believe you because it's the very thing he desires.'

'How can you ask me to go back there when you know how much I hate it?'

He smiled at the shimmer of resentment in her eyes. Not once had she suggested leaving her husband for him. If the thought had crossed her mind, Jackson Stuart was certain she would have instantly dismissed it. It was something her pride wouldn't allow. She was a doctor's daughter who had married above herself. No matter how miserable or wretchedly unhappy she was, Ann

Morgan wasn't about to give up her new-found wealth and status – not for love, especially when he'd told her that he had nothing else to offer her. In her own way, Ann Morgan was just as greedy as he was.

'I want you to go back, my darling, because it's the safest place for us to meet,' he said.

Confusion darkened her eyes. 'The safest? How? If you start coming to the house –'

'Not the house. We'll meet in Tulsa. You make trips into town twice a month for mail and supplies, don't you?'

'Yes.'

'And when you're there, don't you usually take a room at the hotel so you have a place to rest and freshen up?' He already knew the answer to that. In fact, he was certain he knew her habits better than she did.

'Yes.'

'Then, we'll meet there in your room – where we can be alone.'

'But – what if we're discovered?'

'We won't be. The desk clerk's a friend of mine. He'll warn us if anyone comes. And don't worry, my love. We won't have to meet in secret for long . . . just until I can find a way for us to have the kind of life we want,' he said against her lips, then claimed them in another long, drugging kiss. He was already sure of the way, but until he was sure of her, he wouldn't take the final steps.

Ann was at the train station to meet Kell when he arrived that afternoon. And, just as Jackson Stuart had predicted, she had no difficulty convincing her husband that she was homesick. Three days later, the entire Morgan entourage boarded the train to return to Morgan's Walk.

Ten days later, she went to town and took a room at the Tulsa House as usual. She barely had time to remove her dust cloak and hat when she heard a furtive tap on the door. With heart pounding, she hurried to open it. Less than a minute later, it was once again closed and locked and she was in Jackson Stuart's arms.

— 26 —

Mᴀʀᴄʜ 27, 1894

*I fear Chris has found out about us. I shouldn't have gone into
town when I was there only last week, but another seven days
seemed such a long time to wait before seeing Jackson again that
I had to go. Rarely can we spend more than an hour together,
but those stolen hours are what have made my life bearable these
last few months. What a wanton woman I have become, yet I feel
no shame – only guilt at the way I must deceive Kell.*

*And now fear as well that Chris may convey his suspicions to
Kell. I know he must suspect something. He looked at me so
strangely when I opened the door to admit him. And well he
should have, for my clothes and hair were all disarranged from
my haste in dressing, and my chin was reddened by the sharp
stubble on Jackson's face. Next time I must insist that he shaves
immediately before he meets me. Next time. I pray there will be
one, and that all my fears are foolish imaginings and that Chris's
odd silence during the ride home meant nothing. Yet I'm certain
that as quickly as Chris arrived after Jackson had left, he must
have passed him in the hall. Did he see him leave my room as
well?*

He said nothing to me. He didn't even comment on my state of disarray. Naturally I explained away my appearance by claiming that I had been weary from the long ride into town and laid down to rest. I'm not sure he believed that.

Whatever he thinks or suspects, I know he has had no opportunity to speak to Kell as Chris didn't dine with us this evening. After he had escorted me safely back to Morgan's Walk, Chris left again almost immediately – to go to one of the neighbours, he said. Kell seemed to know about it so perhaps that truly is where he went.

What a long, trying evening this has been for me. As usual Kell shut himself in the library with his precious account books shortly after dinner concluded, and I have been alone with my thoughts.

I sit here by the window of our bedroom and look at the rising moon and the first glitter of stars. Somewhere I know that Jackson sees them, too. I wonder if he thinks of me as I think of him. . . .

How odd. I see a horse and rider approaching the house through the trees in the back. Who could be coming to call at such a late hour? And why doesn't he ride up the lane? It can't be Chris. He was astride his Palomino when he left, and this horse looks black, as black as

The sentence was left unfinished. Curious, Flame turned the page, but it was blank – as were all the rest of the pages in the diary. She looked up and found Ben Canon watching her with speculative interest. That bright gleam in his eyes seemed to gauge her reaction, trying to determine the extent of her curiosity. She felt a ripple of irritation at the way she had been manoeuvred into caring. But it was immaterial now. She had to find out the rest of it.

Yet she didn't want to give him the satisfaction of knowing how thoroughly she was hooked. With false calm, Flame closed the diary and laid it on the cherrywood table next to the plate of cold sandwiches.

Flame avoided stating the obvious, aware that Ben Canon had to know precisely where Ann Morgan's diary left off. 'I assume the rider she saw was Jackson Stuart.'

'It was.' With one hand, he removed his reading glasses and slipped them inside the breast pocket of his jacket, drawing her attention to the thick booklet held open in his other hand.

'What happened then?' She studied the age-yellowed pages, fairly certain the booklet wasn't another diary yet unable to make out what it was.

Unhurried, the attorney wandered over to her chair. 'I think it would be best if you learned the answer to that by reading a transcript of your great-grandfather's testimony at the trial.'

'What trial?' Frowning, she hesitantly took it from him.

'The trial of Jackson Stuart for the attempted murder of Kell Morgan.'

Inwardly she faltered at his announcement as her glance raced to the portrait above the mantelpiece. Maybe she should have expected something of the sort, but she hadn't. Attempted murder, Ben Canon had said. That meant Stuart hadn't succeeded. Had it been a deliberate attempt on Kell Morgan's life or had it been the result of an accidental confrontation? From Ann Morgan's diary, Flame assumed that she had recognised her lover and slipped out to meet him. Looking at the hard, proud man in the painting, she could easily imagine the rage, the humiliation and hurt he would have felt if he'd caught his beloved wife in the arms of another man. Honour would have demanded a challenge. Was that what had happened?

The answers to her questions were in the opened transcript she held. She forced her gaze away from the portrait and brought it down to the nearly one hundred-year-old document in her hands.

'Q. Please state your name for the record.

'A. Christopher Morgan.

'Q. You are the brother of the intended victim, is that correct, Mr Morgan?

'A. Yes, sir.

'Q. And you reside at the ranch known as Morgan's Walk along with your brother, is that correct?

'A. Yes, it is.

Q. Will you please tell the court where you were on the evening of March 27th of this year?

'A. In the early part of the evening, I was at a neighbouring ranch – the Bitterman place. It was late when I got back to Morgan's Walk. Probably between ten and eleven o'clock.

'Q. Will you describe to the court what happened when you returned to Morgan's Walk? And, may I remind you that you are still under oath.

'A. Yes, sir. As I said, it was somewhere between ten and eleven. I'd unsaddled and turned my horse into the corral. I was on my way to the house. I noticed there were lights still burning in the library. I realised Kell – my brother – was still up working on the account books. So I came the back way to the house – through the trees. The library's located on that side of the house. I thought I'd check in with him since I hadn't talked to him all day.

'I was probably a hundred and fifty feet from the house when I saw somebody prowling around outside. It was close to payday and I knew we had more cash on hand that we usually keep at the ranch. The thought crossed my mind to raise the alarm, but I couldn't be sure there wasn't someone inside holding a gun to Kell so I slipped closer . . .'

With gun drawn, Chris moved through the trees, then froze against the trunk of an oak as a large patch of white floated across the ground toward the dark figure of a man. It was Ann, a dark shawl thrown over the top of her nightgown. He felt sick inside. All the fight went out of him as he lowered his gun and slumped against the tree.

A hundred times he'd told himself that he was wrong about that afternoon – that Ann was too fine and too good to get mixed up in some illicit affair. She'd been so anxious to go to town that day. There was some lace that she absolutely had to order right away, she'd said. Then when they got there, she hadn't gone to the mercantile store; she'd gone straight to the hotel 'to freshen up'. When she hadn't come out an hour later, he'd gone to see what was keeping her. He wanted to get back to the ranch and over to the Bittermans'.

He hadn't been surprised to see Blackjack Stuart in the hall. The gambler had hung around Tulsa all winter. When they passed each other, Chris had caught the smell of some flowery fragrance and smiled, guessing that Stuart had just passed a pleasant hour or two in the company of a woman.

When Ann had opened the door to him, he'd smelled the exact same perfume on her. And she'd had the dishevelled look of a woman who had just stepped out of some man's arms. She said she'd been resting, but her eyes had been overly bright, her face glowing with the look of a woman who had just been thoroughly satisfied. And he'd seen what a man's whiskers could do to a woman's delicate skin.

He hadn't wanted to believe. He'd fought against it, but there she was running into Stuart's arms. Somewhere back in the trees, a horse snorted in alarm and moved skittishly, rustling the remains of last year's fallen leaves.

Chris looked to the house, his gaze drawn to the lights shining through the glass-panel doors to the library. Kell was there. How could he tell him about his wife? How could he possibly keep it from him? His gut felt all twisted inside, an anger clawing at his throat. He wished he'd never found out. He'd wished he'd never gone to that hotel room. He wished anything that would mean he didn't have to face Kell with Ann's betrayal.

Jackson Stuart heard the whisper of movement a second before his stallion snorted the alarm. In a half-crouch, he whirled to face it, levelling the long muzzle of his revolver at it, then cursed his luck when he saw Ann running across the grass to him. In another minute, he would have had the angle that would have made her a widow, a very rich widow.

He lowered his gun, but didn't holster it, catching her with his free arm as she flung herself at him. 'My darling, I can't believe you're here,' she whispered, pressing a hundred kisses over his neck and jaw as he drew her deeper into the shadows, keeping one eye on the library all the while. 'How could you take such a risk? But I'm glad you did. I needed to see you. I've been so worried.'

But he didn't listen, wishing to hell she'd shut up so he could think how to salvage this. Yet over and over in his mind, he kept thinking that he should have known his luck had changed – he should have known last night when he lost four straight hands at blackjack. He would have lost the fifth if he hadn't palmed an ace. Then he'd nearly got caught. He'd walked away from the table, unwilling to push what was left of his luck any farther.

He should have made his move against Morgan sooner, but he'd wanted to make sure they had the ranch payroll on hand. He could have killed Morgan a dozen times from ambush, but he'd wanted to make it look like a robbery. He didn't want any suspicion thrown on him when he later married Morgan's widow.

The money was there in the library, according to Ann, locked in a cashbox Morgan kept in the bottom drawer of his big mahogany desk. And Morgan was in there, too. Dammit, he'd come so close to making it all work, he couldn't give up now. Tomorrow, he had no choice but to wait until then now that Ann had seen him. Damn her.

Suddenly he tensed, catching a movement in the library. Then Morgan appeared at the double set of doors, his tall, broad frame nearly filling them. He opened one of them and stepped outside. Alerted by the scrape of his boot on the bricked walk, Ann looked over her shoulder and emitted a faint, strangled cry of alarm, briefly pressing closer to Jackson. For an instant Jackson stared at the perfect target Morgan made, backlighted by the lights from inside. His luck hadn't changed he realised, as he raised his gun, thumbing back the hammer.

When Chris saw Kell step outside, his glance immediately raced to the embracing lovers. Not even the deep of the night's shadows could conceal the long white of her skirt. Sick with dread, he knew Kell was bound to notice it. Then he caught the gleam of moonlight on the barrel of a gun. Cold fear shafted through him. Kell wasn't armed. He always unbuckled his gun belt the minute he walked into the house.

'Is that you, Chris?' Kell called out, followed by a questioning, 'Ann?'

Thrown into action by the sound of his brother's voice, Chris brought his gun up and yelled, 'Look out, Kell! He's got a gun!'

Stuart squeezed the trigger just as the full-throated cry of warning shattered the night's stillness, the explosive report drowning out most of it. Ann's scream barely registered as his glance stayed long enough to watch Morgan go down, lost in the dark shadows close to the ground. Then Stuart swung toward that voice out of the night, blood pumping high and hot through him, a steely calm guiding his every move. Morgan's brother stepped out from a tree into the full light of the moon, his gun levelled, looking for a clear shot. Exultant at the thought that he could eliminate both Morgans, he pushed Ann from him, not wanting her endangered by a stray bullet and simultaneously snapped off two quick shots.

He pulled back the hammer on the third and caught Morgan's gun flash. He heard its barking report as the bullet slammed into his right shoulder, the impact spinning him to the side and sending his own shot wild. There was no pain, only a fiery hot burning sensation. He tried to come around and bring his gun to bear on the younger Morgan again, but Ann came out of the shadows, crying his name and throwing herself at him amidst the sound of more gunshots and shouts of alarm. Off-balance, he couldn't absorb the sudden weight of her against him, her momentum driving them both to the ground, the fall jarring the revolver from his hand. Swearing viciously he tried to push her off him and grope for the gun, pain knifing through his shoulder.

A boot came down hard on his wrist, pinning it to the ground. Stuart looked up – into the muzzle of a gun. A handful of half-dressed cowboys stood around him, all in boots and hat, some with braces drooping around their pants and others with belts and holsters buckled around their red flannels. He let his head fall back against the earth's hard pillow. His bid for Morgan's Walk was finished. He'd lost.

In a kind of dazed shock, Chris walked over to them and stared at the dark wet stain that spread slowly from the small hole in the back of Ann's white nightgown. He looked at the gun in his hand. The bullet that had made that hole had come from it. Repulsed by the cold feel of it, Chris let go of the gun, letting it fall to the ground, then crouched down next to Ann. She lay slumped and motionless – like a rag doll partially draped over the man whose life she had tried to save.

'Ann.' Tentatively he reached to touch her. 'I didn't mean to. I didn't see you. Why? Why?'

'What'd he do?' One of the cowboys spoke up. 'Use her as a shield?'

Chris didn't answer, letting them think what they liked and hoping his silence might protect Kell from the dishonour his wife had brought him. He started to pick her up, gently and tenderly, not wanting to hurt her, mindless that she was beyond hurt.

'Don't touch her.'

There was such hoarseness in that voice that Chris hardly recognized it as Kell's. When he looked up, his brother towered over him, his left arm hanging limply at his side, blood dripping steadily off the tips of his fingers.

'Boss, you're hurt,' someone said.

But no one took a step towards him, frozen by the look of stark, white grief that had turned his face to stone. Chris backed away from the body, his mouth and throat working convulsively as he searched for the words to tell his brother how sorry he was. But he couldn't find them and he had a feeling Kell was beyond hearing them.

He watched in a silent agony of his own as Kell sank to his knees beside his wife's body and picked her up with his one good arm, cradling her against his chest and burying his face in the dark cloud of her unbound hair. Those big shoulders heaved, racked by grief, but no sound came from him – nothing at all.

Vaguely Chris was aware that Stuart had been dragged to his feet but he paid no attention to him until one of the men asked, 'What about this guy? Want us t' string him up?'

For an instant, he was tempted to give the order. For an instant, anger boiled inside him. For an instant he wanted to blame Stuart for Ann's death, reasoning that none of this would have happened if it wasn't for him. But hanging Stuart wouldn't erase the guilt he felt. He'd been the one who pulled the trigger, not Stuart. And he couldn't pretend otherwise.

'Tie him up and lock him in the tack room,' he said. 'And, Gus, ride into town and get a doctor for my brother. While you're there, tell the sheriff to wire the marshal and tell him we've got a prisoner for the tumblewagon.'

'She was killed,' Flame murmured absently, a touch of sadness in her voice. 'The poor woman.'

'It was ruled accidental.' The attorney held a match to the bowl of his pipe and puffed deeply, drawing the fire into the tamped tobacco. 'Conjecture is' – he shook out the match and tossed it into the fireplace – 'she saw that Stuart was hit and went to his aid, inadvertently stepping into the line of fire. I find it much more logical and more in character than the supposition that she might have been nobly sacrificing her life to save him.'

Having read Ann Morgan's diary, Flame agreed with that, although she doubted Kell Morgan would have found much consolation in the knowledge. As her glance swung to the portrait, she noticed there were no openings along the outer wall, only a window.

'This room doesn't have any doors to the outside.'

'Not any more.' Charlie Rainwater waved a leathered hand at the panelled wall to the left of the fireplace. 'They used to be there, but about a week after his wife's death, Kell Morgan ordered them walled in and the brick path outside torn up. I figure the sight of 'em probably haunted him, making him remember that night and relive her death all over again.' He tipped his head back and gazed at the portrait. 'From all accounts, he took her dyin' pretty hard. It's not surprising I guess, when you think how much he adored her.'

Ben Canon grunted an agreement to that, then removed the pipe stem from between his teeth to add, 'I doubt if his grieving was made any easier by Stuart's brag from his jail cell in Tulsa about how close he came to having everything that belonged to Kell Morgan – from his money and his house to his wife.' He arched a glance at Flame. 'Which is what prompted Kell Morgan to insert the condition that the property must pass to a blood heir or revert – at that time – to the Creek Nation. Later, after statehood was granted in 1907, he changed it to the State of Oklahoma.'

'I see.' Flame bowed her head briefly, her glance falling on the transcript in her lap. 'What happened to Jackson Stuart?'

'He was tried before Judge Isaac Parker in Fort Smith and found guilty of attempted murder. With typical harshness, the judge sentenced him to thirty years of hard labour. Ten or fifteen years earlier, Parker would probably have ordered him to be hanged on the theory he was guilty of murdering somebody even if he hadn't succeeded in his attempt on Kell Morgan's life. But times had changed, and Parker was no longer the final authority in the territory. Too many of his decisions had been appealed to the Supreme Court and reversed.' A smile rounded his shiny cheeks, ruddy in the fire's glow. 'I suppose you could say that Stuart's luck had returned. A prison sentence was definitely better than a hangman's rope.'

'And Chris Morgan, my great-grandfather?'

'He left Morgan's Walk shortly after the trial was over – never to return. I'm sure you can appreciate the guilt and remorse he felt over Ann Morgan's death. However inadvertent or accidental, it was a bullet from his gun that killed her. And, as Charlie said, Kell Morgan took her death very hard. But it wasn't something he verbalised. In the code of the western man, he held his grief inside and went off by himself for days on end. With the responsibility he felt for her death, Chris Morgan believed – rightly or wrongly – that his presence was a constant reminder to his brother of that night. So, he left.' The attorney paused, gesturing briefly with his pipe in the direction of the mahogany desk. 'There is a letter from him to that effect if you'd like to read it.'

'No, it isn't necessary.' She refused with a silent shake of her head, convinced there was, indeed, such a document to support his statement. Gathering up the photo album, the diary, and the transcript, Flame rose from her chair and carried them over to the desk, placing them on top of it, then turning to confront the two men. 'I admit this was a very interesting story –' she began.

'Oh, but it isn't the end of it, Mrs Stuart,' Ben Canon broke in, again that gleam of supreme confidence in his position lighting his eyes. 'In a way, it could be called the beginning. You see, Blackjack Stuart was released from prison after serving twenty years of his thirty-year sentence. By then little Johnny Morgan had grown up into Big John Morgan. Unfortunately he inherited more than just his mother's dark hair and eyes, but many of her rashly impetuous tendencies as well. At the tender age of sixteen he was obliged to marry the daughter of a neighbouring rancher. Hattie was one of those miracle babies, born six months after the wedding.'

'But she was a chip off the *old* block,' Charlie Rainwater inserted. 'A Morgan through and through. And old Kell spotted that right off. By the time her legs were long enough to straddle a saddle, he was taking her everywhere with him. Some of the old-timers used to tell me about watching this five-year-old tyke out hazing cattle with the best of 'em, cuttin' out a steer or chasin' back a cow that broke the herd. She was Kell Morgan's shadow, all right, and closer to him than she ever was to her pa.'

The foreman made no attempt to disguise the admiration in his voice when he spoke of Hattie Morgan. The mention of her turned Flame's thoughts to the woman lying upstairs – and the accusations she'd made against Chance. She felt her wedding ring, twisting it about on her finger, suddenly impatient again with all this talk that had nothing to do with him.

'I hope this is leading to something.' Pushed by a restlessness and vague irritation, she crossed to the fireplace.

'It is,' Ben Canon assured her. 'As I mentioned earlier, Blackjack – or Jackson Stuart as Ann Morgan preferred to call him – was released from prison in 1914. He returned to an Oklahoma vastly different from the one he'd left. It was no longer a territory.

In 1907, it had joined the Union as the forty-sixth state. The discovery of the Glenn Pool oilfield in 1905 and the Cushing field in 1912 had transformed Tulsa from a dusty cowtown into the oil capital of the world. The city's streets were paved; electric streetcars provided public transportation; and modern 'skyscrapers' – five and six storeys tall – had sprung up all up and down Main Street. There were shops and stores of every kind and description, offering the biggest and best selection there was to their customers.

'And Morgan's Walk . . .' As the attorney paused for dramatic effect, his gaze rested heavily on Flame. 'With statehood, Kell had finally acquired title to the twelve hundred acres that comprise this valley. He owned another two thousand acres of adjoining land besides that, and leased the grazing rights on another five thousand, making Morgan's Walk the largest cattle ranch near Tulsa. It was a showplace for the entire area. The newly oil-rich looked at this house – one of the finest examples of Georgian architecture west of the Mississippi – and built their mansions to rival it.'

Smiling to shift the mood, he went on, 'So it was on a fine spring day in early May that Kell Morgan took his seven-year old granddaughter to Tulsa so she could pick out her birthday present, an occasion made doubly memorable by the fact that he allowed her to sit on his lap and drive his touring car, a Chevrolet, to town . . .'

Young Hattie Morgan kept a firm hold on her grandfather's hand as she walked proudly along the crowded sidewalk. But each time they passed a store window, she couldn't resist stealing a glance at her reflection in the glass and admiring the well-dressed girl that looked back at her. Everything she wore was new – from the shiny patent leather slippers with tailored bows on her feet to the leghorn straw hat adorned with flowers and ribbons on her head, but especially the polka dot dress with its full skirt and lace-trimmed ruffles. Her grandfather had declared she was the prettiest girl in Tulsa in her new outfit. And she felt certain he was right. He'd never been wrong about anything. Either way, these new clothes were at least as wonderful as the hand-tooled saddle he'd given her for Christmas.

Suddenly his hand tightened with punishing force, bringing her to an abrupt stop and pulling her back to his side. 'Well, what a surprise! If it isn't the great Kell Morgan himself.' A stranger stood squarely in their path. Hattie tilted her head back to look at him from beneath the floppy brim of her new hat. White streaked the hair beneath his hat and his face had a hardened, gaunt look about it, but it was the darkly bright gleam in his blue eyes that caught and held her attention. There was something about it that wasn't nice, despite the wide smile that curved his mouth. 'I wondered when I'd run into you, Morgan.'

'What are you doing in town, Stuart?' The coldness in her grandfather's voice was chilling. Hattie knew he only talked like that when he was really angry.

She decided this stranger named Stuart couldn't be very smart because he just kept smiling, too dumb to know how he was riling her grandfather. He'd be sorry.

'The same as you, Morgan – walking wide and free,' he replied. 'Although I notice you don't throw as big a shadow as you used to, not with all these oil moguls around here now.'

Frowning in bewilderment, Hattie turned to her grandfather. 'What's a mogul, Grandpa?'

The stranger immediately turned the inspection of his blue eyes on to her. 'And who do we have here?' He crouched down in front of her, a hand reaching out to flip the lace ruffle on her bertha. 'Aren't you a pretty little lady.'

'I'm Harriet Morgan,' she informed him coolly and importantly. 'But my grandpa calls me Hattie.'

'Hattie. That's a very pretty name.' The man straightened, again turning his gleaming gaze on her grandfather. 'So she's your granddaughter, is she? I heard your son was raising girls out there.' Then he winked at her. 'Maybe I'll just have to wait until she grows up and then marry her.'

'It wouldn't do you any good, Stuart. It wouldn't get you Morgan's Walk – not any more.'

'Yeah, I heard about the change you made – that it has to pass to a blood kin.' His smile widened. 'You'd be surprised what a patient man I am. I'd be just as happy to see it pass to my son.'

Her grandfather was getting angry. She could see the vein standing out in his neck. 'That will never happen, Stuart.'

The man's smile faded. Suddenly he looked dangerous. 'Maybe it will be over your dead body, Morgan, but I swear to you the day will come when a Stuart owns Morgan's Walk.'

*

'Approximately a month later, Stuart married a widow about twenty-five years his junior. She had a hundred-sixty-acre farm back in the hills that her late husband left her. It wasn't much of a farm, with only about sixty acres of tillable bottom land, the rest rock and trees. The speculation was that Stuart had married her thinking there was oil on the place, especially when drilling rigs moved on to the property six months after he married her. Six wells were drilled, but they were all 'dusters' – dry holes. The widow, however, ultimately gave him a son – Ring Stuart.'

'Yeah,' Charlie spoke up. 'And the threat that Miss Hattie had lived with all her life suddenly became very real when her baby sister Elizabeth ran off and married Ring Stuart.' He paused, then added, as if to make sure Flame understood the significance of all this, 'Ring Stuart was your husband's father.'

'And that's it,' she challenged. 'That's the extent of your proof against Chance – a threat that was made seventy-odd years ago. Because he married me, you think he's after Morgan's Walk.'

'Not just because he married you,' the attorney denied, then hesitated a split second, surveying her with a considering glance. 'There are other factors. For instance, how long have you known him?'

'A month, more or less.' She tilted her chin a fraction of an inch higher, fully aware that it sounded like a very short time.

'What a remarkable coincidence,' Ben Canon declared with mock wonder. 'It was approximately a month ago that we learned of your existence and Hattie informed Chance that he would not be her heir.'

'Did she specifically name me?'

'No. But a man with Stuart's sources – and resources – it wouldn't be too difficult for him to learn your identity.'

Unable to deny that, Flame chose to ignore it. 'What makes you so certain he wants this ranch? With his money, he could buy a hundred   a thousand like it.'

'No doubt he could,' Canon agreed. 'That's a question you'll have to ask him. And when you do, ask him why he's bought or optioned all the property adjoining Morgan's Walk to the south and east. Even for him, that's bound to represent a tidy investment of capital. Make no mistake about it, Flame, he wants this land.'

She wanted to deny it, to argue with him, but he sounded much too confident and that made her very cautious. 'Why?'

— 273 —

'You mean he didn't show you his plans for this property when you went to his office Monday morning?'

'What plans?' she demanded, struggling to hold her temper.

'His plans to dam the river and turn this entire valley into a lake, complete with marinas, resort hotels, condominiums, and luxurious lake homes. It's a very impressive project, I understand.'

'I don't believe you.' She shook her head in quick, vigorous denial. 'You're basing all your accusations against Chance on the fact that a Stuart once tried to get control of Morgan's Walk through marriage. Even if Chance wanted this land – which I'm not convinced he does – there are other ways he could obtain it. He didn't have to marry me to get it.'

'True,' the attorney conceded. 'For instance, he could have tried to buy the land from you. Although he couldn't be sure you would be willing to sell it. Which would mean he would have to bring a variety of economic pressures to bear to force you to sell. Or he could use his considerable political influence to have the land condemned. Or he could have contested the will. But any one of those options might take years – with no guarantee at the end of them that the land would be his. But marriage – think how much quicker, how much more certain that must have seemed to him.'

'And I suppose you think it's impossible he might actually love me.' A bitterness crept into her challenge.

'Forgive me, I certainly don't mean to suggest that you are without considerable attractions. I'm sure he found it very convenient to love you.'

She hated him for saying that. She hated to think that she was being used. 'I don't believe you,' she repeated tautly.

'Well, believe this, Flame. He intends to destroy Morgan's Walk. If he has his way, all of this will be under a hundred feet of water. You are the only one who can stop him.'

Footsteps approached the library, their tread heavy and slow. Flame turned toward the doorway as Charlie Rainwater rose from his chair, a tension gripping him and freezing him in place.

The doctor appeared in the opening and paused, his glance sweeping all three of them before it fell. 'She went quietly. There was no pain, Charlie.'

27

CHANCE CHARGED out of the private elevator before its doors had fully opened. His gaze sliced to Molly as she started to rise from her chair, her customary wide smile of welcome missing, in its place a look of anxiety and regret. Chance took no notice of either as he issued a sharp, 'Has anyone located her yet?' He caught the faint negative shake of her head and didn't wait to hear the actual words. Without a break in stride, he swept past her desk to his office door, snapping over his shoulder, 'Get Sam and tell him I want him in my office – now.'

Anger pushed at him as he crossed to his desk, an anger that had a hot spur of desperation to it. At the sound of footsteps, Chance swung back to face the door. Sam walked in with Molly right behind him.

He approached the desk, looking harried and rumpled as if he'd been up half the night – which he had. 'I'm sorry, Chance –' he began.

But Chance had heard all the apologies at three o'clock in the morning when Sam had called to tell him Flame was missing. He'd had a bad feeling when he hadn't got an answer last night at her flat in San Francisco. But Sam had initially assured him there was nothing to worry about; he'd checked with Matt Sawyer and found out that her flight had been delayed in Dallas with a mechanical problem and she wouldn't arrive in San Francisco until well after midnight Pacific time.

'Dammit, Sam, we both know where she is.' Pivoting sharply, he turned to the smoked glass windows, fighting the rage and frustration he felt at coming so close to having it all, then having it literally snatched from him at the last minute. 'She's at Morgan's Walk.'

'We can't be sure of that,' Molly offered in placation. 'She could have changed to another flight in Dallas or decided to spend the night there and catch a morning plane. There are any number of possible explanations –'

'No.' Chance dismissed them all with a firm shake of his head as he stared grimly at the bleak grey clouds that hung over the city. 'Somehow Hattie got to her.'

'Jeezus, Chance, what if she's found out? What if she knows you want the ranch?'

His control snapped at Sam's worried question. He spun on him. 'She wouldn't have found out a damned thing if you had done your job and stayed with her! Hattie wouldn't have been able to get near – Flame.'

She stood in his office doorway, rigid as a statue, gripped by an icy fury that swept all remaining doubt from her. She completely ignored his cohorts in the deception and focused the whole of her attention on the man who had tricked her, used her – betrayed her.

Recovering quickly from his initial surprise at seeing her, Chance faltered barely an instant, then started around his desk to come to her, his expression making a lightning transition from shock to a mask of relief. 'Where on earth have you been? We've been turning half the country upside down looking for you.' Once, the sight of that intimately possessive look in his eyes would have sent her straight into his arms. Now it failed to move her at all. 'I've been half out of my mind thinking something had happened to you.'

'I overheard how worried you were, Chance,' she replied coolly, watching as he came to a stop, a good twenty feet still separating them, his head lifted in wary caution. She started toward him, taking slow and deliberate steps. 'What exactly was it that you were afraid I'd find out? That Hattie Morgan is your aunt? Or that you stood to inherit Morgan's Walk before I appeared on the scene? Or that when I did, you decided the most expedient and expeditious course of action to regain control of the land was to marry me?'

His narrowed gaze was quick in its study of her, taking in the icy green glitter of her eyes and the faintly contemptuous curl of her lips. 'Flame, I know how it must look – how it must sound,' he began carefully. 'But that's not the way it is.'

'Isn't it?' Her challenging voice trembled with an anger she no longer tried to conceal as she stopped in front of him. 'What a pushover I must have seemed to you, lapping up all your lies and coming back for more, honestly believing that you loved me and that I could trust you – turn on the charm and sweep me off my feet. That was your game plan, wasn't it?'

'You're wrong, Flame.'

'No, you're the one who's made a mistake.' She had come here this morning, certain that if she could talk to Chance, he'd clear away all her doubts. He had, but not in the way she'd expected. With a wrenching twist, she pulled off her wedding rings and held them up for Chance to see. 'These don't mean any more to me than they do to you.' Coolly she opened her fingers and let them fall to the floor, taking pleasure in the brief flare of anger in his expression. She started to turn away then paused. 'I suppose I should inform you that your aunt died at twelve-forty-two this morning. Unofficially, I am the new owner of Morgan's Walk, and I swear to you, Chance, that you will never possess so much as one inch of that land.'

This time when she turned to walk away, he grabbed her and hauled her back to him, his fingers digging into the soft flesh of her arms. 'Dammit, Flame, will you listen to me?'

She didn't flinch from him or attempt to pull free. 'What's the matter, Chance? Have you decided that charm won't work so now you're going to resort to violence? Hattie said you'd do anything to get Morgan's Walk.'

He released her abruptly, his jaw clenched, eyes cold. He didn't try to stop her when she walked away. At the doorway, she paused to look back at him.

'The funeral's Saturday morning. Don't come. You won't be welcome.' Then she was gone, closing the door behind her.

He stared at it, then scooped the rings from the floor and held them in his palm. The diamond's sparkling brilliance seemed to taunt him – just as she had. He closed his fingers tightly around them and turned to walk back to his desk.

'Aren't you going after her?' Sam frowned. 'You can't just let her walk away like that. You've got to talk to her – make her understand.'

'Not now. She's in no mood to listen.' He had never seen her like that – so angry, so hurt, all closed to him, and ready to throw his words back in his face.

'Chance is right,' Molly spoke up quickly in his support. 'Right now she feels hurt. And all she wants to do is hurt back. You can't reason with someone in pain. You have to wait – give her a couple of days for it to ease, then talk to her.'

'I hope you're right,' Sam said, none too certainly.

'I am,' she smiled confidently. 'She loves you, Chance. I'm as certain of that as I am that the sun comes up in the morning.'

'But what if you're wrong?' Sam murmured, shaking his head.

'She isn't,' Chance asserted, holding up the hand that clenched the wedding rings. 'I'll have these back on her finger. It may take me some time but they'll be there. I'm not going to lose her – or Morgan's Walk.'

But Sam wasn't to be mollified as he ran a hand though his rumpled hair and sighed. 'This is all my fault.'

The phone rang, the blinking light indicating the call was coming in on Chance's private line. 'I'll get it,' Chance said as Molly started to answer it. 'It's probably either Maxine or Matt Sawyer calling to let us know about Hattie.' He picked up the phone.

'Chance, darling, it's Lucianna.' The familiar melodic trill of her voice came over the line. 'I hope I'm not calling at a bad time, but there's this ridiculous rumour going around that you got married without letting your friends know a thing about it. Is it true, darling?'

He looked at the rings in his hand. 'That seems to be open to argument at the moment.'

28

A SHROUD OF cold grey clouds covered the late afternoon sky, casting its gloom over the imposing three storey brick mansion and adding to its bleak, cheerless look. Dead brown leaves tumbled across the lane in front of Chance's Jaguar, chased by a brooming wind out of the north.

He slowed as he approached the house. There were no cars parked in front of it, indicating that if any of the neighbours had stopped after the funeral, they'd already left. Which meant Flame would be there alone.

He'd debated long and hard about the wisdom of coming out here today. According to Matt Sawyer, Flame was scheduled to fly back to San Francisco tomorrow. He wondered if he should have waited to contact her after she had returned to the city where they'd met, but he didn't think so. The timing now was ideal, too. Sobered by the ritual of the funeral this morning and the opportunity to reflect afterwards, she was bound to be more receptive than she might be another day. And, dammit, he wanted to see her. She was his wife.

He parked the car in front and climbed out. The brisk north wind whipped at his hair and sent more leaves scurrying across the lawn as Chance stared at the house he'd once lived in. A black wreath hung on the front door. There'd been a wreath of mourning on the door the last time he'd stood in front of the house – at almost this very spot. That time it had been for his mother.

Suddenly he was a little boy again, fighting the tears he was too old to cry and feeling the choke of a child's hatred in his throat. His father's hand was hard on his shoulder, the reek of whiskey strong on his breath.

'Did you see her face when you told her someday you'd be back? White, she went. White as them pillars. And you will, boy.' His fingers dug into the ridge of his shoulder, the grip hurting him. 'Look at it. Look at it and remember, because that house and all this land is gonna be yours. And there's nothing that bitch can do about it. Nothing.'

'I hate her.' The words came from the back of his throat, pushed out by all that bitterness and hot emotion. 'I hate her and I hate that house. When it's mine, I'm gonna burn it down.'

'Now you're talking stupid. Bricks don't burn.' He turned Chance away from the house and pushed him toward a dusty pick-up. 'Come on. Let's get out of here.'

'Where are we gonna live, Pa?'

'We'll find us a place. Don't you worry.'

They'd found a place all right – an old shotgun house in Tulsa, a ramshackle relic from the boom days when the oil companies had built cheap housing for their workers. The house had been freezing in the winter and sweltering in the summer and, most of the time, it stunk of his father's vomit. But the rent had been cheap, just about what he'd earned every month on his paper route that year. His father had worked sporadically then, enough to keep food on the table, clothes on their back, and a bottle of whiskey by his bed. By the time Chance turned fourteen, he'd stopped doing even that much. Enough for a cheap bottle of booze, that was all he'd cared about – that and raving drunkenly about Hattie and reminding Chance that all this was just temporary. Two years later he'd finally succeeded in drinking himself to death.

Hattie had done that to his father – taken his pride and self-respect and ground them under her heel. When they'd lived here at Morgan's Walk, Chance had watched his father slowly crumble under the constant lash of her tongue. He'd hated her for that.

Oh, he had yessed her and noed her, but never with respect in his voice – only defiance.

That was a long time ago. Yet, standing here, it didn't seem all that long. Breathing in deeply, Chance mentally shook off the memories and walked to the front door. He lifted the brass knocker and dropped it twice, the wind carrying off the hollow thuds.

Maxine opened the door to him, her look of surprised recognition quickly turning to quiet welcome. 'Chance. I've been thinking about you so often these past two days, and here you are.'

Stepping inside, he took both her hands and smiled at the stout housekeeper who had been his only friend. 'How are you, Maxine?'

The puffiness around her eyes told of the tears of grief she'd already cried, and the brightness of them now indicated more were held at bay. 'She could be such a cruel woman at times, Chance, but she suffered so at the last I –' She bit back the rest as her chin quivered. She forced a smile. 'It's hard to believe she's gone. I expect any minute to hear her yell for me.'

'I know.' His glance swept the grand foyer, finding it exactly the way he remembered it, right down to the celadon vase on the round table. More than that he could feel Hattie's presence, the stirring of old hostility.

'It isn't fair, Chance,' Maxine murmured. 'I always thought the next time you walked through that door, it would be for good. Now . . .' As her voice trailed off, she glanced sideways in the direction of the main parlour.

Instantly Chance knew Flame was there. 'I'm here to see Mrs Stuart, Maxine.'

'She won't see you.' She shook her head sympathetically. 'She gave strict orders that if you called or –'

'Maxine, I thought I heard –' Flame halted in the parlour's framed arch, her gaze locking on him. She wore a long-sleeved black dress, very plain and very elegant, and her red hair was swept back in a classic chignon. No jewellery of any kind adorned her, and only a minimum of make-up. Yet she had never looked more strongly beautiful to him that at that moment. He released Maxine's hands, letting her step back from him and ignoring the housekeeper's guilty, worried look.

'Hello, Flame.'

'What are you doing here?' Perhaps it was the trace of

hoarseness in her voice or the faint lines of tension around her mouth that alerted Chance to the signs of fatigue and stress. He wasn't sure. In any case, he could see that she seemed tired and, he hoped, vulnerable.

'I came to see you.' He moved away from the door and Maxine, angling towards Flame. 'You are still my wife.'

'You'll be hearing from my attorney about that.'

Even though he'd expected something of the kind, he still felt an anger at actually hearing the words. 'By your attorney, I assume you mean Ben Canon.'

'Does it matter?' She was angry, too, but it was the cold kind she'd shown him at his office. 'Whatever reason you thought you had for coming no longer exists. Please leave or I'll have you thrown out.'

'Why are you so afraid to talk to me, Flame?'

'I'm not!' Her temper flared ever so briefly before she battened it down. 'And I don't have to stand here and listen to you to prove that.'

'Hatred is a very contagious thing. It permeates the very walls of this house.' He wandered past her into the parlour, his glance skimming over the room's familiar furnishings – the ebony piano, the Victorian sofa and chairs, and the silk rug on the floor that held traces of the tea he'd spilled on it long ago. 'The place hasn't changed,' he mused, then angled a glance over his shoulder at her. 'I lived here as a boy. Did Hattie tell you that?' She nodded, almost warily. 'I wasn't allowed in the parlour except on very rare occasions, but I used to sneak in here when she wasn't around. She caught me once, jumping off the piano, and took her cane to me. I probably deserved that. But she had no right to refuse to let me see my mother for three days.' Chance paused, remembering, a bitter cynicism pulling at a corner of his mouth. 'It's odd, but it never made any difference to Hattie that my mother was a Morgan. I was born a Stuart, and because of it, she made my life hell. If there's any justice in the hereafter, that's where she is now.'

'Am I supposed to feel sorry for you now?' Flame mocked from the archway, her arms folded in front in a challenging stance. 'Is that what you hoped to accomplish with that poor, abused childhood vignette? Do you know what's sad, Chance?' She walked over to him, never losing that hint of defiance. 'If you

— 282 —

had told me that before – if you had been honest with me – I probably would have believed you . . . and made an even bigger fool of myself. I suppose I should thank you for that.'

He faced her, now wary himself. 'I made a mistake –'

'A big one. You used me. You used me as a quick and easy means for you to get Morgan's Walk. I will never forgive you for that or forget it.'

'You're wrong. When we met, I didn't know you had any connection to Hattie.'

'It doesn't matter when you found out – before or after you met me. The point is you didn't tell me. On the contrary, you deliberately kept it from me.'

'I admit that was wrong. Maybe I didn't think you would understand. Maybe I wanted us to have more time together first. But it wasn't a lie when I told you I loved you.'

She laughed – a harsh breathless sound. 'I can't believe this. After what you've done, do you really think you can come here and tell me how much you love me, and I'll just fall into your arms? Do you really think I'm that stupid – that gullible – that I'll let myself be taken in by you again?'

There was an ominous tightening of his mouth, a muscle leaping along his jaw. 'I expect you to listen to reason.'

'Whose reason? Yours? You make me sick, you lying bastard.' She turned from him, hating him as violently as she'd once loved him.

'Dammit, Flame.' His hand snaked out to seize her arm. She halted, turning rigid at his touch, and stared coldly at the hand on her arm, saying nothing. The silence stretched for several tense seconds, then he removed his hand from her arm. 'You've been infected by the hate that lives in this house, haven't you?'

'Is that why you're so determined to destroy it and build your grand development on it – because you see it as a place of hatred?' Flame caught the faint start that Chance wasn't quite quick enough to conceal at the mention of his proposed development. 'Did you think I didn't know what you planned to do with Morgan's Walk – and all the rest of the land you've bought?'

'Whatever use I may nor may not have considered putting this land to, has nothing to do with why I'm here.'

'Doesn't it?' she mocked. 'You mean you didn't come here to win me back? I'm curious, Chance. How were you going to convince me to flood this valley and destroy Morgan's Walk? Were you going to wait a couple of months, then come to me and say, "Darling, I have this great idea to take that land you inherited and turn it into a fabulous resort complex – think of the millions you'll make from it, so much more than you would ever realise if you maintained its current ranching operation?" Maybe you'd add the incentive: "We'll do it together, darling – work side by side as partners." Naturally I'd be so blindly in love with you that I'd agree. That's the way you thought it would work, isn't it?'

'Why should I answer that when you wouldn't believe me anyway?' he challenged quietly.

'You're right. I wouldn't.'

Reaching out, he gently took hold of her arms. Flame stiffened instinctively, ready to resist if he should attempt to force himself on her, but he didn't. She was almost sorry. There was a part of her that was so raw it wanted to lash out – to kick and scream and claw. But the undemanding warmth of his hands didn't invite it.

'I've hurt you, Flame. I know that.' There was a persuasive pitch to his voice now, softly serious and subtly soothing. 'You have every right to be angry with me –'

'I have your permission to hate you – how nice,' she murmured caustically, deliberately striving to shatter the spell of his voice.

'Dammit, I came here to apologise, Flame – to tell you that I love you – I need you.'

'You need Morgan's Walk – which I now own,' she fired back and watched his head recoil, his eyes narrowing in a probing study.

'Such a sharp tongue you have,' he murmured. 'Who is it you're trying to convince that you don't love me any more – you or me? If it's me, I'm not buying it because I know you still care.'

She felt her first twinge of uncertainty, conscious of the way everything had quickened inside her moments ago, her pulse accelerating, her senses heightening – coming to battle-readiness, she thought. Yet, she managed coolly to meet his gaze. 'As conceited as you are, I'm sure you believe that.'

'Love can't be turned off with the flick of a switch – as much as you might want to convince me otherwise.'

'That all depends on the circumstances,' Flame asserted, but Chance shook his head, rejecting her claim.

'No, the feelings you had for me are all still there – hidden behind a wall of anger and hurt pride. You may prefer to deny it, but you want me every bit as much as I want you.'

When she felt the pulling pressure of his hands, her first impulse was to resist forcibly. Flame instantly rejected that, realising that only by showing complete indifference would she prove anything to him. As he drew her into his arms, she steeled herself not to react. When his mouth moved towards hers, she waited until the last second, then turned her head aside, letting his lips graze her cheek.

Undeterred, Chance simply transferred his attention to the pulsing vein in her neck. Suddenly it all felt achingly familiar – the sensuous nibbling of his mouth, the caressing splay of his hands, and the hard, lean shape of him. She had to force her hands to remain at her sides as she fought the memory of how it had been between them. The child in her wanted him to hold her tightly and kiss away all the hurt. But it required the innocence of a child to believe that kisses would 'make it all better'. And she had lost that innocence long ago. Physical love – no matter how enjoyable and satisfying – was a momentary thing. It couldn't right the damage that had been done. He'd used her, and by using her, he'd betrayed her. She couldn't trust him any more.

She closed her eyes against her inner tremors of longing, not entirely sure how much she could trust herself. 'Are you through?' She injected all the iciness she could into her question.

She felt him pause, then slowly straightened to look at her, but she carefully kept her face averted, unwilling to let him see how fragile her defences against him actually were.

'For now,' he said, that lazy edge back in his voice. 'But you're not as indifferent to me as you'd like me to believe. I'd prove it to you, but – if I did – you'd hate me for it. And it isn't your hate I want, Flame. It's your love.'

Stung by his arrogance, she lifted her head sharply to glare at him. 'Hattie was right. I'm only now beginning to realise how right she was. You'd stoop to anything, wouldn't you? You'd lie, cheat, steal – whatever is required to get your hands on Morgan's Walk.' She shrugged off his hands and stepped back, unable to bear the touch of him. 'I think you'd better leave, Mr Stuart. You're not welcome here – ever.'

For a long second, he made no move at all – said nothing. Just when she thought she might have to summon Charlie Rainwater and some of the boys from the bunkhouse, Chance slowly nodded. 'I'll go. But I'll tell you the same thing I told Hattie. I'll be back. This isn't finished between us.'

'That sounds remarkably like a threat.' She tilted her head a little higher, letting him see that she wouldn't be intimidated.

His lips curved in a smile that was anything but warm. 'I never make threats, Flame. I thought you knew me better than that.'

She stayed exactly where she was, not moving as he walked around her to the foyer. When she heard the front door close, she pivoted slowly to stare after him. Seconds later she heard the growling rumble of his car starting up. Then she was surrounded by the unsettling silence of the house. Made restless by it, Flame ranged over the parlour, then stopped at a window and studied the rolling tumble of dark grey clouds beyond the glass panes.

That was exactly the way she felt inside – dark and churning with a violent turbulence. These feelings had been there, seething below the surface for the last three days. She'd managed to block them out, but seeing Chance again had unleashed them. Flame finally admitted to herself what she'd instinctively known all along. It would never be over between them. Morgan's Walk made it impossible.

If she'd had any doubts that he still wanted the land, his coming here had eliminated them. He was as determined as ever to get it. Hattie had warned her about that very thing before she died. But how could he succeed? Hattie had left it to her.

Flame turned from the window, suddenly troubled. Ben Canon had told her something. She pressed a hand to her forehead, trying to remember what he'd said. He'd mentioned something about Chance contesting the will and – yes, something about applying financial pressure to force her to sell. But he'd talked about a third alternative. Her frown lifted as she slowly brought her hand down – remembering. He could try to get the land condemned. That's what Ben had said.

Why have it condemned? The lake, of course.

She had to stop him. But how? What was this development of his? If she was going to fight him and win, she had to know more about his plans. Against a man like Chance, she needed specific knowledge. Otherwise, she could never hope to block any attempt he made. She couldn't constantly be on the defensive. She had to find a way to take the fight to him.

The instant she thought it, Flame realised that it wasn't enough merely to prevent him from getting Morgan's Walk. If it was the last thing she did, she had to make him pay, for her grandfather's sake as well as her own. It was time a Morgan got even and she was the one who was going to do it.

It was odd the hot calmness she felt; the rawness – the rage – that had consumed her these last three days now finding a channel, a direction. It didn't matter that at the moment she didn't know how she would go about exacting a fitting retribution. That would come. First she had to learn all she could about Chance's plans for the land.

But how? Ben Canon had indicated there were drawings or blueprints of it in Chance's office. How could she get a copy of them? Chance would never volunteer a set. If there was some way she could get into his office . . . She drew in a quick breath, suddenly realising maybe there was.

She'd have to act quickly. Tonight, in fact. And clothes, she'd need evening clothes, something ultra dressy. Nothing she had with her would do. She'd packed for a weekend in the sun, not an autumn week in Oklahoma. The dress she had on she'd bought yesterday for the funeral. Did she have time to go buy something? She glanced at the ancient grandfather clock that stood beyond the parlour doors in the foyer. It was nearly five. Would there be shops open that carried the type of evening dress she needed? And where were they? Flame railed at the time she'd lose looking for one, especially when she knew there were at least three suitable outfits hanging in her closet in San Francisco.

Closet. That was it. Hattie's closet, jammed with an entire wardrobe of clothes for every occasion. If she could find something that worked, it didn't matter how old it was. The style of evening clothes rarely changed. As for size, with a little tucking and pinning, she could make it fit.

As Flame walked swiftly from the parlour, Maxine entered the foyer. 'I heard Cha – Mr Stuart leave. Would you like me to start supper now, Mrs Stuart?'

After faltering briefly, Flame continued to the staircase. 'You don't need to cook anything, Maxine. I'm not hungry tonight.'

'Oh, I don't have to cook. The neighbours brought enough casseroles and salads to last a week.'

'I'd forgotten that.' Flame halted momentarily at the base of the stairs and turned back to the housekeeper. 'If I want anything to eat later, I'll get it myself. There isn't any need for you to stay. It's been a long day all the way around. I'm sure you'd like to go home.'

'I am tired and . . .' Maxine hesitated. 'If you're sure you don't need me any more this evening, I think I will go back to my place.'

'When you leave, would you stop by the bunkhouse and ask Mr Rainwater to come to the house?'

'Of course.'

With that minor detail handled, Flame started up the steps to put the rest of her plan in motion, her thoughts racing ahead as she tried to recall what evening wear she'd noticed in Hattie's closet.

— 29 —

Fʀᴏᴍ ᴛʜᴇ street below, Flame couldn't see any lights shining from the windows of the Stuart Tower's twentieth floor. On a Saturday night, it wasn't likely anyone would be working – unless it would be a cleaning lady. Just the same, she drove slowly around the block for another look.

A quick drive through the underground garage confirmed no Jaguar was parked in the space reserved for Chance. Satisfied that all was safe, Flame drove the ranch's Lincoln around to the building's front entrance and parked at the kerb. She gripped the steering wheel with both gloved hands and breathed in deeply, trying to settle the clamouring of her nerves, heart and senses.

Before she could question the wisdom – or the sanity – of her actions, she stepped out of the car and nervously smoothed a hand over the hipline of the coffee-brown satin gown. Its slim line suggested something out of the mid-fifties, but the simplicity of its style made it almost ageless, and definitely suitable for her purpose since society's critical eye wouldn't be reviewing it. She reached inside the car for the matching evening bag and the full length fox coat. The fur coat had been an absolute find. It wasn't in the best condition, its sleeves and collar showing wear, but it was exactly what she needed.

She draped it around her shoulders and unconsciously cast a

furtive glance down the street, but all was quiet, with few cars moving about in the downtown area. She turned toward the building's glass entrance and the lobby within, brightly lit with fluorescent lights. Pausing, she felt the front of her gown and made sure the orchid brooch of diamonds was securely pinned at the centre of its v-shaped neckline.

Thank God she needed to appear anxious, agitated and upset, because that was exactly the way she felt as she hurried to the doors, moving as quickly as the gown's front-slit skirt would allow. At the doors, Flame stopped and rattled them and tapped repeatedly on the glass. Finally the uniformed guard behind the lobby's security desk looked up, a Hostess Twinkie halfway to his mouth. Flame gave him her most appealing smile and rattled the locked door again.

He hesitated a split second, then laid the Twinkie on its cellophane wrapper, and hastily wiped the crumbs from his mouth with a backhanded scrub, then got up and walked around the desk. The guard was an older man, somewhere in his early sixties, the grey hair beneath his cap cut close to his head in a short butch, and his double chin hanging over the collar of his shirt, the same way his beer belly hung over the belt of his pants. But it was the noisy jingle that caught Flame's attention as he approached the doors, a large metal ring strung with keys and dangling from his hand.

On the other side of the door, he stopped and searched through the keys. Flame glanced anxiously over her shoulder, certain that Chance would drive up any second and she'd be caught in the act. Powerless to hurry the guard along, she waited, mouth dry, nerves screaming with impatience while he separated one key from the rest, and inserted it in the lock. The instant a crack showed, Flame darted inside.

'Is something wrong, Miss?' He eyed her curiously, tipping his head down to look at her through the top of his black-rimmed bifocals.

'You don't know how relieved I am to see you.' She clutched at his arm, drawing him with her as she moved from the door toward the bank of elevators. 'I was afraid there wouldn't be anyone here to let me in. I didn't know what I was going to do. The most awful thing has happened.' Near the security desk, she let go of his arm and unfastened the jewelled clasp of her evening bag. She started to reach inside, then stopped and looked at him as if just realising, 'You have no idea who I am, do you? And here I am rattling on. I'm Flame Stuart – Chance Stuart's wife.'

He immediately brightened, his jowled cheeks lifting in a smile. 'Of course, Mrs Stuart. The whole building's been buzzing with the news of your marriage to Mr Stuart,' he declared. She'd counted on that – just as she'd counted on the slowness of the word getting around that she'd left him. 'Everybody said Mr Stuart found himself a beautiful redhead and they certainly were right about that.'

'Aren't you so kind, Mr –' She glanced at his nametag.

'Dunlap. Fred Dunlap.'

'Mr Dunlap. Let me explain my problem. As I said, the most awful thing has happened,' she rushed on, reaching into her purse again, this time taking out one of the diamond earrings that matched the brooch. 'I've lost the mate of this earring. Chance – Mr Stuart – gave them to me as a gift – along with this pin. I'm supposed to meet him in an hour and he expects me to be wearing them. I've searched everywhere. Then I remembered that I was wearing them the day we came here. Is there any way you can let me into my husband's office so I can see if maybe I left it there? I can't bear the thought of telling him I lost it.'

'I sure can, Mrs Stuart. It's no trouble at all.' He shifted his heavy bulk toward the elevators, again going through the many keys on his ring. 'You just come with me and I'll take you up.'

'You have no idea how grateful I am, Mr Dunlap. I've been half out of my mind with worry over this.' She was certain she sounded like a babbling fool, but she couldn't seem to stop talking as she followed him to the elevators. 'I know the set must have cost him a fortune. But it's more than that. It was the first present he gave me. Well, not the first. He sent me orchids first. That's why he had this pin and these earrings designed in the shape of orchids, because they were actually the first.'

Flame wasn't even sure the security guard was listening as he used a key to open some sort of utility panel and slip some switches inside. The 'Up' arrow blinked on above the elevator directly in front of her and its doors silently glided open. She practically ran into the cage, then waited again for the lumbering guard to join her. He punched the button for the twentieth floor. Seconds ticked by with unnerving slowness before the time-delayed doors finally slid shut.

As she watched the light above the doors blink on the ascending numbers of the floors, the silence seemed worse than her previous chatter. 'I never realised how slow these elevators were,' she declared in utter truthfulness.

'It's always like that when you're in a hurry. Nothing ever moves fast enough.'

'I guess not,' she said and laughed nervously.

Finally the elevator came to a stop on the top floor. With stomach churning, Flame waited in its dimly lit lobby while the security guard went to turn on the office lights. Again the seconds seemed to drag forever before he came back and led her down the wide hall to Chance's office. There she had to wait again for him to find the key and unlock the door.

When he followed her into the office, Flame wanted to scream at him to leave. Instead she forced herself to smile. 'Thank you so much, Mr Dunlap,' she said, turning to face him, letting her body language indicate to him that his presence was no longer required.

He hesitated uncertainly. 'I'd be happy to help you look for that missing earring, Mrs Stuart.'

'That isn't necessary,' she rushed. 'I mean, you've done so much already and I wouldn't want to take you away from your desk. After all, you do have a job to do. It wouldn't be right for me to take you away from your duty.'

'I suppose not.' He nodded a grudging agreement. 'If you should need me though, you just call thirty-one thirty-one. That's my extension and I'll be up here in no time.'

'I'll remember that. Thank you, Mr Dunlap.' She remained where she was, watching as he turned and left, not drawing an easy breath until she heard the distant *ding* of the elevator. Then she hurried over and closed the door – just in case he decided to come back and check on her.

Turning, she swept the long fox coat off her shoulders and scanned the room, trying to decide where to begin her search for the preliminary drawings of the proposed development. She started with Chance's desk, specifically the long credenza behind it. But none of the papers on top of it contained any reference to the project, and a search of the drawers and doors proved equally fruitless.

Aware that time was against her, Flame moved quickly to the

built-in cabinetry along the wall in the informal sitting area. Behind one set of doors, she found a bonanza of blueprints. She wasted precious minutes going through them and, again, came up with nothing.

Where were they? She fought down the momentary panic and widened her search to the bookshelves near the conference table. Nothing. My God, what if they weren't here? What if they were in Sam's office instead?

Then she spied the long cardboard tubes in an upright rack next to the credenza on the other side of the burl table – the kind of tubing blueprints and drawings were kept in! Struggling to control the leap of excitement, Flame went to investigate, flinging the fur and the brown satin evening bag on to one of the conference chairs.

Ten minutes later, three of the tubes had offered up detailed drawings of site plans, preliminary blueprints for the proposed dam, and artists' renderings of the luxury hotel, marina, condominiums and townhouses. And the credenza had yielded an assortment of information – everything from an environmental impact study to a feasibility report. Plus Flame had found copies of several memos outlining the status on additional land purchases Chance was trying to make.

She was stunned by the amount of time, effort and money that had already gone into the project. Which seemed to prove how confident Chance had been that he would get Morgan's Walk – one way or another. Nothing in Ben Canon's remarks had given her the impression that Chance's plans for the development had progressed this far. She wondered if the attorney knew.

Sobered by the discovery, Flame went through all the drawings, blueprints and reports again, searching for duplicates, gathering them in a stack to take with her, and returning the rest to their original places. She doubted that Chance would ever notice there were copies missing. Fortunately there were duplicates of everything with the exception of the coloured renderings, an initial engineering report, and an overall topography map. But there were black-and-white copies of the renderings, a subsequent engineering report that appeared to contain much of the same information as the first, and a contour map showing natural water drainage.

Suddenly, from the outer office, came the muffled *ding* that signalled the arrival of the elevator. She froze. The private elevator – the one that came from the underground parking garage – the one that required a key to operate – the one Chance used! She went cold, her heart leaping into her throat and lodging there.

With discovery imminent, she looked frantically around the room for a place to hide. But there was no obvious place – no closet, no darkened alcove, no shadowy corner hidden from view. The office was too open, too exposed. She couldn't crawl under his desk; he was bound to go there. Hiding behind the sofa was out, too; he'd see her crouching behind it when he walked by.

There were footsteps in Molly's office. She had to act fast. With speed more important than silence, she scooped up the stack of information she'd gathered and dumped it in the corner, hoping it wouldn't be noticed, then grabbed the fur coat and the evening bag off the chair and dragged them with her as she scrambled under the round conference table and frantically pulled the chairs in closer, hoping the forest of legs would obscure her.

As the door to Chance's office opened, Flame made herself as small as possible and pressed close to the centre pedestal. She didn't dare move – or even breathe for fear the satin of Hattie's gown would rustle and betray her presence.

But it wasn't Chance who entered. It was a woman. Flame could see her reflection in the office's smoked glass windows. She almost breathed a sigh of relief, thinking it was the cleaning woman. With her, she could talk her way out of this situation. Then she recognised Molly Malone and knew she didn't have a prayer of convincing Chance's secretary that she was under the table looking for her supposedly lost diamond earring.

'Honestly, these cleaning people,' Molly grumbled aloud. 'Heaven knows how long these lights have been on. If they had to pay the electricity bill here for a month, they wouldn't be so free with them.'

There was a click, then darkness – except for the light shining through the doorway to Molly's office. In the reflecting windows, Flame saw Molly's silhouette briefly outlined in the doorway before she walked through and pulled the door shut behind her, throwing Chance's office into near total darkness.

Flame breathed in shakily and relaxed a little. For the moment she was out of danger – but she was also trapped. She couldn't leave until Molly did. What was she doing here on a Saturday night? How long before she left? What if the security guard came up to see if she'd found the earring? What had made her think she could get away with this in the first place? Why had she taken so much time looking through everything? Why hadn't she simply grabbed what she could find and left? If she had, she would have been out of here and safely on her way back to Morgan's Walk.

She listened to the sounds of Molly moving about in the outer office, file drawers sliding open and clanging shut. A short span of silence was followed by the rapid tapitty-tap of the typewriter. Helpless, Flame sat on the floor under the table, surrounded by an increasingly weighty darkness.

But the sound of the typewriter didn't last long. Then a desk drawer shut and a chair squeaked noisily. Again there were footsteps and more indistinct movement.

How long had Molly been here? Five minutes? Ten? Twenty? In the darkness, Flame had no conception of time, but it seemed an eternity went by before she finally heard the bell-like signal of the elevator doors. Then, all was quiet – except for the loud thudding of her own heart. After making certain no crack of light was visible beneath the door, Flame groped her way out from under the table.

This time she didn't dally, but moved as quickly as the darkness would allow, gathering up the papers and plans and clutching them in her arms along with the fur coat and bag. Feeling her way along the wall, she found the door. It opened at the turn of her hand. She stepped quickly into Molly's equally darkened outer office.

Somehow she managed to make it to the hall without bumping into anything. From there she could see a faint light shining at the far end and knew it came from the dimly lit elevator lobby. She caught up the coffee-brown skirt of Hattie's long gown and ran all the way. It wasn't that far, yet when she reached the elevators she felt winded and weak, her heart rocketing against her ribs. Panic, that's what it was.

She forced herself to drink in deep gulps of air and breathe out slowly, taking the few necessary, precious seconds to calm herself. Then she laid the fox coat on the floor and placed the jumble of reports, plans, and drawings inside it. She wrapped the coat round them, paused long enough to push the button to summon the elevator, then picked the coat up, papers and all, and held it in front of her, doubling the coat nearly in half, draping it over her arm and hopefully hiding the bundle it contained.

When the elevator doors opened, she stepped quickly inside and pushed the button for the lobby floor, then caught a glimpse of her reflection in the wall's mirror and turned to survey her appearance. My lord, but her face looked strained and pale. Hurriedly she pinched her cheeks to put colour into them, then noticed the bareness of her earlobes. The earrings, they were still in the evening bag. Awkwardly she clutched at the unwieldy fur-wrapped bundle with one arm and unfastened the purse's clasp to rummage inside for both diamond earrings. She clipped the second one on her ear just as the elevator doors opened on the lobby floor.

Cautiously, Flame looked out, making certain the security guard was alone at the desk. Then with a bright smile she breezed over to him.

'I found it. Can you believe it?' She turned her head from side to side, letting the diamond earrings flash their fire at him.

'That's wonderful, Mrs Stuart.'

'It is, isn't it?' she declared, hugging the fur tightly to her and turning flirtatiously pleading. 'Would you mind not saying anything to Mr Stuart about this? I'd rather he didn't know I'd misplaced it even for a moment.'

'Don't worry, Mrs Stuart.' The man grinned and winked conspiratorially at her. 'It will be our little secret. My lips are sealed.'

'Thank you, Mr Dunlap. You're an absolute dear,' she said, already moving away from the desk toward the front doors.

She had to wait for him to unlock them again, then practically ran to the Lincoln parked at the kerb. She opened the door, tossed the precious fur bundle on to the passenger seat, and hurriedly slipped behind the wheel. Her hands were shaking so badly she could barely insert the key into the ignition lock. When she turned the key in the switch, the motor growled to life. The guard stood at the glass doors, watching her. She waved to him as she pulled away from the kerb on to the empty street. He waved back.

She felt weak, a mass of jangled nerves exhilarated and relieved all at the same time. When she glanced at the digital clock on the car's lighted dashboard, she realised that only twenty-three minutes had passed. She'd been certain she'd been in the building at least an hour. She'd done it, though. She'd swiped the plans right from under Chance's nose. She started to laugh and couldn't stop.

═ 30 ═

EARLY AFTERNOON on Sunday, Flame emerged from the concourse at the San Francisco International Airport and walked straight to the waiting Ellery, receiving his welcoming kiss on the cheek. As usual, he asked no questions. He didn't need to. By the time they reached her Russian Hill flat, she'd told him the whole galling mess.

Her suitcases stood in the hallway to her rear bedroom, exactly where Ellery had set them down when they walked in. But the long box she'd brought back with her had been sliced open and its contents spread over the glass coffee table.

Flame poured more champagne into her fluted glass. The sparkling wine, a gift from Ellery, had been intended to toast her state of newly-wedded bliss, but it had become, instead, a means to cool the seething anger that continued to churn inside her. She turned to Ellery, so casually elegant in his lavender cashmere sweater as he lounged against the white sofa.

'More champagne?' she asked.

He waved his partially full glass in absent refusal. 'Do you know this is the first time I've drunk champagne at a marital wake? It's a rather novel experience.' But his sardonic smile faded, his glance turning thoughtful and sympathetic as he directed it at her. 'You sounded so blissfully happy when you called me last

Sunday, I must admit I never dreamed –'

'Neither did I.' She cut him off before he could actually say the maddening words.

He leaned forward to study the black and white renderings on the coffee table in front of him, resting his elbows on the knees of his precisely creased trousers. 'This is some development he wants to build.' Then he lifted his head, suddenly curious. 'How did you manage to get all these plans and reports?'

'I have them. What does it matter how?' Flame shrugged.

He responded with a wry smile. 'Why did I bother to ask? It's obvious that under the circumstances, he wouldn't have given them to you. Which means you must have purloined them – to put it delicately.'

'They're copies. He'll never miss them.'

Ellery made no comment to that, and let his attention return to the array of paperwork and plans before him. 'The thing that puzzles me is – why Tulsa? Why Oklahoma? This project has to run into the multimillions. Why would he invest that kind of money in this area?'

'You haven't looked at the feasibility and market study.' Flame walked over and pulled it from the stack. She flipped it open to a map of the United States with the project site marked and circles radiating out from it. 'If you'll notice, the development is within a four hundred and fifty mile radius – approximately a day's drive of every major metropolitan area in the Midwest – Dallas, Houston, Kansas City, St Louis, Denver, Memphis, New Orleans – and Chicago falls a fraction of an inch outside of that magic line. Nearly one-third of the nation's population lives within that circle. He could easily turn this into the vacation Mecca of the Midwest.'

'I believe you're right,' he said, faintly startled by the discovery. 'My God, what a shrewd bastard.'

'But he needs Morgan's Walk to do it.' She riffled through more of the drawings until she found the site plan. 'Because the dam that makes his lake is right here – on what is now *my* land. If Chance has his way, nearly every acre of it will be under water.'

'Exactly what do you intend to do with all these plans and blueprints? Obviously you could pin them to a wall and throw darts at them – or fashion them into an effigy of Stuart and burn it.

But other than that . . .'

'I'm going to a reputable engineering company and have them review them for me.'

'Why?' Ellery frowned, an eyebrow arching. 'You know what they are.'

'But that's all I know. I'm not an engineer. I can't read a set of plans. Maybe there's something here that I'm not seeing. . . . Some way that Chance can get my land.'

'You keep talking as if you believe he'll try to go through with this project. Surely that's impossible now that you've inherited the land. If you won't sell it to him – and I assume you won't – then he'll have to give it up and count his losses.'

'Will he?' she countered. 'You don't know how ruthless he can be. It's bred in his bones. Don't forget he married me thinking it would give him control of the land. He wants Morgan's Walk, Ellery.' Her fingers tightened around the fluted champagne glass, her voice vibrating with her tautly controlled anger. 'His reasons go beyond the time and money he has invested. No, with Chance, it's strictly personal. He hates Morgan's Walk. That's why he searched for and found a way to destroy it. The fact that he'll make millions in the process is merely a bonus. He'll try and keep trying, Ellery. That's why I have to find a way to stop him.'

'This whole thing reeks of a vendetta,' he observed, again with that wry movement of his mouth. Flame stiffened, catching the hint of mockery in his voice. 'Revenge is sweet and all that.'

'No, Ellery, you're wrong,' she declared in an icy calm. 'Revenge is everything.'

≡ 31 ≡

MOLLY MALONE eyed the man standing before her desk suspiciously, covering it with one of her patented, pleasant smiles. 'I'm sorry. Mr Stuart isn't in yet. He plays squash on Thursday mornings which means he'll be late getting to the office.' She pretended to check the day's appointment calendar, which by now she had memorised. 'Unfortunately when he arrives, he has to go straight into a meeting. I'm afraid he'll be tied up all day. What did you need to see him about? Perhaps I can help you.'

'I don't think so. It's personal.' His tan raincoat was stained and worn, a button missing from the front, and the polyester suit under it didn't look any newer, yet the man carried himself with a quiet authority.

'I see,' Molly murmured and took another look at him, trying to guess his age. Somewhere in his early fifties, she thought. And despite the string tie around his neck and the cowboy boots on his feet, she was certain he was neither a rancher nor a farmer. His face didn't have the dark ruddy tan of a man who'd spent his life outdoors and his eyes didn't crinkle at the corners from squinting at the sun all day. 'In that case, why don't you let me make an appointment for you?' she suggested.

'That won't be necessary.' The sack-like pouches under his eyes and the turned-down corners of his mouth gave him the look of a weary, yet extremely patient man. 'I'll wait until he comes.'

'But he has a –'

'That's all right.' He swept aside her objection with an indifferent flick of his hand. 'I won't take more than a couple minutes of his time, and I'm sure he can spare me that much before his meeting.'

Molly clamped her mouth shut, recognising that short of having the man thrown out, he wouldn't be persuaded to leave. She turned in a faint huff and busied herself with some papers next to her typewriter, watching him out of the corner of her eye as he wandered over to study a painting on the wall.

'Molly?' Sam called to her from Chance's office, a perplexed note in his voice.

As she rose from her chair, she shot the man another suspicious look then went into Chance's office. Sam was over by the conference table, a bundle of blueprints under his arm. He turned when she entered the room.

'Some of these plans are in the wrong slots.' He frowned. 'The architect's drawings are where the blueprints for the dam should be, and the dam blueprints are . . . It doesn't matter where they are. But somebody's been in them and mixed them all up. I know Chance wouldn't do it. And I certainly didn't. Who else could have gotten into them?'

'They're all there, aren't they?'

Sam nodded affirmatively. 'That was the first thing I checked.'

'It was probably the cleaning people then. They pick the oddest places to be thorough in their dusting, then leave cobwebs in the corners for everyone to see.' She shrugged it off as unimportant and glanced over her shoulder towards the partially closed door to her office. Lowering her voice, she said, 'There's a man out there who insists on seeing Chance when he comes. He won't give his name or state his business, but I'd swear he's a process server. I can smell them.'

Sam's frown deepened. 'You think someone's sueing the company?'

'What else?' She lifted her hands in an empty gesture, then added, 'I think you should go down and warn Chance before he gets on the elevator. He should be here any minute.'

'I will.' He shoved the rolled blueprints at her. 'Take these and put them in my office.'

Two of them threatened to unroll when he handed them to her. Molly juggled them for an instant, then they both heard the bell-like *ding* of the elevator. They looked at each other, realising it was too late.

'Chance Stuart?' came the man's inquiring voice.

'Yes?'

'This is for you.' The announcement was followed by the sound of footsteps leaving the outer office to enter the hall.

Molly turned to face the door as Chance walked into his office, scanning the legal-looking document in his hands, his forehead creased in a troubled frown. 'A process server,' she said to Sam. 'Didn't I tell you I could smell them?'

But Sam wasn't interested in the accuracy of her guess as he tried to read from Chance's expression the seriousness of this new occurrence. 'We're being sued, I take it. By whom?'

Chance flashed him a quick look, a killing coldness in his eyes, the muscles standing out sharply along his jaw. But he didn't immediately answer the question, striding instead to his desk and tossing the papers on it, then moving to the window behind it and staring out, his head thrown slightly back and his hands thrust in the side pockets of his suit trousers.

'We're not being sued, Sam,' he said curtly. 'Flame has petitioned the courts to have our marriage annulled.'

'Damn,' Sam swore softly.

'Oh, Chance,' Molly murmured sympathetically as she took a few uncertain steps towards him. 'I'm sorry.'

He pivoted sharply, his glare running to both of them. 'I never said I was accepting this as her final answer.'

'Of course not.' Molly stiffened immediately, lifting her head to show him her total support and confidence.

'Who's her attorney?'

'Guess,' Chance countered sarcastically.

'Ben Canon,' Sam murmured, then sighed heavily. 'You're right. I should've known that.' He glanced hesitantly at Chance. 'When you saw her on Saturday, did she give you any inkling at all that she was going to do something like this?'

'Yes. But I didn't believe it would come this quickly.'

'What are you going to do?' Sam frowned. 'What can you do?'

'Stall,' he said and shifted his attention to Molly. 'Get Quentin Worthy on the phone and tell him you're messengering over this

— 303 —

petition. And tell him to find me the best damned divorce lawyer there is, and I don't care where he has to go to get him. In the meantime, I want any action on this petition postponed. Explain to him that I'm trying to get my wife to agree to a reconciliation.'

'You don't really think she will, do you?' Sam questioned sceptically.

'Of course she will,' Molly spoke up. 'She's hurt and angry and upset right now and it's all that Morgan woman's fault. But she loves Chance. I know she does. She'll realise that herself. You wait and see – absence will make the heart grow fonder.'

Sam shook his head at her eternal optimism. 'If you're going to start tossing out clichés, Molly, don't forget – out of sight, out of mind. And there is half a continent between them. You can't get much more out of sight than that.'

'If the two of you are finished trading clichés, then I'd like to know if there are any appointments on my calendar for tomorrow that can't be postponed,' Chance broke in.

Molly flashed him a guilty look of apology and replied, 'You're supposed to have breakfast with the governor in the morning – at the Governor's Mansion in Oklahoma City – but as far as the rest are concerned, they could easily be switched to another day. I don't recall anything else that's pressing.'

'In that case, after you get in touch with Quentin Worthy, call Mick Donovan and advise him that we'll be flying to San Francisco when we leave the capital tomorrow.'

⟨ 32 ⟩

MALCOM POWELL'S driver had the umbrella at the ready, its ribbed canopy opened to shield her from the Thursday afternoon drizzle when Flame stepped from the car. 'Thank you, Arthur.' She flashed him a hurried smile as she took the umbrella from him and held it over her head.

He touched his cap to her. 'See you next week.'

She nodded a brief acknowledgement to that and moved away from the car, cutting across the flow of scurrying pedestrians to reach the entrance to the office building. Ellery was there, holding the glass door open for her, obviously just returning from lunch himself.

Under the shelter of the entrance's overhang, Flame paused long enough to lower her umbrella and release the catch to close it. Ellery sent a glance after the limousine pulling away from the kerb.

'I see you had lunch with the great one today,' he observed.

'Yes.'

His eyebrow lifted at her clipped answer, but she ignored it as she brushed past him to enter the building. In two strides, Ellery drew even with her again, matching her brisk pace to the elevators.

'That bad, was it?'

'I beg your pardon.' She pretended she didn't know what he was talking about.

'You're still gritting your teeth. Which would suggest your luncheon with Mr Powell was something less than a pleasant experience.'

She started to deny it, but what was the point? Ellery knew her moods too well. 'Unfortunately Malcom wasn't as tactful as other clients and co-workers have been.'

'Asked you a lot of questions about your break-up with Stuart, did he?' Ellery guessed.

'That's one way of putting it, yes.'

It had begun almost the moment she'd walked into his office, her long paisley velvet skirt swinging about the calves of her boots. She hadn't crossed the length of the room to the massive antique desk where Malcom stood, instead she'd stopped midway and deposited her handbag on a chair.

'I'm sorry I'm late, Malcom.' She'd talked at him as she tugged off her gloves and unbuttoned her poncho-style raincoat, careful to avoid the probing study of his grey eyes. 'Debbie – my assistant – is home with the flu. I have a temporary in her place. When they rang up to say Arthur was waiting for me downstairs, I was on the phone with another client. And she never passed the message on to me before she left on her lunch break.' She'd sent him an apologetic smile as he moved out from behind his desk, angling towards her.

'I understand.' But the smoothness of his reply had failed to conceal the underlying edge of irritation in his voice, reminding Flame that Malcom Powell wasn't a man who liked to be kept waiting.

When she'd squared around to face him, she'd been confronted by the power of his presence. She'd stared at the muscular swell to his chest, arms, and neck that was impressive, and the broadness of his square jaw and the forceful thrust of his dimpled chin that spoke of his iron will. She'd wondered how she could have possibly forgotten in two short weeks.

The hard gleam in his grey eyes had been difficult to meet. 'Although, I must admit I had started to suspect that you'd run off again with your lover. Or – should I say your husband?'

Stung by his probing taunt, Flame had let her gaze drop and masked it by sweeping off her cape and draping it on the chair with her purse. 'That was a mistake.' She'd fallen back on what had become her stock answer these past few days. 'One that I've taken steps to correct as soon as possible.' She'd feigned a smile of indifference and deliberately glanced at the pocket doors to Malcom's private dining room, slid open to reveal the table set for two within. 'We're having lunch here. How nice.'

'I told you Stuart wasn't the man for you.'

No one else had pursued the subject, taking her reply as the final word on the matter. But not Malcom.

'So you did – and you were right,' she'd admitted, more sharply than she'd intended. 'But if you asked me here today to gloat –'

'Not to gloat, but simply to remind you that I'm here.' His grey glance had wandered over her in an assessing fashion, the look in his eyes turning warm. 'My feelings towards you haven't changed, Flame . . . nor my desires.'

'I think you should be able to appreciate that after making one mistake, I'm not about to make another.'

'And I think . . . that whatever happened between you and Stuart must have been a bitter blow to your pride.'

'It was more than my pride he hurt!' She'd flared immediately, then abruptly turned away, struggling to regain control of her emotions. 'If you don't mind, Malcom, I'd rather not discuss any of this,' she insisted curtly.

'I can see that,' he'd murmured. 'But I can't help being curious. I've never seen this much anger in you, Flame – not even when you've lost your temper with me.'

'Maybe I have cause.'

'Maybe you do,' he'd said in a considering way. 'And maybe a glass of your favourite Chardonnay will cool it a little.'

They'd gone into his private dining room then, but that hadn't been the end of it. Several times during the course of the meal, Malcom had alluded in some way to Chance and her break-up as if he knew, or guessed there was a great deal more to the story than she was telling.

'I think Malcom hoped I'd weep on his shoulder,' she said to Ellery as they joined the crowd of workers waiting in front of the elevators. 'But I don't need his shoulder – or anyone else's.'

'Speaking of shoulders, we'll have the artwork finished on the

Shodderly ad next week.' Interrupted by the arrival of an elevator, Ellery waited until they'd wedged a space inside, then picked up where he'd left off. 'Do you want to take a look at it a week from Friday?'

'It would have to be first thing. I have an appointment in Oakland at eleven that day.'

'What's in Oakland?' Ellery frowned.

'Thorgood Engineering.'

'I've never heard of them. When did the agency acquire that company for a client?'

'They aren't a client. I'm seeing them on a personal matter.' The elevator came to a stop at the agency's floor. 'Excuse us, please.' She squeezed her way through the jam of people to the open doors, with Ellery right behind her.

'This is about those plans of Stuart's, isn't it?' he said.

Nodding an affirmative answer, Flame walked by the receptionist's desk and into the hall that led to her office. 'If nothing else, they can tell me the steps Chance would have to take in order to have my land condemned for his lake.'

'Time is definitely not lying idle in your hands, is it?' Ellery murmured.

'No. And you can bet he isn't wasting any either. Which is why I can't afford to sit back and wait to find out what his first move will be . . .'

He caught her arm, stopping her short of her assistant's office and eyeing her with a knowing look. 'Why do I have the feeling that you already have some scheme in motion? And I don't mean this engineering thing.'

Flame smiled, with just a hint of smugness. 'When I talked to Ben Canon yesterday – my attorney in Tulsa – I asked him to find out whether Morgan's Walk met the criteria for a listing in the National Register of Historic Places. If it does, there might be some objection to having such a house sitting on the bottom of a lake.'

'Very good.' Ellery inclined his head in approval.

'I thought so.' But she also knew it was much too early to be congratulating herself. Still she couldn't help feeling a little pleased as she turned and entered her assistant's office. 'Did any messages come for me while I was gone, Miss Austin?' She didn't trust the temp to pass them on to her automatically after this noon's fiasco.

'Just two.' The bright-eyed brunette promptly plucked them from her desk top and handed them to Flame, then wasted a sidelong glance at Ellery.

'Thank you.' Flame scanned the pair of messages as she crossed to her office door.

'Oh, Ms Bennett, wait.' The brunette's anxious call turned her around. 'I forgot,' she said guiltily. 'There's a man waiting in your office for you.'

'In my office? Who?'

'I believe his name was Stuart. He said you knew him.'

Too furious to speak, Flame longed to strangle the girl. Instead she swung on Ellery. 'I know.' He held up a hand, staving off any need for words. 'I'll call the service for you and have her replaced.'

'Did I do something wrong?'

As Flame swept into her office, she heard Ellery say, 'I think that's a safe assumption, Miss Austin.'

Chance stood at the window, his back to the door when she came through. He looked back, angling his wide shoulders at her, then slowly turned to face her. Just for an instant, under the full impact of his gaze, she felt the tear of old feelings. Just as quickly she blocked them out, and pushed the door shut behind her.

'What are you doing here?' she demanded.

'I believe you asked the same thing the last time we saw each other.' The grooves on either side of his mouth deepened in a mock smile. 'And my answer is the same – I came to see you.'

'I thought I made it clear that I didn't want to see you.' Flame crossed to her desk.

'I can't accept that.' He wandered over to stand in front of her.

'You have no choice,' she snapped. 'And what do you mean coming into my office and making yourself at home as if –'

'– as if I was your husband?'

'That isn't what I was going to say!'

'No, it probably wasn't,' he conceded with a slight dip of his head. 'I decided it would be better to wait here than in the outer office where any number of your co-workers might see me. I thought it might spare you a lot of needless questions.'

'Such consideration would be touching if it came from anyone other than you.' She sat down behind her desk and began going through the stack of mail on top of it, pretending to scan the letters without absorbing one word.

'Flame, I didn't come here to make you upset or angry –'

'Then why are you here?' She finally lifted her glance to his face, taking in the familiar sight of its smooth, rakish lines, so very strong, so very compelling.

'I came to talk to you.'

She arched him a scornful look. 'Don't you mean – to talk me out of Morgan's Walk?'

'No, I don't.' There was a quietness to his voice that she couldn't ignore. 'You've condemned me without hearing me out. I'm not saying that when you do, you'll change your mind. But you owe me that much, Flame.'

'I don't see it that way,' she replied stiffly.

'Maybe you don't, but what harm will it do to listen? Have dinner with me tonight.'

She started hotly to reject his invitation, then another thought occurred to her and she wavered, covering her hesitation by rising from her chair and moving away from the desk and Chance at right angles. 'Where are you staying?'

'The Carrington.'

She wheeled to face him, still gripped with indecision and unwilling to act impulsively a second time. 'Let me think about it and call you later at the hotel.'

Chance sensed she was on the verge of agreeing to meet him. But he also had the feeling that if he pushed her, she'd refuse. He backed off.

'All right.' He nodded slowly in acceptance. 'I'll wait to hear from you.'

She was surprised that he'd given in so easily. She'd expected him to press her for an answer. She wondered why he hadn't as he walked out of her office. Was he that confident she would ultimately accept? Did it matter if he was? He couldn't possibly have guessed the reason she was contemplating meeting him.

Chance had barely left her office when Ellery walked in. His glance ran over her, quick with concern. 'Are you all right?'

'Did you think I wouldn't be?'

'I wasn't sure.'

'I promise you, Ellery, I'm not about to fall apart simply because I saw him again.' She walked back to her desk.

'What did he want?'

Her mouth twisted in a humourless smile. 'He wants me to have dinner with him tonight so we can talk.'

'You refused, of course.'

'Not yet.'

For a run of seconds, Ellery was silent, studying her with a probing eye. 'Some devious wheels are turning in that head of yours.'

Flame smiled. 'He's made his first move. He's going to try to win me back. He convinced me once before that he loved me, why shouldn't he think that he could do it again? What would happen, Ellery, if I let him think he might succeed?' she wondered aloud.

'Do you know what you're saying?'

She ignored his question and continued to talk out her stream of consciousness. 'If I strung him along, he wouldn't dare contest the will – or make any overt move to get control of Morgan's Walk. And think of the time it would gain me.'

'Stuart isn't a man to be easily tricked.'

'I know.' She shrugged that off. 'But he'll also expect me to play hard-to-get. And that won't be difficult at all.'

'This isn't a game,' Ellery warned.

She turned her overly bright green eyes on him, the devil of malice in them. 'Yes, it is. It's called "deceit" – I learned it from an expert.'

Flame deliberately waited until nearly six o'clock to call Chance and accept his invitation. When he offered to pick her up, she refused. 'We can dine at your hotel,' she said. 'I'll meet you in the restaurant at eight.'

In the hotel's multi-tiered dining room, Chance observed Flame's approach as the maître d' escorted her to his table. He paid little attention to the way heads turned when she passed, his own wholly absorbed by the striking picture she made coming toward him, dramatic in a high-necked black-and-white suit in a spotted silk moiré. The lofty way she carried her head and the confident swing of her square shoulders came naturally to her like the fiery gold colour of her hair. That they created a stir and caught the eye was purely incidental. She'd done more than that to him, though. She'd settled much of his restlessness of spirit, she aroused much of his masculine instincts to possess and protect. He hadn't realised how much of either until she'd walked out. He wanted her back. He had to have her back. Chance was as single-minded in this as he was in getting Morgan's Walk.

When she neared the table, he stood to greet her. Her glance swept him coolly as she murmured a greeting, then let the maître d' seat her in the chair opposite him. The waiter arrived instantly to ask if she would like something from the bar. Her hesitation was momentary, her glance running to the glass of Scotch before him, then she ordered a glass of Chardonnay.

Once they were alone at the table, she finally met his gaze with a look of studied indifference. 'I believe this is a first,' she said. 'No peach champagne and no orchids.'

'I didn't think it would be appropriate.' He scanned the strong modelling of her features, looking for a break somewhere in the reserve she'd thrown up against him. But he couldn't penetrate the green mystery of her eyes, so cool and aloof to him now. He would have preferred to face the fire and temper she'd shown him in her office rather than this air of tolerance and disinterest.

'You were right. It wouldn't be.' Then her attention was pulled away from him as the waiter returned with her wine. She thanked him with a smile – the first Chance had seen on her lips since he'd kissed her goodbye the morning he left for Texas – the morning that had signalled an end to the rare happiness he'd known. When she faced him again, all trace of the smile was gone. He felt a sweep of hot anger and immediately clamped down on it, recognising it would get him nowhere with her.

He lifted his glass of Scotch in a toast. 'Thank you,' he said.

'For what?' She held her wine glass, as if unprepared to sip from it until she knew the answer.

'For coming tonight.'

'Chance Stuart – humble?' she mocked. 'I find that extremely difficult to believe.'

He took a drink of his Scotch, the burn of it in his throat matching his own emotional rawness. But he'd learned long ago not to let such feelings show. 'I received my notice that you're seeking an annulment.'

Now she took a sip of her wine. 'I suppose you intend to fight it.'

'If I thought it would do any good, I would.' By his definition, stalling was not the same as fighting.

The cool curve of her lips challenged. 'Don't you mean – if you thought it would get you Morgan's Walk, you would?'

'Flame, I didn't ask you here tonight to talk about Morgan's Walk.'

'Really?' Scepticism riddled her voice.

'I want to talk about us.'

'There is no "us", if you're referring to you and me.' She paused, a glint of derisive amusement appearing briefly in her eyes. 'Of course, by us – you could also be referring to me and Morgan's Walk.'

'Once before I told you I made a mistake in not telling you Hattie Morgan was my aunt – and that Morgan's Walk would have been left to me if she hadn't learned about you. And I made a mistake in not telling you I wanted that land. But that wasn't my biggest mistake,' he said, carefully choosing his words. 'My biggest one was wanting both. I was greedy, Flame. When I said I loved you, that wasn't a lie. If there wasn't a Morgan's Walk, I'd still want you for my wife.'

Something quick and surprised momentarily flickered in her expression, then a wary doubt set in as she eyed him steadily, searching his face. Within seconds, her glance fell to the wine glass, a cynicism edging the corners of her mouth.

'That's a safe thing to say, isn't it, Chance? It almost sounds convincing. There's just one problem – there is a Morgan's Walk. There always will be. So that situation will never arise.' She lifted her glass, her eyes mocking him. 'Aren't you lucky?'

'How can I be when I lost you both?' he reasoned smoothly.

'Perhaps you're right,' she conceded, her glance running over him again. 'But it isn't over, is it? You can still contest Hattie's will. Who knows? Maybe you'll even win.'

He sat before her, dark and elegant in his tailored navy pin-striped suit and pale silk tie, the soft candlelight throwing the planes and hollows of his sculpted face into sharp relief. To-night, perhaps more than any other night, he had the look of a gambler, a man who dared to do what others only dreamed. He was a man who lived on the edge of danger and enjoyed the view. But she wasn't swayed by that as she'd been before, reminding herself that gamblers were notorious for cheating and conning people.

'I don't plan to contest the will, Flame. It wouldn't accomplish anything for either of us, except to tie up the title in the courts for years and cost a fortune in attorney fees.'

She relaxed a little, aware that a court fight was a battle she couldn't afford to wage. That was the advantage Chance had over her; he could outspend her ten thousand to one and not miss a penny of it. At the same time, she didn't dare trust that he truly meant what he said.

'Plans can always change, though, can't they?' she challenged, aware that her only hope was to be able to stall Chance long enough to give Ben Canon time to get the estate settled, a process the Oklahoma lawyer was doing his best to expedite.

'It's possible,' he agreed, 'but highly unlikely.'

'I notice you didn't rule out the possibility,' she said.

'I don't rule anything out. And I'd like to persuade you to do the same.'

'Me?' She frowned, unsure what he meant by that.

He looked at her, something strong and vivid – and unsettling in his gaze. 'Hasn't it occurred to you that I might be telling you the truth, that I might honestly be in love with you, and I would have wanted you for my wife whether you'd been Hattie's heir or not?' As she started to reply, he cut her off. 'I don't want you to answer that, only to consider it as a possibility. Nothing more. Otherwise we'll end up arguing all night. Why don't we call a truce? I won't try to convince you to change your mind about me if you won't bring up Morgan's Walk and the way I tried to deceive you over it. Agreed?'

Flame hesitated, not entirely sure that was wise. Yet to refuse might indicate a vulnerability on her part. 'Why not?' she said. 'At least it will guarantee a quiet dinner.'

Chance smiled at that. 'I think we'll be able to find something to talk about.' He picked up the menu. 'Speaking of dinner, why don't we decide what to order. I'm told the rack of lamb here is excellent.'

Dinner proved to be more of an ordeal than Flame had expected. She'd forgotten how incredibly persuasive Chance could be when he set out to charm. More than once she'd caught herself responding to that seductive smile of his or that lazy glint in his eyes. Habit, that's all it was – an ingrained reaction to the same stimuli. But there was danger in that, even though such inadvertent responses also served her purpose by letting him think that, with persistence, he might succeed in winning her back.

When Chance suggested an after-dinner drink, Flame refused. Once she would have lingered, wanting to prolong their time together, but not any more. Instead she made her excuses to leave, explaining that she had an early day tomorrow and some work to finish tonight in preparation for it. She doubted that he believed her. Not that it mattered. If he chose to think she was running from him, that was all the better.

But Chance didn't make it easy for her to escape, insisting that he see her safely into a cab. She was obliged to wait while he summoned the waiter and signed the cheque. As she crossed the lobby with his hand resting lightly on her lower back, Flame was reminded of the time she'd gone up those elevators with him to his suite. She felt sick and angry all over again when she remembered the way she'd been taken in by all his smooth lies. Never again.

Outside in the night cool, the doorman whistled for a taxi. But it was Chance who stepped forward to open the door for her when it drove up.

'Thank you for dinner,' she said and started to climb in.

The touch of his hand on her arm checked that movement. 'I want to see you again, Flame.' It wasn't a request or a plea, merely a statement of his desires.

She looked at him, conscious of the quiet intensity of his gaze that had once made her believe he cared deeply about her. 'I don't know.'

'I'm flying to Tahoe in the morning – to check on my project there,' he said. 'Will you come with me?'

'In your jet? So you can spirit me off to some far away place for a wildly romantic weekend? No thank you,' she declared with a firm shake of her head. 'I've been through that before.'

'Then join me there,' he persisted.

She hesitated, then drew away from him and slid into the cab. Inside, she glanced back at him. 'I'll think about it.'

He didn't like her answer, but, as she expected, he didn't press her for a more definite one.

*

The mirror-smooth lake reflected the sapphire blue of the sky and the snow-capped peaks of the Sierras. But the postcard-perfect setting was marred by the belching roar of machinery and the rattling whir of riveters' guns as the construction raced to get the steel superstructure up and closed in before the first heavy snows of winter fell.

In a hard hat, Chance walked among the customary construction rubble on the high-rise hotel site, flanked by the structural engineer and the architect, and trailed by his on-site construction manager, the steel contractor and his foreman. He stopped to watch a crane swing a steel beam into place, then questioned the architect about the number of cars that could be accommodated beneath the hotel's porte-cochere, shouting to make himself heard above the racket.

A steel worker hot-footed it across the site, waving an arm to get their attention. Spotting him, Chance paused and waited for the man to reach them.

The steel contractor stepped forward to intercept him. 'What's the problem?'

He looked at Chance and motioned over his shoulder in the direction of the office trailer. 'There's a lady here wantin' to see Mr Stuart,' he yelled his answer.

Chance lifted his head sharply and glanced at the trailer, everything tensing inside him. Flame. She'd come. Without a word, he walked away from the others and headed for the trailer, his stride lengthening and quickening as he neared it. He pulled the door open, his image of her vivid and bright, all his acute hungers revived.

He stepped inside and stopped short. 'Lucianna.' He was angry, frustrated, the bitterness of disappointment strong on his tongue. 'What are you doing here?'

'I came to see you, of course.' All warm smiles and glowing eyes, she came to him. He caught at her, his arms stiffening to prevent the kiss she wanted to give him. 'Sam told me you were here. Now, don't be angry with him. He was thinking of you. This is a time when you should be with friends.'

'You should have called first,' he said tightly. 'I've asked Flame to join me here.'

'Wonderful.' Lucianna shrugged her lack of concern and

smiled. 'When she comes, I promise I'll disappear without a trace.'

But Flame didn't come.

— 33 —

THE OATMEAL knit of her long jacket flared slightly from the matching shaped turtleneck dress as Flame swept aggressively into Karl Bronsky's office at Thurgood Engineering, an eagerness in her stride that she didn't even try to contain. Her glance darted automatically to the drafting table in the corner, then fell on the rolled plans lying on the desk and finally lifted to the thin, tanned man coming around the desk to welcome her.

'It's good to see you again, Ms Bennett. Please have a seat.' Karl Bronsky was a freckle-faced man in his mid-forties with mild eyes and a habit of nodding with each spurt of talk, as he did now. 'The traffic on the Bay Bridge must have been murder. It always is on a Friday with everybody racing to get out of the city for the weekend.'

'It was.' But she wasn't interested in wasting time exchanging pleasantries about the traffic or the weather. 'When I talked to you this morning, you indicated you had finished your review of the plans I left with you.'

'I did.' Again there was that sharp nod of his head as he circled back around his desk.

'What did you think of them?'

'What did I think? I think it's one helluva ambitious project – if you'll pardon my language – the kind every engineer dreams about being a part of.'

'Then . . .' She paused, choosing her words carefully, '. . . you didn't see any flaw in them.'

'You have to understand, Ms Bennett, these are in the preliminary stage. They aren't finished working drawings. Which isn't to say a lot of thought hasn't gone into them. Obviously it has. In my opinion, it's definitely a viable project.'

'I see.' She tried not to let her disappointment show.

'Now, you asked me specifically to look at the plans for the dam.' He began going through the stack of rolled blueprints and drawings on his desk. 'As you know, none of these contain the name of the firm responsible for drawing up the plans – or any reference to its location.'

'I know.' She'd made certain all such references were removed before she'd given them to him for review. She hadn't wanted to run the risk that someone in Thurgood Engineering might know someone with the engineering firm Chance had used. Fields of business tended to be small worlds and she didn't want word accidentally getting back that she was in possession of these plans.

'Anyway, I don't know who engineered the plans on the dam, but he seems to be a highly competent individual – or group of individuals.' He unrolled one of the sets and anchored the corners down with a paperweight, pencil holder, stapler, and desk pen set. 'As a matter of fact, I only question him on one area. Which isn't to say I think he's wrong. It's impossible to second guess somebody when you aren't in possession of all the facts.'

'What did you question?' Flame noticed that he'd unrolled the overall site plan.

He leaned over it, a faintly puzzled look clouding his sunny freckles. 'You did say that you owned this valley and these people had come to you with the proposition for this massive project.'

'Yes.'

'The thing I can't figure out – at least not without more information – is why they chose this particular site for the dam and why they would want to flood the entire valley?'

'What do you mean?' She tried to check the sudden leap of hope, reminding herself it was too premature. 'Where else could they build it?'

'Again, you have to recognise, Ms Bennett, that I haven't seen the actual site. I'm just going by these plans. But when I look at this, the most logical location for the dam would seem to be this neck of hills here' – he pointed it out to her on the plan – 'well north of the present site. Which would leave this entire south section of the valley intact.'

Which was also where the house and all the ranch buildings were located, Flame realised. She stared at the map, too stunned for an instant to react.

'Think of the golf course and country club that could be built in this valley – and what a complement it would be to the rest of the development. It would definitely be an improvement over that rolling dervish of a course they show winding through the hills now.' He raced on with his thoughts. 'Naturally it would change the shape of the lake – send it into this valley to the northwest. To me that would be a better location for the marina and hotel with these hills sheltering it from high winds. Changing the dam site opens up a whole new set of options. You could put in a landing strip for private aircraft, and, Lord knows, a development like this is going to attract the kind of people who have their own planes. The way it stands now, you'd have to flatten a hill to put an airstrip in, and cost-wise it probably wouldn't be feasible.'

'Then, why –' But she knew why. Chance hated Morgan's Walk. He wanted to destroy it. He wanted it at the bottom of the lake.

Karl Bronsky straightened, regret bringing two thin lines to his forehead. 'I shouldn't have gone on like that. Again I have to stress that the engineer who did this work and chose this site over the one I suggested may have very sound reasons.'

'Such as?'

'Test borings could have shown him that this location wouldn't support a dam without costly sub-shoring. Maybe here he can anchor it to bedrock for a fraction of the money.' He shrugged, indicating a multitude of possibilities. 'Without inspecting the site and doing the necessary tests, I'm only guessing, Ms Bennett.'

'Mr Bronsky,' she spoke slowly, playing with all the possibilities in her mind, even the outrageous ones. 'Is it possible that sometime within the next two weeks you could fly to Oklahoma with me and look at the property yourself?'

'Oklahoma – is that where it is?' he said, then breathed in deeply, considering her suggestion with obvious interest. 'I suppose I could arrange my schedule to free up a couple of days.'

'Good, because I'd like to know if it's absolutely necessary for all of my land to be flooded.' She smiled faintly. 'It's not that I don't trust the work of this engineer. I'd just like a second opinion.'

'I don't blame you. In fact, it's probably the smart thing to do.'

The traffic light ahead turned red and the limousine eased to a smooth stop at the crosswalk. From the rear seat, Flame watched as a cable car clanged across the intersection. Idly her glance swung to Malcom's driver Arthur, separated from the rear passenger area by a sliding glass partition. He'd turned the radio to an easy-listening station and the soothing music of an old André Previn tune came softly over the stereo speakers.

Turning her head on the back rest, she looked at Malcom and smiled faintly. 'If I closed my eyes, I think I could fall asleep.'

The cleft in his chin deepened slightly, amusement glinting in his eyes. 'I thought you had.'

'After that marvellous lunch, can you blame me?' Her smile widened, but the wonderfully lethargic feeling remained, making her feel all lazy and replete. 'Right now it wouldn't take much persuasion to turn me into an advocate of siestas.'

With customary keenness his gaze examined her face. 'You do look tired.'

She didn't deny that she was. 'I've been on the go constantly for the last ten days trying to get everything caught up so I can leave tomorrow for Tulsa. This is the first time I've been able to sit back and truly relax in days – and I have you to thank for it.'

'Tulsa. That's Stuart territory you know,' he challenged, closely watching her reaction to Chance's name.

Flame smiled with a degree of cool unconcern. 'He doesn't have an exclusive on it, Malcom.'

'Do you intend to see him while you're there?' he asked, aware that she'd met with him before.

'Possibly.' Although she had agreed to see Chance that didn't mean she would. She'd cancelled meetings with him before. 'It depends on my schedule. There are a lot of legal matters that I need to clear up regarding the settlement of Hattie's estate – documents to be signed, that sort of thing.'

She didn't mention the engineer Karl Bronsky would be flying the day after she arrived to meet with her and look over Morgan's Walk, specifically the proposed dam sites. She had yet to confide in Malcom the reasons behind her split with Chance or the battle ahead of her to prevent Chance from acquiring control of the land he'd married her to get.

Malcom frowned thoughtfully, his gaze narrowing. 'I don't understand why you see him when you keep saying you're through with him.'

She smiled away his remark, a playfully chiding light entering her eyes. 'You make it sound as if he's been my constant companion, Malcom. I've only met him twice. And contrary to recent rumours, there is no reconciliation in the works.'

There wasn't a trace of doubt in her voice. Was she over him? Malcom wondered. It was true she no longer reacted hostilely to the mere mention of Stuart, but a vindictive gleam appeared in her eyes each time his name was brought up.

The traffic light turned green and the limousine rolled forward with little sensation of motion to its passengers. 'How long will you be in Tulsa?'

'Just over the weekend. I'll be back the first of the week.' She glanced at him curiously. 'Why?'

'I was wondering what your plans are now that you've become a woman of property and independent means.' He smiled to conceal the fact that he didn't like the idea of Flame going to Tulsa, even for a brief time – any more than he liked the idea that she might be meeting Stuart while she was there. 'Is this preliminary to a permanent move?'

The possibility she might move out of easy reach . . . beyond his influence . . . had concerned him ever since she'd told him about her inheritance of a large ranching estate in Oklahoma.

'*Modestly* independent means,' she corrected lightly. 'Certainly not enough to induce me to resign from the agency.'

'Good.' Malcom smiled in disguised relief. 'That means I won't have to work with a new account executive.'

She gave him a look of mock reproval. 'Next, you'll be trying to convince me you're only interested in my mind.'

'I admit your company is mentally stimulating,' he replied, matching her bantering tone, then paused, letting his gaze travel slowly down her curved figure. 'Unfortunately I haven't had the opportunity to discover how stimulating you can be in . . . other ways.'

She released an earthy laugh. 'You never give up, do you,

Malcom? If persistence was a virtue, you'd be the most virtuous man I know.'

His smile widened. 'It's called wearing down the opposition.'

'You're definitely an expert at the game,' Flame declared, a hint of amusement remaining in her voice.

His look grew serious and wanting. 'Does that mean I'm finally making progress?'

She started to deny that, then paused to look at him, suddenly recalling how comfortable and at ease she had been with him these last two hours. Wasn't that rare – as rare as the heady excitement she'd known with Chance?

Giving him the most honest answer she could, she said, 'I don't know, Malcom.'

He said nothing to that, simply took her hand and lifted it up to press a kiss in its palm as the limousine came to a stop in front of the agency's building. Arthur stepped out and opened the passenger door for her, extending a hand to help her out. She withdrew her fingers from Malcom's grasp and climbed out of the car, then turned back.

'Thank you for lunch . . . and your company, Malcom.'

'We'll talk again next week after you get back from Tulsa,' he promised, the possessive light in his grey eyes even bolder than before.

Slowly and thoughtfully, Flame turned and walked to the building's entrance.

— 34 —

SUNDAY AFTERNOON, Flame walked the freckle-faced Karl Bronsky to the front door of Morgan's Walk, his preliminary inspections of the land completed. Charlie Rainwater waited outside to drive him to the airport.

'Thanks again for the hospitality,' he said. 'I didn't mean to impose.'

'You didn't,' she assured him. 'We'll talk when I get back to San Francisco.'

'Right.' Then he was out of the door.

Flushed with a feeling of victory, Flame closed the door behind him and turned, barely able to contain her excitement. Then she saw Maxine standing in the foyer watching her.

'Is Mr Bronsky leaving already?' The housekeeper frowned.

'Yes.' She was instantly alert, recalling the foreman's warning that Hattie had long doubted Maxine's loyalty. According to him, she'd never made it a secret that her sympathies were with Chance. If there was any leak at Morgan's Walk, the housekeeper was the likely source. 'Charlie's taking him to the airport to catch his flight.'

'It seems to me it was hardly worth his time to fly out here,' the woman declared. 'He arrives in time for supper last night, then he takes off with Charlie first thing this morning and stays gone most of the day. He couldn't have spent more than an hour with you. That's a funny way to treat your host, if you ask me.'

'Karl's a city boy. He's never been on a working ranch before and he was fascinated by it. Maybe he always dreamed of being a cowboy when he grew up.' Flame shrugged to indicate her lack of concern.

'What does he do for a living?' Maxine asked curiously.

'What does anybody do who lives in a city? He works in an office surrounded by four walls.'

If Maxine noticed her avoidance of a direct answer, she gave no sign of it. 'Ben's waiting in the library to see you.'

'Will you bring –'

'I already took him a pot of coffee, and I included an extra cup for you.'

'Thank you, Maxine. That will be all.' With long, swinging strides, Flame crossed the foyer and walked down the hall to the library, her spirits lifting again with that inner sense of triumph.

She entered the library, then turned, with hardly a break in motion, and drew the pocket doors closed. A fire blazed in the hearth, the cheery crackle of its flames matching her ebullient mood as she crossed to the desk. Ben Canon sat behind it, his diminutive frame dwarfed even more by its massive size. She stopped short when she saw the coffee tray and the spread of legal papers before him.

'The plans. Where are they?'

'I rolled them up and set them in the corner.' With a swing of his balding head to the right, he directed her attention to the plans propped against the bookshelves behind him, half hidden by the walnut stand supporting a world globe.

'Maxine didn't see them, did she?'

'No. I already had them put away when she brought the coffee.'

'Good.' Flame relaxed a little then.

'Did your engineer friend get off all right?'

She nodded absently as she retrieved the site plan and spread it out on the desk. 'Charlie's taken him to the airport. I'm afraid Karl walked poor Charlie's legs off today.' A hint of a smile touched her mouth. 'To hear him tell it, Karl tramped every foot of the hills at both locations, and even climbed down to inspect

— 325 —

the river banks. Just before he left, Karl told me his visual inspection hasn't given him any reason to believe that the dam couldn't be built on the north site. I've authorised him to do whatever test borings are necessary – and I also told him to bring in a crew from the coast, not to use anyone locally. I don't want Chance to find out what we're up to.'

'What are you up to?' Ben Canon rocked back in the desk chair and folded his pudgy hands across his chest to study her with a puzzled, penetrating look. 'As your attorney, don't you think I should know?'

'I want to prove this second dam site is viable. You've already warned me about the political power and influence Chance wields. If we have to fight a condemnation attempt, this might be a weapon for us – an alternative to his proposal that will, at least, save the house and part of the valley.'

She had another idea, too – one she'd been toying with ever since Karl Bronsky had brought up the possibility of another dam site – but she didn't mention it to Ben Canon. She knew how crazy, how impossible it would sound to him. It probably was, but she hadn't been able to convince herself totally of that yet.

'It might work.' He nodded slowly in thoughtful approval. 'Is that it?'

'I was curious about something else,' she admitted and moved the site plan over in front of him. 'This valley here on the northwest side, it doesn't appear that Chance owns it – or has optioned it. I'd like to find out who does.'

'It's probably the Starret place, but I'll stop into the county courthouse and check the tax rolls to make sure.'

'I think it would be better if you didn't do it yourself, Ben. If Chance finds out, he might wonder why you're interested, and we don't want to tip our hand to him.'

'You sound remarkably like Hattie,' the lawyer observed, then humphed a short laugh. 'She's probably turning circles in her grave knowing you've invited him here to dinner tonight.'

'Maybe,' Flame admitted as she began rolling up the site plan. 'And maybe she'd approve.' This would mark the third time she'd met with Chance, and the first time it wouldn't be at a public place. That part didn't concern her. She was confident of her ability to handle him even if sometimes she momentarily let herself be attracted to him again. No, not to him, she quickly corrected that thought. She was attracted by the memory of how it had been between them before she'd discovered he was only using her. That sense of loving and being loved had been powerful then.

Ben Canon rocked forward in his chair, a rare grimness pulling at the corners of his mouth. 'I wish you could persuade Stuart to tip his hand.'

Aware that the crafty old lawyer never made idle comments, Flame glanced at him sharply, noting the look of heavy concentration that creased his brow as he studied the papers before him, the ones he'd been going over when she came in. 'You had a reason for saying that, Ben. What is it?'

'As you know, the inventory and appraisal of all of Hattie's assets has been completed – along with compilation of all the outstanding debts, mortgages, and bank notes. While I was going over them to establish the worth of her estate, I came across something that bothers me.'

'What?'

'The bank sold the mortgage on Morgan's Walk last spring.'

She immediately tensed. 'To whom? Chance?'

'I don't know and that's what bothers me. I have the name of a corporation that's the new mortgage holder, but I can't trace the true owner. Which makes me suspect that I'd find Chance at the end of the maze of holding companies and private trusts. Unfortunately I can't prove it.'

Flame turned away, bitterly realising just how hollow and fleeting that sense of victory could be. 'He knows how to stack the deck, doesn't he?'

'You could say that.'

'I suppose he can call the entire mortgage due.'

'He can and – more than likely – he will.'

'What about the money from Hattie's life insurance policy?'

'There's enough to pay the estate tax and give you about six months operating capital. I'm afraid the only way you're going to be able to pay off the mortgage to Chance is to find yourself another lender. And, I have to be honest, Flame, that isn't going to be easy.'

'Why? The ranch is worth it.'

'The value's there, yes. But good management and the ability to repay – that's what a lender will look at very hard – especially these days with so many family farms and ranches going under. And you know next to nothing about the ranching business.'

'I don't, but Charlie Rainwater –'

'– is old. Old enough to draw Social Security. It's time reality was faced, Flame.' He handed her a sheaf of papers. 'Morgan's Walk is something of a white elephant – especially this old house. As you can see from those cost income statements, the ranching operation itself has shown marginal profits for the last few years. And nearly every bit has gone into the maintenance and upkeep on this building.' He paused, regret entering his expression. 'I know how much Hattie loved this place, and, in my own way, I fought as hard as she did to keep it from falling into Stuart's hands. But realistically speaking, if this house wasn't out here in the country, I'd recommend that you donate to some local historical society for a museum – anything to get out from its costs. I don't mean to sound like the prophet of doom, Flame, but if the cattle market should go down or the calving losses in the spring are high or Charlie's health goes bad and your new manager isn't as sharp as he is, you could be in trouble. I'm telling you all this to make sure that you see you're going to have a tough time of it all the way around ... especially with this mortgage business.'

'I see,' she murmured, then added wryly, 'At least I'm beginning to.' She stared at the papers in her hand. 'May I keep these and look them over?'

'By all means,' Ben nodded. 'Those are your copies.' He set his briefcase on top of the desk and flipped it open. 'I have some documents that require your signature.' He laid them out for her and gave her a pen. 'With luck, and no interference from Stuart, by the end of next week Morgan's Walk and everything on it will officially be yours.'

'Good,' she said, although at the moment she was beginning to wonder about that.

'Oh, and something else.' He reached inside his briefcase again and took out a newspaper clipping. 'This was in a Reno paper recently. I thought you might like to see it – just in case Stuart decides to give you any problems about the annulment.'

The newspaper photograph showed a smiling Chance and beaming Lucianna, and the caption beneath it read: 'Real estate magnate Chance Stuart and diva Lucianna Colton back together

again. Seen at a recent fund-raiser for the performing arts . . .'
Flame didn't read any more, going cold, then hot with rage. All
that talk about how much he loved her and needed her, how
much he wanted her back – for herself – it was all more lies.
And he was coming here tonight to tell her more.

After dinner, Chance stood in front of the parlour's fireplace, a
brandy glass in his hand, and stared at the new flames dancing
and darting over the seasoned logs in defiance of any pattern. It
should have been a cosy setting – brandy and coffee for two, the
flickering glow of the fire, the easy quiet of the house, the low
lights of the room.

A single floorlamp burned, its dome-shaped, fringed shade dif-
fusing the light from its bulb and casting a soft amber glow on the
wing chair where Flame sat, her body angled sideways, knees drawn
up. Turning his head slightly he surveyed her with a sidelong look.

Like a contented cat, she looked, all curled up in the chair, the
sleeves of her intarsia sweater pushed up, the loose fit of her
white slacks clinging softly to her long legs. Her mane of red-
gold hair ran faintly lawless back from her lovely and proud face.
The mere sight of her stirred him profoundly.

Yet, as he looked at her, it wasn't Flame he thought about. His
mind kept playing back the discussion he'd had with Sam today
in his office.

'Chance, a whole month has gone by. Don't you think it's time
we did something?' Sam argued, exasperation and frustration
showing on his boyish features. 'We haven't contested the will. If
we don't do something in the next couple of days, the court's going
to hand Morgan's Walk over to her. You realise that, don't you?'

'Tying up the title to that land isn't going to accomplish anything, Sam. I'm not going to fight her on it, and that's final.'

'You're not going to fight her on that, and you're not fighting
her on the annulment either. Dammit, Chance, I know you love
her and you want her back. I understand that, but – what about
Morgan's Walk?'

'What about it?'

Sam lifted his shoulders in a helpless gesture. 'It just seems
to me that you're counting an awful lot on getting Flame back.
I mean, you're not making any other move to get the land.'

'If I take any action against her now, I can forget persuading her to come back to me. She'd be convinced all I want is the land.'

'Maybe so.' Sam sighed, a heavy, disgruntled sound. 'But I worry about the amount of time going by. I'm not saying you should call the mortgage due, but you could hassle her a little by demanding financial statements and a review of the loan. Put some pressure on her and maybe shake her up a bit.'

'You don't shake Flame up; you just make her mad.'

'I think it's a mistake to do nothing, Chance. How long can we afford to sit on our hands?'

'As long as it takes.'

Sam looked at him. 'Are you making any headway with her? Or is she just stringing you along?'

He hadn't had an answer for that – and he didn't now as he swirled the brandy in his glass, then tossed down most of it.

'More brandy?' The softness of her voice reached out to him, stirring his senses, but it was the politeness of her enquiry that registered.

'No.' He turned the rest of the way around to face her chair, letting his gaze move over her. She seemed vaguely restless under it, her guard lifting, shuttering the green of her eyes and masking her expression with a blandness. 'During the last – almost – four weeks, we've had dinner together, talked, and occasionally even laughed together. So why do I have the feeling that I'm not getting through to you – that you're just going through the motions?'

With an unhurried grace, she uncurled her legs and rose from the chair, her hands sliding into the slanted side pockets of her slacks as she wandered over to the fireplace. 'I think you've forgotten these meetings were your idea, not mine.'

'I suppose they've meant nothing to you – that you've regretted every unguarded smile you gave me,' he taunted, lifting the glass halfway to his mouth and speaking over the top of it. 'And you have given them to me. Granted, they happened at weak moments – when you forgot to hate me.'

'Then they must have been rare, indeed,' she returned coolly.

He smiled at that and finished the rest of his brandy, then walked over to the coffee table and set his empty glass on top of it. He didn't turn back.

'What do you want from me, Flame?' Every sense was sharpened as he waited for an answer that didn't come. He spoke again with a rising energy, his anger close. 'Am I supposed to crawl? Beg? What?'

'I want nothing from you, Chance. Absolutely nothing.'

When he turned, she had her back to him, facing the fire. He stared at the tall, willowy shape she made against the firelight.

'I don't believe you've stopped caring, Flame.' As he walked up behind her, he saw her stiffen in sudden alertness, defending herself against the steady beat of his presence.

'And I don't care what you believe.'

'I've made you laugh. I've made you smile. I've made you angry. And, no doubt, I've made you cry.'

'While you're ennumerating your list of accomplishments, don't forget that you've also made me hate you.'

'But you care. You're not indifferent to me, any more than I am to you.' He touched the soft points of her shoulders, his hands settling gently on to them, remembering the feel of her – and feeling the tensing of her body. Drawn closer by her nearness, he brushed his lips against her hair, breathing in its clean scent. 'I've missed you.' He hadn't meant to say that, but now that it was out, he said the rest, too. 'I've always believed that a woman had to be everything to a man – or nothing. You are everything to me, Flame. Everything.' He let his hands trail down her arms and follow the bend of her elbows to cross in front of her, drawing her back against him. She tipped her head to the side, as if away from him, but he found the slender curve of her neck and the vein that throbbed there. 'I never knew anything about family or love – not growing up here, in this house. But you taught me . . . you showed me how it could be.'

'No.' She wasn't sure what she was saying 'no' to – to him, to her memories, to the physical response he evoked? His words, his voice, his touch were all working on her, undermining the barriers she'd put up against him. She offered no resistance at all when he turned her into his arms.

'Yes.' His glance ran quickly over her.

This close, Chance noticed the long sweep of her lashes and the curvature of her mouth, and the small lines at the lip corners, which made her – when she chose – look wilful and steel-proud. Her breasts were pressed to his chest so he could feel the quick beat of her heart and the quick in-and-out run of her breathing. Her face was set against him, yet he sensed she was disturbed and uncertain – she who seldom was. There was no doubt in his mind, though. He needed her. For him, she was the softness and the endlessness, the fire and the green, cool depths.

'I need you, Flame,' he murmured and kissed her, his mouth coming down hot and firm. Taken by surprise, or suddenly willing – Chance wasn't sure – but she kissed him back, deeply.

Then she pulled herself away and backed up, moving out of his reach. 'You're good, Chance,' she declared, her voice still husky with the level of her disturbance. 'You're very good.' She wondered how she could have forgotten, even for a moment, that the man was an expert at seduction. 'But it isn't going to work, not a second time. Because I know it isn't me you need; it's Morgan's Walk.'

'That's a separate thing.'

'Is it?' She took the newspaper clipping from her pocket – the one with the photograph of Chance with Lucianna – and handed it to him. 'I can see how heartbroken you are over losing me.'

He shot a look at it, then brought his gaze straight back to her. 'This means nothing. Lucianna is an old friend. You know that.'

'Then let her console you. I'm sure she's good at it.'

'Dammit, Flame –' He took a step towards her.

She brought him up short with a cold, 'I think you'd better leave, Chance. You've had your dinner and you've had your conversation, but you're not going to have me.'

He hesitated. She saw the indecision warring in him, the impulse to press his point – and to take advantage of the vulnerability she'd shown him. Then he appeared to change his mind, crumpling the newspaper clipping and tossing it into the fire.

'I'll go,' he said. 'We'll settle this another time.'

She knew better – because there wasn't going to be another time. But she didn't tell him that. She let him walk out of the parlour believing that she would meet him again somewhere, sometime. But there was no more need for that. She'd gained the time she wanted.

When she heard the front door close behind him, she turned to the fireplace and watched the flames leap greedily to consume the crumpled paper. For an instant, the grainy photograph of Chance and Lucianna, arm in arm, stood out sharply. In the next second, it was all black char.

— 35 —

TWICE AFTER she returned to San Francisco, Chance attempted to contact her again but Flame had been tied up in meetings on both occasions and hadn't bothered to return his calls. She knew that sooner or later he'd realise she was deliberately avoiding him, but she hadn't had time to concern herself with that.

Every spare hour – every spare minute – of her days had been taken up by meetings, phone calls, and long discussions with Karl Bronsky and an associate of his, Devlin Scott. The results from the test borings had come back, proving the northern dam site was definitely viable. But Flame no longer regarded it as a weapon with which to fight any condemnation proceedings initiated by Chance. The northern dam site had become the cornerstone for a daring new plan – a plan she had discussed with no one other than Karl Bronsky and Devlin Scott, a plan she had constantly reviewed and refined on her own until she felt it was ready. Even then she hadn't told Karl all of it – certainly not the most critical part.

Deciding that she was as fully prepared as she would ever be, Flame made the final call that would either set her plan into motion or put her back to square one.

'Hello, Malcom. It's Flame.'

'If you're calling to cancel our lunch on Thursday, you realise this will be the second week in a row you've done that.'

'I'm not.' Their Thursday luncheon was the farthest thing from her mind. 'I have a business proposition I'd like to discuss with you.'

'A business proposition.' A note of alertness entered his voice. 'Regarding what?'

'It's personal. It has nothing to do with the agency,' she said. 'And I'd prefer to show you, rather than try to explain it over the phone.'

'When would you like to meet?'

'Any time,' she said. 'In fact, the sooner the better.'

'What about this evening?' Malcom suggested. 'I have a six o'clock meeting, but I should be free by eight. I'm spending the night at my apartment in town rather than drive home to Belvedere. We could meet there at – say, eight-thirty.'

With no hesitation, Flame replied. 'Eight-thirty it is.'

When she hung up, her assistant contacted her on the intercom. 'You have a call on line two, Flame, from a Mr Canon in Tulsa. Do you want to take it or shall I tell him you'll return the call later?'

'I'll take it.' She immediately picked up the phone and pushed the button on the blinking line. 'Hello, Ben.'

'I just received a call I thought you might be interested in.'

'From whom?' She frowned curiously, certain Chance wouldn't be calling him.

'A local real estate agent. He wanted to know if there was a possibility the new owner of Morgan's Walk would consider selling it. It seems he has a party in Texas – Dallas supposedly – who's interested in the property.'

'Really?' she murmured, suddenly angry. 'You can bet Chance is behind this.' It irritated her that Chance would think she was too stupid not to see through this ruse.

'I'm sure of it,' Ben agreed. 'He knows you would never sell to him. More than likely he's hoping you'll sell the land to somebody else to spite him – especially if the offer is generous. Which I'm sure it will be.'

'What did you tell the agent?'

'Basically nothing.'

'Call him back and tell him –' She checked her first angry

impulse in favour of another thought. 'Tell him you don't think the new owner is interested in selling, but to have his Dallas party contact me personally, and indicate you think I could be persuaded if the price was right.'

'If that's what you want, I'll do it.'

'It is.' She smiled faintly. 'There's more than one way to string Chance along.'

Malcom Powell's town apartment on the eighteenth floor of the sleek steel and glass high-rise was small by society's standards, but definitely luxurious. A single spacious room combined the living and dining area with an elaborate entertainment centre. The decor was modern in its approach while possessing classical overtones – Malcom collected marble obelisks and Bedemier wood furniture. Done in a study of greys, the colour scheme was designed to draw the eye to the panoramic view of the city and its glitter of nightlights.

But Flame took little note of either when she arrived at the apartment promptly at eight-thirty. After inquiring politely about his earlier meeting, she wasted no time on pleasantries.

'Do you mind if I use the table for these plans?' Without waiting for his reply, she crossed the floor of pearl-grey marble to the lacquered dining table.

'Not at all.' Malcom followed at a more leisurely pace, then watched with curious eyes as she removed a set of drawings from her large leather portfolio case and spread them on the table. 'Can I pour you a drink?'

She started to refuse, then noticed the glass in his hand. 'Gin and tonic.' When he returned with it, she set the drink aside without taking so much as a sip from it, and opened her attaché case instead, taking out the booklet that contained the summary and analysis of Chance's proposed development.

'After I talked to you this morning,' Malcom observed her actions but didn't step up to the table to look at the material she set out, 'I initially thought you wanted to talk to me about setting up your own agency, but something tells me I was way off the mark.'

'You were.' She threw a quick smile at him. 'As you know, I recently inherited some property in Oklahoma. This' – she indicated the site plans and drawings on the table – 'is what Chance Stuart planned to do with that land.'

Moving up to stand beside her, Malcom glanced briefly at the plans, then angled his shoulders toward her, his gaze intent in its study of her. 'As I recall, you inherited the property *after* you left him.'

'That's true.' It wasn't easy, but she managed to meet his gaze squarely, pride asserting itself despite the bitter blow it had been dealt. 'And I think it's obvious by the amount of thought and work that's gone into these drawings he had planned this project long before he met me. As you can see from this site plan, he's already in possession of these parcels. All he lacked was the valley.'

'And that's why he married you.'

'Yes.' There was no reason to deny it and at this point Malcom deserved to know the truth about Chance – about everything. 'I'd like you to look this over for me, Malcom, and tell me what you think honestly of the project.'

He looked at her at length, as if trying to discern the motive behind her request. Finally he simply nodded. 'All right.'

When he took a pair of steel-rimmed reading glasses from the inside pocket of his charcoal-grey business suit, Flame picked up her drink glass and wandered over to the living room, leaving him to study the information without looking over his shoulder. Oddly enough, she didn't feel nervous. Impatient, yes. Determined, definitely, But nervous, no. She knew precisely what she wanted, why she wanted it, and what she would do to get it – with no second thoughts and no regrets.

She resisted the urge to pace the room and sat down instead on the soft leather sofa facing the dining table and Malcom. She sipped at her drink, tasting none of it, not even the icy wetness of it. She made a concerted effort not to stare at him, yet she was aware of his every move, the recessed lighting overhead flashing on the streaks of grey in his dark hair with each tilt of his head.

The waiting became unbearable. Still, she didn't move from the sofa, the ice in her drink turning to water. When she thought she couldn't stand the tension any more, Malcom took off his reading glasses and paused to take one last look at everything on the table, then turned unerringly in her direction.

'Well?' She prodded him for some comment without budging from the sofa, unconsciously holding her breath.

'I think Stuart would probably have set the real estate world back on its heels again – and pocketed millions in the process,' he said, then paused. 'Or am I assuming too much when I said "he would have"?'

'No, you're not.' She got up from the sofa and walked over to the dining table. There, she opened the portfolio and took out another set of drawings. 'This is the development I want to build.' She spread them out on the table, covering the ones she'd taken from Chance's office and ignoring the sharp look of surprise Malcom gave her. 'As you can see the concept is virtually the same as his. The placement of various things has been changed. The dam site is located farther north on the river, opening this valley which lends itself perfectly to a thirty-six hole course and a hotel/country club with ample room for condominiums and townhouses to be built around it as well as a landing strip for private aircraft. Changing the dam site also necessitates a change in the location of the resort hotel and marina, moving it over here to this area. Actually it's a better location than the one he had since it gives the marina protection from the prevailing winds in the area. And' – she had difficulty keeping satisfaction from creeping into her voice – 'changing the dam site also means that most of the land Chance owns is left – literally – high and dry.'

'You're serious about this,' Malcom realised.

'I have never been more serious about anything in my life,' Flame stated. 'However, I should point out the site for the resort hotel and marina is outside the boundaries of Morgan's Walk. Seven individually owned parcels make up the site including the valley area that will be flooded once the dam's in place. Naturally that land will have to be acquired as quickly as possible.'

'Why are you doing this, Flame?' he asked quietly – almost too quietly. 'It's more than the money you might make, isn't it?'

'Chance still wants my land. The mere fact that he married me to gain control of it proves how determined he is to get it. He isn't going to stop just because that attempt failed. He'll try and keep trying until he succeeds. He already holds the mortgage on Morgan's Walk. I received a call from my attorney today advising me that I'll probably be receiving a very lucrative offer to buy the ranch – supposedly from an investor in Dallas. There's no doubt in my mind that Chance is behind it. When I turn that down, he'll simply call the mortgage due. If I should be successful in obtaining a loan somewhere else – which won't be easy – more than likely he'll buy it up, too. He's going to do everything in his power to squeeze me out. If all I do is fight a holding action, ultimately I'll lose. Which leaves me one alternative,' she concluded. 'I have to beat him at his own game.'

She caught the glimmer of new respect and admiration that appeared briefly in Malcom's look. Then he smiled, ever so faintly. 'And maybe get a little revenge in the process.'

'That's part of it, too,' she admitted with candour.

'And this business proposition you mentioned on the phone – where do I fit in your scheme of things?'

'I need a partner.' She didn't bother to add that he had to be someone with power and financial credibility, regarding that as a given. 'I *might* be able to put this development together by myself, but we both know how difficult – if not impossible – it would be, especially if Chance finds out. But with the Powell name and money behind me, even Chance Stuart would find it hard to go up against you.'

'But why should I back you, Flame? Aside from the money that could be made, what do I get out of it?'

'Me,' she replied evenly.

His smile was faintly sardonic. 'I knew that's what you were going to say.' Flame experienced her first moment of unease. 'However tempting the proposition is – and it is very tempting – I'm not sure I like the idea of being used by you to get back at Stuart.'

'We have always been honest with each other, Malcom,' she said, choosing her words. 'I'm not sure you realise how rare that is. I know I didn't. Never once have you implied to me that you desired anything more than an affair. In fact you openly admitted that you had no intention of ever leaving your wife. I've learned to appreciate that honesty – and many other things as well. I have always respected and admired you, Malcom, both as a business-man and a man. And we enjoy each other's company, too. As you once pointed out to me, we get along well together. What better basis for a relationship is there than a mutual admiration and respect?'

He breathed in deeply, a trace of wariness in his expression. 'I want you, Flame – more than I've ever wanted any other woman. I want you so much that I almost believe what you say. You're very convincing.'

'And I want you. Revenge is part of it, Malcom. I'm not denying that.' Moving slowly she closed the space between them until she stood mere inches from him. Still, she made no move to touch him. 'But it isn't all of it. I'm tired of being alone. I'm tired of being lonely. I want someone I can share things with, whether it's work or play. Is that really so difficult for you to believe?' she argued quietly.

'No.'

'Then . . . can we be partners?'

In answer, his hands closed on her arms and drew her the last few inches to meet his descending mouth. She responded to his kiss, although admittedly without the passion and intensity of feeling that she once had given Chance. But she'd learned the painful way, it was better to love wisely, safely, than to be swept away by emotion. She swayed against him and wound her arms around him, answering the forceful pressure of his kiss.

When he led her into the bedroom, another quiet composition in grey, a part of her regretted that in the order of things, it had to be next that they make love. As she undressed beneath his heated glance, she reminded herself there would be time enough later to discuss strategy and options. Now there was this. It was not a passive lover he wanted and she knew that. She sincerely tried to give what he did want. She met his force with her own and urged him to drive away her memories. After all, it was part of the bargain.

If his hands and lips were not as quick to seek out and find her pleasure points – if he relied more on strength than finesse to show his desire – if the satisfaction from their coupling was less than that she'd known before – she blocked it out. Afterwards, lying in his arms, her head resting on his powerfully built chest, she felt a measure of contentment and ease. That was enough for her.

— 36 —

SAM WALKED out of his office and threw a quick glance at the closed doors to Chance's suite, then hesitated and went over to Molly's desk. 'Is Chance busy?'

'Busy?' She sighed and glanced at the lighted button on the telephone indicating one of the lines was in use. 'He's in there trying to get a hold of Flame again.'

'And all he's getting is the usual runaround, right?' Sam guessed, and shook his head, joining Molly in her troubled sigh. 'In the last two months, he's spoken to her exactly once, and I'd be willing to bet that was an accident. If she'd known he was calling, she would never have picked up the phone.'

'He worries me, Sam,' Molly declared. 'Have you noticed the weight he's lost? And he isn't sleeping nights either. It's no wonder he's so irritable and –'

'– impossible to talk to,' he finished the sentence for her.

'Why is she treating him like this? Doesn't she know what she's doing to him?'

'You're as bad as Chance,' Sam murmured, looking at her with a mixture of sadness and disgust. 'It doesn't seem to occur to either one of you that she just might not give a damn.'

'Maybe I was wrong about her.' Such a concession coming from Molly bordered on the monumental and Sam knew it. 'She seemed to be genuinely in love with him. Maybe it was an act. That's the only explanation that makes sense.'

'There might be one or two others.' But Sam didn't go into them. Molly would never admit that part of the blame for Flame's present attitude might belong to Chance for the way he'd deceived her about Morgan's Walk. As far as Molly was concerned, she should have forgiven him for that.

'I thought that Hattie woman was cruel and heartless,' Molly said, an anger showing in the tight working of her jaw. 'Now I'm beginning to think it runs in the family. The amount of suffering those two women have brought into his life . . .' She sighed again and looked at Sam. 'What are we going to do?'

'I don't know about you, but I have to go in there and tell him that I finally heard from J.T. If he's in a bad mood now, it's only going to get worse.'

'What happened?' she asked, then immediately guessed. 'She refused to sell.'

'Something like that.' He walked over to the doors and knocked once.

But Chance didn't hear it as he slammed the receiver down, cutting off the voice on the other end of the line as she started to explain that Ms Bennett was in a meeting and couldn't be disturbed, an excuse he'd heard too many times to believe any more. No woman had ever rocked and tore at him like this, until he could think of nothing else but having her back. She was like a hammer beating at his strength. Cursing under his breath, he ran a hand through his close cropped hair as he leaned on his desk, his shoulders hunched against the ache that wouldn't go away.

'Chance?' Sam's voice intruded, bringing his head up sharply.

'What is it?' he snapped, turning his chair away while he fought to regain his composure.

'I just finished talking to J.T. in Dallas.'

He spun the chair back around. 'Has he met with Flame?' He checked the impulse to ask how she was and demanded instead, 'What did she say? Has she agreed to sell Morgan's Walk?'

'No.' Sam paused briefly. 'Her exact words to him were – and I quote – "Tell Chance Stuart that Morgan's Walk isn't for sale at any price." Naturally J.T. denied that you were in any way involved in the offer. But I guess she just smiled and showed him the door.'

'Damn.' The curse was barely more than a whisper.

'Don't you think it's time we took the gloves off, Chance?'

He leaned back in his chair and reached in his jacket pocket, taking out the set of wedding rings he'd carried with him every single day since Flame had dropped them at his feet. He closed his fingers around them, feeling the edges of the diamond cut into his palm.

'Call the mortgage due,' he said, then slowly pulled open the centre drawer of his desk and dropped the rings inside. He pushed the drawer shut, and wished he could be as successful in shutting Flame from his mind. 'Cut off all credit to Morgan's Walk. Call in every favour and apply whatever pressure you have to, but get it done. I want to drain her cash, and hopefully leave her nothing to operate on. While you're at it, hire away all the ranch help you can.'

— 37 —

Hᴇᴀʀɪɴɢ ᴛʜᴇ turn of a key in the lock, Malcom lowered the newspaper and took off his reading glasses, his glance turning to the entrance hall in his apartment. The closing of the door was followed by the firm tap of high heels on the marble floor as Flame strode into view, still dressed in the brown-and-white wool Adolfo suit she'd worn earlier in the day, a combination made all the more striking by the red of her hair.

'I expected you an hour ago.'

'I know, darling.' She gave her wool and alpaca coat a toss, flinging it on to one of the chairs, then crossed to the back of the sofa and bent down to give him a quick kiss. 'I'm sorry. My meeting with Ellery took longer than I thought. There were simply too many things to go over. Would you like me to freshen your drink?' she asked, reaching for his glass.

'Please,' he said as she crossed to the drinks cart, his glass in hand.

'I have to spend most of tomorrow at the agency.' Using the tongs, she plucked cubes from the ice bucket, dropped some in his glass and the rest in hers. 'I'm not going to have any choice unfortunately. I have too much work backed up.'

'You're spreading yourself too thin. It's time you gave the agency notice.'

Watching as she splashed more whiskey into his glass, Malcom could see she didn't look the least bit tired, mentally or physically. On the contrary, he'd never seen her look so vibrantly alive, driven by a restless energy. The impression was reinforced when she turned back to him, giving him the direct effect of her green eyes. In that moment, he saw her then as she was to him, the shape and dream of beauty, the image of a still fire burning in the night, perfect and pure-centred with a white heat. He wanted to believe he was responsible for that bright glitter in her eyes. But he knew better and her next words confirmed it.

'I can't, not for a while yet. I don't know how closely Chance is watching me. If I quit the agency, he'll start wondering what I'm going to do.' She walked over and handed him his drink. 'And we can't risk arousing his suspicion too soon.' She kicked off her alligator pumps and sat down on the sofa cushion beside him, curling her silk-clad feet under her and angling sideways to face him. 'Besides, my workload with the agency isn't that heavy now that I've managed to turn most of my clients over to other account execs in the firm – with the exception of Powell's, of course.' She reached out to touch him, her fingers tracing the lobe of his ear then trailing over the square line of his jaw.

'Of course.' He smiled automatically while silently wondering if he'd ever cease resenting the way every third sentence of hers contained some reference to Stuart. The man was an invisible presence constantly with them. The bed was the only place he didn't appear – and Malcom wasn't entirely certain about that. Endless times he'd found himself wondering if he pleased her in bed as fully as Stuart once had. His virility had been something he'd never doubted . . . until now. Over and over he reminded himself that Flame was with him – not Stuart. Yet he couldn't shake the feeling that she would never have come to him if it wasn't for her desperate thirst for revenge. He probably should be grateful to Stuart, but he was beginning to despise the man as much as Flame said she did. In truth, he was eager to tangle openly with Stuart and prove who was the better man.

'Speaking of Chance' – the ice cubes in her drink clinked against the sides of the glass as she idly swirled the gin and tonic – 'the notice came last week calling the mortgage due. I have sixty days to come up with seven hundred-odd thousand dollars.'

'Last week.' Malcom frowned. 'You never said anything about it.'

'I forgot, what with all the meetings we had with the engineers and the land planners. We have plenty of time to come up with it so it really doesn't matter. And I have no intention of paying it until the very last minute. I'm sure he believes he's created a problem for me and I want him to go on thinking that.'

'You're a cunning woman, Flame.' At the same time that he realised that, he also recognised that her every thought, her every move was dictated by what she expected Stuart's response or reaction to be.

'It's going to take cunning – and an element of surprise – to beat him.' Again her restlessness surfaced as she uncurled her legs and rolled gracefully to her feet, avoiding his gaze. 'Which reminds me – did Karl drop the new site plan by your office? He said he'd have it ready today.'

'It's on the table.'

'Are there many changes?' She walked over to study it for herself.

'A handful, but they're all minor ones.' Malcom hesitated, then set his glass down on the coffee table and joined her in the dining area. 'He has the plans for the dam finished as well. I gave Karl the name of my contact in Washington and told him to fly there next week so he can look them over.'

'Aren't you being premature –'

'No.' Malcom overruled her. 'If we're going to run into any major snags, it will be with the dam. And I want to know about them as soon as possible.'

She shrugged her acceptance of his decision, but he could tell she didn't completely agree with it. 'Has your attorney heard anything further from any of the real estate agents in Tulsa?'

Malcom had instructed his attorney to utilise the services of seven different real estate agencies to buy the seven parcels where the resort hotel and marina were to be built. 'Not as of yesterday.'

'I wonder what the problem is. It bothers me that we've been able to acquire options on only three of them. They've been working on it almost a month now.'

'Has it ever occurred to you they might not be anxious to sell?' he chided.

'But I'm anxious to buy,' she stated, then glanced at him. 'Malcom, do you realise that you have never seen Morgan's Walk?

These site plans and drawings are all you've ever seen of the property. Why don't we arrange to fly out there for a couple of days?'

'I suppose I could rework my schedule.' It was the idea of having Flame to himself for two or three days that appealed to him more than looking at the development site itself.

'We could meet with the real estate agents while we're there and find out what the hold-up is. If it's a matter of price, we can authorise them to increase the offer. If it's something else, we can figure out a way to deal with it,' she said, thinking out loud. 'I think the trip is definitely a good idea. The last time I talked to Charlie he mentioned he was having some problems. He's lost most of his help on the ranch,' she added in a quick aside. 'And there was some difficulty with feed stores. Maybe I can get that ironed out too while we're there.'

'It's always business with you, isn't it?' Malcom murmured, realising that very little about their relationship had changed.

For an instant, she went absolutely still. Then she turned, all the stiffness flowing from her. 'No, not always.' A smile played with the corners of her mouth. With a supple lift of her arms, she draped them around his neck and let a finger play with a strand of dark hair at his nape. 'I distinctly remember numerous occasions when business was the farthest thing from my mind. Don't you?' Lightly she brushed her lips across his, then brought them back, letting the tip of her tongue moistly trace their unyielding line.

For an instant, he resisted, then he pulled her roughly against him and crushed her lips in a hard kiss, hoping this time to block the sensation that there was someone else with them.

— 38 —

EVERYTHING IN the latest status report indicated that his Tahoe project was progressing well ahead of schedule, but Chance could find little satisfaction in the figures and construction projections. They didn't fill the empty places in his body and his spirit, the wild and lonely ones that bred his restlessness and short temper. He felt the stir of memories and firmed his jaw against it. She wasn't coming back to him. He'd accepted that – just as he'd accepted that the rest of the days would have an emptiness, haunted by the memory of the time he'd had with Flame. It was something he couldn't change. He had no choice but to live with his bitter regrets.

Without warning, the door to his office opened. Chance looked up from the report, made irritable by the intrusion. 'Dammit, Molly,' but it wasn't Molly who posed briefly within the frame, then boldly entered the room. 'Lucianna.' He stood up, rankled by her unannounced arrival and showing it. 'What are you doing here?'

'That's no welcome, Chance,' she chided, dramatically clad in a leopard print cashmere coat trimmed at the collar, sleeves, and hem in fox with a matching fur toque covering the black of her hair. Casually she deposited her purse on a chair and came around his desk. 'You should say: "Lucianna, darling, what a wonderful surprise to see you here."'

When he failed to kiss her, she slowly withdrew her hands, skilfully covering whatever rejection she might have felt with a proudly indifferent expression. 'I've come to take you to lunch. And don't tell me you're too busy. I've already checked with your dragon lady and you have no appointments for the next two hours. As a matter of fact' – a knowing smile curved her wide mouth – 'your schedule is relatively free for the next four days – no trips, no important meetings, nothing. Which will take us right into the weekend, maybe beyond.'

'I thought you were supposed to be in Europe this month.'

'I was,' she admitted, almost too casually, and turned away from him to stroll to the window. 'But there is a small problem with my throat. The doctor has told me I must give my voice a complete rest for three months – and I told him I would cancel all engagements for *one* month only.'

Catching the hint of fear in her voice, Chance relented. 'Three months,' he said. 'They'd have to put you in a straitjacket and tape your mouth shut, wouldn't they?'

She swung back to him, her dark eyes turning soft at his understanding. 'That's what I told him,' she said, then lifted her hands in an empty, helpless gesture. 'But here I am with an entire month. And I said to myself: who better to spend it with than you. It will be like old times, won't it?'

He looked at her, recalling the high passion that had once filled their days together, and recalling, too, the loneliness of his life now – and how grim that loneliness was. 'Maybe it will,' he conceded, then smiled faintly. 'In any case, you're welcome to stay.'

Not pressing the point, Lucianna drew back, her expression confident and warm. 'Where are you going to take me for lunch?'

'As I recall, you were taking me.'

'In that case' – she walked over and hooked her arm with his – 'I'll have to find some place *very* cosy and *very* quiet.'

As she started to draw him away, Sam barged into the office. 'Chance, I –' He stopped short, frowning in surprise at the woman on Chance's arm. 'Lucianna. What are you doing here?'

She sighed in mock exasperation. 'The welcomes I receive here leave a great deal to be desired. I expected better from you, Sam.'

'I'm sorry, I –' A look of boyish chagrin briefly raced across his expression, only to be replaced by the troubled frown he'd worn when he came in, his attention swinging once again to Chance. 'Fred Garver just called me and wanted to know what was going on. His friend Zorinsky, with the Corps, claims there's another set of plans for the dam being circulated in his department.'

'That's impossible.' Chance automatically dismissed it. 'Somebody probably saw a similarity in the place names and confused the two.'

Sam nodded, 'That's what I said. Fred did, too, but Zorinsky swears it isn't the case – that he triple-checked to be sure before he called Fred. The plans call for a dam to be built on Morgan's Walk, but this dam is located almost a mile north of our site. The house and most of the valley won't be flooded.'

'What?' Chance frowned, suddenly wary, his scepticism fading as he unconsciously slipped free from Lucianna's hold. 'Where did these plans originate? Did Fred find that out?'

'They were done by an engineering firm called Thurgood. Fred's pretty sure it's a West Coast company. That has to mean Flame's behind it.' He paused, then went on with rising energy. 'A lot of things are starting to make sense, Chance – like some of the comments that filtered back to us from the ranch hands we hired away from Morgan's Walk. Remember they said some men had been there taking soil samples. At the time I shrugged it off, figuring she'd contacted some oil and gas companies and arranged to have their geologists come out to see if there was the potential for any oil or gas on the property, but obviously –'

'– they were doing test borings for the dam,' Chance finished the sentence for him.

'Exactly.' Sam punched the air with his finger, emphasising the point. 'And something else is adding up, too. Fred said that with the dam moved up the river, more of the land to the northwest will be flooded. Remember the rumours we've been hearing about a lot of real estate activity going on there. Somebody's buying – or trying to buy up that hill land. And we thought somebody had gotten wind of our development and was doing some speculating. We also said almost the same thing when we heard those rumours about a big resort development going on somewhere in the Midwest. We thought they were talking about *our* project. But I'll bet you anything she's got something in the works along the same line.'

'You have a problem with that theory, Sam,' Chance said. 'She hasn't got the money to do it. We've seen her financial statement. Excluding Morgan's Walk and her apartment in San Francisco, she has only about twenty thousand dollars that she can get her hands on readily. She might have used some of the proceeds from Hattie's life insurance to have the plans drawn up for the dam, but, Sam, she hasn't been able to raise the money yet to pay our mortgage demand. So where is she going to get the money to buy all this property?'

'From Malcom Powell.' Lucianna sat in the chair next to Chance's desk, holding her compact open with one hand and applying a fresh coat of lipstick to her already red lips with the other, her purse lying open on her lap. Briefly she met the glance he shot her. 'He's the logical choice, darling, since the two of them are in the midst of a torrid affair.'

'That rumour was thick when I met her,' he replied impatiently. 'Their relationship is purely business. She handles his advertising account with the agency, and that's all.'

'It may have been all *then*.' Lucianna shrugged with feigned idleness and recapped the tube of lipstick. 'But it's a fact now. Oscar told me they've been seen together almost constantly.'

'I told you she handles the account for his stores,' he snapped. 'Naturally she has to meet with him.'

'Naturally.' She smiled at him in a look of mock acceptance. 'And I'm sure that's the reason he gave her a key to his apartment in town – so they could have private business conferences in the bedroom instead of the boardroom.'

'I don't believe you,' he murmured coldly.

'About the key or the fact that they're lovers? They are, you know. But you don't have to take my word for it.' She returned the compact and lipstick to her purse and closed it with a definite click of the clasp. 'Call Jacqui Van Cleeve – or read her columns these past few weeks. That woman doesn't print anything that isn't the absolute truth. And believe me, she has a network of spies that are the envy of the KGB.'

He looked at her for a long, challenging moment, demanding that she admit she was wrong – that she'd exaggerated. She looked back at him, in her dark eyes a sadness, a hint of pity, and regret that she'd been the one to tell him. Then it hit him. She was telling the truth. A hot swell of jealousy ripped through him.

He turned from both of them, his hands doubled into tight fists, wanting to strike out at something, anything – but there was nothing, just a hard pressure squeezing at his heart.

'Chance, I –' Sam began tentatively.

Chance stiffened, then turned slowly. 'Call Fred back will you? Tell him if he can't get a copy of those plans, I want him to draw his best guess of the new lake's location. And I want it now,' he ordered, conscious of the flatness, the deadness in his voice.

'Right.' Sam nodded, backing towards the door.

He pushed the intercom button. 'Molly, will you come in here.'

From her chair, Lucianna murmured, 'I have the strange feeling our lunch has been cancelled.'

He ignored that as Molly entered. 'Get hold of Kelby Grant. Tell him to get over here. I have some land I want him to buy for me – yesterday,' he said grimly.

'Yes, sir.'

'And Sam,' Chance called him back before he got to the door. 'Tell Fred I want a finished set of drawings on our dam site as fast as he can get them done for me. And I want the Corps' stamp of approval on them the day after – and I don't care how he gets that done.'

'But he can't complete the plans without doing test work on the site itself,' Sam protested.

'Tell him to get a crew out there and get it done.'

'But we don't own the land.' He looked at Chance as if he'd taken leave of his senses.

'Haven't you ever heard of trespassing, Sam?' he replied tiredly. 'As soon as you get Fred lined out, call Matt Sawyer. Tell him I want everything he can get me on Malcom Powell.'

'Will do.'

Molly was on his heels when he exited the office. 'Sam, what's all this about? What happened?' In the briefest of terms, he explained it to her. When he'd finished, Molly looked properly outraged. 'What does she know about building a development? Malcom Powell's money or not, she'll never succeed.'

'I don't know about that Molly. From everything I've read about Malcom Powell, he could match Chance dollar for dollar. If that isn't bad enough, it's old money. Chance doesn't have the phone numbers of half the people Malcom Powell calls by their first name. With him backing Flame, this is going to turn into one helluva war. And Morgan's Walk is going to be the battle-ground for it.'

'She's got to be stopped.'

'How?' he asked, and shook his head over the lack of an answer.

'Well, someone has to try,' she insisted.

'I know.' A troubled sigh broke from him. 'I can't help feeling this is all my fault, Molly. If I hadn't let Chance down – if I'd kept a closer watch on Hattie, we would have found out about Flame right from the start. Then maybe none of this would have happened.'

'Wishing won't change the past,' Molly replied curtly. 'So don't waste valuable time dwelling on it. Concentrate instead on finding a way to stop her. Which reminds me . . .' She turned to her desk. 'There was a note in today's mail from Maxine. The new duchess of Morgan's Walk will be arriving on Thursday – with two guests. It will be interesting to find out who they are.'

— 39 —

EXHILARATED FROM the brisk gallop back to the barns, Flame walked back to the imposing brick manor house of Morgan's Walk with her arm linked around Malcom's waist and the weight of his resting possessively around her shoulders, a quickness and a lightness to her steps that matched her new mood. As they approached the front door, she drew apart from him and waited, allowing him to open the door for her, then swept into the entrance hall. There she stopped and turned back to him, pulling off her riding gloves as he closed the door behind them.

'What a marvellous ride,' she declared, leaning into Malcom when he returned to her side, curving his arm to the back of her waist and asserting his claim on her once more. 'How about a drink to top if off?'

He shook his head. 'I think I'll shower and change instead. Why don't you join me?'

'Not this minute, but I'll be up directly,' she promised. 'I want to check with Maxine and see if there were any calls, then find out what Ellery's doing.'

Ellery called from the parlour, 'Do I hear my name being bandied about?' Flame pressed a quick kiss on Malcom's cheek in parting, then moved to join Ellery in the parlour. 'I see the Lone Rangeress and her powerful companion have returned. Hi Ho

Silver and all that,' Ellery observed dryly, lounging with his usual ease on the sofa in front of the fireplace.

'And it was wonderful, too,' she stated, ignoring his jesting remark. 'There was a blush of green over the whole countryside. I had the feeling that any moment every tree and bush was going to burst into leaf. We rode up to the dam site and I showed Malcom where the lake will be.' She walked over to the drinks cart and poured some tonic water in a glass, adding some ice cubes from the insulated bucket. 'You should have come with us.'

'No thanks. When I go riding, I prefer to have the horses under the hood of a car.'

Something crackled. Belatedly, Flame noticed the daily paper lying open on his lap. 'You've been reading the newspaper,' she accused. 'You said you didn't want to go because you wanted to work on the sketches for the golf course.'

His eyebrow lifted at the hint of impatience in her voice. 'I can't make up my mind whether this project of yours is turning you into a shrew or a slave-driver.'

'A shrew?' She frowned, faintly indignant. 'How can you say that, Ellery? I have never behaved like a shrew.'

'Really?' His eyebrow arched even higher. 'I think you've forgotten how rudely you berated those poor people on the phone this morning.'

'You mean those real estate agents?' She remembered that earlier sharpness of her tongue – without regret. 'They deserved it. The ones who weren't waiting to hear back on the offers they'd made were waiting for a little time to go by before making another offer – so they wouldn't appear too anxious and drive up the price. Why should they care? They aren't buying the land. I am. Ben warned me that people were laid back around here, but this morning was ridiculous.'

'We are testy, aren't we?' Ellery murmured.

She started to snap an answer at him, then sighed. 'Sorry. It still irritates me when I think how much time has gone by – all because they didn't want to look as though they were trying to pressure anybody to sell. Believe me, they aren't going to be concerned about that any more.' She took a quick drink of the iced tonic water, then wandered over to the fireplace. 'You managed to avoid my question about the sketches. Did you get anything done on them?'

'Even though this was supposed to be a pleasure trip, yes, I did sketch for my supper,' he mocked. 'They're on the table by the window.'

Flame walked over to look at them. Altogether there were six different views – all in pencil – of the valley, its pastureland and shade trees turned into the manicured green of a golf course.

'Ellery, these are very good,' she declared as she went through them again.

'Then I won't have to go hungry tonight.'

She turned, smiling at him in amused exasperation. 'Will you stop that? I'm trying to pay you a compliment.'

'Thank you.' He bowed his head in mock docility.

Shaking her head at him, she laid the sketches down, mentally reminding herself to show them to Malcom later. 'Seriously, Ellery, they are good. Sometimes I think your talent is going to waste in the art department of Boland and Hayes.'

He dismissed that with a careless shrug. 'Speaking of art' – he picked up the newspaper in his lap – 'have you seen today's paper?'

'I haven't had time to look at it. Why?'

'There's a small piece in here I found interesting.'

'What's that?' She crossed to the sofa and glanced over his shoulder, her attention drawn first to the article near his right thumb. 'You mean the story about the tenor Sebastian Montebello guesting in the Tulsa production of *Otello*? I think I saw a poster about that some –' She faltered, her eye caught by the photograph in the left hand corner, a photograph of Chance Stuart and Lucianna Colton. Flame stared at the warm and lazy smile on Chance's face, a smile she'd once believed he reserved exclusively for her. Now Lucianna was the recipient of it, The caption beneath mentioned a minor throat ailment that had sidelined the renowned coloratura soprano and stated her intention of attending *Otello* – in the company of real estate magnate, Chance Stuart – to see the performance of her dear friend, Sebastian Montebello.

'I wonder if it's too late to get good seats,' she murmured.

'You're surely not thinking of going?'

'Why not?' she challenged. 'I'm certainly not going to stay away simply because he'll be there.'

'Heaven forbid,' he murmured.

'If Malcom and I can get seats, do you want to go?'

'My dear Flame, I wouldn't miss this for the world.'

Arriving patrons of the opera filled the foyer of Chapman Music Hall, the subdued chatter of their voices punctuated by an occasional trilled greeting. From the hall itself, Chance could hear the muted and discordant notes of the last-minute tuning of instruments by the orchestra. He took another deep drag on his cigarette and exhaled the tangy smoke in a rush. Not for the first time, he wondered why he'd agreed to come. He glanced at his watch. Eight more minutes before the overture was scheduled to start.

Beside him, Lucianna caught the slight movement of his wrist, and his downward glance at his watch. 'You aren't too bored, are you, Chance darling?' she murmured soothingly.

'No,' he lied.

'I'm sorry I had to drag you here tonight,' she said, explaining again, 'Unfortunately Sebastian found out I was in Tulsa. He would never have forgiven me if I hadn't come tonight. I wouldn't care, but I have to sing *Aida* with him this fall. And I shudder to think the hell he could create for me on stage if he chose to be spiteful. It's bad enough putting up with his endless practical jokes.'

'And you're the perfect victim for them, aren't you?' Chance guessed. 'You approach everything with such intensity, even rehearsals, completely immersing yourself in the role, you open yourself up to it.'

'He does it to destroy my concentration so he looks good and I look bad,' she declared, then sighed, casting him a sideways glance. 'As much as I don't want to, I have to go backstage before the performance and wish him well. Will you come with me?'

'Of course. Only I think you're about to be waylaid,' he said, spotting the tall anorexic brunette making a beeline through the crowd toward them and realising that he should have known Gayle Frederick would be waiting to descend on Lucianna the instant she saw her. The woman fancied herself a patron of the arts. Which meant she was too rich to be called a groupie.

'Chance, how wonderful to see you.' She sailed up to him and kissed him on both cheeks with typical theatrics.

'Gayle,' he murmured in acknowledgement.

'And Miss Colton,' she gushed, turning to Lucianna. 'You don't know what a thrill it is to meet you. What a night this is going to be – Sebastian Montebello on the stage and Lucianna Colton in the audience.'

'How very kind you are,' Lucianna smiled, putting on her 'diva' face.

'Not at all,' she insisted. 'If anything, I'm lucky. Although not as lucky as you,' she added, sliding a quick look at Chance. 'I mean, here you are with the throb of every heart in Tulsa.'

'I am lucky,' Lucianna agreed, her hand tightening ever so slightly on Chance's arm.

Catching the minor stir of activity at the entrance, Chance glanced in that direction. A fine tension, different from the impatience and irritation he'd felt before, held him motionless as he found himself looking at Flame. The months and days since their first meeting at the cocktail party seemed to drop away. Again he was staring at her from across a crowded room, drawn by that arresting combination of red-gold hair and jade-green eyes.

Yet, tonight she looked untouchable – somehow distant and aloof. Frowning at the change, Chance studied her closer. She was wearing her hair differently. Instead of cascading in a luxuriant mass around her face and shoulders, it was smoothed back and caught in a wide clasp at the nape of her neck. The style wasn't severe, yet its effect was to subdue the fire with high sophistication. That wasn't Flame. Neither was the strikingly chic and elegant suit of quilted copper lamé that she wore, unrelieved by any jewellery. The straightness of its long jacket completely hid the ripeness of her figure, giving Chance the impression that she had gowned herself in a suit of copper armour.

Someone moved into his vision, blocking his view of Flame. For an instant Chance tried to look through the man, then the cleft chin, the square jaws, and the iron eyes registered their image. It was Malcom Powell – her new lover. Chance looked at the glowing tip of his cigarette, a tightness coiling through him.

When he lifted his glance again, he caught the smile she gave Malcom . . . so warm, so admiring, so damned intimate. He had tried to convince himself that she had turned to Malcom out of spite, that it had been a means of getting back at him . . . maybe even an attempt to make him jealous. But the way she looked at Powell . . . With a hint of savageness he turned and stabbed the end of his cigarette in the ashtray, burying it deep in the fine white sand.

'Look, Malcom Powell and his party have arrived,' Gayle Frederick declared as Chance straightened and turned back. He stiffened in alertness when he saw they were coming directly towards them, although he doubted Flame had seen him yet. 'Didn't I tell you this was a night,' the brunette added, her low voice riddled with excitement. 'You know him, don't you, Chance?'

'Yes.'

Lucianna's fingers dug into his arm. 'Perhaps –' she began. But Chance, anticipating her suggestion that they leave before Flame and Powell reached them, silenced her with a faint shake of his head. The anger in him wanted a confrontation with Flame.

'He's visiting friends in the area,' Gayle issued the quickly whispered aside even as she turned to snare the approaching party that included, Chance noticed, Ellery Dorn. 'Mr Powell, how delightful to have you with us this evening. Let me be – if not the first, then the most recent – to welcome you to Tulsa.'

'Thank you . . . Mrs Frederick, isn't it?' Powell replied with a suggestion of a bow.

'Yes,' Gayle confirmed, preening a little at his recognition. 'And I believe you know the marvellous diva, Lucianna Colton, and – of course – Chance Stuart.'

'Indeed.' The grey eyes turned on him, iron-smooth and blatantly measuring.

'Powell.' Nodding once, Chance returned the look and briefly gripped the man's hand, aware of the strength and power that lay in more than Powell's hand.

Continuing with the introductions, Gayle said, 'And this is Flame Bennett from Morgan's –'

But Flame broke in. 'Mr Stuart and I have met before.'

Her coolness grated at him as Gayle swung toward him, red firing her cheeks. 'Oh, dear,' she murmured, remembering precisely who Flame Bennett had been.

'It's all right, Gayle,' he said, masking his anger with a smoothness. 'The ex-Mrs Stuart has a habit of bringing up the past that is better forgotten.' Deliberately, Chance held Flame's gaze. She tried to conceal it, but he saw the flash of anger in her green eyes.

'I am so sorry –'

'Don't apologise, Mrs Frederick,' Flame inserted coolly. 'It isn't necessary – Mr Stuart isn't known for the accuracy of his memory.'

Chance turned to Powell. 'Is it business or pleasure that's brought you to Tulsa?' he inquired, letting his glance slide back to Flame, and catching her slight tensing.

'I believe you could call it a working vacation,' came the smooth reply.

'Flame takes care of the advertising for you – doesn't she?' he said, pausing fractionally. 'Among other things, I understand.'

His pointed barb completely escaped Gayle Frederick as she pushed her way back into the conversation. 'I do hope you're considering Tulsa as a location for one of your stores, Mr Powell. With Neiman-Marcus and Saks here already, all we're missing is a Powell store.'

'We'll see,' he replied, a complacent and confident gleam in his eyes as he took Flame firmly by the arm, asserting the closeness of his relationship with her. 'Shall we go, Flame darling, Ellery.' Then to Chance, 'If you'll excuse us, I think it's time we took our seats.'

As they moved away to join the line of people drifting into the theatre, Gayle sighed. 'How awful. I never did get to meet the handsome gentleman with them. Is he someone important, do you know?'

Chance ignored the question, turning his attention instead to Lucianna. 'You said you wanted to go backstage.'

'How good of you to remember that,' she murmured somewhat archly. 'Especially when I thought you'd forgotten all about me.'

'There's nothing wrong with my memory, Lucianna.' Although at the moment he wished there was.

Flame tried to concentrate on the tenor's performance, but her glance kept straying from the lighted stage to the rows of silhouetted figures in front of her. Covertly she scanned them again. She wished she knew where Chance was sitting. The way the back of her neck was prickling, she was almost certain he was somewhere behind her.

Again she asked herself why she had let that newspaper photograph of Chance and Lucianna goad her into coming here tonight. Had she wanted Chance to see her with Malcom so he would know she had a man in her life? Or had she wanted to see for herself that all the gossip in the papers about his affair with Lucianna Colton was true – that his alleged *good* friend had become his lover again?

If it was proof of the latter she'd wanted, she'd certainly got it. The way Lucianna had been moulded to his side, as if they were connected at the hip, and that arrogantly triumphant gleam in her dark eyes that said 'He's mine' – and the possessive curve of his arm around her waist; all of it had combined to make the intimate status of their relationship blatant to the most casual observer. Had Lucianna been his lover all along – even when he'd been pursuing her? Flame went cold at the thought, hating both of them now.

Applause broke out around her. Belatedly Flame joined in as the house lights slowly came up, signalling the start of intermission. She feigned a casual glance over her shoulder. But too many people were moving about; standing, stretching, turning to chat to someone, or wending their way to the aisle. If Chance was back there, she couldn't see him.

Squaring around, Flame hesitated, conscious of an enveloping tension, then stood up, tucking her lizard purse under her arm and smiling briefly at Malcom. 'I think I'll get some fresh air.'

Malcom started to warn her that she'd likely run into Stuart out there, then he realised she knew that – just as she'd known Stuart would be at the opera tonight. He nodded instead and said nothing, remaining in his seat and smouldering in his own private hell. Oh, he had her, but he had never really had her.

Outside the wind had died to a whisper and the night was warm with the promise of spring. The city lights of downtown Tulsa had blurred the stars to a dusting of pale specks overhead, too faint to compete with the bright lights shining from the windows of the monoliths that loomed in front of the Performing Arts Centre.

In the distance a horn honked, but there were few cars on the downtown streets. The only hum of traffic came from far away. Flame breathed in the quiet of the night, feeling its calmness smoothe over her as she gazed across the precisely landscaped green of the Williams Centre.

'I've been hearing some rumours lately.' The lazily seductive drawl of Chance's voice seemed to reach out from the night and stroke her.

The calm fled, leaving a high alertness. Somehow Flame managed to restrain the impulse to spin sharply around and, instead, continued to gaze into the night. 'Have you? she countered, certain he was alluding to her relationship with Malcom.

'Yes.' A soft footfall warned her that Chance was directly behind her.

She took a quick breath and caught the fragrance of his cologne, earthy and masculine. Slowly she turned to face him, recognising that not only was she ready for this confrontation, she was also looking forward to it.

He stood before her, dark and elegant in his black evening attire. 'Very interesting rumours they are, too.'

'Really?' She tried to read his expression, but it was too bland, too hooded.

'Yes, all sorts of talk about dams, resort hotels, marinas.'

She stiffened, her heart rocketing. That was the last thing she'd expected him to say. How had he found out so quickly?

As if reading her mind, he said, 'Did you think I wouldn't hear about your project? Sometimes it really can be a small world, Flame.'

'So it would seem,' she murmured tightly.

'You don't really think you're going to succeed, do you?'

'You surely don't think you're the only one capable of building it, do you?' she challenged.

'Initially I didn't put much stock in the rumours – until I found out who your partner was.' He tipped his head at a considering angle. 'You got into bed with Powell literally as well as figuratively, didn't you?'

Angered, she asserted, 'It must gall you to know that I'm going to build the development you planned and still keep nearly all of Morgan's Walk intact.'

'Assuming you succeed.' His smile mocked her.

'I will.'

'Will you? You've dealt yourself into a game with the big boys, Flame. And in cut-throat competition, there aren't any rules.'

'Is that supposed to frighten me?' Flame taunted.

'You've already made a beginner's mistake. You should have bluffed – pretended that you didn't know what I was talking about until you found out for sure how much – or how little – I knew about your project. But you admitted it.' There was a wry and lazy slant to his smile. 'You tipped your hand, Flame.'

'That makes us even,' she retorted. 'Because now I don't have to wonder any more whether you know what I'm doing. You've told me.'

'This is the only warning you're going to have, Flame,' he said quietly. 'For your own good, you'd better get out while you can.'

'And let you take over Morgan's Walk? I'll see you in hell first,' she declared with a faint, but defiant toss of her head.

He dismissed that with a vague, shrugging motion. 'I've been there most of my life anyway.' He paused. 'When you see Powell, tell him there's nothing to be gained by waiting. He might as well write me out a cheque for the mortgage balance. I never did like to spend my own money. I might as well use his to stop you.'

'You'll get it when it's due and not before.'

'Suit yourself.' He started to turn away, then swung back. 'Speaking of Powell. Is he enjoying the bedroom benefits of your partnership as much as I did?'

Stung by that remark, she struck hard at his face, the impact jarring every nerve in her arm. Instantly she was seized, his fingers digging into the quilted fabric of her copper sleeves and bruising her arms. Refusing to struggle and give him the satisfaction of overpowering her physically, Flame stood silent and unyielding, meeting the icy glitter of his blue eyes.

'Does he make you furious like this?' he demanded.

'You'll never know.' She observed the brief flexing of the muscles along his hard jaw and knew her jibe had got through.

'Won't I?' he mocked. 'You're too cool. Which tells me he doesn't ruffle you at all. You don't *feel* anything with him, do you?'

'I trust and respect him – which is more than I could ever say about you,' she hurled bitterly.

But Chance just smiled. 'Trust. Respect. Those are lukewarm things. Not like this.'

He hauled her against him, his mouth coming down on her lips before she could turn away. The angry and demanding passion of his kiss drove at her. Despite all the twisting and turning of her head, she couldn't elude its heated force. Then came the shocking recognition that some part of her didn't want to end this moist rocking together of their lips. Pride wouldn't let her respond, but a hunger inside wouldn't let her break it off.

Abruptly Chance pushed her from him. Dragging in a deep breath, she threw back her head to look at him, taut-jawed and grim-lipped. Could he see the brightness of her eyes? she wondered. Did he know it was caused by hot tears?

'Do you realise how ironic it is, Flame?' he challenged, a harshness tightening his voice. 'You condemned me for using you to get Morgan's Walk. Yet you can justify the way you're using Powell because he's your means of keeping it.'

She trembled, angered that he would dare to make such a comparison. She wanted to shout at him that it wasn't the same at all. There was no pretence of love in her affair with Malcom – not on either side – and no attempt at deception either. Theirs was an arrangement that suited both of them. But Chance had already walked away from her. She glared after him, watching as he disappeared inside the building, and hating him for trying to paint her with his own devil-black brush.

Turning her back on the lighted hall, she drank deeply of the night air and fought to cool her temper. Why did she let him rile her like this? Why didn't she simply ignore his pointed jibes? There was no truth in them.

'Have you had all the fresh air you want?' Malcom tried but he couldn't keep the accusing edge out of his voice.

It wasn't the fresh scent of the night air he caught when he halted behind her, but the heady tang of a man's cologne that mixed with her perfume. Swinging around at the sound of his voice, she faced him, all heat and fire. He had the satisfaction of knowing that whatever Stuart had taken, it had been without her consent. Yet he was irritated, too, by the deep emotion Stuart had succeeded in arousing when he had barely created a ripple in all this time with her.

'He knows, Malcom.' Her voice was made tight by her attempt to keep all feeling from it.

'He knows about what?'

'Our development.'

'You told him?' He eyed her in surprise.

'I told him nothing that he didn't already know.' She gripped her small purse with both hands, her knuckles whitening with the pressure. 'This changes things, Malcom. He'll be out to stop us now.'

'I'll handle him. Don't worry. As soon as we get back, I'll get Bronsky moving on an approval for the dam – and place a few calls of my own to clear the way for it. I have the financing for the project virtually in place now. I can't think of any obstacles he can throw in our path that will stop us.'

'But you don't understand,' she insisted urgently. 'He's going to come after us with everything he has. This isn't a fight we can win by waging it at long distance. One of us will have to stay here in Oklahoma from now on. Obviously that has to be me.'

He disagreed with her logic, but he didn't think logic had anything to do with her decision. She claimed to hate Stuart, yet she wanted to be here to do battle with him. Silently, he studied her – so rigid and proud. He wanted to kiss away that stiffness, but he doubted that he would like the taste of another man's lips.

'That's what you've wanted all along isn't it? To move out here,' he said with a certain fatalism.

'No,' she denied as if stunned he should even suggest it.

'That's what you planned to do when you married him.'

'Well, I'm not married to him now,' she replied angrily.

'Yes, I know. But I wondered if you remembered that.' He took her arm. 'Let's go back inside. The night air doesn't seem to be agreeing with either one of us.'

= 40 =

IN LESS than a week's time, Flame flew to San Francisco, packed her things, notified the building manager of her intended absence for several months, arranged for her mail to be transferred, resigned her position at the agency, cleared her desk, and caught a flight back to Tulsa. Fortunately, she had been grooming Rudy Gallagher to take over the Powell account, the only major client she had continued to handle personally the last few months, so the actual transference of her accounts had been the least time-consuming of her tasks. The rest had been hectic and harried, evey minute crammed with something that needed to be done.

And the pace hadn't slowed up when she arrived back at Morgan's Walk. Friday morning the freight service delivered the boxes of personal items she'd arranged to have shipped to her. She sorted through them, separating the three marked with the letter 'P', indicating they contained either her paperwork or office supplies, and carried them into the library. The rest she gave to Maxine to unpack.

Weary from jet lag and too little sleep in the last five days, Flame stood in the middle of the library and stared at the three boxes, then shook her head at her inability to decide which to unpack first. What did it matter? Ultimately she had to unpack all three.

Using the scissors from the desk, she cut through the packing tape and unfolded the cardboard lids. From the grand foyer came the pounding thud of the front door's brass knocker. At almost the same instant, the telephone rang.

Hearing the rapid clumping as Maxine hurried down the stairs, Flame called out, 'I'll answer the phone.' Leaving the opened box on the floor, she crossed to the desk and picked up the phone on the second ring. 'Morgan's Walk, Flame Bennett speaking.'

'I know what you are trying to do.' Startled by the strange sounding voice on the line, Flame pressed the receiver closer to her ear and frowned. 'You had better stop or you will be very sorry.'

'Who are you?' she demanded angrily. '*What* are you?'

But the line went dead. She held the phone away and stared at it. Something about the threatening call was vaguely reminiscent of the hastily scrawled messages she'd received in the past. The hawk-faced man – she hadn't thought about him in weeks. But that had all happened back in San Francisco – before she married Chance. Had he followed her all the way to Tulsa? If so, why had he broken the pattern and called her instead of leaving her another one of his menacing little notes?

That voice, it sounded alien, mechanical . . . like a robot's. It was definitely not made by a human. No, some kind of voice synthesiser had been used, obviously to protect the identity of the caller. But she'd never heard the hawk-faced man speak. She couldn't have recognised his voice.

She mentally shook the whole thing away and returned the receiver to its cradle, telling herself that she was making too much out of it. More than likely the call was some adolescent's idea of a prank. As far as she was concerned, a very unamusing one.

'I see I've caught you in the midst of settling in.'

Flame spun around and stared for a blank instant at Ben Canon standing in the doorway, materialising out of nowhere, like the leprechaun he resembled.

'Maxine said you were in here.' His gaze narrowed sharply on her, his remark reminding her there'd been someone at the door when she answered the phone. 'Is something wrong?'

'No,' she denied quickly, then gestured toward the phone.

'Some crank called. That's all,' she said, shrugging her shoulders in an attempt to dismiss the threatening phone call. 'Come in, but you'll have to excuse the mess. As you can see, I have moved in bag, box, and baggage.'

'Yes, I noticed part of it in the foyer.' He smiled in sympathy as he walked over to a wing chair.

'What brings you all the way out here?'

'I have some good news.' He set his briefcase on the chair.

'I could use some.' Especially in the wake of that phone call, but she didn't say that as she skirted the box at her feet and joined him in front of the fireplace, conscious as always of the portrait that watched her.

The lawyer took a letter from his briefcase and handed it to her. 'Morgan's Walk has received preliminary approval to be listed as an historic place. I stress preliminary. It could still be rejected. Unfortunately we can't claim Will Rogers slept here – or that Edna Ferber wrote part of *Cimarron* in one of the guest bedrooms. We could be certain of acceptance then. Still I think this is a good sign.'

'So do I.' As Flame started to glance through the letter, Maxine walked into the library, carrying a coffee tray, the thick rubber soles of her orthopaedic shoes making almost no sound on the hardwood floor.

'You didn't say, but I figured you wanted coffee,' she declared, throwing a pointed look at the attorney.

'That's thoughtful of you, Maxine.'

She sniffed at his compliment. 'I decided it was better to bring it now than get all the way upstairs and have you holler for me to get it.' Just as she set the tray down on the cherrywood table, there was another knock at the front door. The housekeeper left the room muttering, 'This house is turning into Grand Central Station.'

'Are you expecting someone?' Ben glanced at her curiously as he helped himself to a cup of coffee.

'No. But I wasn't expecting you either.'

Almost immediately, Maxine was back. 'It's some real estate man named Hamilton Fletcher.' She handed Flame his business card. 'He asked to talk to you, but he wouldn't say about what.'

Flame recognised the agency name on the card as one she'd commissioned to buy land for her. Ignoring Maxine's probing look, she said, 'Show him in.'

With a white straw stetson in hand and gleaming black cowboy boots on his feet, Hamilton Fletcher looked the part of a gentleman rancher, quiet and unassuming with a thin, almost scholarly face. 'I don't mean to be barging in on you like this, Ms Bennett,' he apologised immediately, talking in a soft drawl. 'We've talked on the phone, but we've never met. I'm Ham Fletcher . . . with the Green Country Real Estate Agency.'

'Of course, Mr Fletcher. I remember you,' Flame replied, then introduced him to Ben Canon whom he already knew.

'I've just come from the Crowder place, the one you wanted me to try to buy for you,' he said. 'Since I was so close, I thought I'd stop and see if I couldn't straighten something out. After I talked to you on the phone last week, I went to see the Crowders and made them another offer. When I stopped by today, they said they weren't interested in selling . . . and that they'd already told the other fella that.'

'What other fella?' She frowned.

'That's what I was wonderin',' he replied with a troubled smile. 'If you've got someone else trying to buy their land for you, it'd be best if I backed off and not muddy up things. I know you were upset that I was taking so much time –'

'Mr Fletcher –' she interrupted him. 'I don't have anyone else trying to buy the Crowder place for me.'

He lifted his head, his hazel eyes rounding slightly. 'In that case, ma'am, there must be somebody else who's wanting to buy that land, too.'

'Then let me suggest that you go back to the Crowders and make another offer – a substantially higher one,' Flame stated crisply.

He hesitated, slowly turning his hat in his hand. 'The last offer I made them was a hundred dollars an acre more than the land's worth.'

'Then make it five hundred,' she replied. 'I want that land, Mr Fletcher.'

He drew back his head. 'I don't think there can be any doubt about that – not with that high of an offer.'

'Good. Then if there's nothing else, Mr Fletcher . . .' she murmured, raising an eyebrow at him.

He took the hint. 'I'm on my way to the Crowders. I appreciate your time, Ms Bennett, Mr Canon.' He nodded to both and left.

The agitation and impatience she'd managed to contain in Fletcher's presence, broke free the instant he walked out of the library. She whirled from the doorway and started to pace. 'Chance has found out I need that valley.'

'I think that's a safe bet.' Ben Canon nodded.

'And I think I know how,' she said grimly, turning to face him. 'The day before I left San Francisco, I met with Karl Bronsky. It seems our application and plans for the dam have mysteriously disappeared. We have to submit everything all over again. If Chance doesn't actually have our original plans in his possession, then he has copies of them. Which means he knows everything.' Just as she had once known everything about his project. 'Which is why he has someone out there trying to buy the rest of the valley before we can. Thank God we already have three of the parcels under option. But that Crowder piece is pivotal. We have to have it.'

'I'm sure Stuart knows that, too.'

'What do you know about the Crowders, Ben?'

He gave her an empty look and shook his head. 'They're just a name on a county plat to me. You need to ask Charlie that question. He knows everything about everybody living within twenty miles of Morgan's Walk.'

Spring was a busy time of year at Morgan's Walk. Between the demands of Charlie's schedule and hers, Flame wasn't able to talk to him until the following day. Then she went to him, joining the foreman at the corrals – ketchpens Charlie called them – where the ranchhands were ear-tagging, vaccinating, and branding the young calves and castrating the bull calves.

Charlie stood at the fence, his arms draped over the top rail and his boot hooked on the bottom one. When she walked up to stand beside him, he glanced sideways at her and nodded, the white of his moustache lifting in a quick smile.

'You gettin' all settled in, Miss Flame?' he drawled, not bothering to raise his voice above the bawl of the white-faced calves and their mothers.

'I'm getting close.' She watched a cowboy on the ground prodding at a bewildered calf, urging it farther into the narrow chute.

'How are the new men doing?'

Charlie made a sound of contempt. 'Most of 'em are about as worthless as tits on a boar.' Then quickly shot her an apologetic look. 'Beggin' your pardon, Miss Flame, but that's what they are. I gotta watch 'em every minute or I'll find 'em sittin' on their brains.' Red dust swirled as a calf charged past them, newly released from the chutes. Charlie instantly straightened and yelled impatiently at one of the cowboys. 'Holstener! You let that calf go without taggin' his ear. Run him back through.' Then he relaxed again in his negligent pose against the fence and muttered sideways at Flame, 'See what I mean?'

'Yes.'

'Don't you worry about it though. I'll get the work out of 'em.'

'I know you will.' She paused briefly, then asked, 'Charlie, what do you know about the Crowders?'

'Which ones?'

'The Crowder family that owns that valley farm north and west of us.'

'Old Dan Crowder and his wife, you mean.' He nodded. 'Yeah, they're still livin' there on what they call the homeplace. Although I hear their daughter and her husband are doin' most of the farmin' since Ol' Dan took sick. They had two boys, but they're both dead now. They lost the oldest when he was just a pup. The other boy was killed in an automobile accident ... must have been ten years ago. Now they've got just the girl. 'Course, she's got three younguns. I can't remember what her name is ... Martha ... Mary ... Marjorie. It's something like that.'

'You said Mr Crowder's ill?'

Charlie nodded. 'Operated on him last year for throat cancer. That family's had a rough time of it one way or another. But they're good people – honest, hard working. Makes you wish folks like that had a decent place to live.'

'The farm's not worth much?'

He shook his head. 'The soil's too poor. Sittin' in the valley like that, you'd think it'd be good bottom land, but it ain't. They probably make enough from farmin' to keep their heads above water and that's about all.'

'You'd think they'd sell it and buy somewhere else.'

'You'd think so. But there's been a Crowder workin' that

land since before this territory became a state. Course there was already a Morgan here when they came.'

'Hey, Charlie!' a cowboy shouted. 'Reckon we can have the cook fry us up a mess of mountain oysters for supper tonight?'

Charlie shouted back, 'At the rate you boys are movin', we'll still be here come daybreak.'

'I'll let you get back to your work, Charlie,' Flame said, encouraged by the information he'd given her about the Crowders. The father's recent illness and surgery had to have placed the family in some financial straits. She felt certain they'd find her generous offer for the farm much too tempting to resist.

But a phone call to the real estate agent, Ham Fletcher, later that day failed to provide her with an answer – good or bad. He said he'd left the offer with Mrs Crowder and planned to call back the first of the week if he didn't hear from them in the meantime. He promised he'd call her the minute he had an answer one way or the other.

But Sunday came and went without a phone call from him.

Flame frowned in her sleep at the blaring ring that tried to waken her. She tried to shut it out. For a time, she was successful. Then it came again, louder and shriller than before. With a groan, she rolled over, certain it couldn't be morning already. She felt as if she'd just fallen asleep. Then her grogginess faded as she realised it wasn't the alarm going off; it was the telephone ringing.

She groped for the pull-chain to the lamp by her bed and peered blearily at the green-shining numbers on her digital alarm clock. Eleven-thirty-six p.m., they read.

'Malcom, there's a two hour time difference,' she moaned and lifted the receiver, carrying it to her ear. 'Hello,' she said, trying to force the sleep from her voice.

'You did not listen to me,' came that strange mechanical voice over the line, its monotone oddly distorted and tinny. Flame sat bolt upright in the bed, fully awake. 'I warned you. You had better stop now or you will be sorry.'

'If this is supposed to be funny,' she declared angrily into the phone, 'I am not amused.'

But there was no reply, nothing but the hollow sound indicating the connection had been broken. Flame gripped the receiver an instant longer, then slammed it down. Who was doing this? The hawk-faced man? But why? First he had warned her to *stay away from him.* By that she had assumed he meant Chance. Had he? Now he was warning her to *stop.* Stop what? It didn't make any sense. The two didn't seem to connect.

But if it wasn't the hawk-faced man, then who? Chance? He had tried to warn her off that night at the opera, hadn't he? Was this some tactic of his to scare her away? Perhaps. Yet, try as she might, she couldn't imagine him deliberately frightening her like this.

On Wednesday, Flame sent Maxine home early. Twenty minutes after she left, the telephone rang. Flame stiffened instantly, a high tension leaping through her nerves. She stared at the phone on the desk and listened to it ring a second time, reminding herself that she hadn't received any threatening calls in the last three days. Did that mean they had stopped? Or was this one?

Hating her jumpiness, she picked up the phone. 'Who is this?' An instant of silence followed. 'I –'

'Flame? Is that you?'

'Malcom.' She recognised his voice and immediately felt foolish for sounding so combative. Those calls had bothered her more than she realised. 'I'm sorry. I didn't know it was you.'

'Who did you think it was?'

'It doesn't matter.' She didn't want to go into it just now. There were too many other – more important – things she had to talk to him about. 'I'm glad you called. I was going to try to reach you later tonight. How are you? Is everything all right there?'

'Everything's fine . . . although lately my luncheon meetings have become very dry and boring affairs.'

'It must be the company you're keeping nowadays.'

'I'm sure of that,' Malcom replied.

'Listen, I have some good news. We've been able to secure an option on another parcel. At least, it's verbally secured. Ben's drafting the agreement now and I'm having dinner with him tonight to go over it. Hopefully we can telex it to you in the morning.'

'Why don't you bring it with you when you fly back on Friday? One more day shouldn't hurt anything.'

For a moment she didn't know what he was talking about.

Then she remembered she'd originally said she would fly back this weekend to wrap up any loose ends. 'I won't be able to come Malcom. I'm sorry. I have too many things to do here.'

'It's amazing, Flame,' he said in a tone that revealed his ill humour. 'You were too busy to see me before you left. And now you're too busy to come back. In all the times we've talked this last week, I have yet to hear you say you miss me. We made an agreement, Flame, and this long distance communication wasn't part of it.'

'Believe me, I don't like it either. I do miss you, Malcom. Maybe I haven't said it, but you don't know how many times I've wished you were here. I need you, and there's so much we need to talk about. It appears we're going to have a problem acquiring the Crowder property. They turned down our last offer. I know they need money. They don't have medical insurance and they owe the hospital a small fortune for the operation Mr Crowder had last year. With the doctor's bills and the ongoing treatment he's needing, they have to be deeply in debt. I'm trying to find out how much they owe. That's one of the things I wanted to go over with you. Maybe if we offer them enough money to pay off all their bills and have a little nest egg left, we might be able to induce them to sell. What do you think?'

'It sounds logical,' he replied, cynically thinking that she missed talking to him all right — about business. Why couldn't she have said she missed him — and left it at that?

'It means we'll be paying more than the farm's market value. But that land is so crucial to us I think ultimately it will be worth whatever we have to pay.' There was a slight pause, then she said, 'Malcom, why don't you fly here? Once I get all the figures together, it will be so much easier to go over them with you in person than trying to do it over the phone.'

'It certainly would, wouldn't it?' he murmured dryly.

'This isn't a decision I want to make without you, Malcom. Can you come?'

'Not this weekend. I have a board meeting to attend Saturday morning.'

'What about the following weekend?'

Malcom hesitated. Opening Day was the following weekend, signalling the start of the yacht season in San Francisco. In all the years he'd been married, he and Diedre had never failed to participate in the event, frequently holding a party on their boat. But he wanted to see Flame. Out of all those years, what harm would it do to miss one Opening Day?

'I might be able to arrange that,' he said at last.

'Wonderful. We can turn the air-conditioner on and spend a cosy evening in front of the fireplace with lights turned down low and a fine old brandy I found.'

She sounded happy. Malcom wondered if Diedre was right when she said he was getting cranky and difficult to please. After all, Flame had asked him to come. And she'd never been the helpless, clinging type. That's part of what had attracted him to her in the first place – her pride and independent spirit.

'Where can I reach you later tonight?' she asked.

'What time?'

'I don't expect my dinner meeting with Ben to last much longer than a couple of hours. I should be back at Morgan's Walk by ten at the latest. Ten o'clock Central time, that is.'

'Which means eight o'clock here, and I'll be at the DeBorgs' having dinner. Why don't you call me in the morning at my office?'

'First thing,' she promised. 'And try to come next weekend, if you can, Malcom.'

'I will. I want to sample that brandy by the fire . . . and you.'

⟞ 41 ⟞

WHEN FLAME walked out of the downtown restaurant, her glance went automatically to the towering black monolith in the next block. The ebony gleam of its marble façade seemed to loom over her, the distinctive gold 'S' of the Stuart logo taunting her with its presence. Abruptly she turned and waited for Ben Canon to join her.

'Thank you for dinner,' she said. 'I enjoyed it.'

'After all the evening meals you've had alone at Morgan's Walk, I thought it might be a pleasant change.'

'It was.' She opened her purse and took out her car keys. 'I'll call Malcom in the morning and advise him that you'll be telexing the final draft of the option agreement first thing.'

'I'm going back to my office right now and make those few minor revisions we discussed tonight,' he replied, holding up the folder in his hand that contained the document. 'Where did you park? I'll walk you to your car.'

'I'm in the lot across the street.' She nodded in the direction of the light blue Continental parked directly beneath a light. 'You don't need to walk me over there, especially when your office is in the opposite direction.'

'Just trying to be a gentleman,' he shrugged indifferently, accepting her refusal of his company.

'Be my lawyer instead and get that option agreement finalised before Chance slips in and buys that land out from under my nose.'

He chuckled at that. 'You're sounding more like Hattie every day. Good night, Flame.'

He waved the folder at her and set off with a jaunty stride. Smiling absently, she watched him for a moment, then angled across the street to the parking lot. A security light cast its bright glow over the sky-blue Lincoln parked next to its tall pole, banishing all the night's shadows.

As Flame paused in its light to unlock the driver's door, she felt a prickle of unease; that odd, uncomfortable – and much too familiar – sensation that she was being watched suddenly claiming her. She hadn't had that feeling since she'd left San Francisco back when the hawk-faced man had been following her. She looked around, scanning the lot and the street, half expecting to see the hawk-faced man shirk out of sight. But there was nothing: no one walking along the sidewalk, no one sitting in a parked car, no dark shape lurking in the shadows of the buildings nearby.

Almost angrily she shook off the feeling, blaming it on those threatening phone calls that had her imagination working over-time as she unlocked the car door and quickly slipped behind the wheel. Yet it remained, cloaked in the need for haste that had her accelerating out of the parking lot on to the street.

Four blocks from the restaurant, the rear-view mirror reflected the glare of bright headlights behind her. Flame immediately tensed. Where had that car come from? She was certain there'd been no vehicle waiting to turn at the last intersection. How had it appeared like that – as if out of nowhere? Then she realised how paranoid that sounded and chided herself for seeing a threat in something so innocent as a car behind her on a public street. The entrance ramp for the interstate was just ahead, for heaven's sake. Naturally there'd be more traffic around it, even in this quiet downtown area.

Flame honestly tried to ignore the car behind her, yet she was aware that it turned on to the interstate when she did. But so did a second car behind it.

The fifteen-mile stretch of highway to her exit seemed much longer tonight. Along the way, she passed slower-moving traffic and other vehicles passed her, yet the glare of headlights in her rear-view mirror remained constant. Over and over again, Flame told herself that it didn't necessarily mean it was from the same car.

When it took the same rural exit she did, she began to wonder if her first instinct was right – that the car was following her. It was five miles to Morgan's Walk from here – five miles on a narrow, two-lane highway that carried very little traffic, especially at night.

With her uneasiness growing, Flame slowed the Lincoln, trying to force the car behind her to pass. But it slowed down, too. When she speeded up, it did, keeping the same close distance behind her. Her palms began to sweat. The hawk-faced man had never been this obvious when he'd tailed her before. Why now? Then she realised that whoever was back there wanted her to know she was being followed – he wanted her to be worried . . . frightened. The worst of it was – he was succeeding.

Straining, she tried to see beyond the bright beams of her headlights into the blackened night, searching for a landmark that would tell her how much farther it was to the turn-off for Morgan's Walk. Ahead the highway curved sharply to the right. From that point, Flame knew it was less than a mile to the ranch's drive. She flexed her fingers, trying to ease their knuckle-white grip on the steering wheel, as she slowed the Lincoln to make the curve.

But the car behind her didn't, its headlights suddenly looming closer, the reflection of their glare nearly blinding her.

'Are you crazy?' Flame cried out. 'Don't you know there's a curve up ahead?'

A second later it slammed into her from behind, the impact jolting her, pitching her forward against the steering wheel, and sending the Lincoln shooting into the curve. She was going too fast! The car would never hold the curve!

As she braked frantically, the Lincoln briefly skidded sideways, crossing into the other lane. She fought desperately to control it, fear tightening her throat, nerves screaming. But she couldn't hold it on the road. The car careened wildly into the ditch on the opposite side. There was a split second of terror when she thought it was going to roll. Somehow the Lincoln righted itself and plunged up the other side of the ditch, bouncing and roughly tossing her from side to side.

It came to a shuddering stop in an open pasture twenty yards from the road. Flame sat there for a full second, her fear-frozen hands gripping the steering wheel. Then the shaking started, tremors of relief vibrating through her as she realised how very close she had come to disaster. She sagged against the seat back, then stiffened, remembering the car that had forced her off the road. All she could see of it was the red of its taillights in the distance.

She had no idea how long she sat there with the engine idling, the transmission in park – something she had no memory of doing – waiting for the shock to subside. Finally, on shaky legs, she got out and inspected the damage. All she found were some dents in the chrome bumper and clods of earth and clumps of grass caught here and there.

Aware that there was little hope of anyone driving by at this hour, she realised that she either had to walk for help or drive out of here and back on to the road herself. She chose the latter.

That mile to Morgan's Walk was the longest she'd ever driven in her life, her arms, her shoulders, her neck aching from the banging about she'd taken. She was certain she'd wind up with several lovely bruises, but at least that was all. It could have been much worse – and that was the scary part.

The telephone started ringing the minute she walked into the house. She stopped short, dread sweeping over her as she stared at the beige telephone on the foyer table. Slowly she walked over and picked it up.

'Hello,' she said, a wary tension in her voice. That alien voice replied in its eerie monotone, 'You were warned. You may not be so lucky next time.'

Flame gripped the phone, unable to speak, unable to move – paralysed by the significance of that message. As the line went dead, she could feel every aching bruise and strained muscle in her body – and the fear rising again in her throat.

Fighting it, she quickly depressed the button and heard the familiar hum of the dial tone. Hurriedly she punched a set of numbers, but in her haste, she inverted two of the digits and had to stop and start all over again.

'Ben.' She held the receiver with both hands. 'Someone . . . someone deliberately ran me off the road.'

'What? When?'

'Just now. On my way back to Morgan's Walk. It was deliberate, Ben. Somebody's trying to kill me.'

'Flame, where are you? How do you know it was deliberate? What makes you so certain?' The questions came rapid-fire, the shock in his voice evident.

'I'm here at . . . Morgan's Walk. I just got a phone call telling me –' She stopped, catching the edge of panic in her voice, and started again, forcing a calmness. 'Telling me that I'd been warned – and that I might not be so lucky next time.'

'What?' Ben sounded as stunned as she had been. 'Who was the call from?'

'I don't know.'

'Is it a man's voice? A woman's?'

'It's a robot's,' she replied and laughed nervously, trying to shake off her fear.

'What? Be serious, Flame.'

'I am. Somebody's using some sort of voice synthesiser to make these threatening calls.'

'*These* calls,' Ben repeated. 'There have been others?'

'This makes the fourth – or maybe it's the fifth. I can't exactly remember now.'

'Dammit, Flame, why didn't you tell me about them?'

'I didn't think they were important. I thought they were a prank. Now . . .' she breathed in deeply, 'now I think I should notify the police.'

'I'll do it. You stay there and I'll bring a detective out to talk to you. As soon as you hang up from me, call Charlie. I don't want you alone in that house.'

She started to protest that such a precaution wasn't necessary, then thought better of it and agreed to call Charlie.

'I'll be there in thirty minutes – forty at the outside,' Ben promised.

Flame sat in the parlour with both hands wrapped around her third cup of the strong black coffee Charlie had made for her when he arrived. Time and the potent brew had managed to push most of the fear to the back of her mind, and enabled her to regain control of her emotions, allowing her to go over the events again and again with the detective from the Tulsa police department.

'No. I told you I couldn't see what kind of car it was,' she repeated her previous answer to the unsmiling man in the loose-fitting blue serge suit whose I.D. read: Thomas Bartholomew Barnes. 'He followed too close. The glare of the headlights –'

'*He*? The driver was a man?'

'That was merely a figure of speech,' Flame insisted, her patience waning at this endless picking over every little detail. 'I couldn't see the driver. I don't know if it was a man or a woman.'

'And there weren't any other cars on the road?'

'None,' she said, shaking her head. 'Not before or after I was forced off the road.'

'Let's go back over these threatening calls you say you've been receiving.'

'Again,' she murmured, sighing in irritation.

'Yes, ma'am, again,' he confirmed, his voice remaining unmoved and continuing its stubborn and polite run. 'What did the caller say?'

'He –' Flame caught herself. 'It warned me that I'd better stop or I'd be sorry – or a variation of words to that effect.'

'Stop what?'

'I don't know!' As the answer exploded from her, she took a quick breath and tried to control her rising temper.

'You must have assumed something,' the detective persisted.

'I *assumed* the calls were a prank.' She shoved the coffee cup on to the end table and pushed off the sofa, too agitated to remain seated any longer. She crossed stiffly to the fireplace, ignoring the throbbing protest of her right knee at the renewed activity, then turned back to confront the detective. 'Somebody tried to kill me tonight, Mr Barnes, and I want to know what you're going to do about it!'

He leaned back in the chair, resting his head against the rose brocade upholstery. 'Who would want to kill you, Ms Bennett?'

Flame hesitated a fraction of a second. Abruptly, she turned her back on the detective and stared at the ornate fireplace screen. 'I moved here only a few weeks ago. I don't know many people here.' She hesitated again and turned back to face him. 'I'm not sure if there's any connection, but – before I moved here – when I was in San Francisco, I was followed by this man. Twice he slipped me threatening messages.'

The detective looked at her with sharpened interest, his pen poised above his small black notebook. 'What did he look like? Can you describe him?'

'He was . . . of average height and build, in his late forties. I think he had brown hair and I believe his eyes were hazel. And there was a very pronounced hook to his nose. I always thought of him as the hawk-faced man.'

'And these messages, were they the same as the phone threats you've been receiving?'

'No, they were different. That's why I'm not sure if it means anything. The hawk-faced man was always warning me to – I quote – "stay away from him".'

'Who were you to stay away from?'

'I –'

'Excuse me,' Ben Canon spoke up. 'I think I can clear up this matter. You see, on behalf of my late client Hattie Morgan, I engaged the services of a private detective in San Francisco – a man by the name of Sid Barker – first to locate Ms Bennett, then to . . . look out after her.'

Flame swung around to stare at him. 'You hired him to follow me!' she demanded, reacting with a mixture of shock and outrage.

His smile was meant to calm. 'You were the heir to Morgan's Walk at that point. And Hattie was anxious that . . . nothing happen to you.' His deliberate hesitation made it obvious to Flame that Hattie had been trying to warn her away from Chance.

'Why didn't you tell me this before?' But it was too late to be angry about it, especially when she knew how right Hattie had been to warn her about Chance.

'It never occurred to me,' Ben said ruefully. 'I'm sorry.'

'Then who's making these calls? Who's trying to kill me?' She didn't want to think Chance was behind all this. But, with the hawk-faced man eliminated, who else could it be?

'There must be someone, Ms Bennett,' the detective insisted. 'An ex-husband, a former boyfriend, a jealous lover, an angry wife – someone.'

Diedre. Did Malcom's wife feel so threatened by her affair with him that she would do something this drastic? No, it wasn't possible. She was in San Francisco; that was much too far away. The same was true with Lucianna . . . unless she or Diedre had hired someone. But Flame rejected that possibility too, unable to visualise either woman actually hiring someone to kill her.

She lifted her head in challenge. 'My ex-husband is Chance Stuart. Does that help you?'

He breathed in deeply at that. 'Stuart, eh.'

'Yes,' she said, her voice clipped and sharp, betraying her strained nerves. 'Tell me, Mr Barnes, exactly what are you going to do about the attempt on my life tonight?'

His shoulder lifted in a vague shrug. 'Check your car over, see if the lab can pick up any traces of paint from the other vehicle that might help us identify at least the make of it.' He paused briefly. 'But to be perfectly honest with you, Ms Bennett, even if we are lucky enought to track down the owner of the car, it still doesn't mean he or she was the driver of it. And even if we could, it's doubtful that they could be charged with anything more than reckless driving.'

'But what about the phone calls? The threats on my life?' she demanded. 'You can't simply disregard them.'

'To make a case for attempted murder, we'd have to be able to prove the driver of the car made those phone calls. We could put a tap on your line and monitor all your calls, but – from what you've told me – the caller never stays on the line for more than fifteen or twenty seconds. Which means there wouldn't be time enough to trace the call.'

Flame read between the lines, a fine tension gripping her. 'And if you could, what then?'

The detective had the grace to look uncomfortable as Ben Canon spoke up. 'The caller would probably be charged with a misdemeanour.'

'A misdemeanour.' She repeated in a stunned voice.

'That's assuming we can't prove the caller was the driver of the car that tried to run you down,' the detective explained. 'I'm sorry, Ms Bennett, but until a felony is actually committed –'

'You mean until – this person – actually kills me, there's nothing you can do,' Flame accused, trembling now with an anger born out of this awful feeling of helplessness.

He said nothing to that, instead closing his notebook and slipping it into his jacket pocket. 'If you think of anything else that could be useful, you have my card. You know how to get ahold of me. And if you receive any more threatening calls, mark the time and the exact message, and keep me informed.'

Ben stood up. 'I'll see you to the door, Mr Barnes.'

'That isn't necessary.' The detective rose from the wing-backed chair and nodded politely to Flame. 'I can find my way out.'

There was silence in the parlour, broken only by the sound of his footsteps in the entrance hall, then the final click of the front door closing behind him. Flame was conscious of both Charlie and Ben watching her.

'I think it's obvious the police aren't going to be much help in this.' She tried to sound nonchalant, cynical, but the words came out stiff and brittle.

'You think it's Chance, don't you?' Ben said.

'I don't know what to think,' she insisted, agitation putting a sharp edge on her answer. She didn't want to believe it was Chance even though he was the only one it could be. And he had vowed to stop her. Yet she couldn't imagine him resorting to violence to accomplish it. Could she be that wrong about him?

'Flame, I –' Ben began.

Briskly she interrupted him. 'I'm sorry, but I don't want to talk about it any more. I'm tired and I . . . just want to get out of these clothes.' And forget, she thought to herself, but she knew that was impossible even as she ɑlked from the room.

— 42 —

WITH THE ease and deftness of long experience, Charlie
Rainwater reached down and unlatched the pasture gate without dismounting from his horse. Flame waited on her mount
while he swung it open for her. She rode through the opening,
then reined her horse in on the other side and watched as he
swung his horse through and closed the gate, again from horseback. Satisfied it was securely fastened, he straightened in his
saddle and looked for a moment at a pair of white-faced calves
cavorting about under the contented eyes of their Hereford
mothers.

'That's a sight these old eyes of mine never get tired of seein','
Charlie declared as he turned his horse away from the gate and
walked it up to hers. His faded blue eyes studied her thoughtfully.
'Are you really goin' through with your plans for that development?'

'If I can.' Assuming she didn't get killed first, Flame thought,
the memory of her near brush with death too fresh yet.

These last five days, she'd thought of little else, becoming
tense and on edge – and suspicious of everyone. She'd sworn
Charlie and Ben to secrecy, extracting their promise not to mention the threatening phone calls or the attempt on her life to
anyone – not even Malcom. If he found out, she knew he'd

insist that she return to San Francisco. In her mind, to run from these threats would be the equivalent of giving up, and she wasn't about to do that. Neither could she totally discard the possibility that Malcom's wife might be the one behind them. Or Maxine who had looked after Chance as a child and believed he should have inherited Morgan's Walk. Or Lucianna Colton who might want Flame completely out of Chance's life. Or some crazy environmentalist who didn't want the river dammed and made into a lake. Dammit, it could be anybody. It didn't have to be Chance.

Frustrated and confused, Flame pointed her horse towards the imposing brick mansion that crowned the gentle knoll and overlooked the entire valley – the mansion her great-grandfather had designed and built. Suddenly it hit her. Morgan's Walk had to pass to a blood relative! All along Chance had been the obvious suspect, but now she realised that he had an even better reason to want her dead – Morgan's Walk would automatically pass to him. The facts seemed inescapable; he was the only one who stood to gain if she either gave up the fight – or was killed.

Yet, when she remembered the times she'd been with him, the tender strength of his arms, the loving stroke of his hands, Flame tried but she couldn't imagine Chance actually trying to hurt her, not physically. He was trying to scare her. That's what he was doing. He thought he could frighten her off. She was angry then, angry that he thought she could be intimidated by the threat of violence. But why should that be a surprise? It wasn't the first time he'd underestimated her.

So engrossed in her own thoughts, she barely heard Charlie when he said, 'Every time I look at those Herefords scattered across that green pasture, I try to picture a bunch of rich folks riding around in those electric carts chasin' a dimpled ball. But it just won't come to me. I just keep seein' the river, the trees, and the cattle.' His horse snorted and pricked its ears in the direction of the house. 'Looks like you've got some company, Miss Flame.'

'What?' Frowning, she gave him a blank look.

'I said you got company.' He nodded in the direction of the dusty pick-up parked in front of the house.

'I wonder who it is?' Someone was at the front door – a woman.

Maxine appeared to be arguing with her. Flame lifted her horse into a trot and cut across the front lawn, the thick grass reducing the echo of hoof-beats behind her to a dull thud as Charlie followed.

Nearing the house, she heard the woman's voice raise in angry challenge. 'I know she's in there. You just march right back and tell her that I'm not leaving until I see her!'

'But she isn't here,' Maxine protested. 'She went –' She stopped, catching sight of Flame riding up with Charlie.

The woman turned, giving Flame her first good look at her as she reined her horse to a halt short of the portico steps. Somewhere in her early thirties, she was a tall woman, a solid woman, dressed in a pair of polyester knit slacks, the kind with the elastic waistband and stitched-in creases, an overblouse of print cotton giving her upper body an extra heaviness. Her light brown hair was cut short and curled in a tight frizz that required little care. She faced Flame in a tight-lipped anger.

'What seems to be the problem, Maxine?' Flame swung down from her horse and passed the reins to Charlie.

'This woman –' Maxine began but never got a chance to finish.

'So you're the Bennett woman – the new duchess of Morgan's Walk,' the woman spat with contempt. 'This place was big enough for Hattie. Why isn't it big enough for you?'

'I don't believe we've met.'

'No. You're too high and mighty to come yourself. You send that agent of yours instead to dangle all that money in front of us.' She took a step closer, her broad face taut with resentment. 'And in case you haven't guessed, I'm Martha *Crowder* Matthews.'

'The daughter,' Flame murmured, unintentionally out loud.

'Yes, the daughter,' the woman snapped. 'And I'm telling you to your face that our farm isn't for sale! I don't know who you think you are to come around here waving money in our face and thinking we'll snatch at it. Four generations of Crowders have farmed that land, and some day my sons or daughter will work it. My great-grandfather and my grandfather are buried there, and when my father passes on, he'll be buried there, too. Everybody's wondering what's happening to the family farm when it's people like you who are destroying it.'

'Mrs Crowder – Mrs Matthews,' Flame quickly corrected herself. 'I'm not trying to destroy –'

But the woman wasn't interested in listening. 'I sent that real estate agent of your's packing this morning. If he ever comes back to badger my father again about selling and making him feel bad because he can't take care of his family the way he'd like, you're going to answer to *me*! Now, I'm warning you to stop – and you'd better listen.'

Flame stiffened, the phrasing almost an exact echo of the threatening messages she'd received. Was this woman the one who'd made all those calls? And nearly ran her down? Remembering those terrifying seconds when the car had been bearing down on her, Flame grew angry.

'Don't threaten me, Mrs Matthews.'

'I'm not threatening anything – I'm telling you!' she said and stormed off the portico, straight to the pick-up truck, coated with a film of red dust.

Spinning tyres spat gravel as the truck lurched forward under a heavy foot. Flame watched it speed away from the house.

'Looks like you aren't going to be able to get the Crowder land,' Charlie observed, leaning loosely on the saddlehorn.

She flashed him a sharp glance, any sympathy she might have felt towards the woman banished by yet another threat. 'We'll see about that.'

'What's he talking about?'

At Maxine's probing question, Flame turned, realising the housekeeper had overheard everything. 'Nothing that concerns you,' she said curtly and climbed the portico steps, removing her riding gloves. 'Have you cleared away all those boxes from upstairs? I don't want that mess there when Mr Powell arrives tomorrow evening.'

'No, ma'am, but I will.'

Thunder rumbled in the far distance, nearly masking the sound of the car's engine as Charlie drove the ranch's Lincoln around to the front of the house. Crossing the foyer, Flame glanced out of the window at the ominous black clouds that darkened the sky. As yet, it hadn't begun to rain, so she left her raincoat draped over her arm and her umbrella closed.

She stopped at the foot of the staircase and called up,

'Maxine, I'm leaving to pick up Mr Powell at the airport. When you're through laying out the extra towels, you can go home.'

A muffled reply came from one of the upstairs rooms, acknowledging the message. As Flame started for the door, the telephone ran. She hesitated, then walked over to the table and picked it up.

'Morgan's Walk.'

'You have been warned,' the mechanical voice intoned. 'Why have you not listened?'

'You don't frighten me,' she retorted angrily, but as usual, the connection had already been broken. She slammed the receiver down and stood there, vibrating. Why had that Matthews woman called again? Did she think she hadn't made herself clear yesterday? Then Flame grew still, realising it was an assumption on her part that the Crowders' daughter was the one behind the threatening calls. She had no proof. Again she felt the rawness of anger. Who was doing this to her?

'Ms Bennett?' Maxine stood at the top of the stairs, frowning in surprise. 'I thought you'd left.'

'Not yet.' She glanced sideways at the phone. 'Maxine . . . have you taken any . . . strange calls?'

'Strange? What do you mean?' She started down the stairs, studying Flame with a puzzled look.

'Peculiar sounding voices – or maybe they hang up as soon as you answer.'

'No.' She shook her head without hesitation. 'There haven't been any calls like that.' She eyed Flame a little closer. 'Are you sure you feel all right, Ms Bennett?'

It almost sounded as if she thought Flame was losing her mind. 'I'm fine,' she retorted and crossed immediately to the door.

Charlie Rainwater was coming up the steps as she walked out. 'There you are,' he said. 'I wasn't sure you heard me drive up with the car. Here's the keys.'

'Thank you.' She took them from him and started to walk to the car, then hesitated and turned back to him. 'Charlie, do you know what kind of car the Crowders have?'

'They don't have a car – leastwise not any more. They sold it last fall to pay some of Dan's medical bills. All they got now is that pickup their daughter was drivin' yesterday.' Then he frowned. 'Why?'

'Just curious.' She shrugged off the question and resumed her course to the Lincoln, more troubled than before. Maybe she hadn't seen what kind of car had almost run her down, but she was positive it hadn't been a pick-up truck. Assuming the woman had borrowed a neighbour's car, that still didn't explain how she'd known Flame was at the restaurant – unless, of course, she'd followed her there. Yet that didn't seem logical – not for a woman with a husband and children at home and a sick father to care for. And why hadn't the Crowder woman confronted her as she had yesterday instead of trying to run her down? That was backwards.

Flame sighed heavily as she slid behind the wheel of the Lincoln. If she eliminated Martha Crowder Matthews as a possibility, that left Chance again.

Halfway to the airport, the clouds opened up and sent down cascading sheets of rain. Terrific claps of thunder mixed with jagged bolts of lightning to show Flame the awesome power of a Midwest storm.

The violent rain delayed the arrival of Malcom's private jet. Flame used the time to contact Detective Barnes at the police department and inform him that she had received another threatening call, giving him the exact time and the brief message. As she returned to the lavishly furnished waiting room in the F.B.O. Building, she cynically wondered why she had bothered to call him. There was nothing the police could do about the threat, except to file it away. She sat down in one of the leather chairs and listened to the hammer of the rain on the roof and the ominous rumble of thunder.

The rain came down in sheets, drenching Chance as he dashed from the silver Jaguar to the covered entrance of his villa. He paused long enough to shake off the excess water, then reached for the door. But it was opened from the inside as his houseman Andrews appeared, clad in a raincoat with a black umbrella in hand.

'Mr Stuart. I was on my way out with the umbrella.' The sombrely competent man gave Chance a look of mild reproval for not waiting.

'I don't need it now,' Chance replied briskly.

'Obviously,' Andrews murmured, stepping back to admit him and observing the water that dripped from him.

'Where's Miss Colton?' Automatically he handed his briefcase to the houseman, his glance sweeping the marble foyer of his Tulsa residence. 'I didn't notice the Mercedes when I drove in.'

'She returned from shopping about forty-five minutes ago, sir.' Andrews took a handkerchief from his pocket and wiped the bottom of the case before setting it on the imported marble floor. 'She was caught in the rain as well and went upstairs to change. I'm relieved you made it back safely, sir. With this violent storm in the area, I thought you might be delayed several hours.'

'We landed about an hour before it moved in.' He ran a quick hand through his hair, combing the wet strands away from his face with a rake of his fingers.

'You've been back that long,' Lucianna accused from the grand, curved staircase, pausing in a dramatic fashion midway down, then descending the rest of the way, the long, tunic-style jacket to her satin lounging pyjamas flowing out behind her. 'Why didn't you call and let us know you were back? You have no idea how worried I've been thinking you were up there in those clouds with all that thunder and lightning. Where have you been all this time?'

'I had some things I needed to go over with Sam and Molly.' His quick smile at her approach failed to erase his vaguely preoccupied air.

Ignoring it, Lucianna started to slide her hands around his neck, then felt the dampness of his suit jacket and drew back. 'Darling, you're soaked to the skin.'

'It's raining outside – remember?' he murmured, an ironic twist to his mouth.

Lucianna turned to the houseman. 'Andrews, draw Mr Stuart a nice hot bath,' she instructed peremptorily.

'Don't bother, Andrews,' Chance said, vetoing her order. 'Just lay me out some clean, *dry* clothes.'

'Very good, sir,' the houseman replied inclining his head in a movement that fell somewhere between a bow and a nod.

'Are you sure, darling?' Lucianna murmured softly, sidling closer to him while taking care not to let her satin lounging suit come in contact with his wet clothes. 'I was going to volunteer to wash your back ... among other things.' She slipped her hands inside his jacket and smoothed them over his custom-made shirt as Andrews silently climbed the staircase to the master suite.

Chance caught her hands and set them away from him. 'Maybe another time,' he said, rejecting both her advance and her suggestion.

Momentarily taken aback, she laughed to cover it and took him by the hand to lead him to the stairs. 'You'll regret that someday, Chance Stuart. I don't make offers like that very often.' When he failed to respond with some equally teasing rejoinder as they started up the bleached oak staircase, Lucianna eyed him thoughtfully, trying to discern this oddly preoccupied mood he seemed to be in. After all these years, she thought she knew his every mood, but this one puzzled her. She finally asked, 'Is something wrong, Chance?'

'Of course not. What makes you think there is?' he shot back, the very abruptness of his answer making it ring false.

'This feeling I have that something's bothering you.'

And the guarded look he gave her, masked by a lazy smile, heightened the feeling. 'Woman's intuition, I suppose.'

'Darling, you can't deny I'm a woman. And my instincts tell me that something's upset you and put those lines of tension around your mouth,' she replied confidently, her glance flicking to the unusually thin line of his lips.

He looked at her, for a moment neither denying nor confirming her observation. Then a loud clap of thunder vibrated through the house, setting the wall sconces' pendants of Nesle crystal to tinkling.

'Blame it on the storm then – and the violence in the air,' he said.

Suddenly she knew that, whatever was bothering him, it had something to do with Flame. Rage flashed through her, jealous rage. She looked away, aware that it was useless to confront him. Flame Bennett was one subject Chance refused to discuss with her – not even in the most general terms. Had he seen her? Talked to her? But that was impossible. He'd come directly from the airport. No – he'd met with Molly and Sam before coming home. Then the meeting must have been about her. She had never hated anyone as much as she hated that woman. But she knew how to make Chance forget her. It merely required setting the proper scene.

Twenty minutes later, Chance stood beside the king-sized bed and tucked the tails of his striped shirt inside the waistband of his Italian slacks. Outside, the storm had subsided to a steady rain. Lightning flashed, drawing his glance to the rain-coated window.

In his mind's eye, he saw again the jagged bolt of lightning that had lit up the night sky as he'd been leaving the airport after meeting with Sam and Molly – the bolt of lightning that had revealed the light blue Lincoln in the parking lot and the woman walking away from it, an umbrella tipped against the sheeting, wind-whipped downpour. The long shape of her, the familiar way she moved – it was Flame; he'd known it immediately even though he couldn't see her face. There was only one possible reason for her to be at the airport: Malcom Powell was flying in to spend the weekend with her.

From the adjoining sitting room came the distinctive *pop* of a champagne cork, shattering the mental image of that rainy scene. Abruptly Chance turned away from the bed where she'd slept with him for those few precious nights as his wife, turning his back on those memories as she had spurned him.

A set of double doors led into the sitting room. He crossed to them and pulled them open. Andrews glanced at him briefly then continued to pour champagne into the two fluted glasses, a serving towel deftly wrapped around the bottle to absorb the bubbly foam. When Lucianna saw him, she undraped herself from the brocade sofa she'd been lounging on and assumed a seductive pose, her hands gripping the plump edges of the sofa cushions, her shoulders hunched forward and her head thrown back.

'Feel better, darling?' Her dark gaze slithered admiringly over him.

'Drier,' Chance replied and strolled the rest of the way into the room as she picked up the two glasses and rose from the sofa to cross to him. 'Champagne. What's the occasion?' he said, taking the glass she handed him.

'Darling, when has there ever had to be an occasion for us to drink champagne?' she challenged and touched the rim of her Baccarat crystal glass to his.

Chance lifted the glass to his mouth, but the effervescent wine had barely touched his lips when he jerked the glass away. 'What the hell –' he bit off the rest of the expletive, flashing a furious glance at Lucianna.

She laughed at his reaction. 'It's peach champagne, darling, not poison.'

He swung on the houseman as he folded the towel neatly around the bottle nestled again in its bed of ice in the champagne stand. 'How much more of this do we have, Andrews?'

'You instructed me to purchase two cases when –'

'Throw it out. All of it!'

Andrews blinked at the appalling waste. 'But, sir –'

'I said – get rid of it!' Chance set the fluted glass on the contemporary acrylic table with such force the crystal neck broke, spilling champagne on the écru rug and sending the rest of the glass shattering to the floor. Yet he seemed mindless to it as he strode to the door.

'Chance. Where are you going?' Lucianna called, still stunned and confused.

He stopped at the door and turned. The look in his eyes cold – so cold it burned. 'To the library.' Then his glance cut to Andrews. 'Hold my calls. I don't want to be disturbed.'

Lucianna flinched at the loud slam of the door when he pulled it shut behind him. Slowly she focused on the peach champagne in her glass. 'He told you to buy this when he brought *her* here to live, didn't he, Andrews?' she murmured the accusation.

There was a slight pause before the houseman answered, 'It may have been around that time, yes, ma'am.'

She walked over to the champagne stand and poured the contents of her glass on to the ice, then glared at him. 'Why are you standing there? You heard Mr Stuart. Get rid of it. Now!' She swung away from him and folded her arms tightly in front of her, still holding the empty champagne glass.

There was a rustle of movement, then the almost silent click of the door latch. Alone in the room, Lucianna looked at the glass in her hand. In a fit of rage, she hurled it at the wall and shut her ears to the sound of the expensive crystal shattering into fragments.

As Malcom stepped out of his Lear jet, Flame went forward to meet him at the bottom of the stair. When he reached her, she quickly shifted the umbrella to cover both of them from the down-falling rain and gave him a quick kiss in greeting, which he immediately lengthened into something warmer.

'You're definitely all in one piece,' she smiled at him. 'I wondered if you would be.'

'So did I,' Malcom replied.

'Was it very turbulent up there?' she asked, surveying him with some of her earlier concern.

'We were able to fly around the worst of it.'

'Good. My car's in the lot,' she said. 'We'll come back for your luggage.'

'Come back? From where?'

'We were supposed to meet Ben Canon and Ham Fletcher ten minutes ago,' she said, water splashing about their feet as she hurried him across the tarmac to the parking lot across from the F.B.O. Building. 'Ham Fletcher's the real estate agent who's been trying to buy the Crowder land for us – with absolutely no success. He insisted it was important that he talk to us. I started to meet him by myself, but I thought it would be better if you hear firsthand whatever it is he has to say rather than for me to try to repeat it.'

'Where are we meeting them?'

'At the hotel here by the airport.'

Irritation rippled through him as Malcom ducked inside the car and settled in the passenger seat. 'I fly all this way, just to step off the plane straight into another meeting. You know this isn't what I expected, Flame,' he challenged. 'What happened to that fine old brandy and our cosy evening in front of the fire – the one you described to me over the phone?' And the one that had persuaded him to come out here.

'I'm sorry, darling, but I promise we'll do it another night,' she said, then immediately started telling him about the latest development with the Crowders. Malcom pretended to listen, but he didn't hear any of it. He remembered the perfunctory kiss she'd given him when he'd stepped from the plane. With a touch of irony, he recalled the way he had always imagined an affair with Flame – that it would bring passion and an escape from stress into his life. Instead it had brought him more pressure. He talked business sixteen hours a day as it was. And he'd flown all this way to do more of the same. He laughed silently at himself, realising that he'd given up a rare leisurely weekend on his boat for this.

His smile faded as he recalled Diedre's reaction when he'd told her he wouldn't be there for Opening Day. He'd waited until two days ago to tell her. He wasn't sure why. Maybe to make the trip sound more urgent. But he hadn't fooled her for a second.

'This Friday. That means you won't be here for Opening Day,' she'd said, her acute disappointment plainly visible.

'I'm sorry, but it can't be helped,' he'd insisted.

'Where do you have to go?'

He'd hesitated a fraction of a second before answering. 'Tulsa.'

In that instant she'd known exactly who he was meeting and why, although she hadn't said a word. The hurt that flashed so briefly in her eyes had said it all. She'd turned away from him then, her shoulders hunching slightly as if to hold in the pain.

'If you have to go, you must,' she'd said, with an attempt at lightness. 'There'll always be next year.' Then in the tiniest of voices, she'd asked, 'Won't there?'

'Of course.' He'd been gruff with her – gruff to hide that twinge of guilt.

He wondered what she was doing now.

'Here we are,' Flame said, rousing him from his thoughts. 'Ben arranged for us to use one of the hotel's meeting rooms. He said he'd meet us in the lobby.'

A glass pitcher of iced water and four glasses sat on a tray in the middle of the long table. Next to them on a separate tray was an insulated carafe of coffee, styrofoam cups and packets of sugar and powdered cream. The rest of the table was taken over by opened briefcases, notepads and ashtrays.

Malcom sat back in his chair at the head of the long table, his fingers linked together resting against his middle. At the opposite end, smoke spiralled from the briar pipe clenched between the attorney's teeth. Like Ben Canon, Malcom mostly watched and listened as Flame conducted the meeting, exhibiting a hard intensity and determination. She reminded him of a corporate tiger, seizing on any point that might give her the end she sought.

'But, Mr Fletcher, you just said you believed Mr Crowder would like to sell.'

'I know what I said,' the agent replied. 'But his daughter won't let him.'

'What right does she have to tell him whether he can sell or not? The title is in his name. He doesn't need her permission.'

'Yes, he does. She has control of everything.'

'That's ridiculous. She's his daughter,' Flame said, with considerably more than a trace of impatience.

'I don't know how it works exactly. Maybe Mr Canon can explain it better, but she's . . . I guess, you'd call her his legal guardian. They set it up when he went in for that cancer surgery last year. And that's still the way it is. The poor man can barely make himself understood, and he's so sick and weak most of the time from that medication he has to take that he can't write more than a word or two at a time, then he has to rest. And Mrs Crowder, she's beside herself worrying over him and all the bills, not knowing how they're going to pay and what's going to happen.'

'What is wrong with that woman?' Flame pushed to her feet. 'Can't she see that if she would accept our offer, then her parents could have some peace and security in their last days instead of all this worry over bills? Instead of being so concerned about where he's going to be buried when he dies, she should be thinking about how he's going to live.'

'You'd think so,' the agent agreed. 'But she's determined to hang on to that farm no matter what.'

'This guardianship – or whatever it is,' she said, turning to Canon. 'Can it be revoked?'

'Possibly.' He took the pipe from his mouth to answer. 'You'd probably have to take her to court and prove she was unfit to do it. And you're talking time there. Mr Crowder might be dead by then.'

'What if he signed a sales contract, agreeing to sell at our price, could we make them honour it?'

'I doubt it.'

'They aren't going to sell, Ms Bennett,' the agent stated. 'I think you'd better accept that. And if you have thoughts of making them another offer, you'll have to find yourself another man to take it to him. She came after me with a shotgun the last time I was out there, and she was crazy-mad enough to use it. Next time she might. And no commission – regardless of the amount – is worth my life. I'm sorry, but that's the way it is.'

'I understand.' But her look called him a quitter.

He stood up, closed his briefcase, and picked up his cowboy hat, holding it respectfully in front of him. 'I wish you luck.'

'Thank you.' She remained standing, her gaze following him as he walked from the room.

Ben Canon thoughtfully poked at the charred tobacco in his pipe bowl and sent an upward glance at Flame. 'There's one consolation in all this. If she won't sell to us, she won't be selling it to Stuart either.'

She turned on him roundly. 'That isn't good enough. We have to have that land. It's absolutely essential to the development. Which means we have no choice,' she declared firmly. 'We have to buy their mortgage and force them out.'

'Why?' Malcom studied her with critical eyes, catching her stunned glance that quickly flared into bewildered anger.

'What kind of a question is that?' she demanded. 'You know very well why!'

'Do I? I wonder.' All of his business life he'd heard statements very similar to hers. Yet he resented hearing such ruthlessness coming from her. 'Those people want to keep their land. But you're going to force them off it.'

'I am not that cold-blooded, Malcom,' she said, her indignation rising. 'I want to buy their mortgage and force them to *sell*, not throw them off the land without a penny. We'll pay them much more than the land is worth.'

'Is that how you justify it?'

'What is going on?' she demanded. 'If you have another alternative, tell me, because I can't see that we have any other choice except to give up. And if we do that, Chance –'

'I wondered how long it would be before Stuart's name was mentioned,' he murmured.

'Malcom, who do you think we're fighting? Who do you think is out there trying to get Morgan's Walk – any way he can?'

'And who do you think is becoming just as ruthless as Stuart?'

'I have to be!' she cried in anger. 'It's me he's trying to destroy.'

'And that makes it all right for you to destroy the Crowders' lives.'

'I am not – *we* are not destroying their lives. Ultimately we're helping them,' she argued.

'And you're going to *make* them accept that *help* whether they want it or not . . .'

'When did you become so righteous?' she demanded. 'How many stores have you forced out of business or into bankruptcy? How many companies have you taken over? The iron man isn't exactly lily white.'

'That was business. With you, it's purely vengeance. It's taken me a while to realise that everything you do revolves around getting even with Stuart. Maybe I didn't want to see it before.'

'That isn't true,' she denied, made restless and impatient by his accusation.

'Isn't it?' Malcom replied, a little sadly. 'The only reason you're with me, Flame, is because I can help you get back at Stuart. You're using me . . . in much the same way he used you.'

'How can you say that?' The fullness of her temper moved darkly over her face, clouding the green of her eyes.

'Because it's the truth. And I've discovered I don't like it.' He got to his feet, amazed that all he felt for her at the moment was pity. 'Go ahead and buy the mortgage, force the Crowders into selling. Do whatever you like, Flame. You've changed. You've become vindictive, twisted by your desire for revenge. And I want no more part of it.'

When he started for the door to leave, she demanded, 'Where are you going?'

He paused near the door and turned back to her. 'Back to San Francisco – to spend the weekend on my boat with my wife. And believe it or not, I'm looking forward to it.'

She stiffened, her chin coming up. 'Are you pulling out on me, Malcom? I thought we were partners.'

A smile tugged at the corners of his mouth. 'You once told me that you wanted our relationship to be strictly business. You've got what you wanted. The next time you need to meet with me, call my secretary. She'll schedule an appointment for you.'

Flame spun away, not watching him walk out the door, her hands gripping the back of a chair, his accusation ringing in her ears. She felt Ben Canon's eyes on her.

'He doesn't understand,' she insisted defensively, but it was too late to explain to Malcom about the threatening calls she'd received.

'I can see that,' he replied, idly puffing on his pipe.

She grabbed up her things and started for the door. 'You heard what he said. Buy the mortgage on the Crowder farm – the sooner the better.'

Still smarting from the injustice of Malcom's remarks, Flame swept out of the room and down the hall to the hotel lobby. She had a brief glimpse of his familiar profile, the silver tips in his dark hair flashing in the light, as he slid into a cab. Resentment, hot and galling, raced through her again. She'd been honest with him. She'd told him from the start that getting even with Chance was part of this. Hadn't he believed she was serious? Had he thought it was some game she'd get tired of playing in a few weeks? Was that why he had twisted everything around and tried to make it sound as though she had somehow deceived him? She hadn't, not once. She suspected that the real truth was their relationship hadn't lived up to his fantasy of it, so – with typical arrogance – he blamed her. Let him.

She pushed through the lobby doors and paused long enough outside to drape her raincoat over her head, not bothering with the umbrella, and ran through the rain to her car. With windscreen wipers slapping at the steady rainfall, she drove out of the hotel lot, on to the street, heading for the freeway entrance a block away. Driving down the on ramp, she spotted a gap in the blur of red taillights and accelerated quickly to highway speed to fill it.

There was a release in speed and the power at her command – a release from the anger and frustration that had no other outlet. She gripped the wheel, fingers clenching and unclenching, her lips pressed tightly together as she stared through the pouring rain at the gleaming taillights in front of her.

A car came up behind her, its headlights on full beam. Flame winced at the painful glare of them in her rear-view mirror, a brightness that seemed to be magnified by the rainy black night.

She muttered irritably at the unseen driver, 'Didn't anyone ever tell you, it's common courtesy to dim your lights when you're behind another car?' She flashed the Lincoln's headlights from low to high beam and back again, then gestured in the rear-view mirror for the car behind her to do the same, but the driver didn't get the message. 'Dammit, will you dim them?'

In an attempt to escape them, Flame swung the Lincoln into the passing lane. But the other car swerved with her, staying right on her tail. She switched back to the right lane and slowed down, hoping it would pass her. But the full, reflected glare of its blinding headlights was there again, directly behind her.

This time Flame realised, all her previous irritation and anger fleeing as alarm surfaced, that she was being followed . . . more than likely by the same person who had forced her off the road the last time. And just as before, whoever was back there wanted her to know he – or she – was there.

'Dammit, who are you?' she cried in a mixture of fear and frustration.

She tried, but between the sheeting rain running down her rear window and the harsh brightness of its headlights, she couldn't see what kind of car it was – if it was Chance's silver Jaguar or something else. Flame spotted the interstate sign indicating an exit one mile ahead – and the one after it promising gas, food, and lodging at the exit . . . and, more importantly, help.

She pushed her foot down on the accelerator and raced for the exit. Her stalker stayed right with her. She didn't slow down or signal her intention as she neared the off ramp. Instead, she waited until the last possible moment then swerved the Lincoln on to the exit, and began to brake.

She was surrounded by darkness and pouring rain. The glare of the headlights – they weren't there any more! The car hadn't followed her. With a quick turn of her head back towards the interstate, Flame tried to catch a glimpse of the car before it disappeared beneath the interstate overpass.

But she couldn't see it. It wasn't there. At the same instant, she had that eerie feeling she was being watched. Some sound, some motion, some instinct told her the car had pulled alongside her on the wide off ramp. She automatically slammed on the brake as she turned to look.

There was a faint, explosive sound as her windscreen fractured into a glass mosaic of a thousand tiny pieces. She couldn't see!

Fighting the waves of panic, Flame brought the car to a full stop. That's when she noticed the two small holes in the windscreen – bullet holes – and the corresponding holes that had also shattered the glass in the driver's window.

The next day, the sky was blue and clear, the sun shining brightly, the water puddles standing around Hank's service station at the interstate exit offering the only lingering evidence of last night's storm. But the nightmare of it was very real to Flame as she watched a man from the police lab measuring the diameter of the bullet holes in the windscreen of the sky-blue Continental.

When she shuddered uncontrollably, Charlie touched her arm. 'Are you okay?'

She thrust her chin a little higher, but carefully avoided looking at him. 'Somebody's trying to kill me, Charlie,' she murmured tightly. 'Hattie warned me he'd stop at nothing – not even murder. But I didn't believe her.'

═══ 43 ═══

RUNNELS of perspiration streamed down his face and neck, plastering the cotton T-shirt against his chest. Drawing the racket back, Chance channelled all of his strength into his swing at the fast-flying ball and rocketed it back at the wall. Immediately he moved back, shifting to a ready stance, totally intent on the ball yet aware of his opponent, one of the trainers at the gym. The man made a diving swing at the careening ball – and missed. Game point.

Chance straightened, lowering his racket, muscles relaxing, the wind drawing in and out of him deep and even. He looked at his opponent lying sprawled on the squash-court floor. Slowly, tiredly, he pushed to his feet and glanced at Chance, shaking his head.

'That's it. I've had it,' he said, admitting defeat. 'Man, I don't know who you're mad at, but you're out for blood.'

The image of Flame came to his mind, proud and strong, the flare of icy defiance in her green eyes. He dropped his glance and turned away to get his towel. 'Hard day at the office, I guess.'

'I guess,' came the answering echo of full agreement. 'Remind me never to play you at the end of the day again.'

His mouth moved in a semblance of a smile as Chance scooped up his towel from the corner and rubbed it over his face and neck, letting its thickness sop up the sweat. Out of the corner of his eye, he caught the movement of the door to the court swinging open and turned, in absent curiosity. When Sam walked in, Chance checked the downward stroke of the towel along his neck, an alertness coursing through him, then continued to wipe at the perspiration.

'What's up?' he asked.

But Sam glanced at the trainer. Taking the hint, the man lifted his towel in a parting salute and headed for the door. 'See ya.'

Chance lifted his head in an acknowledging nod, then brought his full attention to bear on Sam, noting immediately Sam's unwillingness to meet his gaze. 'What happened?'

'I was three hours late.' Grimness and guilt moved over his boyish features. 'She's locked up the Crowders' mortgage. The bank said she was there this morning to sign all the papers.'

'Damn that woman.' He swore in frustration, throwing back his head to glare at the ceiling and bringing his hands to rest on his hips, the racket against his side.

'I thought we had her when we managed to buy those two parcels this last weekend, but they aren't vital to her project. We needed the Crowder piece,' Sam said, his glance finally seeking Chance's eyes. 'She's won, hasn't she?'

'Not if I can help it.' He pulled the towel from his neck. 'Get Donovan on the phone and tell him to get the jet ready. I'm flying to Washington tonight and push for an approval on our dam myself.'

'It's no good.' Sam shook his head, then explained. 'I talked to Molly before I came over here. That's how I knew where you were. Fred called to say he'd heard from Zorinsky. Morgan's Walk has been listed on the National Registry for Historic Places. He says there's no way you're going to get an approval now.'

This time he said nothing. He stood there silent and staring, his mind racing. She'd blocked him.

Sam shifted uneasily. 'Do you want me to wait?'

'No.' His voice was hard and flat. 'I have some thinking to do.'

Sam hesitated then left him standing alone in the court.

═══ 44 ═══

DARKNESS PRESSED its black hands against the library windows. Flame held the telephone firmly to her ear and waited for that voice to finish its threat, an anger like ice freezing her motionless. When a faint *click* signalled the connection was broken, she hung up and pushed the rewind button on the tape recorder she'd hooked to the phone. There was a quick whir of the tape, then a snap as the machine shut itself off. She played back the message, making sure she'd recorded all of it, then rewound the tape, and picked up the phone again, dialling the number in her address book.

'Yes, Stuart.'

That hard, impatient voice belonged to Chance. She smiled coldly. 'Isn't it amazing? You must have been sitting on top of the phone to answer it so quickly. Or maybe you just finished making a call.'

'Flame?' Surprise ringed his voice.

'You didn't expect to hear from me, did you?' she murmured smoothly. 'I thought I would call and tell you I know exactly what you're doing. But it isn't going to work, so you can stop making your threatening calls. You aren't going to get Morgan's Walk even if you succeed in killing me. I've seen to that.'

'Kill you? What are you talking about? What calls?'

Her smile widened. 'I didn't expect you to admit anything. After all, you were the one who told me I should have bluffed and pretended I didn't know what you were talking about.'

'Dammit, I don't know,' came the angry retort. 'What threats? What calls?'

'Maybe this will refresh your memory.' She held the telephone to the tape recorder and played the message for him, a slight shiver of dread breaking through her control as the alien-sounding voice spoke in its flat monotone. 'Your luck has run out. I will stop you for good.'

'My God, that voice – what is it?'

'It certainly isn't yours, is it?' she retorted. 'And much safer than trying to disguise your own. But it isn't going to save you. The police will receive a copy of this tape. They know about the other attempts on my life. And if anything happens to me now, Chance, the police will come directly to you. And I'll have the satisfaction of knowing that you'll never get Morgan's Walk.' She paused slightly, recalling the message. 'You aren't going to stop me for good. I'm going to stop you.'

She hung up, surprised to discover that her hand was trembling. She gripped it for a minute, then ejected the tape from the recorder and took an envelope and a sheet of paper from the desk drawer. Not letting her mind think, she swivelled her chair around and slipped the paper into the portable typewriter she'd brought with her. With an eerie detachment, Flame noted the pertinent details: the time of the threat, its content, her subsequent call to Chance, and her current action. She took the paper out of the typewriter, signed and dated it, then slipped it along with the tape into the envelope and sealed it shut.

With an odd feeling of finality, she laid the envelope aside and leaned back in the chair, gazing at the portrait of Kell Morgan above the mantel. 'I promise you,' she murmured, 'a Stuart will never have Morgan's Walk.'

She felt flat, drained, no emotion left. She'd fought so hard against believing Chance would want to harm her that finally accepting it had taken everything out of her. She realised that, deep down, she'd actually believed that he'd cared for her a little, despite his deception and trickery. But he hadn't. She knew that now. The last illusion of his love was gone.

She continued to stare at the painting. 'It was the same for you as well, wasn't it?' she realised. 'Ann didn't love you either. And, like me, you ended up alone in this house. Your parents had died years before, and you'd driven Christopher away with your pain and hatred the same as I –' she closed her eyes, a tightness gripping her throat. 'The same as I drove Malcom away with mine.'

My God, what had she become? A cold, bitter woman, obsessed with revenge. She remembered the Crowder family and the daughter's determination to keep their land – and her own fierce determination to get it from them. Malcom was right – she had become ruthless and vindictive. She hated Chance, but was she any different from him?

It was funny, she felt dead already – beyond feeling, beyond caring. There were things she should be doing, but they seemed unimportant as she sat and stared at the portrait.

The dull bonging of the grandfather clock in the foyer, chiming the hour, finally aroused her. She sat up and rubbed a hand across her forehead, then picked up the report from Karl that she'd been reading when the phone had rung. But she couldn't seem to concentrate on it.

From the rear of the house came a creaking sound, like the hinges of a door squeaking. Flame paused, listening for an instant, then dismissed the noise as the normal groans of an old house. But it heightened her sense of hearing, making her conscious of a dozen other sounds – from the loud thudding of her heart to the soft whisper of the paper in her hand.

When something rustled in a bush outside, she started at the noise. There was a face in the window! Chance. In shock, she stared into the glowering blue of his eyes, the expression on his hard, lean face lined with impatience and anger. Then she saw the gun in his hand. Her glance flew to the portrait above the mantel and saw the fear in Kell Morgan's eyes. She looked back at Chance. He shouted at her and pushed at the window, but the thick glass muffled his voice.

The report forgotten, she grabbed the phone and tried to reach Charlie at the bunkhouse, but there was no dial tone. She beat at the disconnect switch. It was no use. The line was dead. As she scrambled out of the chair, he pounded at the window, trying to get in. Her legs felt like leaden weights and the desk seemed to grow bigger and wider as she tried to run from behind it and get to the doors.

He yelled, this time loud enough that she could hear, 'Flame, no!!!'

She faltered no more than a split second to glance at him, then turned back to the hall doors. A figure, clad all in black, blocked the opening, a gun in her hand. Flame had that one glimpse, then something slammed into her. Dimly she heard an explosion and the crash of breaking glass as she fell down . . . down . . . down . . . into a swirling black abyss.

══ 45 ══

S TRONG FINGERS squeezed her hand, the warmth of them penetrating, causing her to stir. She surfaced slowly as if wakening from a deep sleep. She opened her heavy eyes, focusing them on the figure of a man standing next to the hospital bed.

'Ellery, I thought –' She had a fuzzy memory . . . that figure in black . . . the gun . . . Chance had tried to kill her. She was in the hospital. She remembered a nurse smiling over her and saying she was out of surgery, that she was going to be fine. She looked at the i.v. bottle on the stand beside her bed, a tube running to her hand, then frowned at Ellery. 'How did you get here?'

'Ben called Malcom, and Malcom called me. I caught the red-eye flight, and here I am.' His usually cynical mouth curved into a tender smile. 'You gave us quite a scare, but you're going to make it. The bullet nicked an artery, but no vital organs. You lost a lot of that San Francisco blue blood, but the doctor tells me you'll probably be up and around in a couple of days.'

'Did they . . . did they arrest Chance?' She forced the question out, needing to know yet not wanting to.

'Chance?' An eyebrow lifted in momentary bewilderment. 'Why should they?' His expression took on a wryly gentle look. 'Or is it a crime in Oklahoma for someone to save your life? Because, my

dear, if it wasn't for Stuart you would have bled to death before
the ambulance got there.'

'But' – she frowned, trying to make sense of this – 'he was
there, Ellery. He had a gun. I saw him.'

'Poor Flame.' Affectionately he gripped her hand a little tighter,
a pitying light in his eyes. 'You thought he was in it with her,
didn't you? He wasn't. He was there to stop her.'

'Her?' Her confusion deepened as she searched his face, wanting to believe him, yet afraid. 'Who are you talking about?'

Her mind raced. Was it the Matthews woman – or Maxine? But
if it was true that Chance had come to stop one of them, then
how would he have known of her intent . . . unless he had plotted
with her? Could it have been Lucianna? But why would she want
her dead? Chance didn't love her . . . did he? There was so much
fragile hope in those two little words that Flame felt the aching
start all over again. If it was true he'd saved her, didn't that mean
he still cared? Oh, God, she wanted him to.

'I'm talking about Stuart's secretary Molly Malone,' Ellery replied, his voice again marked with gentleness.

'Molly?' Shock splintered through her, followed by even more
confusion. 'But why? Why would she want to kill me? I never did
anything to her.'

'Not to her – to Stuart.'

She breathed in sharply at his answer, the memory instantly
flashing into her mind of Chance saying, 'Molly's the closest
you'll come to a mother-in-law' – and Sam's remark that Chance
was the sun in her life and her world revolved around him, that
his enemies were her enemies.

Ellery went on, 'From what I understand, she believed that
Morgan's Walk rightfully belonged to Stuart and – by eliminating
you, she'd be rectifying the situation. And, at the same time,
she'd be preventing another Morgan woman from hurting him
any more.'

'Like Hattie,' she murmured and pressed her head back against
the pillow to stare at the ceiling, the sting of tears burning her
eyes.

She remembered Hattie's hatred for him – and the number of
times Ben Canon had told her she sounded just like Hattie. She
recalled the one occasion Chance had talked about his childhood
– the day of Hattie's funeral – telling her how cruel Hattie had

been to him, and how it hadn't made any difference to her that his mother was a Morgan; he carried the Stuart name, so she hated him. And her own reaction had been bitter scorn.

'I've made such a mess of things, Ellery. Just look what I became.' She gazed at him through the wash of tears and tightened her hold on his hand. 'It makes me wonder why he bothered to stop her.' She tried to smile at her question, but the quivering of her chin made it a futile attempt. 'How did he even find out what she planned to do?'

'Evidently you called him and played some sort of tape that sounded like a talking computer his company recently acquired for a blind office worker. First he tried to reach Molly to ask her about it, then came out to Morgan's Walk. When he discovered her car parked a half-mile down the lane . . .' Ellery paused, smiling crookedly. 'Actually the whole thing sounds like a Dashiell Hammett novella.'

She made another feeble attempt at a smile. 'I guess it does.'

He squeezed her hand. 'They told me I could only stay for a couple minutes. I'm afraid my time's up.'

'You'll come back?'

'Tonight, after you've had some time to rest.' He lifted her hand and pressed her fingers against his lips, then hesitated, holding her gaze. 'Stuart's outside. In fact, the nurses tell me he's been camped out there ever since they wheeled you back from surgery. He wants to see you.'

She caught back a little sob of joy and tried not to let her expectations get too high. 'I'd . . . I'd like to see him.'

'I'll send him in.'

When Chance walked through the door after Ellery left and Flame saw the hard, smooth lines of his face, faintly shadowed by a night's beard growth, she wanted to cry. But she had too much control, too much pride, even now when she realised how wrong she'd been. He came to the side of the hospital bed and stopped near the foot of it, his blue eyes hooded and dark. She noticed his right arm was in a sling.

'You were hurt.'

He glanced at the sling as if he'd forgotten it was there, then touched it briefly with his other hand. 'A minor flesh wound. This will come off tomorrow, if not sooner.'

'I'm glad.' She hesitated, conscious of the tension, the strain, the awkwardness that was between them, and wishing there was a way to erase it. 'I'm sorry about Molly. I know how close you were to her.'

'You know then.' His gaze probed her expression, a hint of anguish and regret surfacing in his eyes.

She nodded. 'Ellery told me. He said you saved my life. I –'

'It was my fault you were in jeopardy in the first place.' Guilt – was that what he felt? She couldn't tell as he moved a step closer, briefly bowing his head before lifting it again to look at her, his jaw line held rigid. 'Flame, I want you to know that . . . Morgan's Walk is yours.' She felt her hope start to crumble at his words. Again it was the land. 'There will be no more attempts by me to take it from you. I swear it was never worth your pain – and God knows it was never worth your life to me.' Conviction vibrated through his voice, deepening its timbre.

'But I don't want it either,' she protested, a little stunned to discover she meant it. 'There's been too much pain, too much bloodshed, too many wrongs committed in its name – on both sides.'

'I came to the same conclusion last night,' he said, nodding slowly and watching her.

'In a day or two,' she said, thinking out loud, her gaze clinging to him, 'I'll talk to Ben about possibly deeding it to the State . . . maybe for a park.'

'Tell him that . . . that I'll lend any support he needs.'

'I will.' Yet it seemed the final break. Without Morgan's Walk between them, she'd have no other excuse to see him. And she wanted to see him. Dear God, she still loved him.

A nurse walked in, her starched uniform rustling crisply. She smiled politely but firmly at Chance. 'I'm sorry, but you'll have to leave now.'

As he looked at her one more time, then turned to go, Flame knew she couldn't let him walk out. 'Chance.' Her fingertips caught at his hand. He turned back, his thumb coming down to hold on to her fingers, something stark and painful flashing over his face. 'Is . . . Is it too late for us, Chance?'

Just for an instant there was a bright flare of blue – that same warm look he used to give her. Then he glanced down at her hand curved over his. 'It's never too late, Flame, if we don't want it to be.'

— 411 —

Behind his guarded reply, she detected the emotion-charged tightness in his voice and hope soared. 'I don't want it to be.'

He looked at her as if to make sure she meant it. 'And I never have,' he declared huskily.

Wordlessly she pressed her hand more tightly on to his and watched his mouth curve into that lazy warm smile that had always tugged at her heart. For the first time, she honestly believed it wasn't too late.

The nurse interposed again, 'I'm sorry, sir, but –'

'I'm going,' Chance said, his gaze remaining fixed on Flame, that warm glint in his eyes. 'But I'm coming back.' He leaned down and pressed his lips against her forehead, then whispered against her skin, 'Till next time.'

'Till next time.' As she echoed his words, she felt a strong, rich eagerness. There was hope, dear God, there was more than hope.